ALSO BY MICHELE CAMPBELL

It's Always the Husband
A Stranger On the Beach

she was the quiet one

....

MICHELE CAMPBELL

St. Martin's Paperbacks

Published in the United States by St. Martin's Paperbacks, an imprint of St. Martin's Publishing Group.

SHE WAS THE QUIET ONE

For information, address St. Martin's Publishing Group, 120 Broadway, New York, NY 10271.

www.stmartins.com

Library of Congress Catalog Card Number: 2018004833

ISBN: 978-1-250-25278-4

Our books may be purchased in bulk for promotional, educational, or business use. Please contact your local bookseller or the Macmillan Corporate and Premium Sales Department at 1-800-221-7945, ext. 5442, or by email at MacmillanSpecialMarkets@macmillan.com.

Printed in the United States of America

10 9 8 7 6 5 4 3 2 1

For Meg

Acknowledgments

I am deeply grateful to my editor, Jennifer Enderlin, for her vision, guidance, patience, and perseverance through the writing of this book. She always knew what the book needed, always had amazing ideas, and never considered even for a second settling for less than my best. She makes me the writer I want to be.

I'm grateful, as always, to my agent and friend Meg Ruley, to whom this book is dedicated. Meg not only makes my books possible, she makes the journey wonderful. I have been fortunate to work with her for many years, and it's one of my very favorite things about being an author.

Thanks to my kids for inspiring me. They show me how to live creatively, and with enthusiasm. And endless gratitude to my husband, who helps and supports my writing in so many ways. I couldn't do this without him.

The only quiet woman is a dead one.
—SYLVIA PLATH

part
one

....

1

February

They locked her in the infirmary and took away her phone and anything she might use to harm herself—or someone else. The school didn't tout this in its glossy brochures, but that's how it handled kids suspected of breaking the rules. Lock them in the infirmary, isolate them, interrogate them until they crack. Usually you got locked up for cheating on a test or smoking weed in the woods. In the worst-case scenario, hazing. Not murder.

She lay on the narrow bed and stared at the ceiling. They'd given her sedatives at first, and then something for the pain. But her head still pounded, and her mind was restless and foggy all at once. A large lump protruded from the back of her skull. She explored it with her fingers, trying to remember what had caused it. At the edge of her consciousness, something terrible stirred, and she pushed it away. If she turned off the light, she would see it, that thing at the edge of the lake.

That thing. Her sister. Her twin.

All across campus on this cold, dead night, silence reigned. She was being accused of a terrible crime, and there was nobody to speak in her defense. They'd called her grandmother to come defend her. But her grandmother believed she was guilty. Even her closest friends suspected her, and she had to admit, they had reason to. She and her sister were close once, but this awful school had changed that. They'd come to doubt each other, to talk behind each other's backs, to rat on each other for crimes large and small, to steal from one another. Mere days earlier, they'd gotten into a physical fight so intense that the girl who interceded wound up with a black eye. That girl hadn't told—*yet*. But she would now.

It wasn't fair. Just because they'd had a fight didn't mean she would kill her sister. How could she? Her sister was the only family she had left. Everybody else had died, or abandoned her. Why would she hurt her only family, her only friend? But every time she closed her eyes, she saw the blood on her hands, the stab wounds, the long hair fanned out. Her sister's face, white and still in the moonlight. She was there when it happened. Why? It couldn't be because she was the killer. That wasn't true. She was innocent. She knew it in her heart.

But nobody believed her.

2

The September Before

Sarah Donovan was a bundle of nerves as she fed her kids a rushed breakfast of instant oatmeal and apple juice. Four-year-old Harper and two-year-old Scottie were still in their pajamas, their good clothes hidden away among half-unpacked boxes. Today was opening day at Odell Academy, the prestigious old boarding school in New Hampshire, and Sarah and her husband, Heath, had just been appointed the dorm heads of Moreland Hall. They'd been laboring in the trenches as teachers for the past five years, and this new job was a vote of confidence, a step up into the school's administration. It came with a raise and faculty housing and the promise of more to come. Sarah ought to be thrilled. Heath certainly was. Yet she couldn't shake a sneaking feeling of dread.

"Hurry up, sweetie, two more bites," Sarah said to Scottie, who sat in his high chair playing with his food, a solemn expression on his funny little face. Scottie was like Sarah—quiet, observant, a worrier, with a lot going on behind his eyes—whereas Harper was an open book. She met life head-on, ready to dominate it, just like her dad.

"If you're done, Harps, go brush your teeth."

"Mommy, I'm gonna wear my party dress," Harper announced as she climbed down from her booster seat. She was beautiful, and she knew it, with big blue eyes and a wild mane of curls, and she loved to dress up and show off.

"You have to find it first. Look in the box next to your bed."

Harper ran off, and Sarah glanced at the clock. They had a half hour till the students and their families began to arrive. Sarah had spent the afternoon yesterday preparing for the welcome reception, and as far as refreshments and party supplies were concerned, she was all set. Five large boxes from Dunkin' Donuts sat on the kitchen counter, along with multiple half gallons of apple cider and lemonade, napkins and paper plates, party decorations and name tags. All that remained was to move everything to the Moreland common room and plaster a smile on her face. So why was she so nervous?

Maybe because the stakes were so high. Heath and Sarah had been brought in to clean up Moreland Hall's unsavory reputation, and the task was daunting. Bad behavior happened all over Odell's campus, but it happened most often in Moreland. Sarah thought it must have something to do with the fact that a disproportionate share of Moreland girls came from old Odell families. (Moreland had been the first dorm at Odell to house girls when the school went coed fifty years before, and alumni kids often requested to live in the same dorms their parents had.) Sarah had nothing against legacy students per se. She was one herself, having graduated from Odell following in the footsteps of her mother, her father, aunts, uncles and a motley array of cousins. But she couldn't deny that some legacy kids were spoiled rotten, and Moreland legacies notorious among them.

At the end of the last school year, two Moreland seniors made national news when they got arrested for selling drugs. The ensuing scandal dirtied Odell Academy's reputation enough that the board of trustees ordered the headmaster to fix the problem, once and for all. The previous dorm head was a French teacher from Montreal, a single guy, who smoked two packs of cigarettes a day—hardly the image the school was looking for. He got demoted, and Heath and Sarah—respected teachers, both Odell grads themselves—were brought in to replace him. A wholesome young couple with two adorable little kids to set a proper example. That was the plan, at least. But there was a problem. Neither Sarah nor Heath had a counseling background. They knew nothing about running a dorm, or providing guidance to messed-up girls. Sarah had spent her Odell years hiding from girls like that, and—to be honest— Heath had spent his chasing them. That was all in the past of course. The distant past. But it worried her.

When Sarah raised her concerns, Heath soothed them away and convinced her that this new job was their golden opportunity. How could they say no? Heath had big plans. He wanted to advance through the ranks and become headmaster one day. The dorm head position was his stepping-stone. He didn't have to tell her how much he wanted it, or remind her how desperately he needed a win. She knew that, too well. Teaching high school English was not the life Heath wanted. There had been another life, but it crashed and burned, and they'd barely survived. With this new challenge, Heath was finally happy again. She couldn't stand in his way.

And he *was* happy. He strode into the kitchen now looking like a million bucks, decked out in a blue blazer and a new tie, with a huge smile on his handsome face.

"Ready, babe?" he said, coming over and planting a kiss on Sarah's lips.

"Just about. You look happy," she said, lifting Scottie down from his high chair.

"You bet. I've got my speech memorized. I've got my new tie on for luck—the one you got me for my birthday. How do I look?"

"Gorgeous," she said.

It was true. The first time Sarah had laid eyes on Heath was here at Odell, fifteen years ago, when he showed up as a new transfer student their junior year. He was the most beautiful thing she'd ever seen back then, and, despite the ups and downs, that hadn't changed.

Heath checked his watch, frowning. "It's after nine. You'd better get dressed."

Sarah had thought she *was* dressed. She'd brushed her hair this morning, put on a skirt, a sweater and her favorite clogs, as she usually did on days when she had to teach class. But looking at Heath in his finery, she realized that her basic routine wouldn't cut it in the new job. She'd have to try harder. That wasn't comfortable, any more than it had felt natural earlier this week to give up their cozy condo in town and move into this faculty apartment. Moreland Hall was gorgeous, like something out of a fairy tale. Ivy-covered brick and stone, Gothic arches, ancient windows with panes of wavy glass. The apartment had a working fireplace, crown moldings, hardwood floors. But it didn't feel like home. How could it? It didn't belong to them; not even the furniture was theirs. Not to mention that the kitchen window looked directly onto the Quad. Anybody could look in and see her business. Life in a fishbowl. She hoped she could get used to it.

"Harper's getting dressed," Sarah said. "I'll take care of Scottie. Can you move the refreshments to the common room and start setting up?"

"Sure thing. And, babe, don't be afraid to do it up, okay? You look hot when you dress up."

Heath grinned and winked at her, but Sarah couldn't help completing the thought in her mind. *Unlike the rest of the time, when you look like you just rolled out of bed.* But Heath hadn't said that, and didn't think it. That was Sarah's insecurity speaking.

It took fifteen minutes to clean up Scottie, coax him out of his pajamas and into some semblance of decent clothes. Five more minutes were spent swapping out Harper's Elsa costume (which was what she'd meant by "party dress") for an actual dress. That left Sarah ten minutes to dress herself. She dug through boxes, but couldn't find her good fall clothes. She ended up throwing on a flowery sundress because it was the only pretty thing she could lay hands on, but topping it with a woolly cardigan against the September breeze. Not her most polished look, but it would have to do. She swiped on some bright lipstick, gathered the kids and the dog, and set out for the common room.

They were only a few minutes late, but when she got there, the room was empty, the tables and chairs were missing, and Heath was nowhere to be seen. She had a minor heart attack, until she caught the sound of Heath's rich laugh floating in through the open window, and looked out onto the Quad. Her husband stood on the lush, green lawn, surrounded by the missing furniture, and a gaggle of leggy, giggling girls.

"Hey, what are you doing out there?" Sarah called, laughter in her voice as she stuck her head out the window. With Heath, you could always expect the unexpected.

He turned, flashing a movie-star grin.

"Here's my lovely wife now. Girls, may I introduce your new dorm cohead, the amazing and brilliant Mrs. Sarah Donovan. Babe, come on out. It's a beautiful day, I thought, why not party on the Quad?"

Party on the Quad? Girls whooped and high-fived at that. Did Heath understand who he was dealing with? Sarah had some of these girls in her math classes in years past. They were the worst offenders, the delinquents, the old-school Moreland girls, accustomed to bad behavior and few repercussions. She'd have to sit Heath down and have a talk about setting an example.

Sarah led her children and the dog down the hall and out the front door of Moreland Hall. They stepped into the sunshine of the perfect September day. Harper ran to her daddy, who hoisted her up onto his hip. Max, their German shepherd mix, ran circles on the lawn, as Scottie chased after him, squealing. Music filtered out from a dorm room farther down the Quad. And those Moreland girls—the same ones who surfed the Web in her classroom and snarked behind her back—made a fuss over her, and said how much they liked her dress. She didn't buy the phony admiration. As they circled around her, long-legged and beautifully groomed, drawling away in their jaded voices, Sarah felt like they might eat her alive.

3

It was the first day at a new school for Bel Enright and her twin sister, Rose. Bel hated Odell Academy on sight. But she'd promised Rose to give it a real try, so she kept silent, and smiled, and pretended to be okay when she wasn't.

It was early September. Their mother had died in May, and Bel was still reeling. The cancer took their mom so fast that Bel couldn't believe she was gone. Mom had been Bel's best friend, her inspiration. She'd worked in an insurance company to support her girls, but the rest of the time, she was an artist. She painted, and made jewelry from found objects. She wrote poetry and cooked wonderful food. They lived in a two-bedroom apartment in the Valley with thin walls and dusty palm trees out front. But inside, their place was beautiful, furnished with flea-market finds, hung with Mom's landscapes of the desert, lit with scented candles. *Mom* was beautiful—the raven hair and green eyes that Bel had inherited (where Rose was blond like their father), the graceful way Mom moved, her serene smile. And now she was gone.

Bel had this fantasy that the twins would go on living in the apartment, surrounded by Mom's things, by her memory. But they were only fifteen, and it was impossible. Rose was the practical one, and she made Bel understand this. In the week after Mom died, Bel lay in bed and cried while Rose made funeral arrangements and phone calls. Mom was a dreamer, like Bel, and hadn't provided particularly well for the twins' future. Who expected to die at forty, anyway? She'd left no will and no guardian, only a modest insurance policy, which Rose insisted they save to pay for college. Bel didn't know if she wanted to go to college. But she understood that they needed a place to live, or they'd wind up in foster care. Rose called all of Mom's friends and relatives. Her brother in San Jose, her cousins in Encino, her BFF from childhood, her girlfriends from work. Rose also called Grandma—Martha Brooks Enright, their father's mother, whom they hadn't seen since Dad died when they were five. Bel objected to that. Why invite Grandma to the funeral when she hadn't bothered to see them all these years? She wouldn't even come. But Rose said they had to try because there was no telling who'd be willing to take them in.

All the people Rose contacted came to the funeral, including Grandma. Mom dying so young, leaving the twins orphaned, tugged at people's heartstrings. Everybody cried, and said pretty things, but it was empty talk. The only person who actually offered to take them in was their grandmother—who was Rose's first choice, and Bel's absolute last. Grandma gave Bel a cold feeling. She was so remote, in her tailored black dress and pearls. She was also the only person who didn't cry at the funeral. Bel noticed that. She noticed that Grandma didn't seem to like Mom much, based on how she talked about her. Grandma, being such a blue blood, maybe hadn't been happy about her son marrying a girl from the wrong side of the tracks. Bel's parents had met in college, at an event honoring the Enright family for endowing a major scholarship. Mom was one of the scholarship recipients. That's how different their situations were. John Brooks Enright was there representing his rich family, and Eva Lopez was there to say a required thank-you. But opposites attract. They fell in love.

When Dad died, Mom moved the twins back to California, and they didn't see Grandma again, or even talk to her on the phone. She sent checks on their birthday; that was it. After the funeral, when Grandma took them to a restaurant and offered to have the girls come live with her, Bel confronted her. Why hadn't Grandma come to see them all those years? Wouldn't you know, she claimed it was all Mom's fault, that she'd tried to visit, but was told she wasn't welcome. Bel didn't believe it for a minute, and afterward, she told Rose so. But Rose thought maybe Grandma was telling the truth. And besides, what choice did they have? Grandma was the only one willing to take them in.

At the end of May, a week and a half after Mom died, the twins went east to live with their grandmother in her big house in Connecticut. Grandma let them keep one painting each to hang in their rooms, but everything else went to Goodwill. They got on the plane with just one suitcase. Grandma would buy them new clothes better suited to life in a cold climate. It turned out that Grandma was very, very rich; something their mother had never told them. Rose thought they'd won the lottery. But to Bel, it all felt wrong. The Mercedes, the big house with its echoing rooms and elaborate décor, the housekeeper who came every day but barely spoke. She tried to settle in, to get used to the strange new circumstances. Maybe eventually she would have succeeded. But then the rug got pulled out from under them all over again when Grandma announced that she was shipping the twins off to boarding school come September.

Boarding school was something rich people did, but to Bel, it just seemed cold. Not only would they go to some pretentious prep school, but they would *live* there, and come home only for holidays. The whole idea was the brainchild of Warren Adams, Grandma's silver-haired, silver-tongued boyfriend. Warren was a lot like Grandma: good-looking, dressed fancy all the time, talked with an upper-crusty accent. Bel didn't trust him. Warren claimed he was merely Grandma's lawyer, but if that was true, why did he hang around her house so much? He said he'd been a close friend of Grandpa's, but then why was he moving in on Grandpa's wife? And he insisted that boarding school was the best place for the twins, but Bel suspected that Warren wanted them out of the way, so he could have Grandma and her money to himself. Rose didn't care. She didn't care if Warren wanted them gone, or even if Grandma did. Odell Academy was one of the top schools in the country, and Rose wanted to go there. She was ambitious like that, and Bel was too depressed to argue. They applied, they got in, and now the day of reckoning had arrived.

That morning, Grandma woke them early. They packed their fabulous new belongings into the Mercedes and drove the three hours from Connecticut to Odell Academy in New Hampshire, where they drove through imposing brick-and-iron gates onto a lush, green campus. Beautiful as it was, Bel felt like she was going to prison.

"Isn't it lovely?" her grandmother said with a sigh. "I remember bringing your father here."

In the back seat, Bel fought tears. But she could see Rose sitting next to Grandma in the front, staring out the window, awestruck.

"It's the most beautiful place I've ever seen," Rose said reverently.

They drove past perfectly manicured lawns, following signs to registration at the Alumni Gym. The gym parking lot was full of luxury cars with plates from New York and Connecticut and Massachusetts. The gym itself was housed in a grand marble building that looked like a palace. It made Bel miss her humble high school gym back in California, with its scarred floor and grimy lockers. She missed her old friends, the beach, their little apartment. Most of all, she missed her mother. A tear escaped and ran down her cheek.

"I want to go home," she blurted.

Grandma met her eyes in the rearview mirror, look-ing alarmed.

"Isabel, dear, we've been over this. Odell is one of the top schools in the country."

"I know I can't go back to California. Just let me come home with you, Grandma. I'll go to the public school. You'll save so much money. Please."

"It's not about the money, darling. Odell is a family tradition. Your father and grandfather went here."

Why did Grandma think that would matter to her? She'd never met her grandfather, and barely remem-bered her father. It was Mom who raised them. Mom had gone to public school, and she was the most intel-ligent and wonderful person Bel had ever known.

Rose reached across the seat and squeezed Bel's hand. "Belly, you're just nervous," Rose said, using her childhood nickname. "First-day jitters. It'll be okay. I'm here. We're in this together."

Bel tried to take comfort in that. It was true, she had her twin. Even if they were different, and didn't always see eye-to-eye, Rose was family. Bel nodded, and swiped a hand across her eyes.

"Okay."

Bel took a deep breath, and the three of them got out of the car. Inside, the Alumni Gym wasn't just a gym, but an entire athletic complex, complete with an Olympic-size swimming pool and indoor tennis courts. Registration tables had been set up on the basketball court, a cavernous space surrounded by bleachers and flooded with light from tall windows. Bright blue ban-ners crowded the walls, trumpeting Odell's many

championships against other prep schools The room
vibrated with voices and laughter, as kids and their
parents greeted and hugged. Rose and Bel were coming in as sophomores, which meant that most kids in
their grade knew each other already, but Bel tried not
to care. Look at them—all stuffy and preppy, in head-
to-toe Vineyard Vines. Who needed them? There must
be other, cooler kids here somewhere. Kids like her
friends back home, who smoked weed and surfed and
let their hair grow wild. She and Rose had moved in
such different crowds. Rose was a good girl. She got
perfect grades, and did Model UN and stocked shelves
at the food pantry. Her friends were dweebs like her—
Bel meant that in a kind way. She loved her sister. Still,
she wouldn't be surprised if Rose fit right in at this
stuck-up school.

The twins picked up their registration packets, which
included dorm assignments, class schedules, IDs, and
a campus map. Bel and Rose had been assigned to the
same dorm, Moreland Hall.

Grandma studied their placement forms, nodding
approvingly. "They usually separate siblings, but I requested that they keep you together, because of your
loss. I'm so glad they listened."

They got back into the car and followed the map to
Moreland Hall. As they drove up to the turnaround
behind the dorm, a group of pretty girls, with long
hair and long legs and wearing matching blue Odell
T-shirts, waved signs that read: WELCOME HOME
MORELAND GIRLS! *Home.* As if this place could ever
be that for Bel. The dorm was vast and built of dark

brick, with arches and turrets and mullioned windows. Like a haunted house. It gave Bel the creeps. But she'd promised to try, and she would.

The twins got out of the car. One of the T-shirted girls stepped forward. She was blond and perfect-looking, but when she flipped her hair, Bel caught the unmistakable tang of cigarette smoke, which piqued her interest. Smoking was against the rules here, supposedly. But maybe not everyone followed the stupid rules.

"Hey, I'm Darcy Madden," the girl said. "We're the senior welcome committee. So, welcome, I guess."

"Hi, Darcy! I'm Rose Enright, and this is my twin sister, Bel," Rose said, stepping forward and smiling eagerly.

Darcy rolled her eyes.

"Right, the orphan twins," Darcy said. "I heard all about you. It's a scam, right? You don't even look like twins to me. Bel's got black hair and Rose has, hmm, what would you call that? Dirty blond?"

"We're definitely twins," Rose said, coloring. "But we're fraternal, not identical. I look like my dad's family, Bel looks like our mom."

"Twins, maybe, but orphans? Since when do orphans wear Lacoste?" Darcy said, looking at Rose's pink polo with its tiny alligator, a glint of amusement in her eyes.

"I am so an orphan. The definition of that is your parents dying, and mine did," Rose protested.

Darcy caught Bel's eye, and they both laughed at Rose's earnestness. Bel then immediately felt guilty for laughing at her sister. But come on, Rose was uptight. A little teasing would do her good.

"She's just joking," Bel said to Rose.

"Yeah, sorry, kidding," Darcy said. "Come on, or-phans, we'll help unload your stuff."

Darcy beckoned, and more welcome-committee girls ran over. The extra hands were useful given the moun-tain of suitcases and boxes stuffed into the trunk of Grandma's car. The last couple of weeks had been one massive shopping spree, as Grandma got them prop-erly outfitted—her word—for Odell. Rose loved the pastel polo shirts Grandma suggested, the wool sweat-ers and boat shoes and Bean boots, the formal dresses for dances and dinners. Bel thought they were frumpy and boring. She'd made a stink, and when that didn't work, she'd begged and pleaded. In the end, Grandma relented and bought Bel some cute things—tops and leggings, jeans, a moto jacket, black suede boots, a couple of minidresses. Both girls also got new phones and laptops, bedding and desk lamps, shower caddies and under-bed storage bins. Grandma didn't stint, and Bel liked the stuff so much that she got over her hesita-tion at blowing so much cash. If Grandma didn't mind, why should she?

Rose and Bel grabbed suitcases. The welcome-committee girls took boxes and they all headed into the dorm, as one girl held the door open for the others. Manners were a thing here, apparently. Bel was sur-prised not only at how much help was offered, but how respectfully the girls treated her grandmother. Then again, her elegantly dressed, beautifully coiffed grandma fit right in at Odell, better than Bel did. The girls refused to let Grandma carry a thing, and a girl was deputized to take her in the elevator and show her the twins' rooms so she wouldn't have to hike up the steep, slippery marble steps.

Bel had hoped that she and Rose would be rooming together. But they were on different floors, Rose on two, Bel on three. Darcy ordered another girl to help Rose, while she hauled Bel's box up the extra flight of stairs to show Bel to her room.

"Thanks for the help," Bel said.

"No worries, we always do it," Darcy said, huffing. "You're in a double. All sophomores are. It can be grim or it can be fun, depending on who your roommate is."

"Who's my roommate?" Bel asked.

"Some dork, probably. C'mon, let's go see."

They walked down a long hallway, lined with closed doors on either side. It was dingier than Bel had expected given the beautifully manicured grounds, with old carpeting, dark wainscoting, and a stale, musty smell. Cards were pinned to each door with the occupants' names carefully written in calligraphy. Darcy stopped in front of Room 305.

"This is you. Looks like you're with Emma Kim," Darcy said. She braced the box on her knee and flung the door open.

The room was empty, and extremely tidy. Light streamed through the enormous bay window opposite the door. Bunk beds were crammed in along the wall where they entered, so the open door smacked up against them. Emma had moved in already, claiming a bunk, a dresser and a desk. Her things were neatly laid out, and the bottom bunk was made up with a pretty duvet and pillows. A poster for a boy band hung over her desk.

"Emma's probably out on the Quad. There's a welcome reception you need to get to," Darcy said.

"What's Emma like?" Bel asked dubiously. From her stuff, she was a neat freak with awful taste in music.

"Kind of a nerd. Not much money. Plays the violin. But she's pretty, and not a narc. Anyway, if you don't like her, you're welcome to hang with me and the seniors."

The offer gave Bel a warm buzz. This cool, older girl liked her. Maybe it wasn't so bad here.

"Really? I might take you up on that," Bel said.

"People'll tell you we're a bad influence, but don't get scared off."

"It's not true?" Bel asked.

"Oh, no. It *is* true."

Bel laughed, and Darcy smiled at her approvingly.

"You know," Darcy said, "when I heard we were getting twins from California, I thought, This could be cool. Then when I heard you were Enrights, I got really excited."

"You know my family?"

"Oh, yeah. My mom and your dad practically grew up together. They belonged to the same country club in Connecticut, and were at Odell at the same time. They even *dated*. Your dad was a hottie, and something of a wild man, apparently. Then he ran off with this gorgeous Mexican girl he met in college, and my mom was devastated."

"That ended up being my mom. She's from California, but yeah, she was beautiful."

"I can tell that by looking at you. Your sister, though? Kind of a dweeb, no?"

"Rose is all right. She's just quiet," Bel said, feeling defensive on her sister's behalf. Though she couldn't resist adding, "We're pretty different."

"Family. Can't live with 'em, can't kill 'em. My fam's cool, though. Mom lived in Moreland back in the day, not long after the school went coed. This dorm always had the raddest girls. But now they're trying to break our spirit."

"Who is?"

"The brass. The headmaster and the trustees. They brought in these new dorm heads to straighten us out, which, trust me, is an impossible task. *Besides*—"

Darcy looked at Bel meaningfully, and laughed.

"What?" Bel asked.

"They screwed up royally, and they don't even know it," Darcy announced, stepping over to the bay window. "C'mere. See that guy in the blue blazer?"

Bel looked down onto a wide, rectangular lawn, surrounded on all sides by graceful brick buildings. Tables and chairs had been set out in the shade cast by Moreland's walls. Students and their families were gathered around, listening to an extravagantly good-looking man, who stood a little apart, talking to the crowd, gesturing gracefully with his hands. Bel couldn't take her eyes off him.

"Who *is* he?" she asked, breathlessly.

"Heath Donovan, the new dorm head, well, *co*head, along with his mousy math teacher wife," Darcy said. "He teaches English, too. Is he the bangin'est thing you ever laid eyes on? All the girls want him. I swear I get tongue-tied around him, and normally I don't shut up."

"He's gorgeous. Why do you say it was a screwup to make him the dorm head?"

"A guy like that, in a dorm like this? Come *on*. By tradition, the Moreland seniors like to cause trouble. It's practically a graduation requirement. We're like the biggest beasts, and we have the best pranks planned. Want to hear our crazy idea, inspired by Heath the Hottie?"

"Of course."

"You have to promise not to tell."

"I would never," Bel said.

"It's a *contest*. Which senior girl can bed Donovan first."

It took a second for Darcy's meaning to sink in. A contest to hook up with the dorm head? Bel hoped she wasn't serious. Yet, when Darcy laughed uproariously, Bel joined in. Who was she to judge? She'd made a cool, new friend. She ought to go with the flow.

4

Classes didn't start until tomorrow, and they already had homework. How was that even possible? Rose only found out because her roommate came back from dinner and started FaceTiming with some boy on her laptop, complaining about the reading for English.

"Wait, what? There's homework already?" Rose said, panicking mildly.

Rose's roommate was Skyler Stone from New Jersey. Skyler had long brown hair and wore a lot of makeup to cover her iffy complexion. Other than her skin, she was pretty and well-dressed enough to make Rose feel like a frump by comparison. Then again, most of the Odell girls made Rose feel like a frump. Skyler had been a freshman last year, and acted put-upon to be rooming with a newbie.

"If you want to see your homework," Skyler said, in a snippy tone, "log on to campus net. It's posted there in your academic module."

Rose had no idea what any of that meant, but she was hesitant to annoy Skyler by asking another question. Instead, she grabbed her laptop and headed up the stairs to the third floor to find her sister. There was virtually no chance that Bel knew how to look up homework assignments on campus net already. But Skyler's sharp tone had stung, and made Rose homesick for her sister.

Rose was the older twin by twenty minutes, and she tried to look out for Bel, though Bel didn't always appreciate it. Bel had poor judgment sometimes. Mom had worked full time. To make extra money, she taught landscape painting in the evenings and sold jewelry at craft shows on the weekends. When Mom was too busy to look out for Bel, Rose took that responsibility on herself. She could handle it. Rose was intelligent and levelheaded. She got good grades, and was careful in her choice of friends. Bel was moody and immature and ran with a bad crowd. She'd cut class and go hang out on the beach to get high. Rose knew it for a fact. She'd even had words with Bel about it, more than once. When Bel told her to mind her own business, Rose went to Mom. But Mom was sick by then, and had other things on her mind. Besides, Mom wouldn't hear a word against Bel, even if it was true. Bel was her pet. So, for the six months that their mother was sick before she died, Bel ran wild. Rose was disgusted by it, frankly. If there was a silver lining to the tragedy of her mother's death, it was getting Bel away from bad influences, and into a situation with stricter supervision.

Rose knocked on the door of 305.

"Come in."

Bel's roommate, Emma, was alone in the room. They'd met earlier at the welcome reception. Emma was beautiful and cool, and had been so nice to Rose at dinner tonight. Bel's room was great, too—the only sophomore double with one of the huge bay windows that Moreland was famous for. Rose was jealous that Bel wound up with the better room and the better roommate. But if having such prime stuff helped her sister settle in here, then Rose didn't mind.

"Hey, Rose. Bel's out at the moment," Emma said.

"Do you know where she is? Apparently, there's homework already."

"Yeah, welcome to Odell. There's always homework."

"I just wanted to make sure she knows."

Emma smiled. "You're such a good sister."

She wore leggings and an Odell sweatshirt, which seemed to be the uniform for hanging around the dorm at night. Her shiny black hair hung over one shoulder in a long braid. Rose made careful mental notes of these details so she could copy them later. The new clothes she'd been so excited about seemed wrong once she got here. No surprise really, since they'd been picked mainly by Grandma. Bel had pushed back on what Grandma chose for her, but Rose had been afraid to rock the boat. Why make Grandma mad over a few pieces of clothing? But now Rose realized that she'd ended up with a prissy wardrobe. Bel's clothes were way cooler. Maybe her sister knew best sometimes, after all.

"I wanted to ask Bel if she knows how to log on to

campus net to see the assignments, and also borrow a few of her things. Which dresser is hers?" Rose asked.

"That one," Emma said, pointing.

Rose rummaged quickly in Bel's dresser and took a couple of pairs of leggings, a flowy top and a cardigan sweater with leather trim on the front. Bel had so much stuff. She wouldn't miss this.

"I don't know when Bel's coming back, but I can show you how to log on to campus net if you like," Emma said.

"That would be great, thank you."

Rose handed Emma her laptop. Emma proceeded to demonstrate how to log on to the school-wide network and navigate it. Rose was surprised to find that she had not only homework assignments, but e-mails.

"Wow, I got an invitation to tea with Mrs. Donovan," Rose said. "Did you get it, too?"

Emma read the e-mail over Rose's shoulder. "No, it's just for you," she said. "The e-mail says she's your advisor. You're lucky. Mrs. Donovan is so nice. I had her for Algebra last year. The Donovans are a huge improvement over the last dorm head. Thank God they fired him."

"Did he do something wrong?"

"He let Moreland get totally out of control. This dorm has a rep, you know. It's the slut dorm."

"Seriously?"

"I hate to use that word, since it shames girls for behavior boys get high-fived for. But, yeah. Which brings me to a rather awkward subject."

"What's that?" Rose asked, alarmed.

"You may have noticed that Bel and I haven't exactly hit it off. At dinner, I invited her to sit with me, and she went and sat with those seniors instead. You know. Darcy and Tessa?"

"I'm so sorry. I apologize for her rudeness."

"Oh, I don't care about that. I have more friends than I know what to do with. But I feel it's my responsibility to warn you that Bel's hanging with a bad crowd."

"Really?"

"Yes. Darcy Madden and her cohorts are notorious. Trust me, you don't want your sister messed up with them. You need to say something."

"I'll try," Rose said, shaking her head. Just when she'd been feeling like they'd dodged a bullet by coming to Odell, history started repeating itself. "I don't know if it'll do any good, though. This has come up before."

"What do you mean?" Emma said.

"Oh, well—"

Rose realized she was on the verge of saying too much. She liked Emma immensely, but she didn't know yet whether she could trust her. If Rose blabbed, Bel might get in trouble.

"Nothing," Rose said. "I didn't mean anything."

"No, really, Rose. You should tell me. I live with Bel. You don't. If I know there's something to watch out for, I can help keep her on the straight and narrow."

Emma had a point there. Rose was on a completely different floor, and wouldn't be able to look out for Bel as much as she would like.

"Okay, well, back home, when our mother was sick, Bel got . . . a bit wild."

"Wild, how? Drugs? Boys?"

"I'm not entirely sure. She would cut class, though. You shouldn't hold it against her. It wasn't her fault. She had no guidance."

"You didn't cut class, did you?"

"Oh, no. I wouldn't do that."

"You can't cut class at Odell. You get a demerit every time, along with early check-in for a week. Two demerits and you can't compete for the school in sports or other activities. Four demerits is a suspension."

"I'll let Bel know," Rose said.

"You should. I will, too. Word is the Donovans are planning a big crackdown. If Bel doesn't get her act together, she could get DC'd."

"'DC'd'?"

"Sent to the Disciplinary Committee. That happens for serious infractions, and then it goes on your record for college applications. You can even get expelled."

"That would be awful. You're right. I need to say something to her."

"You seem very loyal," Emma said. "I wish I had you for a roommate instead of her. She strikes me as a real flake, but I bet you and I would be a great fit."

Rose flushed with pleasure, though she felt guilty for talking about her sister like that with Emma. Then again, Bel *was* flaky. You couldn't deny it. Rose shouldn't feel bad if Emma had figured it out for herself.

5

Rose woke up on the first day of classes to find that a perfect ray of sunlight was streaming through a crack in the window blinds. It felt like an omen. Life started fresh today. She jumped out of bed and hurried to get dressed, humming under her breath. Skyler groaned and pulled the covers over her head.

"Are you always this cheerful in the morning?" Skyler said. "I can't handle it."

"I'm just excited to go to class."

Rose had stayed up late last night doing her introductory assignments, but she didn't feel tired in the least. On the contrary, she was energized. Every word she'd read was emblazoned on her brain, and she couldn't wait to get into the classroom to talk about the material. Like all the great boarding schools, Odell used the Harkness Method. Rose had read up on the Harkness Method before starting here, and it sounded like the perfect fit for her. Small classes, discussion-based learning. At her old school, she'd hated the big, chaotic rooms. The teachers turned their backs and talked to the chalkboard while kids surfed the Web or goofed around. If Rose spoke up in class, kids rolled their eyes. Odell was different. She could be herself here. She could be smart, and learn a lot, and people would like her for it.

It was a perfectly cool September morning. Delicate light filtered through towering elm trees as Rose walked to her first-ever Odell class. She couldn't get over the beauty of the campus, its vast expanse. She'd walked five minutes from her dorm to get to breakfast, and then ten minutes back in the opposite direction to get to Founders' Hall for class, all on brick paths that crisscrossed dew-covered lawns. When she stepped into Founders' Hall, she felt the weight of centuries in the air of its dark paneled hallways, redolent of books and dust. Yet kids rushed by her on the stairs, laughing and goofing around as if the grandeur was old news. Rose couldn't imagine getting to the point where she took this place for granted, and yet, she wished for it to happen, because that would mean she belonged.

The walls of the social studies classroom were lined with framed maps from another century. A marble bust of George Washington watched her from a pedestal in the corner. The teacher was eloquent and thoughtful, and the discussion lively from the start. Rose made her first comment about ten minutes in—something about how the Constitution was the result of compromise—and Mr. Mendez liked it so much that he wrote it on the board. For the rest of the class, kids kept referring to "Rose's point," and she was so proud of herself that she had to take care not to act cocky. English class second period was amazing, too. Mrs. Sunderland went around the room and asked each of them to name a favorite book and say how it had influenced them. Rose talked about the *Little House* books, which she'd read obsessively between the ages of ten and fourteen. Not only did nobody roll their eyes at her, but two other girls piped up to say they'd read those books over and over, too, and loved them just as much.

French was the best of all. Mademoiselle LeBlanc was a native speaker who insisted that the students speak only French in the classroom. (She also had a chic haircut and beautiful suede boots.) Rose was terrified at first. She'd been studying French since middle school, and had never been asked to do more than conjugate verbs on paper. Miraculously, when her turn came, her tongue knew what to do. *"Bonjour, mademoiselle,"* Rose said, the words flowing out almost effortlessly. *"Je m'appelle Rose Enright. Je viens de Californie."* The teacher nodded approvingly, and Rose suddenly had a new ambition. She would become fluent in French, speak with a perfect accent, live in Paris. Odell had a study-abroad program where you could live with a French family for a summer. She would convince Grandma to send her. Oh, life was exciting.

Emma Kim was in Rose's French class, and when the period ended, she fell into step beside Rose, as if it was perfectly natural for them to walk to lunch together. The cool morning had become a bright, sunny day, and the Quad smelled of warm earth. Rose chatted and laughed with her new friend as they headed to the dining hall. Emma was a returning sophomore like Skyler, but didn't seem to mind that Rose was new. Rose cherished the hope that they would become close friends. The girls she sat with at lunch in her old school had never been much more than acquaintances. They didn't hang out, didn't text, didn't invite her shopping or to the movies. It wasn't like she hadn't tried. She didn't really understand why they didn't want to be closer; maybe they didn't consider her fun. Here at Odell, she hoped, the definition of fun would be different. Rose herself would be different here. If this morning was any indication, she would fit in, have friends, be liked and admired.

The new part of the dining hall, known simply as *the New*, was a soaring, modern space, all glass and white walls, with brightly colored flags hanging from the high ceilings (Odell had students from thirty countries). Giant photos of local flora decorated the walls. To Rose, the New looked like some space-age art gallery with tables. As they walked in, a warm buzz of conversation washed over Rose, and her heart lifted. Bel was here somewhere in the crowd. Rose wanted to find her, to gush to her twin about this amazing place. She searched the crowd as she followed Emma to the food line, but didn't see Bel.

She noticed something else interesting, however.

"What's that writing on the walls?" Rose asked Emma.

"The names of every graduating senior are carved on the panels."

"Since when?"

"Going back, like, to the beginning of time. This is the new part of the dining hall, but if you go to the Commons, where they have the formal dinners, you'll see names dating back to the early 1800s."

"Seriously? My father and grandfather went here. Do you think I could find their names?"

Emma looked impressed. "Of course, you just need to know their class year. I had no idea you and Bel were legacies. She never mentioned it."

"Oh, Bel doesn't care about that sort of thing."

"Not care? That's crazy. My parents grew up in Korea, and even they knew Odell. Once my name gets carved on the wall, I'm not letting anybody forget it."

They got their food, and made a beeline for a table where some other sophomore girls from Moreland were sitting. Apparently, students sat by class year. Seniors rated the best tables, farthest from the glass doors that admitted cold blasts of air during the bitter New Hampshire winters, closest to the food line. Emma told Rose to never, ever try to sit there. They would chase you away, your name would be mud. Freshman were relegated to the outskirts, to an area they called Siberia. The other grades filled in the middle. Kids in the fast, popular crowd tended to sit at coed tables, whereas your normals were more likely to sit single-sex, like the Moreland table they were at now.

Skyler was at the Moreland table, sitting next to a girl named Lucy Ogunwe, who ran track and sang in the choir, and was in Rose's civics class. There were girls Rose recognized, and others she hadn't met yet. Emma introduced her around, but the glow of welcome was diminished by a flicker of worry when it hit home that Bel wasn't here. Bel was nowhere to be seen, in fact. At their old school, when Bel didn't show up to lunch, it usually meant she was ditching.

Toward the end of lunch period, a loud whoop went up from the tables where the seniors sat, and Rose turned to look. A muscular boy with a prominent forehead was wiping a gob of whipped cream from his face while kids around him laughed.

"You're gonna regret that," he said, his loud voice carrying in the sudden quiet.

Darcy Madden, identifiable by her bright blond hair, stood beside him, doubled over laughing. The boy grabbed Darcy and smeared the gob of whipped cream on her face. Darcy squealed, then struggled and broke loose, and the two of them ran from the room.

"That's like something that would happen in my school in L.A.," Rose said. "Lunch was out of control there."

"Yeah, well, it's not normal here. That was Darcy, the one I warned you about, and her boyfriend, Brandon. Those two really push the envelope. Disruptive behavior can get you demerits, you know. The teachers don't look happy."

"I'm not surprised."

"Do you see your sister?"

"What? Where?"

"She's sitting right there," Emma said, nodding toward the table Darcy had fled from.

Rose following Emma's gaze and saw Bel, who was fully ensconced, chatting and smiling like she'd known those people forever.

"*Oh.* That's where she went."

Rose was actually relieved to see Bel in the lunch-room. At least she wasn't off in the woods somewhere, ditching school. But Emma apparently didn't see it that way.

"Like I was telling you last night," Emma said, "those seniors are bad news. You need to *do* something."

"What should I do?"

"Go over there, talk to her."

"Now? Really?"

"Yes, really. She's your twin sister, right? It's on you to look out for her reputation. If Bel gets in trouble, it'll reflect badly on you."

That was a new concept to Rose. Back home, the school was big and impersonal, and nobody cared who your family was, unless they were rich or famous. But what Emma said made sense. At Odell, everybody knew everybody. Heck, her ancestors' names were carved on the wall. And she didn't want Bel to get in trouble. She wanted to be a good sister, and help her find her way here.

"You're right. I'm going to say something," Rose said.

Rose got up and marched across the dining hall toward the senior tables. Bel saw her coming, and narrowed her eyes, shaking her head slightly to tell Rose to keep away. Rose hesitated. She didn't want to embarrass her sister in front of the seniors, but she was also conscious of Emma and the other Morelanders watching to see what she would do. She had to do something, right? Emma had said so. She strode up to the senior table.

"What are you doing?" Bel asked, looking alarmed.

"What are *you* doing?" Rose replied.

"What does it look like? I'm eating lunch."

"Come sit with the sophomores."

"Why? I'm happy here."

"You shouldn't sit at a senior table. It's not done."

A tough-looking girl with wavy red hair looked at Rose with a bemused expression. "Who is this chick?" she asked Bel.

"My sister," Bel said.

The redhead reached over and patted Bel on the head playfully. "It's cool, sis. Darcy said Bel could sit with us. She's like our new mascot."

Mascot? That sounded a bit condescending, and yet, Rose felt a tentacle of jealousy stir. She met her twin's eyes pleadingly.

"Bel, come sit with me, *please*. I need to talk to you about something."

"Get lost, Rose. I'm busy."

In front of strangers, no less. Bel was probably just showing off for her new friends, but still, that really hurt. Rose was only trying to help. Couldn't Bel see that? Why didn't she just come along, instead of turning this into a scene?

"You don't have to be so nasty," Rose said.

"Hey, is that my sweater you're wearing?" Bel said.

"Yeah, it's cute. I borrowed it."

"Without asking?"

"Since when do I have to ask?"

"Since when do we share clothes? We don't like the same things. We're not the same size. Give it back."

"Fine, I'll give it back tonight," Rose said.

"She means now," the redhead said, in a snarky tone. "You *are* big, sis. You'll stretch it out."

Rose's cheeks burned. This nasty girl had just called her fat in front of a table full of seniors. Not only did Bel not rise to her defense. She actually *smirked*.

"Screw you, Bel. I don't want your skeevy clothes anyway."

Rose tore the sweater off and threw it in her sister's face. The look of shock in Bel's eyes gave Rose a sick thrill as she turned on her heel and fled back to the Moreland table. Rose had always been the loving sister, had always looked out for Bel. Come to think of it, she didn't get much in return, did she? Bel never repaid the favor, never invited Rose to hang out with her cool friends. To the contrary. She'd been willing to humiliate Rose in front of the seniors.

The Moreland girls had left already, which came as a relief. Hopefully they'd missed the conclusion of that awful scene. Rose's tray sat alone on the table, the half-eaten taco swimming in a pool of congealing orange grease. She bused her tray, worrying kids would gossip about her now. Her fabulous first day of classes had been ruined; and her self-confidence, which had been soaring this morning, was now in tatters. All because of Bel. As much as Rose loved her sister, she would struggle to forgive her for this.

6

Transcript of Witness Interview conducted by Lieutenant Robert Kriscunas, State Police—Major Crime Unit, and Detective Melissa Howard, Odell, NH, PD, with Miss Emma Kim.

Kriscunas: Miss Kim, I'm confirming for the record that your parents have given us permission to speak with you, and that you're being interviewed solely as a witness. You're not a suspect, target or person of interest in this case.

Kim: I should hope not.

Kriscunas: That's just something we say for the record. Okay, let's get started. Can you tell us, how well did you know the Enright sisters?

Kim: Pretty well. We were in the same grade. Bel was my roommate, although we weren't exactly friends. Rose, I was quite friendly with.

Kriscunas: When you say you weren't friends with Bel, do you mean that you didn't get along with her?

Kim: I get along with everybody, Detective. But with Bel, we moved in different crowds, and to be honest, I didn't always approve of her behavior. I kept my distance.

Kriscunas: Yes, and we want to go into detail about Bel's bad behavior. But for now, let's stick to the state of the sisters' relationship. What can you tell us about that?

Kim: Once they came to Odell?

Kriscunas: Anything you can tell us about their relationship would be helpful, as far back as you know.

Howard: For instance, if you know, were Rose and Bel close growing up?

Kim: From what Rose said, I think they were friends to each other. But my sense is, they weren't close, because they're so different—were so different.

Kriscunas: In what way were they different?

Kim: In every way. I mean, here at Odell, kids couldn't believe they were actually twins. First of all, they look nothing alike. Bel was this sultry brunette and Rose was fair, but beyond that—I mean, Bel was drop-dead gorgeous. And Rose was, well, normal. Pleasant-looking. Some might say plain.

Kriscunas: Did that cause problems between them?

Kim: Problems, how?

Kriscunas: Jealousy?

Kim: Oh, so girls are all catty and jealous if one is pretty and the other isn't? I'm sorry, but that narrative is so trite.

Howard: I don't think the lieutenant meant it that way, Emma. We're interested in specific instances of bad feelings between the Enright sisters, that you were aware of.

Kim: If they were jealous, then they were each jealous of the other. I think they both wanted to be more like the other. Rose was really into school, and she was very successful at Odell from the start. Teachers liked her. She was especially close to her advisor, Mrs. Donovan.

Howard: Yes, we're going to be speaking with Mrs. Donovan.

Kim: Rose studied really hard, did lots of extracurriculars. Her grades were good. Where Bel struggled academically, and I think it bothered Bel that Rose was so into school.

Howard: Bothered her, how?

Kim: Like, she found it annoying and prissy, but she was also jealous. Bel, on the other hand, immediately got accepted into this fast, popular clique. Rose didn't like that. She worried Bel would get in trouble. But deep down, she was jealous of Bel's social life. On a Saturday night, Bel would be off partying, but you could always find Rose in the library.

Kriscunas: Rose was quiet, Bel was wild?

Kim: Mmm, that's too simplistic. In some ways, Bel was the quiet one. She hung out with the older kids, but she was a follower, not a leader. Like with the attack—you know, the slipper incident?

Kriscunas: Yes, we're going to go over that in some detail in a moment.

Kim: Okay, that was all Darcy Madden's doing. Bel was just along for the ride. Like I said, a follower. Also, Bel barely ever talked in class, which is somewhat unusual here, and part of the reason she didn't do well academically. Bel and I didn't have any classes together, because I'm on the Honors track, and she was definitely not *on the Honors track. But I heard from other kids that she'd sit there like a bump on a log, terrified to open her mouth. Except in* English.

Kriscunas: You say that like it was important.

Kim: Well. Let's just say that Mr. Donovan *was her English teacher. I can talk about that if you want to. Uh—but Rose was very self-confident. Honestly, even though you could say she wasn't as popular as Bel, Rose fit in better here.*

Kriscunas: When you say Bel was popular, you're talking about with those seniors she hung out with?

Kim: Yes, exactly.

Kriscunas: You say they were a fast crowd.

Kim. Yes, I mean, come on. Darcy Madden and Tessa Romano—you know what they did, right?

Kriscunas: Absolutely, and that's on the agenda. We think that incident could be quite important in terms of motive. Tell us more about Bel and the seniors. How did Bel come to hang out with them? And did it cause the tension with Rose?

Kim: How they started hanging out, I don't know. It was just like that from Day One. I remember the very first day of classes, Bel was already sitting with the seniors, which was pretty unheard of. My guess is, Darcy took a shine to Bel, and since Darcy was the queen bee, that meant Bel was in. Anyway, I told Rose that Bel was headed for trouble, hanging out with that crew. Those girls were notorious for doing drugs, smuggling boys in, pulling pranks, that sort of thing. Rose tried to talk sense into Bel, but Bel wasn't having it.

Howard: Were there specific incidents you recall where they argued over it?

Kim: Oh, they fought about it all the time. Rose felt like her sweet sister was taken over by pod people, you know? But nothing she said made any difference. You have to understand, showing up here as a newbie sophomore is not easy. To have Darcy Madden favor you with her attention—Bel's head was turned. It made her feel special. Those weren't just any friends. They were the most powerful friends you could have at this school, socially speaking. Until it all went wrong, with the attack.

Kriscunas: We understand that the sisters were on opposite sides of that incident. Do you think it's what caused the rift between them?

Kim: The rift had been developing for a while. And not just over Bel hanging with Darcy's crew. There were other reasons, too. Fighting over clothes, over boys—over a particular boy. But yeah, it was the attack that caused the most serious breach between them.

Howard: Serious enough to lead to murder?

Kim: You're the police. You tell me.

Kriscunas: Miss Kim, you were the student who had the best access to both sisters. We're interested in hearing what you think.

Kim: Honestly? I think there are several possible explanations. There was more going on here than you realize.

Kriscunas: Like what?

Kim: Well . . . you say you're going to talk to Mrs. Donovan?

7

To sweet, beautiful Sarah," Heath said, raising his champagne glass. "'One half of me is yours, the other half yours, and so all yours.' Happy thirty, darling, I love you more than ever."

"I love you, too. So much," Sarah said, her eyes sparkling with happy tears.

They clinked glasses, took sips, then leaned across the table and kissed lingeringly. His lips were cool and delicious from the champagne. It was the Saturday night after the first week of classes, and the dining room at Le Jardin glowed with flowers and candlelight. Soft music played in the background, and Sarah felt lucky. She would have settled for putting the kids to bed, making a pot of spaghetti and opening a bottle of red wine. But this was a milestone birthday, and Heath had surprised her with dinner at her favorite restaurant, expense be damned. Life with him had its ups and downs, but it was never less than exciting.

"What you said just now, was that Shakespeare?" Sarah asked.

"Yep. The Bard of Avon never fails to impress. There *are* some benefits to being married to an English teacher, you know."

He ducked his head sheepishly, and she read his thoughts. Heath loved his work, but he was ashamed of the size of his paycheck. He'd never intended to spend his life as an English teacher. There had been a more fabulous, lucrative goal once, and he'd come achingly close to achieving it. Heath was supposed to be a famous novelist by now. On the bestseller list, winning literary prizes, opening fat royalty checks at a house on Martha's Vineyard. But things had gone terribly wrong, and they'd fled back to Odell in disgrace. (A private disgrace, with a confidentiality agreement to ensure it stayed that way.) Back to a safe place, where they'd first met. Now, a fancy dinner out was a rare treat. Sarah wasn't disappointed with their lot in life. They had each other, the two babies she'd always dreamed of, the dog, jobs that were rewarding if not glamorous. But Heath was disappointed, and he didn't hide it.

"There are many wonderful benefits to being married to Heath Donovan," she said, lifting his hand and kissing it.

His smile reached his eyes, and she was grateful for it. In the past few weeks, since they'd gotten the promotion to dorm head, Heath had found his way again after years in the wilderness. An ambitious man of a literary bent and few practical skills could do worse than rising through the ranks at a prestigious boarding school like Odell. Heath had a plan. Dorm head today, but tomorrow, head of the English department. Then dean of faculty, and eventually, headmaster. It would take time, but at least he was dreaming again. Heath wasn't Heath when he didn't dream. Sarah was starting to believe that the demons were banished, but she wouldn't say it out loud, for fear of jinxing it.

They sipped champagne, and chatted about their week. There were a couple of new girls in Moreland, twins, who'd been orphaned. Heath and Sarah had taken them on as advisees, and would keep a close watch. They both remembered their early days as students at Odell. How tough the place could be, how hard it was to get your feet under you. Sarah hadn't been thrilled about the dorm head job. She took it for Heath's sake. But if this job gave her the chance to help girls like the girl she'd been once—shy, insecure, daunted by the school and everyone in it—then something good could come of it.

Heath opened his menu and studied it, an adorable wrinkle forming between his brows. Sarah paused to appreciate his face—the elegant bone structure, the intense blue-green eyes. Even his ears were perfect—small and neat and dignified.

He looked up and caught her staring. "What?"

"Just thinking how lucky I am."

"Me, too, always, love," he said. "Hey, what do you say we split the seafood tower for the first course?"

She looked at the price and raised an eyebrow.

"Oh, come on, we just got raises," he said. "YOLO, am I right?"

She laughed. "You sound like a Moreland girl."

"Uh-oh, it's starting to rub off. Seriously, it's your birthday, so I'm making an executive decision. We split the seafood tower. You get the Dover sole because I know you want it. I get the filet mignon. Then we order the chocolate lava cake with a candle and two spoons."

"Mmm, you always know what I like," she said.

"That's why you married me. So, what do you say?"

"You've got a deal."

They placed their orders, and Sarah pushed the thought of money from her mind. It wasn't something she'd worried about much, before the setbacks of the past few years. Sarah came from a tight-lipped, old-money, old-Odellian family. She grew up in a stately house in a wealthy town in Massachusetts, where life was comfortable, but cold and restrained. Nobody showed off, nobody cried or danced or displayed much emotion of any kind. Her mother wore sensible shoes and tweed skirts, and belonged to the Junior League. Her father commuted into Boston, to a law firm that his own father had worked at before him, and that he would work at till he retired, or died in the harness, which-ever came first. They went to dinner at the country club and to church on Sundays, and talked about trimming the hydrangeas and how the neighbors' house needed painting. Money was never discussed—which was pos-sible only because they had plenty of it, of course.

Heath arrived at Odell like a whirlwind in junior year, on a tennis scholarship. Most kids who came late in the game never made it to the golden circle, but Heath was different. Kids were bored with each other by then, and Heath—so good-looking, so athletic, so charming—was a sensation. Sarah got assigned to be his peer tutor in math, or she never would've gotten near him. They had no classes together, and Sarah didn't run with the popular crowd. Not that she wanted to; they were a rotten bunch. The same beautiful mean girls Heath sat with at lunch had tormented Sarah since freshman year. Yet Heath took a shine to Sarah, despite the disdain of his friends. Maybe he took a shine to her *because* his friends didn't like her, because she was different from them—low-key and nonjudgmental. Heath found refuge in talking to Sarah. He was confident on the surface, but that was an act. His parents were going through a brutal divorce. His father had left his mother for another woman, and Heath's mother— who'd doted on him and raised him to believe in his own greatness—tried to kill herself. There were lawyers involved, involuntary commitment to a mental institution, money problems. Nobody at school knew except Sarah. She kept Heath's secrets, and loved that he trusted her. Once he kissed her, that was it, she was done. Though they didn't get engaged till the end of college. Her parents were none too happy. They thought Heath was beneath her.

Their first few years as newlyweds were bliss. They lived in the city. She worked in a consulting firm, he freelanced for magazines and wrote his novel on the side. Sarah thought Heath was a literary genius, even if his novel hit a bit too close to home for comfort. It was the story of a relationship between a wealthy young woman and a penniless young man that began at an

East Coast boarding school. The boarding school details were lifted straight from their Odell years. The couple was even named Henry and Sophia—*H* and *S*, Heath and Sarah. But the resemblance ended there, and the latter half of the book—in which Henry and Sophia move to France and get caught up in a decadent, expat social scene that ends in murder—was searingly brilliant. Sarah wasn't the only one who thought so. Heath got a book deal, a major one, and had a famous director interested in the film rights. They were on the way to realizing their dreams—well, his dreams. Heath's big break was well deserved. He was a rare talent, a genius. They'd both known it since high school. The world had now caught on, and was giving him the recognition he deserved.

They were so happy.

Then the accusation of plagiarism surfaced. An early reviewer caught it. Whole passages lifted directly from Fitzgerald's *Tender Is the Night,* not the revised edition, but the first, convoluted one, that wasn't widely read. Heath denied it, and Sarah believed him with all her heart. It was only when the publisher pulled the book, prior to publication, that she went out and bought a copy of *Tender Is the Night* and compared for herself. Heath must've thought that nobody would check, because when you put the pages side by side, the plagiarism was obvious. She was almost as angry about his carelessness as his lies. How could he have been so cavalier about something so important to their future? He was used to being admired and adored; that was why. Heath was confident that his transgressions would be overlooked, or forgiven. And she tried to forgive. But it was hard.

Heath was asked to pay back the advance, which was a problem since they'd already spent it. That hadn't been Sarah's doing. She was frugal by nature, but Heath wanted things. A lot of things. New clothes, a car, a better apartment, restaurants, parties. Who was she to say no, when he'd felt so deprived, growing up? Her parents stepped in and lent them the money to pay back the publisher—and never let them forget it.

Her father had thankfully managed to hush up the scandal, or else Heath would've been unemployable in teaching at any reputable school. If it came out, even now, a school like Odell would have no choice but to fire him. Some nights Sarah lay awake, worrying. About the past coming back to haunt them. About Heath's mental stability, how despondent he'd become when things went wrong, and whether he was susceptible to falling into that deep, dark pit again. She didn't think so. She prayed not. She was grateful that, with the dorm head job, he'd found something to feel excited about again. She wanted him to be happy. Heath wasn't a dishonest person. He'd just wanted to succeed so badly—to impress Sarah, to impress her parents—that he'd taken a shortcut to get there. Then he got caught, and felt ashamed, which was why he'd lied. It was a unique situation, far in the past, and unlikely to repeat itself. Besides, they had the children to think about now, and Heath adored his children. He wouldn't let himself get out of control emotionally again, she was certain.

Maybe not certain. But hopeful.

The waitress headed for their table, carrying the seafood tower. Heads turned to admire the dramatic presentation, just as they'd turned when her handsome husband walked in the door a half hour before. People were naturally drawn to Heath. The Moreland girls were crazy about him already. A colleague had said to her that very afternoon: Whenever I see your husband, he's trailing a gaggle of pretty girls. Sarah didn't let it bother her. She trusted Heath, and besides, it wasn't his fault. If she was a student here, she'd follow him around, too. Just look at that incredible smile, as the waitress presented the seafood tower. It was wonderful to see. Heath's happiness was the only gift Sarah needed.

8

Bel sat in Mr. Donovan's classroom in Benchley Hall, watching the hands on the old wall clock creep toward two-twenty, when English class would end. She had a meeting scheduled with Mr. Donovan then, and the thought of it made her queasy. Though she'd been feeling off all day anyway in this awful, sticky heat. Everyone said that the heat wave was unusual, but that didn't help her sleep at night or eat anything more substantial than a piece of fruit. Heat in L.A. had never bothered her, but the climate here was just evil.

The fan buzzing in the corner lulled her, and her eyelids drooped. But then Mr. Donovan spoke, and she bolted upright, her eyes flying open. Heath Donovan was the one thing in this new life that made Bel feel wide awake. He stood at the whiteboard, writing out a line from Shelley and explaining the concept of synecdoche. English was her favorite class just because she liked watching him and listening to his voice. Every day, Bel noticed new details about him. A small scar above his eyebrow, a beauty mark on his cheek, how his eyes crinkled when he smiled, the whiteness of his teeth. She paid attention not only to what he said, but how he moved, when he laughed, what he wore. Today he was wearing khaki pants and a blue-check dress shirt with the sleeves rolled up. The outfit looked amazing on his tennis player's body. He wasn't overly jacked like so many of the jock boys. He was lean and elegant. She didn't try to notice these things. He just made an impression on her, whether she liked it or not.

Mr. Donovan turned to recite the line to the class.

"'Its sculptor well those passions read,'" he quoted, in his deep, rich voice, "'which yet survive, stamped on these lifeless things, the hand that mocked him.'"

He asked for a volunteer to identify the synecdoche in that line, and Bel averted her eyes. If she tried to speak, she'd stutter and blush and generally make a fool of herself. Not because she hadn't done the reading—this was the one class she always prepared for. But because she was shy in front of these hyper-verbal Odell kids, and because Mr. Donovan unnerved her. That part was Darcy Madden's fault. Normally Bel would never stoop so low as to get a crush on a teacher, but Darcy and her posse of Moreland seniors were obsessed with Mr. Donovan and talked about him nonstop. Naturally their obsession had rubbed off on her. Bel listened to Darcy, and followed her lead in all things. Darcy was older, sophisticated. She understood how things worked around here. Bel felt fortunate to have been taken under her wing.

Yet, she had to laugh, because the seniors' contest to seduce Mr. Donovan had gone *nowhere*. Girls went to his office hours or cornered him in the dining hall. They flirted shamelessly, made heavy eye contact. The bold ones flashed some cleavage or bared a thigh in a short skirt. And they got no response. Zero. Donovan didn't seem to notice at all. He was apparently loyal to his wife, though nobody understood why. Darcy said the wife was a total mouse, a real loser. That she must have some unnatural hold over him. Maybe it was money, or some secret she was using to blackmail him. Otherwise, he'd be susceptible to the seniors' charms, like any man would be. To Darcy's own charms, anyway. Bel had to agree—Darcy was killer. She had those perfectly regular features: the long, swinging blond hair; a sharp tongue hidden behind a wide smile. Everybody danced to her tune. To Bel, she was the Oracle of Moreland, not to be contradicted. Yet, Bel thought Darcy was wrong about Mr. Donovan. His love for his wife was pure, and Mr. Donovan was chivalrous. Honorable, like a knight of old. He would see Darcy's sharp edges, and keep his distance. Which made him all the more attractive in Bel's book.

The bell rang. Class ended, and Bel gathered her things, hesitating. Was she supposed to go up to him, or wait for him to speak to her? Would their meeting happen here in this room, or should she go to his office? Talking to teachers wasn't Bel's thing to begin with, and *him*, well, she couldn't imagine speaking to him alone. Well, she could imagine it, but the things she imagined were unlikely to happen.

A couple of kids went up to the front of the room to talk to him, and Bel breathed a sigh of relief. Kids at Odell loved to hang around after class and suck up to teacher. Back home, being smart made you uncool, but here it was the opposite. Everybody spoke up in class, and competed to get noticed. Everyone except Bel, who kept her mouth firmly shut unless a teacher called on her, and then struggled to get a word out. Back home, teachers hadn't cared what she thought, not enough to put her on the spot anyway, and she preferred it that way.

With Mr. Donovan distracted, Bel took the opportunity to slink toward the door, hoping to escape before he noticed. She could claim she forgot, or that something suddenly came up, or—

"Bel," Mr. Donovan called. "Hold on. I'll be done in a minute."

Crap. Bel waited, palms sweaty, heartbeat skittering. Once they were alone, she'd be struck dumb, she knew it.

After a few minutes, the students left to go to their sixth-period classes, and he came over to her.

"Were you going to my office?" he asked, with a puzzled smile. Up this close, his teeth were so white, his eyes so blue, and he smelled so good that she felt dizzy.

"Um. Sorry?"

"I saw you leaving. You remember we have our first advisory meeting now, right?" he asked.

"Oh. Right. Yes. No, I didn't forget, I just wasn't sure, uh, where to, or—what to do," Bel said, her cheeks burning. She sounded like the biggest idiot.

"It's so warm today. I thought we could grab an iced coffee and sit outside. My office is like an oven, but there should be some breeze if we go over to the Art Café. Come on."

Coffee? With Mr. Donovan? Alone? The Moreland girls would be pea-green with envy.

They went to the snack bar in the basement of the Art Studio, which was empty at this hour, since most kids were in class. (Bel had scheduled the meeting for her free period.) Mr. Donovan bought two iced coffees, which he carried to the patio out back. They sat down facing each other at a small iron table in the shade of a tall tree. (The trees in this place were insane. All that chlorophyll, she could gag on it.)

"Since this is our first advisory meeting, I thought I'd start by explaining the role of advisor here at Odell, which is not exactly the same as a guidance counselor in a public school," Mr. Donovan said.

Bel was relieved that he was talking about official-sounding stuff. If she was lucky, she could sit here and enjoy listening to him and never have to say a word.

"At Odell, we're fortunate to have professionals for every function," Mr. Donovan continued. "There are counseling services at the health center if you're having emotional or mental health issues. You'll be assigned a college counselor starting next year. My job is to advise you about academics, and more generally . . ."

She got distracted by the color of his eyes. They were such an intense shade of aqua-blue that they almost seemed fake. Was it possible that he wore colored lenses? But they went beautifully with the long, sooty lashes, and the rich, dark color of his hair, so maybe they were real after all.

"Bel, are you listening?"

"Oh, I'm sorry. I apologize. I just—" She blushed furiously and shook her head.

"No. You know what? It's my fault, droning on like a page out of the handbook. No wonder you zoned out. Let's start over. I'm Heath, and I'm your advisor, nice to meet you."

He reached across the table, and she realized he intended to shake her hand. Had he just given her permission to call him by his first name? Their eyes met, and she put her hand in his. The warmth of his grip jolted her.

"And you are—?" he asked.

"Isabel Enright. *Bel*. Call me Bel. I'm your, um, your student. Nice to meet you, too."

The exchange was so silly that she laughed, and felt less awkward after that. Maybe he wouldn't prove impossible to talk to after all. She simply had to concentrate on what he said, not how he looked.

Easier said than done.

"Think of me as your guide to Odell," Heath said, releasing her hand. "You come to me with a question or a problem, and it's my job to help you. Maybe you have an academic issue, or a personal problem, or maybe you just don't know which extracurricular activity to try. If I can help you, I will. If it's out of my wheelhouse, I'll find the right person for you to speak to. Odell can be so confusing at first, and the point of the advisor is to help you feel comfortable right away. Odell is your home now, and we're your family, your school family, that is. I want you to know, Bel, that you have a support system in me. I'm here for you."

Such kind words would have reached her no matter who said them. But to have Mr. Donovan say them—wow. His sympathy hit her hard; it released something. She'd been holding her feelings in for weeks now. Acting like she didn't care that her grandmother sent them away. Hanging out with a fast crowd because she'd fallen in with them at the beginning, acting the role of wild child to keep up, but having big doubts about it. Fighting with Rose—God, she hated to fight with her sister, but ever since they'd gotten here, things between them felt so wrong. Suddenly it was all too much. Bel's lower lip started to quiver. She looked at Heath for one long, terrible second, and burst into tears.

"Oh," Heath said, flushing. "Jesus, I'm an idiot. I'm so sorry. I know you lost your mother. I should have been more careful. I was only trying to make you feel better, but I put my foot in it."

"No, it's okay," she whispered, but her shoulders were heaving, and she couldn't stop crying.

Heath handed her a napkin from the table, and she blotted at her eyes, her body wracked with sobs. He looked at her with such concern that Bel saw the tragedy of her plight reflected in his beautiful eyes, and the worst moments flooded back. Her mother's face when she told them the diagnosis. Seeing her mother get thinner, lose her hair. The day her mother died. Hearing her grandmother tell them they had to go away to school. Being mean to Rose in the dining hall, feeling terrible about it, and having Rose refuse to speak to her afterward. Now she really couldn't stop crying. Heath dragged his chair around the small table, until he sat beside her, an inch away.

"Bel," he said softly.

She looked up at him, and she realized she wasn't afraid of him anymore, or nervous around him. He felt like a friend.

"I'm sorry," she said, through tears. "I'm embarrassed to flake out on you like this. But my life is just— It's so fucking dark."

He glanced around at the empty patio, then reached out and squeezed her shoulder. "You can tell me. Nobody's here. You can say anything."

"Why did both my parents have to *die*?" she said. "Why *me*? Like, who does that happen to? First my dad when I was little. Then my mom. It's so unfair."

"I agree. Very unfair."

"I'm being punished."

"That's not true. How could it be? You're a child. You've done nothing wrong."

"I'm ungrateful. That's what Rose says. I ought to be glad our grandmother took us in, and sent us here, but I'm not. I'm angry."

"There's nothing wrong with how you feel," he said. "It's completely normal."

"What I'm really saying is, I don't like Odell. I actually kind of hate it."

"I understand. This place can grind you down. Make you feel like you're not good enough. It did that to me, at first."

"Really?"

"Yes. It took me a long time to prove myself here. To find my place."

"Wait. You went to school here?"

"You didn't know? I was actually very happy at Odell—not right away, but eventually. Right? I mean, I came back to teach, though sometimes I think I'm still trying to *show* them. Maybe that's why I came back. I could tell you stories about what it was like, what I went through. I've been low, myself. I've been so low. You can't imagine."

She looked up into his eyes, holding her breath, afraid he would stop confiding in her.

"Tell me," she whispered.

"I shouldn't. I can't—well, maybe I'll tell you another time. But believe me when I say that bad things have happened in my life. Here at Odell, and elsewhere. Things that almost pulled me under, that I thought I would never recover from. But I did. I got past it. And you can, too. You remind me of myself, you know."

"I do? How?"

"Maybe I'm projecting. But the way you're so quiet in class, and yet, I can tell how deeply you're feeling things. You're a dreamer. So am I."

"Yes. You see. You understand me." Her eyes filled with tears again.

"That gives me some insight into how to help you, Bel. You need something to dream about. A focus, something special to work toward. If you could find that, I think you could be successful here. I think you could even be happy. Will you try?"

"I want to, Heath. I worry that I'm not up to it," Bel said.

There, she'd used his name. Was he going to rebuke her? But no, he took her hand, and she held on, like he could save her from the flood.

"Don't sell yourself short. If you could see the girl I see, I know you'd believe in yourself. You *are* up to it," he said, and there was so much sympathy in his voice that she nearly melted.

"But I'm not as smart as the kids here," she said.

"It's not true. I've seen your file. I admit, your grades aren't anything to write home about. But your scores are off the charts. You're very smart, Bel. You just have to do the work, and you'll succeed."

"That's not the only problem," she said. "People are mean here. Everyone's a poser. I feel so lost."

"You have your twin sister to fall back on, don't you?"

"Not really. Rose and I used to be good friends, but this place is driving us apart. She doesn't like who I hang out with. She doesn't approve of my behavior. We fight all the time. I hate it."

"Odell can put pressure on relationships, it's true. You have to ignore the noise. Find some time when it's just the two of you, and hash things out. Will you try?"

"I want to make up with her. I do. I've been feeling so alone."

"You're not alone, Bel. You have your sister. You also have me."

Bel wiped her eyes, and gazed at him. "You mean that?"

"I do mean it. I'm your advisor, and it's my job to help you be happy here. As a matter of fact, I have a suggestion."

Bel was hoping for something intimate and personal, like the two of them having dinner together. Now *that* would give her something to live for. Instead Heath suggested that Bel join the cross-country team, which he coached. It would get her out in nature, and the endorphins generated by long-distance running would improve her outlook. *Yada yada yada*, she thought. But then she realized that he couldn't ask her to dinner even if he wanted to. It would look weird, and it was probably against the rules. But if she joined the team he coached, she could spend more time with him, and not just time, but time in the woods on the running trails, maybe even alone.

"I'd love to," she said.

"Good, it's settled. Come to the field house this afternoon at three forty-five, and we'll get you squared away with a uniform."

He glanced at his watch, which made her sad. She didn't want their meeting to end.

"I have to get going," he said. "It's later than I thought. I'm glad we had this talk, Bel. Everything's going to be all right. You're going to be happy here, I promise. Okay?"

"If you say so."

"I do say so." He stood up and glanced around quickly, making sure that nobody would see. "C'mere, you seem like you could use a hug," he said, holding out his arms.

Bel didn't hesitate. She stepped into his embrace and

gloried there, letting herself bask in the warmth of his body, his breath against her hair. She drank in the scent of his shampoo, which made her think of the ocean, of sandalwood. She would've stayed like that forever, but he released her, and stepped away.

"Okay, see you at the field house later," he said.

Then he was gone.

The air felt cooler now—fresher, sweeter, and it smelled of flowers and grass. Somewhere somebody mowed a lawn, and the buzz of the lawn mower was cheerful to her ears. Bel started walking toward Moreland, and the deep green of the trees and the grass was pleasing to her now. There would always be a before and an after. A before and an after their talk. A before and an after their embrace. Before, she was lost, but now, a light shined on everything she saw. Bel could go tell Darcy and the seniors what happened, and bask in their envy. But she wouldn't. She didn't want to share this. Her friendship with Heath Donovan was her secret, hers alone.

9

H e just got glasses yesterday, poor thing, and doesn't quite know what to make of them," Mrs. Donovan said.

Rose sat at the Donovans' kitchen table, holding little Scottie in her lap. The air was fragrant with the scent of the chocolate-chip cookies fresh from the oven. The child fidgeted with the bright-green eyeglasses attached to his head with a strap, so Rose held him away from her and made funny faces to distract him. He watched her solemnly, his eyes behind the lenses wide as saucers.

"You're so good with him," Mrs. Donovan said. "Do you babysit?"

"I'd babysit for this guy anytime. He's the sweetest," Rose said, lowering her nose and drinking in the scent of the child's flaxen hair.

Mrs. Donovan laughed. "I'll take you up on that. He *is* a sweetie. He was a preemie, you know. He doesn't talk much yet. He's a little delayed. Watch out, though. His sister is a holy terror, and it's a package deal."

"She seems so fun. Is she here?"

"Harper *is* fun. She's a handful, though. She's in her room playing Goat Simulator on the laptop, so we can have some peace and quiet."

"Playing *what*?"

"Goat Simulator. It's this video game where the kid pretends to be a goat running wild in a town. It's actually a pretty good metaphor for Harper's life, come to think of it. Anyway, she's obsessed with it."

Mrs. Donovan placed a plate of cookies on the table in front of Rose. Max lounged at Rose's feet, his tail thumping back and forth with the rhythm of a metronome. This afternoon tête-à-tête was like a dream come true. To be invited into a teacher's home, and to have it be so cozy and adorable. The kitchen had an old-fashioned gas stove, a tile backsplash and pretty curtains. Mrs. Donovan had the nicest smile, and was so easy to talk to. In Rose's old school, the teachers barely knew her name. Rose couldn't believe her luck in getting Mrs. Donovan as her advisor.

"Tea?" Mrs. Donovan asked.

"I'd love to, but I'm holding the baby," Rose said.

"Oh, I'll take him, so you can enjoy your refreshments."

Mrs. Donovan brought mugs of tea over to the table. Why did people say she wasn't good-looking? She might not be flashy or blingy, but she had a fresh, wholesome prettiness—like a mother should. Rose's mother had been glamorous, yet Rose had never felt comfortable with her eccentric, arty style. Done up in thrift-shop finds, with a big tattoo of angel wings on her arm for their dad. She cooked up pots of organic quinoa for dinner, but never baked cookies. Rose had secretly wished for a normal mom, someone more like Mrs. Donovan. She felt guilty thinking that, yet, if Rose was honest, here in this delightful kitchen with Mrs. Donovan, she didn't miss her mother much at all.

Scottie went to Mrs. Donovan happily. Rose took a bite of a cookie. It was warm and gooey inside. *Bliss.*

"These are divine. Thank you so much for baking for me. You didn't have to!" Rose exclaimed.

"Oh, it was no trouble. Harper helped. She loves baking—today, anyway. Five minutes from now, she'll be on to something else."

"It must be so special for them, growing up at Odell," Rose said.

"People think that," Mrs. Donovan replied, frowning. "But being a faculty kid makes for a strange childhood. We eat most of our meals in the dining hall, with a million people all around. Scottie gets overwhelmed by the excitement, and Harper eats it up. Literally. Yesterday I found three brownies in her pockets. Students sneak her extra dessert."

Rose laughed. "That's adorable."

"Not when she's bouncing off the walls at bedtime from all the sugar. Besides, it's a control thing. How can I teach her *no* when there are so many teenagers around who say yes?"

"Yes, but—it's so wonderful here, with beautiful

grounds to play in. I grew up in an apartment complex in the city. Everything was concrete. We couldn't have pets. To me, Odell feels like paradise."

"You're not alone in thinking that. Some people see the campus, and it's love at first sight. My husband was like that. He lived and breathed Odell when we were students, and that's still true. Even if he wasn't sure about being a teacher, he knew he wanted to be *here*," Mrs. Donovan said, and laughed sheepishly.

"He doesn't like being a teacher?"

"Oh, I, uh, didn't mean it that way," Mrs. Donovan said, coloring slightly, as if she'd said too much. "Heath loves his work. Especially now that we're dorm heads, and truly immersed in the community. He finds it very fulfilling."

There was a false note in Mrs. Donovan's voice that made Rose wonder how she herself felt about Odell.

"And you? Do you like your work?" Rose asked.

"Thank you for asking. I love teaching math. But I'm a bit of an introvert, so the dorm head job, living here on campus, doesn't come as naturally to me as it does my husband. But I think it's important work, so it's satisfying in that sense. Historically, Moreland has had challenges. I had run-ins with girls from this dorm when I was a student here. It just seems to attract the mean girls."

"There are mean girls here now," Rose said.

"I realize that. And I want to be part of fixing the culture. Heath and I are trying to foster a healthy atmosphere in Moreland. But it's tricky. We have to identify the girls causing the trouble, hopefully before they do anything too disruptive, and get them to change their ways, if possible."

Rose wondered if Mrs. Donovan had heard the gossip. There was a rumor going around that the Moreland seniors—the same girls Bel hung out with—were engaged in a competition to seduce Mr. Donovan. Rose was so outraged when she heard that that she wanted to hit somebody. If it was true, they ought to be expelled. She had half a mind to tell Mrs. Donovan about it right now, and put a stop to it. But how awkward was that— telling Mrs. Donovan other girls wanted to sleep with her husband? It was too embarrassing, and would spoil their cozy tea date.

"Enough about me," Mrs. Donovan said. "How are *you* doing, Rose? You've been through so much with your mom's passing. Odell can be a tough transition in the best of times. Are you settling in all right?"

"Yes. I love it here. I couldn't be happier."

Mrs. Donovan looked at her skeptically. "I'm very glad to hear that, but you don't have to say it if it isn't true. I know you're off to a great start academically. You're doing excellent work in math class. I've also heard from some of your other teachers that you're a confident speaker at the Harkness Table, which is a big indicator of success at Odell."

Her teachers said good things about her. Rose nodded, arranging her features so she wouldn't look too pleased with herself.

"I *adore* my classes, Mrs. Donovan. I feel so engaged, like I'm really learning."

"What about outside of class? Are you feeling comfortable socially?" Mrs. Donovan asked.

"I'm doing so much fun stuff," Rose said cheerily, grabbing her backpack, and pulling out her notebook. "Here's my list so far. Auditioning for the fall play. I joined the debate team. I'm working on the literary magazine. Joined Model UN and French Club. Oh, and I might audition for the chorus. I've never sung in front of people except for karaoke, but I was pretty good at that."

Mrs. Donovan looked at her in astonishment. "Rose, that's a wonderful list. I'm very impressed. But you have be careful not to take on too much."

Rose felt it should be obvious that she could handle anything she took on. Was Mrs. Donovan selling her short because of her background? Odell was a clubby place, and though Rose's father's family were old Odellians, and Grandma had money, Rose and Bel had been raised by a single mom in modest circumstances. Compared to her classmates, with their summers filled with golf and tennis, their vacations abroad and tutors for every subject, Rose had grown up underprivileged. But she intended to keep up with the Joneses in every way, and she didn't want Mrs. Donovan doubting her.

"Don't worry, I'm very organized. When my mother was sick, I bought the groceries, I did the laundry and the cooking. I dealt with the doctors. I even the paid the bills, with help from my grandmother. And I still got straight A's, although admittedly, my old school was easy compared to Odell."

Mrs. Donovan's face softened with sympathy. "You

poor thing. To be burdened like that, at your age. No wonder you're trying to be superwoman. We have excellent therapists in the health center. You should talk to someone."

"That's not necessary."

"It can help you process your grief over losing your mom."

"I try not to dwell on things that make me sad. I put them out of my mind, and go on the best I can."

"Everybody needs to talk things out, Rose. That reminds me. I've been meaning to ask about your sister."

"My sister?"

"Yes. Is everything all right between you and Bel?"

"Everything's fine. Why?" Rose asked, alarmed.

"I heard through the grapevine that the two of you had a falling-out."

Damnit! Kids had been gossiping about that incident in the dining hall, and it must've gotten back to Mrs. Donovan. Rose had been livid about the whole incident, to the point that she hadn't spoken to Bel since, despite Bel's multiple attempts to apologize. This whole mess was Bel's fault, and Mrs. Donovan needed to know that.

"There was an incident in the dining hall the first day of classes," Rose began.

"Go on."

"Bel . . . Well, she can be immature, and she doesn't always have the best judgment. We were talking a minute ago about mean girls in Moreland. I'm afraid Bel's fallen in with that crowd. Darcy Madden, and her friend Tessa, that redheaded girl. She was sitting with them at lunch, and I tried to get her to move tables. I'm worried they'll get her into trouble."

Mrs. Donovan looked at Rose with concern in her eyes.

"I can't comment specifically on other students' disciplinary history. But you're right about that group being a problem. So that caused trouble between the two of you."

"We haven't spoken since," Rose said, conveniently omitting the fact that she was the one refusing to speak to Bel, not the other way around.

"I'm sorry to hear that," Mrs. Donovan said.

"Is there anything you can do?" Rose asked.

"Do?"

"To get Bel to stop hanging out with them."

"Well. I suppose I could ask Heath to mention it to her. He's her advisor."

"That would be great. I'll be honest, if Bel gets in trouble, I'm afraid it'll reflect badly on me."

"Rose, you keep mentioning Bel getting in trouble. Is she doing something she shouldn't? Something specific, not just socializing with the wrong crowd. If you're aware that other students are breaking the rules, you're supposed to report them. Even if it's your sister. The Honor Code requires it. Do you understand?"

Rose thought again about the contest to seduce Mr. Donovan. Bel's new best friend was behind it. She hoped that didn't mean her sister was involved with it. But she didn't have proof, and she was afraid to say anything. Not only would it be terribly awkward to bring this up with Mrs. Donovan, but Rose could wind up with a reputation as a rat. That was social suicide at Odell.

"I haven't heard anything specific," Rose insisted. "Nobody tells me anything because I'm known as a girl who follows the rules. I just worry about my sister."

"I understand. I'll ask Heath to speak to her about the company she keeps. But there's something I need to ask of you in return."

"Okay."

"Make up with Bel. Talk through your differences. You two are both new here. You've been through a lot. You need each other. Can you do that, Rose? Please? For me?"

Rose hesitated. She was hurt and pissed off enough that she really didn't feel like making up with her sister. Not yet. Still, she couldn't refuse Mrs. Donovan's request, when Mrs. Donovan represented everything that was good and kind in the world.

"I'll try," she said, taking another cookie. "Promise."

10

Bel had a stalker. Zachary Cuddy from her Spanish class wouldn't leave her alone. She'd hooked up with him the second week of school, on the night of the opening dance, and immediately realized her mistake. She'd been trying to shake him ever since, but he wouldn't take no for an answer. Zach seemed to think he owned her, even though they hadn't done more than fool around briefly in the woods. Yet nearly every day, he'd claim the seat next to her at morning convocation, or wait for her after Spanish to escort her to her next class. Yesterday, she'd turned around in the lunch line to find Zach standing right behind her, literally breathing down her neck. She nearly screamed. She'd tried ignoring him, laughing at him, running in the opposite direction, telling him to knock it off or she'd tell a teacher—nothing worked. He'd just look at her with puppy-dog eyes and beg her to tell him what he'd done wrong, so he could fix it.

Zach was one of several mistakes in Bel's brief Odell career that could be laid at Darcy Madden's door. Bel did whatever it took to please Darcy, and unfortunately the things that pleased Darcy had a certain twisted quality. Yet, Darcy's friendship cast a circle of light so bright that Bel ignored the consequences. To be inside Darcy's circle was to be among the chosen. Most Odell kids were earnest and square, but Darcy's friends were different. They laughed, and did wild things—bad things even—but they were bulletproof, and never suffered. Darcy and her crew hailed from old Odellian families with gobs of money. If they misbehaved, or broke rules, Mom and Dad met with the headmaster, and the kid got sentenced to counseling or, at worst, rehab. Bel had already seen this, with a girl named Mia who got suspended for alcohol the first week of school. She went home for three days, and came back smiling, with a tan, a new pair of Saint Laurent boots, and a fifth of bourbon that they drank the same night in Darcy's room. Life in Darcy's circle was a big joke. The terrible pressures of Odell—the crushing workload, the college-admissions race, the insane three-hundred-page code of conduct manual—vanished at the flick of Darcy's shiny, blond hair. Bel *needed* to be part of that. It wasn't the money that turned her head, or the privilege. It was the freedom from fear.

Bel didn't stop to calculate the cost of doing Darcy's bidding, but in the back of her mind, she knew it was adding up. Under Darcy's influence, she'd turned her back on her sophomore classmates (a bunch of uptight bores), allowed her sister to be insulted in front of the entire dining hall (Rose was too sensitive, anyway), worn pajamas to class on a dare (so hilarious, even though she'd gotten two demerits, and four meant suspension), and snuck out of the dorm to smoke weed out at Lost Lake (*so* chill, though getting caught could mean expulsion). Bel felt bad about those things, and yet, she also felt good—carefree, young, and most of all, flattered to be included. Being Darcy's pet made her somebody important, where otherwise, Odell would grind her down.

The Zach hookup happened because Darcy decreed it. Darcy worried that her boyfriend, Brandon Flynn, was paying too much attention to Bel. *You're like the new toy*, Darcy had said threateningly, *better watch you don't get chewed*. Bel had done nothing to encourage Brandon's attention. She found him repugnant, actually. Husky build, sandy hair, a Frankenstein forehead, Brandon was a mouth-breathing delinquent. He was also very, very rich, his dad being a real-estate billionaire, and Darcy was very possessive of her Mr. Moneybags. She refused to believe that Bel wasn't interested in Brandon, or that Bel was only nice to Brandon because he was Darcy's boyfriend. That couldn't be true, Darcy said, because Brandon was the only guy Bel gave the time of day to.

That's when Bel let slip that there was someone else she pined for. It slipped out, and then it was too late to take it back. Bel couldn't tell Darcy about her Mr. Donovan obsession without getting roped into their awful contest. She had to make up another boyfriend. That's where Zach came in, in a major miscalculation.

On the night of the opening dance, the Alumni Gym was dark, stuffy and jammed wall-to-wall with kids swaying to Rihanna. Bel was milling about with Darcy and Tessa, waiting for Brandon to text them that he'd scored weed, so they could all meet up at the lake. From the corner of her eye, Bel saw Zach Cuddy heading her way, and immediately knew that he was going to ask her to dance. He'd been harassing since the first day of class. Her first instinct was to turn away and pretend not to see him, but she saw her opportunity, and caught herself.

"Hey, here comes my crush," Bel said to Darcy.

Darcy followed Bel's gaze. "Him? He looks like a loser."

Zach was tall and thin, with a shock of dark hair and mild blue eyes behind professorial-looking eyeglasses. Some people might call Zach handsome, but Bel and Darcy were not among those people.

"I think he's cute," Bel insisted.

"Whatever, girl. It's your coochie. Invite him to the lake if you want."

"Uh—"

Bel *didn't* want to go as far as inviting Zach to the lake. But Darcy shot her a skeptical look, and she knew she had no choice. She stepped onto the dance floor and intercepted him.

"Hey," she said.

"Hey, I'm Zach from your Spanish class."

"Duh, I know. Why do you think I'm talking to you?"

"Oh. Excellent. Would you do me the honor of dancing with me?"

"No."

His face fell.

"I don't want to dance right now," Bel said, glancing over her shoulder to make sure Darcy was watching. "I need some air. My friends are going down to the lake. Why don't you come?"

Zach looked over at Darcy nervously. "I'm not sure that's a good idea."

"Why?"

Zach hesitated, lowering his voice. "Um, when you say *friends*, you're talking about Darcy Madden, right?"

"Yeah, so?"

"I'd love to hang out with *you*. But I'm not looking to get wasted or anything."

"Who said anything about getting wasted?"

"It's just, from what I hear—"

"What you hear. Do you judge people based on gossip?"

Zach looked taken aback. "No."

"Don't judge her, then. People just say stuff about her because they're jealous. It's a pretty night. Come outside with me. Please?"

Bel took Zach's hand and gave him her sweetest smile. His eyes lit up.

The loudspeakers started making an awful screeching noise, which distracted the chaperones. Darcy and Tessa slipped out the back door, and Bel pulled Zach along, hurrying to keep up. Outside, the night was warm, lit by a fat harvest moon hanging low in the velvety sky. There was a loud sound of crickets chirping, and the smell of mulch and wet leaves, as they headed for the path into the woods. Zach's hand trembled in hers.

"Are we seriously going to the lake? I've never been there at night," he said.

"I have," she said. "It's gorgeous. Come on, hurry."

Darcy and Tessa had been swallowed by the trees. Bel raced to keep up, flicking on the flashlight on her phone to light the way.

The Odell campus bordered a thousand-acre nature preserve—pristine land made up of dense forest, open fields, hilltops, valleys and babbling streams, all criss-crossed by a network of hiking trails. Lost Lake sat about a mile into the nature preserve from the border of campus. The path that led there was dark and mysterious, but with her friends in front of her and a boy by her side, Bel felt safe. More than safe, she felt happy to be alive. It was a beautiful night, and she was on a crazy adventure, with a slight edge of hysteria, as if she was high already even though she hadn't smoked anything. That was the effect Darcy's shenanigans had on her.

Bel stumbled on a root, giggling as Zach caught her.

"Are you okay?"

"*Fine*. Relax, Zach. You're too uptight," she said.

They didn't talk again until they reached the wide meadow that bordered the lake. Zach caught the view across the open water, sparkling in the moonlight, and drew a sharp breath.

"See?" Bel said. "It's worth it. C'mon."

They headed for the wooden hikers' lean-to that faced the lake. It had been the favorite rendezvous point for Odell kids looking to sin since time immemorial. Zach seemed to know that as well as Bel did. Or else he just smelled the pot.

"Uh, no, I can't," he said, stopping in his tracks.

"You don't smoke weed?"

"Not on campus I don't. Surest way to get caught."

"This isn't campus."

"Not technically. But if you think the faculty doesn't know about the lean-to, you're mistaken. They raid it regularly."

Darcy had never told Bel that, but that didn't mean it wasn't true. "Are you sure?" Bel asked.

"Positive. A bunch of guys from my dorm got caught drinking here last spring. They all got kicked out."

"Wow. I had no idea."

"Yeah, although, they were nobodies. And two of them were black. I'm not saying the school excessively punishes poor, black kids. It's the opposite. If you're somebody important, you get away with stuff that normal kids get punished for. Those friends of yours—I know who they are. They're connected. Maybe you are, too. But I'm not, so I should probably go."

Bel felt sorry for Zach. Plus, she hadn't come this far just to turn around and leave without putting Darcy's Brandon concerns to rest.

"We don't have to get high," Bel said. "Let's just go in the woods and hook up. You can't get expelled for that, right?"

He smiled. "I don't know, but it's a risk I'm willing to take."

"Hold on. I'm just gonna let Darcy know that we're going someplace more private."

She did. And they did. Their make-out session, which stopped well short of actual sex and was so forgettable to Bel, was now imprinted on Zach's brain forever, to the point where he was making her life unbearable. She had to do something to get rid of him.

11

Rose had promised Mrs. Donovan that she would make up with her sister. But as the days passed, she couldn't bring herself to fulfill that promise. She was still smarting from that incident in the dining hall on the first day of class, when Bel allowed one of her new best friends to humiliate Rose, and didn't speak up in her defense. It was on Bel to apologize to Rose for that first, and *then* Rose would meet her halfway. Okay, Bel had tried to apologize the day after it happened. But that was too early. Anybody could see that. The wound was too fresh; Rose had cut her off and walked away. Now that more time had passed, Bel ought to understand that it was time to apologize again. This time, Rose would graciously accept her apology, and they could make up. But Bel kept her distance, and things between the sisters remained icy.

As angry as Rose was with her twin, she also missed her very much. Odell was a tough place, for all its glory. The pressure was intense, and the competition was crushing enough to pierce Rose's healthy self-confidence. At Odell, one needed allies, and Rose didn't make friends easily. Her pleasant rapport with Emma Kim was moving slowly toward friendship, but it would never match the history she shared with her sister. Bel wasn't a natural soulmate for Rose; they were too different. But she was family, and nothing could change that.

On a chilly evening in early October, Rose walked back to the dorm alone. She'd left dinner early, overwhelmed by the feeling of being alone in a crowd. Emma had disappeared from the dining hall lately because she was rehearsing nonstop for the fall orchestra recital. That left Rose to navigate the Moreland sophomore table on her own. She knew she ought to try harder to make other friends, but she was too proud to put herself out there. So tonight, and too often lately, she'd ended up sitting quietly while conversation swirled around her, feeling left out.

The sharp chill in the air as she walked toward Moreland, the deep shadows cast by the setting sun, the empty paths, pressed on Rose's heart. When she caught a glimpse of Bel in the distance, climbing the steps to Weston Library, suddenly that incident in the dining hall seemed frivolous. She couldn't let it destroy her relationship with her only sister. If she and Bel could be friends again, Rose wouldn't feel so lonely.

Rose hurried up the steps and onto the dramatic main floor of Weston Library, with its three-story atrium and enormous windows. Bel stood by the reference desk, talking to a boy named Zach who was in Rose's biology class. As Rose approached, Bel actually smiled at her.

"Hey," Bel said.

"Hey," Rose replied, surprised at the warmth of her sister's greeting. Bel had barely acknowledged her in weeks.

"Look, I have to go. I have plans with my sister," Bel said to Zach.

"Rose is your sister?" he asked.

It made Rose stupid happy to realize that Zach Cuddy knew her name. He was worlds above your average Odell prepster dude, and the only boy she'd met so far who piqued her interest.

"That's okay, I can wait," Rose said. "Or maybe the three of us should—"

"No," Bel said. "I need to talk to you. Now. Come on."

She grabbed Rose by the arm and yanked her toward the front door. Rose glanced back at Zach helplessly as they exited the library.

"I'm so glad you want to talk," Rose said, falling into step beside Bel out on the path. "I feel like we've been mad at each other long enough."

The sky was nearly dark, and the yellow glow of the lampposts illuminated the paths. Bel sighed with irritation, her entire demeanor changed from how she'd been a moment earlier.

"So, you're finally gonna forgive me? I apologized weeks ago, by the way," Bel said, shaking her head irritably.

Her sister's tone annoyed Rose. Bel still didn't get how hurtful her action—or her inaction—had been.

"Put yourself in my shoes. Getting called fat on my first day of school in front of the entire dining hall. It was awful."

"Come on, she didn't call you fat, and practically nobody heard her."

"Don't minimize."

"Look, I said I was sorry, and I am sorry. Tessa's a bitch, but that's not my fault."

"If she's such a bitch, why do you hang out with her?"

"Because she's Darcy's friend."

"Why are you friends with Darcy?"

Bel whirled to face Rose. "If this is going to turn into a rant about my poor choice of friends, then we're never gonna make up. I miss you, Rose. I want us to be closer. But you have to back off with the judgment stuff."

"I miss you, too. I'm just worried about you. Those are, like, the most reckless kids in the school, and they're bound to get you in trouble."

"Maybe I don't care."

"How can that be? I don't understand that."

"We're different, okay?" Bel said, her eyes in the lamplight sparkling with unshed tears. "You have everything figured out. I'm just trying to get through my days. Darcy makes me feel like there's some fun left in the world, since Mom died. Can't you understand that?"

Bel's words hit home. Bel had been much closer to their mother than Rose had. Rose had resented their bond, and had felt left out. But Rose shouldn't let that lingering resentment blind her to Bel's real grief. Bel had taken their mother's death much harder than Rose had. Rose reacted by trying to think about Mom as little as possible, and being grateful for her new life, where she could have a substitute mom like Mrs. Donovan. A better mom, really. Whereas Bel thought about their mother constantly. Rose had to admit, Bel's reaction was the more normal one. It worried Rose sometimes, how little grief she felt. It was almost like there was something wrong with her.

"You're right," Rose said. "You and I experience Mom's death differently. I take all my sadness and put it into succeeding here."

"Is that the explanation? Because you seem so fine with everything that, sometimes, I wonder if you really loved Mom."

Sometimes, Rose wondered that herself. But she would never admit to such a socially unacceptable emotion as not loving her own mother.

"God, what a mean thing to say," Rose said. "That hurts. Don't you get it? We can both feel grief, but show it differently. I'm doing my best to understand your way, and that you're acting out—misbehaving— because of sadness. Meanwhile, instead of trying to understand me, you accuse me of not loving Mom? That's low, Bel."

"I'm sorry. You're right. I need to try harder to see your perspective."

"Thank you. I would appreciate that."

"Let's be friends again, okay?" Bel said.

"Yes. That's all I want. I'll get off your back about Darcy, too, promise."

Bel smiled tearily. "Okay. Deal," she said, and held her arms out.

They hugged for a long time, right there in the middle of the path. Rose had to swallow hard in order not to cry, which made her feel relieved. At least when it came to Bel, Rose still had a heart.

"Hey," Rose said, disentangling herself. "I have Oreos in my room. Want some?"

"You know I do."

They linked arms, and walked back to Moreland together.

12

By mid-October, Bel's schoolgirl crush on Heath Donovan had morphed into something more powerful, and more dangerous. After their iced-coffee date at the Art Café, she just couldn't shake the memory of their embrace. She still felt his arms around her, and wanted to experience that again. But how? She'd sit in English class and stare, letting his voice wash over her. Bel worried that kids in her English class would notice, and tease her. Or worse, that Darcy and the Moreland seniors would find out. If the seniors realized she was mad for Heath, not only would they mock her relentlessly, but they'd force her to play their tawdry game, which she absolutely refused to do. She didn't even like hearing about it anymore. What they were doing was childish and degrading. What Bel felt for Heath was real. Bel now understood that Heath knew how she felt, and was glad of it. This amazing realization dawned on

her in English class, on a stormy afternoon in late
October, as they discussed one of Shakespeare's sonnets.

Rain sluiced against the mullioned windows as
Heath read aloud to the class from a poem about summer, and love.

"'If happiness were like the flowers of June,'" Heath
quoted, in his beautiful, resonant voice, "'then I would
take the best of them, roses and columbine, the lilies,
and bind them in your hair . . . I think of you as the day
wanes, and as the sun sinks deep into the ocean, and as
the stars turn round above.'"

And just then, as the clock on the wall ticked to the
beat of Bel's heart, Heath looked up and caught her
eyes. He'd been gazing down at the page, then those
incredible blue-green eyes flicked up and settled on
Bel, at the precise moment he spoke of binding flowers in her hair. Their gazes met, and held. Everything
else faded away, and she was transported with him to
a field on a perfect June day. She could smell the grass,
as she had that afternoon they sat together on the patio,
when she told him her troubles, and he comforted her.
She could feel the breeze, and feel his arms around her
again, his breath on her hair. And she finally understood
that Heath Donovan wanted her to love him. Otherwise, why—out of fifteen students in the room, seven
boys, eight girls—why would he look directly at *her* at
the very moment he said those words? This wasn't just
a foolish crush. It wasn't a one-way street. She meant
something to him, too.

There were other signs.

Bel had joined the cross-country team at Heath's

urging, and he was teaching her how to run. (Okay, he was teaching all the girls on the team, but he paid special attention to Bel. She wasn't imagining it.) There was so much more to running than she'd known. Form, pacing, strategy. Appreciation for the terrain. The sprawling Odell campus was situated in a valley ringed by rugged hills. The nature preserve, and its hiking trails, were their own private wilderness to train in. After a brutally hot Indian summer, the weather had turned wet and raw, and Bel's afternoons were spent slogging through the muck on the trails with twenty other girls. They had practice five days a week, rain or shine, and meets on Saturdays. At first, it was torture, and she did it only to be near Heath. But as the weeks went by, calluses formed on her feet, muscles hardened in her legs, and she got faster, until she was keeping pace with the best girls on the team, and with Heath himself.

Heath ran alongside them on practice days. He was that kind of coach: He didn't spare himself, even in the worst weather. He'd start at the front of the pack and slowly drop back, checking on each runner or group of runners in turn, giving them pointers, boosting their spirits. Bel made sure to run alone. She wanted to be certain that, whenever Heath caught up with her, they would have privacy. She'd get ten or fifteen minutes alone with him on a long run—more than he gave any other girl. They'd set a pace where they could comfortably maintain a conversation. The gray skies and whistling wind would drop a cloak of intimacy over them as they ran. Other girls might be in sight, but they were out of earshot, and Bel could say anything. She looked forward to these runs as if they could save her life, and in a way, they did. Bel told Heath all her troubles. He was the only person on earth she could talk to; with everyone else, Bel put on an act, full of snark and bravado. None of her friends or even her own sister suspected how lost she felt inside. But Heath knew the true her.

Out there in the woods, just the two of them and the wind, Heath listened like he really cared. He told her things about himself, too, personal things. As successful as Heath Donovan had been during his student days at Odell, he'd felt like an outsider then, as Bel did now. Heath got into Odell on a tennis scholarship, and he came late, not till junior year. As soon as he got there, his parents split, and money was tight. He couldn't keep up with the rich kids—not even with Mrs. Donovan, who was his girlfriend then, and later became his wife.

That was the only time he mentioned his marriage. He didn't speak of his children to Bel, either, even though she could see him with them in the dining hall on any given night. She understood this to mean that he was being sensitive to her feelings. She couldn't bear that he belonged to these other people and not to her. Heath understood that, so he didn't shove it in her face, and for that, she was grateful.

If there was a doubt in Bel's mind that Heath knew her feelings, and maybe even felt something in return, it was put to rest the day she blew out her knee during practice. It happened just a couple of days after the moment that their eyes met in class. (Bel was still floating from that.) They were out for a six-mile run, the trails slick from days of rain. The weather had turned dramatically colder. Bel was running by herself, wondering when Heath would catch up with her, when her foot flew out from under her on a steep, icy stretch of trail. She hurtled downward, trying desperately to arrest her fall, and landed hard against a granite out-cropping with her leg twisted underneath her. A bolt of pain shot through her right knee, so bad that it took her breath away.

Lucy Ogunwe, one of the faster girls on the team, came up to Bel from behind, and bent over her, panting.

"Hey, are you okay?" she asked.

Tears flooded Bel's eyes. She was too stunned to reply.

"No worries, Donovan's right behind," Lucy said, nodding toward the trail above. "Hey, Coach, Enright fell," Lucy called out to him. "I think she's hurt."

Heath ran up to them, taking in Bel, crumpled on the ground, clutching her knee, the sheen of ice all around her.

"Do me a favor," he said to Lucy. "Go back and tell the girls behind you that there's an ice patch here. Tell them to slow it down to a walk. Stay safe."

"Got it," Lucy said, and set off in the direction Bel had come from.

Through a scrim of pain, Bel realized that Heath had just sent Lucy away. They were alone now. He knelt down beside her.

"Where does it hurt?" he asked, tenderness in his voice.

"My knee."

"Can you sit up and lean back against the rock? Here, let me help you," he said.

Heath put his hands on her waist and gently lifted her to a sitting position. The motion tweaked her knee, and she cried out.

"Did I hurt you? I'm sorry, sweetheart," he said.

The endearment was too much for Bel. Something came loose inside her. As Heath bent over her, his face mere inches from hers, his eyelashes wet with rain, she reached out and laid her hand on his cheek.

"I love you," she said.

He stopped dead, looking at her so intently that she felt like he must see straight into her soul.

"Are you part of that ridiculous game? I know about it, you know. I'd be very disappointed in you, Bel."

Despite his words, Heath didn't move away, or shake off her hand. The warmth of his cheek under her cold fingers spurred her on.

"Never," she said, her words tumbling out in a rush. "I hate those girls. They're childish. What I feel for you is real, Heath. It's not a game. I know you feel it, too. Please, tell me you do."

His eyes, as they locked on hers, were troubled. "I'm married. You're a kid. You're my student. It can't be," he said.

That wasn't a denial. He wanted her. She could see it in his eyes. Bel's lips parted, and she leaned in, desperate to feel his mouth on hers.

"Tessa," Heath said, snapping back abruptly.

Tessa Romano had just come over the top of the hill. Tessa was the sturdy redhead with freckles and a potty mouth who'd caused so much trouble in Bel's relationship with Rose. Bel couldn't think of a worse girl to discover them like this. Tessa didn't really like Bel. Of all the Moreland seniors, Tessa was most likely to spill her guts to Darcy the second she got back to the dorm.

"What have we here?" Tessa asked, her eyes lighting up luridly.

"Bel took a fall and hurt her knee," Heath said, his facing going stony, as if a mask had dropped over it. "Come here, please, and give me a hand. Let's see if we can get her to her feet without her putting weight on the right leg."

They got on either side, and Bel draped her arms over their shoulders. Leaning on them, she managed to stand up and hobble down the steep slope. Every step was a blur of pain and anxiety. What must Heath think of her now, that she'd been so undisciplined, in such a risky situation? Would Tessa tell people? Could Heath get in trouble? He must hate her now.

Thirty awful minutes later, they reached the bottom of the hill. Heath had called ahead, and they emerged from the woods to see a security department car waiting on the road to whisk Bel to the infirmary.

Heath helped her into the back seat. "I'll call the infirmary later to check with the doctors. You'll probably need to go on the injured list. Would you like Tessa to stay with you?"

I want you *to stay with me*, she thought. But she couldn't speak the thought aloud. If people started to talk, he might never spend time with her alone again.

"I'm fine," Bel said curtly.

Heath closed the door with a sharp *click*, and the car drove away.

At five-thirty, Bel was alone in her room back in Moreland, lying on Emma's bunk, because she couldn't climb up to her own. She could hear girls passing by in the hallway, on their way to family dinner in the Commons, the old part of the dining hall. Family dinner was this awful thing that happened once a week, where kids had to dress up and sit at tables with faculty members. If Bel's injury had an upside, it was that she'd gotten excused from attending tonight. She was supposed to keep her leg elevated and a cold pack on her knee for the rest of the evening. The pain pills the doctor had given her dulled the ache in her knee, but not the sick feeling in her heart. He'd almost kissed her; they'd been that close. But now, their bond was shattered, their great love affair over before it started.

Suddenly the door banged open, and Darcy stormed in, blond hair flying, her pretty cheerleader's face red with pique.

"What the fuck, Enright. When were you planning to tell me you have something going on with Donovan?"

Shit. Tessa must have told Darcy what she saw, and Darcy had a big mouth. This story would be all over school the second Darcy walked into the dining hall. If Bel wanted to protect Heath from the fallout, she needed to convince Darcy that nothing had happened out on the trail this afternoon.

"I don't know what you're talking about," she protested, widening her eyes innocently.

"Don't give me that BS. Tessa saw you with him in the nature preserve this afternoon. She said you were practically in a lip-lock."

Bel pointed to the bandage and ice pack on her knee. "Uh, hello, you see my injury? I fell and blew my knee out. Mr. Donovan helped me up. That's all Tessa saw. He had to put his arms around me to lift me. He's the coach. He's not gonna leave a runner lying on the ground."

Darcy looked at Bel's knee and frowned. "That's not what she said. She said he pays all sorts of attention to you. The other girls are jealous."

"Well, she's lying then—exaggerating anyway."

"Tessa's been loyal as a dog for three years at this school. You, I've known for like five minutes, and you expect me to believe you over her? Sorry."

"I swear, Darcy, nothing's going on. I would never horn in on your contest. Not without your permission."

"I should hope not. I don't need anybody cock-blocking me, especially not you, after all I've done for you. If I thought you were trying to steal my prize—"

"I would never. Tessa has a wild imagination, and she misinterpreted, that's all. Swear to God."

Darcy put her hands on her hips. "I don't know who

to believe. What you're saying makes sense on the surface, but I get the feeling you're holding out on me."

Bel placed her hand over her heart. For a skeptic and a liar herself, Darcy was surprisingly susceptible to flattery. Bel laid it on thick. "Believe that I'm your true friend, Darcy. There's nothing but love and gratitude in my heart for you."

"Okay, then prove it."

"How?"

"It's almost November, and the Moreland seniors haven't pulled any good pranks yet. We need to keep up our reputation, and I have something radical in mind for tonight. A revival of a prank my mom's gang used to pull back in the day. You'll see."

"You want me to help with that tonight? You see the shape I'm in. I'm not mobile."

"Aww, your widdle boo-boo huwts? Tough titties, Enright. Take a Vicodin or smoke some weed, whatever you need to do, but you're not getting out of this one. Time to earn your keep. If you want the benefits of hanging out with me, you have to do some dirty work."

That gave Bel a chill. Darcy at her worst could be savage.

"What exactly is this prank?" Bel asked.

"It's a surprise," Darcy said, snarkily. "Be at my room at midnight, and you'll find out."

She turned on her heel, and was gone.

Bel laid her head on the pillow and wished she'd never come to this damn school. The two things that had kept her going had both fallen to shit today. Her friendship with Darcy was supposed to be easy and fun, but now it just seemed sick and twisted. And her love for Heath—which just a couple of hours ago she believed was reciprocated—would never amount to anything now that her conduct had exposed him to gossip and ridicule. Everything was ruined, and she couldn't face it.

Her glance fell on the bottle of pain pills on the dresser.

13

Transcript of Witness Interview conducted by Lieutenant Robert Kriscunas, State Police—Major Crime Unit, and Detective Melissa Howard, Odell NH, PD, with Mrs. Sarah Donovan.

Kriscunas: Mrs. Donovan, you and your husband were the dorm parents for Moreland Hall, so that meant you were in charge of supervising these girls, correct?

Donovan: Uh, sure, yes. We ran the dorm. We did curfew check, room check, ran dorm meetings, that sort of thing. We did milk-and-cookies socials in the common room two nights a week. But there were forty girls in Moreland. Or—thirty-nine, after the, the— My point is, we couldn't possibly know everything that was going on with each girl. If you're suggesting—

Kriscunas: This isn't about your job performance, ma'am. We're investigating a murder. I'm trying to get the background on these two sisters, and how closely you monitored them. This is standard procedure. Just tell the truth, and it'll all be fine.

Donovan: Yes, of course I'll tell the truth.

Howard: Now, Rose Enright—she was your advisee, correct? You must've known what was going on with her.

Donovan: Yes, I knew Rose quite well, much better than I knew Bel. I have only the most wonderful things to say about Rose.

Kriscunas: What can you tell us about Rose's relationship with her sister? Conflicts they might have had with one another? Or other people who got drawn into their conflict, who might wish harm to one of them because of a relationship with the other, if you see what I'm getting at?

Donovan: All I can say is, Rose told me from when I first met her that she and Bel were very different. But those differences were not enough, in my view, to explain this murder. Rose was very responsible, and believed in following the rules. Bel's judgment was not as good. She made friends with some questionable elements in the dorm, and that got her into trouble. Those people ought to be looked at. This is not necessarily about the relationship between the sisters. If you focus too much on that, you may miss other important aspects of the Enright girls' lives.

Kriscunas: Don't worry. We'll get to the other stuff. This is just background right now, so we can understand the relationship between Bel and Rose.

Donovan: To understand it, you need to know that

they tried to be friends. Rose made a great effort to be closer to Bel, and not to criticize her. They got along fine right up until the slipper attack.

Kriscunas: The slipper attack drove them apart?

Donovan: It was a huge deal, and they were on opposite sides of the incident. There were repercussions, terrible repercussions for a number of students, and for the school itself.

Kriscunas: We think this incident is very important to the case. You were in a unique position to know what happened that night. So, if you could, walk us through that incident in Moreland Hall, in detail.

14

Those girls are up to no good.

Sarah sat at the head of one of the Moreland Hall tables in the Commons, eyeing Darcy Madden and Tessa Romano as they smirked behind their hands. Once a week, in imitation of bygone days when masters and students dined together, the entire school gathered in the old dining hall, affectionately known as the Commons, for a formal meal called family dinner. The Commons—with its cathedral ceiling and stained-glass windows, dark paneling and dusty chandeliers—was a suitably grand and gloomy setting for the occasion. Everybody got dressed up and made polite conversation. In her own student days, Sarah had found family dinner excruciating to sit through. She was sympathetic to students who got the squirms or the giggles. But Darcy and Tessa were not your average students. They were a bad lot, and they'd been planning a sick piece of mischief that targeted Sarah and her family personally. She thought it had been nipped in the bud. Heath had told her so. But if it had, why were they smirking like that?

The girls looked pointedly in Sarah's direction and burst into a raucous fit of laughter.

"Darcy, is there something you'd like to share with the rest of us?" Sarah asked, fixing the girl with a cold glare.

Darcy gave a brazen smile. "Yes, Mrs. Donovan. I was just saying that the cod is especially tender tonight."

Tessa guffawed, and some of the other girls at the table shook with suppressed laughter. Sarah's face went hot. She was blushing, just like when the mean girls were nasty to her back in her student days. She'd never mastered the art of the snappy retort, and had never succeeded in putting a girl like Darcy Madden in her place. Then again, she hadn't expected to be dealing with high school bullies at her age.

"I wish you would set an example for the younger girls, and behave appropriately at the dinner table," Sarah said. "You're a senior. You ought to understand basic decorum by now."

Darcy had the good sense not to reply this time. Sarah turned back to her food, but her appetite was gone. She was upset about more than disruption at the dinner table. Earlier today, the head of the math department had knocked on Sarah's office door and passed along some disturbing news.

Patricia Banks had been mentoring Sarah since the day she'd started teaching. They weren't exactly friends, since Patricia, or Pat, as she was called, was her boss and much older, but Sarah was always grateful for her advice and her company.

"Free for lunch?" Pat asked.

"I'd love to, but I have a pile of grading to do, so I'm eating at my desk. Rain check?" Sarah said.

"Fine. But there's something I need to talk to you about right away."

Pat stepped into the office and closed the door behind her. She was a trim woman, conservatively dressed, in her late fifties, with graying hair. She reminded Sarah a bit of her own mother—practical, competent, with a reserved way about her that could be off-putting. Especially at a moment like this, when her tone was ominous.

"What's wrong?" Sarah asked.

"I heard a rumor about the girls in your dorm. I thought I should pass it along, in case there's any truth to it. They may be plotting something pretty crazy."

"Drat, and here I was thinking we were keeping a lid on things."

"You have been. The faculty is very impressed that there haven't been any incidents in Moreland yet this year. But it's a challenge to keep it that way with some of the girls you've got. Then I heard this crazy rumor— so crazy, I hesitate to repeat it. But I thought, What if it's true?"

"What is it?" Sarah asked, nervously.

"Eduardo Mendez heard it from one of his students," Pat said, "and brought it to me since he knows I'm close with you. Neither of us felt comfortable raising it with Heath directly. We thought it would be best if you did that."

"With Heath? I don't understand."

"Eduardo's student claims that Darcy Madden is sponsoring a contest among the Moreland seniors to seduce your husband."

Sarah gave a shocked laugh. "A contest? Like, with prizes and everything?"

"I don't know about that part. But girls are supposedly being dared to—and please, forgive me, Sarah, I know this is embarrassing. It's embarrassing for me to raise it, so I can only imagine how you feel. They're being dared to *come on* to him. I have no doubt that even if this is true, your husband would behave impeccably. But given the sensitive nature—well, Eduardo worried it might sound like an accusation if he brought it to Heath. Nobody means it that way. Your husband is known as a completely upstanding, honorable man. I'm sure he'll be as horrified to hear this as the rest of us. *But*, if this is true, these girls could put him in a compromising position, through no fault of his own. Defensive measures may be called for. That's why I felt I should warn you."

Sarah shook her head in amazement. "I expect bad behavior from Darcy. Drinking, boys. But this? It's bizarre."

"I know."

"Who did Eduardo hear it from?"

"The girl didn't want her name used. He says she's not in your dorm, and she's not involved in this herself.

But she has friends in Moreland, and she heard it from them."

"He believes her?"

"Yes, which doesn't make it true. Maybe it's a joke, maybe the student misunderstood. We can always hope. Still, my advice to you is to raise it with Heath. Better safe than sorry. If he's noticed unusual behavior, we can go to Liz Geller to discuss what steps should be taken."

Liz Geller was the dean of students, just below the headmaster in the chain of command at Odell. But Liz had recently been diagnosed with breast cancer.

"Isn't she on health leave?"

"Oh, you're right. Well, let me know what Heath says, and we can take it from there."

"Thank you. Really, Pat, I mean it. Thanks for looking out for us."

"Happy to. You two have taken on a lot with Moreland. Everyone on the faculty is pulling for you. Let me know if there's more I can do."

As soon as the door closed behind Pat, Sarah got out her phone and texted Heath that she needed to talk to him right away. He wrote to say he was at lunch; she should come to the dining hall.

Grading the tests could wait. Sarah had to find out if Heath had noticed any odd behavior from the Moreland seniors. Pat was right: Those girls could cause trouble. Ever since that first day, when Heath moved the welcome reception to the Quad and rebranded it as a party, Sarah had worried that he was too innocent for this job, too easygoing. His approach to reforming

Moreland seemed to be to make friends with the girls, to be their buddy. He didn't see the pitfalls. The dorm head job hadn't been her idea. But she wanted them to succeed; she wanted *Heath* to succeed. Sarah needed to protect him.

Sarah looked around for Heath when she got to the dining hall and didn't find him right away. Then she spotted him, near the conveyor belt where trays were bused, talking to a dark-haired girl whose back was turned to Sarah. Bel Enright, maybe? As Sarah approached, something in Heath's expression caught her attention. The intensity of his gaze, the rapt way he listened as the girl spoke—he looked . . . *enthralled*. She looked at Bel, and saw why. Bel possessed an epic sort of beauty that Sarah never had, even in girlhood. The willowy limbs, the lustrous skin, the long, shiny hair. Sarah felt a momentary pressure in her chest, as if she couldn't breathe. Then the girl walked away, and Heath looked up and saw Sarah watching. He smiled at her like everything was normal.

The gossip is making you paranoid.

"Hey, babe," Heath said, walking over and giving Sarah a peck on the cheek. "What's up? Your text sounded urgent."

"Can we find somewhere more private to talk?"

He looked concerned. "Sure. The Commons is empty. Come on."

"Was that Bel Enright I saw you talking to?" she asked as they walked.

"Uh-huh."

"What were you talking about?"

"Tomorrow's reading assignment," he said. "Why?"

"Just curious," she said.

He shot her a puzzled glance. She decided not to elaborate because, really, there was no basis to worry. Heath had never given her cause to think he'd cheat. And certainly not with a kid. He would never do that, in a million years. The warning about Darcy Madden's contest was messing with Sarah's head. She needed to get a grip. Focus on the problem at hand.

The Commons was deserted, echoing and dim. They sat down facing each other at a long, empty table.

"What is it?" Heath said.

"Pat Banks told me something crazy, and I need to ask you about it. Supposedly Darcy Madden is running a contest to see which Moreland girl can seduce you first. Do you know anything about this?"

She'd expected Heath's jaw to drop, or for him to burst into hysterical laughter. Instead, he nodded.

"Yes, but it's nothing. Don't worry about it," he said.

"Wait a minute. You *knew* about it?"

"It's just talk, among a bunch of silly teenage girls. No need to get upset."

"Is it true, or it's not true?"

"Is what true?"

"Is there a contest to seduce you, or not? And if there is, how did you find out about it?"

"Honey, it's nothing. I noticed some of the girls acting strangely around me, just within the past couple of weeks. They'd flash some thigh or twirl their hair seductively, then giggle. I could tell something was up, so finally I said something to one of them."

"To who?"

"To *whom*. To Ashley Wetherby. She's captain of cross-country this year, and I know her fairly well."

"I know who she is. She's part of Darcy Madden's gang. Are you saying Ashley made a pass at you?"

"I wouldn't call it a pass. She was just acting silly. She came to my office one day wearing these itty-bitty shorts and a sports bra, and leaned on the edge of my desk. I said, Wouldn't you be more comfortable in the chair, aren't you cold, and by the way, what's up with all you girls flashing me lately?"

Sarah could picture the scene. Ashley Wetherby was petite and curvaceous, with long strawberry-blond hair. If girls like that were throwing themselves at her husband, Sarah wanted to know.

"And? What did she say?" Sarah demanded.

"She said it was a game, that Darcy started it. I told her to cut it out, and to tell that to the rest of them, or else I might start to think I was being harassed, and feel compelled to report them. I'm pretty sure she delivered the message, because they've cooled it noticeably. So, problem solved. Nothing to worry about."

"I can't believe this happened and you didn't tell me. I'm your wife. The mother of your children. *And* the cohead of Moreland. I deserve to know."

Heath took her hands and looked deeply into her eyes. "Darling, you're right, I'm sorry. That was a mistake."

"How could you withhold that?"

"To be honest, I'm worried that you're not happy with the new job. That you only took it for me, because I wanted so badly to get into the administration. I feel guilty about that. When something comes up that seems particularly annoying, or stupid, I want to protect you from it. The bottom line is: I handled this stupidity on my own, so as not to upset you."

So, he wanted to protect her from the unpleasant aspects of the dorm-head job. Sarah wished it was that easy. As much as she adored Heath, and appreciated his efforts to take care of her, she didn't always trust his judgment. In this case, keeping Darcy's little plot to himself could have serious consequences. Sarah took her hands away.

"Your heart was in the right place," she said. "But in the future, please, don't shelter me. Think about how dangerous this situation is. If it comes out that this contest was going on, and that you knew but did nothing, it might look like you condoned it. It still might. In fact, I think we should say something. Report it."

Heath's eyes darkened. "Sarah, it's resolved. I told them to cut it out, and they did. I mean, what do you suggest we do? Complain to Simon?" he asked, referring to the headmaster. "Go to the Disciplinary Committee? Then it becomes a federal case, and suddenly our spotless record for keeping order at Moreland is no longer so spotless."

So that was it. Heath had made a calculated decision not to take further action, on the theory that informing the school about Darcy's "contest" would reflect badly on their management of Moreland. He had a point there. It wasn't just Pat; other teachers had commented to Sarah that Moreland seemed finally to be on a good track this year. People were already crediting Heath and Sarah with achieving a miraculous turnaround. She knew how much that meant to him. If she insisted on reporting this, she'd undermine their success. *His* success. She couldn't do that to him. Not when he was feeling happy and excited about his career for the first time in years.

Heath had a strategy. They would follow it.

"I didn't think about how reporting this might look bad for us," Sarah said. "I understand your point now. We won't report it. This time. But if anything else happens—"

"Yes, of course. Thank you. Now, what about Pat?"

"What about her?"

"I think you should go back to her and say there's nothing to the rumor. You asked me about it, and I hadn't noticed anything. Otherwise, she might talk. We can't have this getting around."

"Heath, that would be a lie."

"I know, but what else can we do? If we tell her the truth, she'll tell us to report the girls to the Disciplinary Committee, and then everybody says, Oh, the Donovans can't handle Moreland."

"I don't want to lie to her. She's my boss."

"Then I'll talk to her myself, and finesse it so I don't have to lie directly. Okay?"

"All right," Sarah said, though she didn't see how Heath could throw Pat off the scent without actually lying.

The whole mess made for a pit of dread in her stomach. Heath had bent the truth on matters of importance before, and it hadn't ended well. He wasn't a liar, per se. He just really wanted to get ahead, and sometimes he took shortcuts. Sarah understood that he was trying to prove himself to her, and to support their family, so she forgave him for it. But it made her nervous.

"In the future," she said, "when something happens in Moreland, with these girls, promise you'll keep me in the loop."

"Absolutely. I'll tell you everything, always. We're teammates, love."

He smiled and leaned in for a kiss, and she felt much better.

Now, at family dinner, as Sarah watched Darcy and Tessa behave like coconspirators plotting an imminent attack, her confidence from the afternoon dried up and blew away. Heath was an optimist who saw the best in people. Sarah envied him his sunny outlook, and his blithe confidence in the world, but she couldn't share it. Whether those girls were still working on their outrageous contest, or whether they had some other mischief in mind, she didn't know. But she knew she'd better keep her eye on them, or their scheming would come back to bite her, and her family.

15

At family dinner on Friday night, Rose sat next to Lucy Ogunwe, who told her that Bel had gone to the infirmary after slipping and falling on a patch of ice during cross-country practice. She'd hurt her knee pretty badly, Lucy said, and wouldn't be coming to dinner tonight.

Rose was more upset to hear that than the injury really warranted. She understood that a knee injury couldn't possibly be life-threatening. But their recent reconciliation had left her feeling protective enough of her twin that the thought of Bel laid up, in pain, was terrible. Rose jumped up and went to the head of the table to talk to Miss Chaudry, a science teacher who was one of the dorm associates in Moreland Hall.

"I just learned that my sister was hurt in an accident this afternoon," Rose said. "She's in her room, all alone. May I be excused to take dinner to her?"

"That's very sweet of you, Rose. Go ahead, you have my permission," Miss Chaudry said.

Rose went up to the buffet and filled a plate for Bel, making sure to add extra rolls and a brownie because Bel liked them especially. She covered the plate with a napkin, and carried it down deserted pathways, all the way back to Moreland Hall, where she climbed the stairs to the third floor.

There was no answer when she knocked on Bel's door. She peeked in and saw Bel fast asleep in the bottom bunk, with bandages and an ice pack strapped to her leg. Rose went into the room and looked down at her sister, watching her breathe. Bel's breathing seemed strangely shallow, and her mouth hung open like she was in a stupor. Was that normal? Rose hadn't watched Bel sleep in years. She wished she could ask somebody for a second opinion, but everyone was at dinner. The dorm was empty. Rose put the plate of food down on Bel's desk, and came back to feel her forehead. Bel didn't have a temperature. How bad could it be if there was no temperature? This was a simple knee injury. You couldn't die from it. She went back to the desk, tore a sheet from Bel's math binder and left a note.

Hey, Belly, sad you got hurt! I brought you some dinner. Text me when you wake up, and I'll bring you Oreos. Hugs! Rose

On the way out, she leaned down and kissed her sister on the forehead.

• • •

Rose opened her eyes in the semidarkness, feeling like she'd heard a noise. Something had woken her up. She strained to listen and heard only Skyler Stone's regular breathing, coming from the bottom bunk. Ever since her mother's illness, Rose had become a light sleeper. That didn't serve her well in the dorm, where the presence of twenty girls per floor made creaks and cracks and bumps in the night inevitable. She sighed and turned toward the wall, pulling the covers over her head.

There it was again.

She'd definitely heard something this time. Rose turned back over, her heart thumping. Someone was in the hallway, standing outside their door. There was creaking, breathing, suppressed laughter.

The door banged open. Rose sat up in a panic and whacked her head on the ceiling, grunting with pain. The light flicked on in the room. It took a moment for her vision to clear and her eyes to adjust. There were people in the room, three of them, wearing ski masks. A robbery! She screamed, but in her terror, it came out more like a croak. Then she heard girls laughing and whispering, and realized this was something else entirely.

"Get Stone first," Darcy Madden said, her voice unmistakable through the ski mask. "She's such a bitch."

"I thought we came for the sister," Tessa Romano replied.

"She's next. C'mon, move."

What the hell—? Rose lay down quickly and pulled the covers up around her, pretending to be asleep, as Darcy and Tessa converged on Skyler's bunk. Rose heard the thud of a body against the floor. They must have dragged Skyler from her bed. Were they physically attacking her? Rose peeked out from under her blanket, trembling.

"Wha's happen?" Skyler mumbled.

"Old Moreland tradition. You're getting spanked. Rip her clothes off," Darcy said.

Rose watched in horror as Darcy grabbed Skyler's arms from behind, while Tessa tugged at her top. It tore with a loud ripping sound, exposing her small breasts.

"Her pants, idiot," Darcy said. "I'm not spanking her tits."

"You said *clothes!*"

"God, do I have to do everything around here?"

Tessa proceeded to strip Skyler completely naked, while the third intruder slumped against the wall near the door and watched.

Skyler was wide awake now, thrashing on the floor like a hooked fish. "Perverts! *Stop! Rose, help!*"

"Ooh, she's a wild one," Darcy said, laughing. She looked over at the third girl. "C'mon, Snapchat it. They're waiting."

The third girl raised her iPhone, moving in a strangely unhurried way, as if she was drugged, or wading through deep water. Rose saw the brace on her knee, the dark hair tumbling from the ski mask, and realized—that it was *Bel. Shit!*

Darcy pulled a fuzzy pink slipper from her pocket,

as Tessa grabbed at Skyler's thrashing legs. Skyler kicked and flailed, trying desperately to cover herself with her hands, but it was two against one.

"Rose, she's filming me! Make her stop."

Skyler was right: Bel had a phone in her hand, pointed at Skyler, whose privates were exposed for the whole world to see. For all her Jersey attitude, Skyler was modest, and changed in the bathroom rather than let Rose see her naked. If Darcy was to be believed, they were Snapchatting it—streaming it to someone who wasn't in the room. A boy? Multiple boys? Fucking savages. This would destroy Skyler.

Rose grabbed her pillow and jumped down from the top bunk, landing on top of Darcy, who yelped. Panting, Rose whacked at Darcy and Tessa with all her might, but they didn't stop. They were *laughing*, the monsters.

Darcy raised an arm to fend off Rose's blows. "Get this crazy bitch off me!"

But the others were too preoccupied to try to stop Rose. Tessa had flipped Skyler over onto her stomach and was struggling to hold her down to be spanked. As Bel continued to film, Darcy administered a series of quick, sharp taps to Skyler's naked behind with the slipper. Skyler shrieked loud enough to wake the dead, but nobody came to help them.

"Got her! Ha, slippering returns to Moreland Hall!"

Rose faced the open door and yelled at the top of her lungs. "Help! We're being attacked!"

"*Attacked*? Oh, for Chrissakes. It's a slipper, you little priss! Zoom in on her ass, Enright!" Darcy said to Bel.

Bel moved in closer and raised her phone. Rose was breathless with shock that Bel would do something this mean, this stupid. She was going to end up expelled, and she deserved to. Rose whirled on her sister, pummeling her with the pillow.

"How dare you? You're as bad as them. Get out, get out now!"

Bel raised her arms and retreated, moving jerkily, as if not fully in command of her body. Rose suddenly remembered Bel's heavy stupor when she'd visited her room earlier tonight. Was there something going on beyond the knee injury?

"Hey. Are you all right?" Rose said, lowering her pillow.

Bel didn't reply. She hadn't said a word the whole time. She backed away and slipped out the door, limping, ski mask still on. Rose poked her head out. A couple of freshman who lived next door, and some seniors from a few rooms down, were milling in the hallway.

"What's going on?" a freshman asked, a frightened look on her face.

"Darcy and Tessa attacked us," Rose said.

One of the seniors made a snorting noise. "*Attacked*? You can't take a joke, can you? And you," she said to the freshman, "mind your business. Go back to bed."

Rose ducked back into the room.

"Where'd Enright go?" Darcy said, getting to her feet. "That wuss ran out on us! Oh, she's gonna pay for this."

Tessa jumped up. Skyler was in a heap on the floor, naked and sobbing. Darcy and Tessa headed for the door, but Rose stepped in front of them, her head hot with rage. How dare they? She lashed out viciously with the pillow, whacking Darcy in the face.

"Fucking psycho, get away from me," Darcy said, reeling back, but Rose wouldn't let up.

"You're the psycho. Get out of here!"

Darcy and Tessa pushed past Rose and out the door.

"I'm telling!" Rose screamed after them.

"You better not, or I swear to God you're dead," Darcy said, over her shoulder.

Rose helped Skyler up. She stumbled to her bunk, crying quietly and tugging her pajama bottoms up. Rose got her a sweatshirt to cover the ripped camisole.

"Here, put this on."

"What the hell just happened?" Skyler said, sniffling. "They hit me with a *slipper*?"

Rose sat down next to Skyler and hugged her close. "It was some kind of hazing ritual, I think. Are you hurt?"

Skyler was shaking all over. "Yes, I'm hurt. Not, like, going to the hospital hurt, but I'm so upset. Did they film it?"

"Yeah, I think so," Rose replied.

Skyler gave her a sharp look. "You *think* so?"

"Yes. They Snapchatted it."

"Who did they send it to?"

"I don't know."

"Did they send it to boys?"

"They didn't say."

"That was your *sister* who filmed me. You know it was."

What was the point in lying? Rose couldn't've protected Bel if she wanted to. And she didn't want to.

"Sky, I can't believe she did that. I'm so sorry."

"I think they were targeting *you*."

"It can't be. Bel and I have been good lately. Just tonight, I brought her food. I think it was random."

"You can't possibly think that. They targeted our room. You know I'm right. Your sister's as much of a psycho as those other two. I'm going to the dorm heads," Skyler said, standing up unsteadily.

"It's the middle of the night. Shouldn't you wait until the morning?" Rose asked.

"Why? You're not protecting her, are you?"

"No."

"Yes, you are."

"No. I just think— Do you really want to wake up the dorm heads?"

"I don't give a shit if I wake them up. I want to catch those assholes with the evidence. I want that video erased."

"If it's Snapchat, it's already gone."

"Fine, but there's evidence," Skyler said, mopping at her wet face with her sleeve. "I bet you a hundred bucks they're sitting in Darcy's room right now, high-fiving and laughing at me. They'll still have the ski masks. The Donovans can catch them before they get rid of the proof. I want them kicked out of this friggin' school. I don't give a shit if one of them is your sister."

"Look, I understand. If you want to go to the Donovans tonight, I won't stop you."

"Not only won't you stop me. You're coming with me. I need a witness to back me up."

Rose hesitated.

"I heard you tell Darcy you'd report her," Skyler said. "Were you just blowing smoke? Pretending to be tough?"

"No. But I—I can't. It's my sister."

"So the fuck what? After what she did."

Ratting on girls as connected as Darcy and Tessa would be social suicide. But ratting on her own sister— even if she deserved it—felt like a real betrayal.

Then again, hadn't Bel betrayed her?

"Come on, you just defended me like a total badass," Skyler said. "Don't pussy out on me now. You can't feel sorry for Bel after what she did to us. She's an evil bitch, just like the others."

Rose did feel sorry for Bel. Or, not sorry—protective. It was an old instinct, and hard to shake. Yet, what Bel and her friends had just done was no joke. It was a physical assault, a rape, almost, and Bel was just as guilty as the other two, even if she'd only filmed it.

Only? Rose ought to stop making excuses for her twin. If Bel shared a video of Skyler, naked, getting attacked, that was despicable. And a huge violation of school rules. All that social-media stuff got you in trouble worse than anything. But that was the problem. If Rose ratted, Bel would get expelled.

"I hear you, I really do," Rose said, sighing. "But she's my sister, and I feel like there must be another explanation."

"Then you're a fucking sap. The explanation is: She's

a lowlife. She agreed to attack you. They came here for both of us. If you hadn't fought them off, *you* were gonna be next. They said it."

Skyler was right. Rose had been personally targeted, not just Skyler. Tessa said so at the beginning. *We came for the sister.* Rose knew that in her heart. Bel had sided with her delinquent friends over Rose. After everything Rose had done, after how hard she'd tried to be a good sister, Bel betrayed her. Rose didn't want to believe it. But it was true. Bel was on Darcy's side now. She had to be stopped.

"You're right," Rose said, with a sad sigh. "I'll go with you to the Donovans. Now, before I get cold feet."

16

Transcript of Witness Interview conducted by Lieutenant Robert Kriscunas, State Police—Major Crime Unit and Detective Melissa Howard, Odell NH, PD, with Miss Skyler Stone.

Howard: *Thank you for sharing your story with us, Skyler. I know the incident itself was traumatic for you. But it's important to our investigation, so we really appreciate you talking to us.*

Stone: *Okay. But there's something I want to get straight. I'm not taking the fall here.*

Howard: *Taking the fall for what? I don't understand.*

Stone: *For the murder. People on Facebook are blaming me.*

Kriscunas: *How is that possible, when you were no longer at the school at the time of the killing?*

Stone: *I know, right? But kids are putting out there that I started the feud between Rose and Bel. I pressured*

Rose to squeal to the Donovans, and that made the twins turn on each other. Total BS. Rose wanted to go to the Donovans as much as I did. She hated her sister after that attack. But not just because of the attack. The twins hated each other, and the slipper thing was only part of it.

Kriscunas: Tell us what you know. Why did the twins hate each other?

Stone: Stupid shit. Emma Kim'll tell you Rose made a habit of stealing Bel's clothes. Bel had really cool clothes. She had an eye, a style about her. Rose used to go in and quote-unquote "borrow" them—all the time. They had a fight about that in the dining hall on the first day of school. Ask anybody. But it wasn't only clothes they fought over. There was a boy, too. Those girls were at each other's throats.

Kriscunas: Which boy?

Stone: Rose was crazy for Zach Cuddy. I mean, obsessed with him. She went on and on about him all the time. She would Web-stalk him.

Kriscunas: Web-stalk?

Stone: You know, chase him on Facebook and Snapchat and Insta. Like, any time he was on or posted something new, she'd try to chat him up. But Zach wasn't having it, because he was obsessed with Bel. Honestly, I never thought Bel was as gorgeous as people say, but you know, that kind of dark and sultry look gets them. The big lips, the witchy eyes.

Kriscunas: You say the twins fought over this Zach—spell his last name?

Stone: C-U-D-D-Y.

Kriscunas: They had actual arguments over him?

Stone: Oh, I don't know. Ask Zach. But there's something to it. He was stalking Bel, too.

Kriscunas: Zach Cuddy was stalking Bel. Actually *stalking her, physically, not just online?*

Stone: Yeah. Kids were saying that. I even heard Bel say it.

Kriscunas: Thank you. That sounds significant. We'll look into it.

Stone: Good, because I'm tired of being the scapegoat.

Howard: During the slipper attack itself, you mentioned that Rose fended off the girls by hitting them with a pillow. Did that include hitting her sister? What we're trying to get at is, previous incidents of violence between the twins.

Stone: Look, Rose went after Bel, but she did it for me. I was begging Rose to make them stop filming. Do you understand—they sent out nude pictures of me!

Howard: Yes. That's terrible. We're very sorry.

Stone: I don't know why more isn't being done about that.

Kriscunas: That case is currently pending. Detective Howard and I are not personally involved in investigating it, but we can put you in touch with—

Stone: My dad and the lawyers are handling it. I'm just saying, Bel was the one holding the camera. At first she was kind of slumped over, but Darcy egged her on, and she ended up Snapchatting the attack. Supposedly she was high on painkillers. I don't buy that, but they used that as an excuse.

Kriscunas: Who did?

Stone: The administration, when they made the disciplinary ruling. Complete BS. I mean, come on, Bel basically made child porn when she Snapchatted me. If she was sober enough to work the phone, then she was sober enough to pay for what she did. Rose always said, Bel gets away with murder.

Howard: Rose said Bel got away with murder?

Stone: Yeah, and she hated her for it. Bel attacked me, and Rose was the one who suffered. *After that night, the whole school decided we were snitches. They turned on us. It ruined our lives. My family took action to protect me, at least. Rose's family turned on her. Personally, I think Bel was behind that. She wanted the grandmother's money for herself. No wonder Rose hated her sister so much.*

Kriscunas: There were issues over the grandmother's money?

Stone: I don't really know that for sure, but I did hear that the grandmother was pissed. She's friends with Darcy Madden's folks. Speaking of Darcy, have you looked into her? Darcy didn't take it lightly, getting ratted out. She was livid—at Bel and Rose, both. Since Bel didn't get in trouble, kids thought she snitched, too. Bel's very close to Donovan, tells him everything.

Kriscunas: Hold on, slow down. You're saying—

Stone: I'm saying, you should question Darcy, and Tessa Romano, too. They're the biggest criminals who ever set foot on this campus. They posted threats on Facebook, you know.

Kriscunas: We didn't know. Threats against whom?

Stone: Against me and Rose. I never saw them, but I heard.

Kriscunas: You're saying Darcy and Tessa posted threats against you?

Stone: Darcy did, but then her lawyer made her take the post down. That's what I heard.

Kriscunas: All right, we'll look into that.

Stone: You should. Boy, were they ever pissed off about what happened. I wouldn't put it past either of them to kill someone.

17

"Sarah. Sarah, wake up. Somebody's at the door," Heath said, shaking her shoulder.

"Who— What, what time is it?"

Sarah sat up and rubbed her eyes. There were tears in them. She'd been dreaming that Heath had left her for another woman.

"It's quarter to one. You get the baby, I'll get the door," he said.

Scottie was screaming, and the dog was barking. How had she managed to sleep through that? She threw a robe on and ran to the kids' room. It was close inside, smelling of the diaper pail. Scottie stood grasping the bars of his crib and sobbing, his face bright red in the glow of the night-light. He raised his arms to her.

"Shush, shush, little love, don't wake Sissy."

Sarah lifted him out, found his pacifier, popped it into his mouth. He immediately quieted. She walked with him over to the bedroom door, cradling him

against her shoulder and swaying soothingly as she
strained to hear. He was wet; she could feel the heavi-
ness in his diaper. She caught the high pitch of a girl's
voice, speaking in an alarmed cadence. What the hell
was going on? Whatever it was didn't sound good. She
remembered Darcy and Tessa's behavior at dinner
tonight.

Sarah was eager to hear what was happening, but if
she took Scottie into the living room, he'd be up for the
rest of the night. It took ten minutes to get him changed
and rock him back to sleep. Sarah finally emerged,
bleary-eyed, to find Rose Enright and Skyler Stone
sitting on the edge of the sofa, looking tired and upset. Heath stood over them, shifting impatiently from
one foot to the other, like he couldn't wait to get out of
there.

"What's going on?" Sarah asked.

"I need to fill Mrs. Donovan in and consult her about
this. Give us a minute," Heath said.

Heath pulled Sarah down the hall to the kitchen and
flipped on the light. She sat down hard on a chair, keyed
up with fatigue, and pulled her robe tight around her.

"What happened? They look upset," Sarah said.

"Darcy Madden and Tessa Romano came into their
room while they were sleeping and spanked Skyler with
a slipper. Apparently, they filmed it, too, and she's worried that they'll show the video to boys. Or already did."

"Goddamit, I *knew* they were up to something. We
should have intervened sooner. Do you want to call
Simon, or should I?"

Simon Barlow, the headmaster of Odell Academy,

had hired them to be dorm heads, and presumably could fire them as well if they didn't measure up. Given what had just happened, he might decide to do just that. Sarah was starting to think it wouldn't be such a bad thing.

"I don't want to call Simon yet," Heath said. "Let's get the facts first."

"What facts do we need?" Sarah said. "This sounds like a classic case of slippering. You remember slippering from when we were at Odell, don't you, Heath? *I* do. Some seniors slippered me freshman year. They didn't even take pictures, and it was still humiliating."

Slippering was a hazing ritual that started before there were even girls at Odell, at the now-defunct finishing school down the road, known as Miss Chase's. Legend had it that a few of the more precocious Miss Chase's girls threw a slumber party and took Polaroids of themselves spanking each other with slippers. The Polaroids circulated among Odell boys like so many nudie postcards, and a tradition was born. When the two schools merged in the seventies, slippering arrived at Odell in full force, though it grew less popular over the years. Sarah assumed it had died a well-deserved death long ago, but apparently everything old was new again.

"Darcy Madden's mother was an old-time Moreland fast girl," Heath said. "Darcy's probably gotten the message at home that pranks like this are all in good fun, and she's trying to revive the tradition."

"That's no excuse."

"I'm not saying it's an excuse."

"Then, what are you saying? It's our job to address

this, and we're screwing up. This very afternoon, I said we should report Darcy over that contest idea, and you talked me out of it. If we'd done that, this never would have happened."

"You're saying it's my fault that Darcy attacked Skyler Stone?"

"This isn't about blame, it's about doing our jobs. We were hired to clean up Moreland. You're the one who wanted this job, and yet when these girls misbehave, all I see from you is laughing it off and making excuses."

"Sarah, what's gotten into you?" Heath asked. "I feel like you're turning on me. Are you angry about Darcy's contest?"

"I think I took that pretty well, actually—learning that a gang of teenage girls is trying to seduce my husband. But shrugging it off was a mistake. We took no action, and now look. The same girls have gone and attacked another student. We need to take this incident seriously, Heath."

"I agree. But it's a mistake to wake Simon up at one o'clock in the morning, before we've done any investigation. It's bad optics, it creates a crisis atmosphere, and who knows, it may turn out not to be necessary. Let me get a handle on the situation. I'll gather the facts, and, I promise, I'll present them to Simon first thing in the morning."

"What are you planning to do exactly?" Sarah asked.

"Talk to Darcy and Tessa. Interview them, is a better way to put it. My guess is, they'll admit to it. Hell, they'll probably brag about it. Once they confess, I can institute a disciplinary lockdown, and send them to the infirmary for the rest of the night. You keep Skyler and Rose here for now. I don't want them mingling with the girls who did this to them. When I go to Simon in the morning, I can say it's under control. We can bring this to Simon tied up in a neat little bow."

"Okay," Sarah said grudgingly.

She had to admit, that sounded like a good plan. But as soon as Heath left, Sarah realized it wouldn't be so easy to keep Skyler Stone contained while Heath did his investigating. Sarah invited Rose and Skyler into the kitchen, and made them tea and toast. Almost immediately, Skyler started to get antsy.

"How long do you expect me to wait?" Skyler said.

"It may be a little while. Have some tea," Sarah said.

"I don't want *tea*. I want justice. I want to call the police."

Police? The blood drained from Sarah's face. Getting the police involved would turn this into a full-blown scandal. Even Sarah didn't feel up to taking that on, not without consulting the headmaster first.

"Skyler, listen," Sarah said. "I know you're upset, and you have a right to be. Mr. Donovan is sending the girls who did this to the infirmary on disciplinary lockdown. He's gathering information, so we can get the headmaster and the Disciplinary Committee involved first thing in the morning. The headmaster will make the determination about whether it's appropriate to call the police. There's a protocol for when that's done."

"I don't care about your frigging protocol. How about picking up the phone and dialing the goddamn number?"

"If you want to call, I won't stop you. I'm just saying, there's a way the school handles this, and I personally can't go around the procedure. You can, if you want to."

"I'm calling my dad. He'll sue the pants off those bitches."

Sarah glanced pleadingly at Rose Enright, who'd been sitting silently beside Skyler, listening to the conversation.

"Sky," Rose said, "I think she's right. Let's wait till Mr. Donovan comes back, and hear what he has to say. Then, when you call your parents, you can tell them what the school is doing about this. Seriously. Drink some tea. It'll help you calm down."

Thank God for Rose. She had a good head on her shoulders, and reminded Sarah of herself at that age. If only more Odell girls were like Rose, Sarah's job would be easy.

It was a half hour before Heath got back. He walked into the kitchen, looking weary, and tossed two ski masks onto the table.

"They admitted to everything," Heath said. "You girls can go back to your room now and rest easy. Darcy and Tessa are spending the night in the infirmary on lockdown, so they won't bother you. In the morning, I'll convene the Disciplinary Committee, and request that they be suspended from school."

"Suspended? That's it?" Skyler demanded.

"Suspension is a serious punishment. It'll go on their permanent records. Colleges see it," Heath said.

"You think that's enough?" Skyler said, her face crimson with rage. "They should be in jail. Not just

Darcy and Tessa. Bel, too. Bel Snapchatted the whole attack. That's like making child porn. Why isn't *she* locked in the infirmary?"

"Bel?" Sarah said, turning to Heath, her stomach knotting. "Bel Enright was there? You didn't tell me that."

Heath held up his hands. "Hold on a second. Bel is in the infirmary, too. But there're extenuating circumstances in her case. She got hurt yesterday on a practice run and had a bad reaction to the pain medication they prescribed. While she was under the influence, Darcy and Tessa pressured her into participating in the attack. They're guilty, and I assure you, they'll be brought up before the Disciplinary Committee. Bel will, too, but her involvement is different."

Around the table, everybody's jaws dropped, including Sarah's. *We can bring this to Simon tied up in a neat little bow*, he'd said. Was this what he'd meant? He'd needed time to cover for Bel Enright? Otherwise, why hadn't he mentioned Bel to Sarah when he gave her the rundown on the attack in the kitchen earlier?

"But you're going to tell the Disciplinary Committee she was there, right?" Skyler asked.

"Of course. I'll tell the Committee everything. Who knows, maybe they'll disagree with my assessment and think Bel deserves to be punished, too. I care about what happened to you, Skyler. I take this very seriously, and the girls who did this will get what they deserve."

Heath told the girls to expect to be called before the Disciplinary Committee to give their accounts of the attack. In the meantime, they were not to discuss it with any other students. Heath seemed like he was in a hurry to shoo the girls out the door. When they'd left, Sarah tidied the kitchen quickly, then got into bed beside him, feeling uneasy. Heath turned to flick off the lamp.

"Wait a minute, there's something I have to ask you," she said. "Why didn't you tell me about Bel Enright?"

"Didn't I tell you about her?" he said.

He couldn't really think that? Could he? Heath had a funny expression on his face—one of watchfulness, of careful listening, like he was trying to avoid some pitfall.

Was she being paranoid?

"You most certainly did not. You said Darcy and Tessa attacked Skyler. You never mentioned Bel."

"Maybe I forgot to mention Bel. I'm sorry, honey. My mistake. I was muddled from being woken up."

"Bel filmed the attack. She may have even shared the video with other kids. What did she say when you asked her that?" Sarah said.

"I didn't ask her. I told you, Bel was whacked-out on pain meds. She was in no condition to be interviewed."

"Wait, you didn't ask her if she shared the video? Did you confiscate her phone?"

"Honestly, that didn't occur to me. I was focused on getting medical attention for her. I didn't want to say this in front of the other girls. Especially Rose—I didn't want to upset her. Bel's in bad shape. Dr. Mehta almost sent her to the hospital to get her stomach pumped, that's how bad of a shape she was in."

"You're saying she abused prescription drugs."

"We don't know that. It may have been an accident. It may have been a suicide attempt. The one thing I *do* know is, the meds were prescribed to her by the Odell infirmary, for an injury that Bel sustained during a cross-country practice that *I'm* responsible for. She could turn right around and blame the school, blame me personally. Sue us, even. You want me to accuse her of drug abuse, now? Be reasonable. I'm trying to handle this situation in a way that's fair, but without making *us* look bad, you and me."

"We already look bad, for not reporting Darcy's contest."

"Nobody knows about that. And nobody has to."

"If we lie. I don't want to be part of a cover-up."

"Sarah, a cover-up, really? These are kids we're talking about. *Kids*, fantasizing about a teacher. Spanking another kid with a bedroom slipper. It's stupid stuff, and besides, I already said I'm going to Simon first thing in the morning. Nobody is covering up anything. Why are you questioning me like this? Don't you trust me?"

Heath looked at her with hurt in his eyes. The fact was, she didn't entirely trust him. She worried that he was cutting corners again to get ahead, like he'd done years ago, with his novel. The glibness, the willingness to bend the truth when it suited him, to take the easy way out. He was doing it all over again. She could see it. Yet, Heath reacted so badly when things went wrong. She had to remember how vulnerable he was to failure. Mentally fragile, like his mother had been. She had no choice but to back him up. Otherwise, she might undermine his confidence, and the consequences might be terrible.

They couldn't go through that again.

"You're right, sweetheart," Sarah said. "You promised to go to Simon first thing. That's good enough for me. Tell you what. I'll come with you, so we can present a united front."

"Uh, but I'm the one who interviewed the girls. I know what happened."

"Sure. You can do the talking. I'll be along for moral support."

"Oh."

"Heath, I need to. We're coheads of this dorm. Don't exclude me, please, or I can't be comfortable in the job."

"I understand. You're right. We'll go together. Now, let's get some sleep. I'm beat."

Heath kissed her and snapped off the light. Sarah lay in the darkness, staring at the ceiling.

Something still didn't feel right. Heath had held out on her. He didn't tell her about Bel Enright's involvement, and he appeared to be letting Bel off easily compared to the other girls. Maybe there was a reasonable explanation. Maybe it had slipped Heath's mind to mention Bel, given that Darcy and Tessa were the ringleaders. And maybe Bel was really under the influence of meds prescribed by Odell, and Heath was legitimately worried about liability for that.

Or, maybe not.

Sarah needed to take a deep breath, and stop doubting her husband so much. That stupid bad dream about Heath leaving her was still messing with her head.

Things were under control. They were going to the head-master in the morning with the facts. If Bel warranted punishment, she'd be punished. Heath was very ambitious. He might even be willing to withhold information from higher-ups in order to advance his career. But he wasn't a cheater, and he'd never look twice at a young girl. She was confident of that.

Then, why couldn't she sleep?

18

Bel opened her eyes and saw Heath sitting in a chair beside her bed. She was in a private room in the infirmary. It was dingy and narrow, but cozy. A bar of light fell from the window and illuminated Heath's perfect face. From the quality of that light, Bel guessed it was late afternoon. Had she missed the entire day of classes?

"You're awake," Heath said, leaning forward in the chair.

Bel nodded, which made her head pound. Her arms and legs were heavy with fatigue. When she moved even slightly, pain shot through her right knee. The pain sharpened her mind, bringing her memory back. Certain things, she saw clearly. Slipping and falling on the icy downhill yesterday. How Heath had cradled her in his arms, how she'd touched his face. Tessa coming along and discovering them, and Darcy threatening to tell the whole school. Whatever Bel did last night, she did to protect Heath. But what *had* she done? That memory was wrapped in cobwebs. Something bad, presumably, or Heath wouldn't be here.

"What happened?" she asked.

"That's what I need to ask you," he said. "Are you up for a conversation? How do you feel?"

"I'm really tired, and I have an awful headache," she said. "Oh, and my knee hurts like hell. Other than that, I'm fine."

He smiled at her indulgently. "All right. You're so pale. Let me get you some water, and something to eat, first. Then, we'll talk."

Heath left the room. Bel sat up against the pillows and ran her fingers through her hair. It felt greasy. She must look awful. Her throat was dry, and her breath smelled funky. Sitting up cleared her mind, and last night started coming back to her. Instead of going to Darcy's room at midnight, as she'd been instructed, Bel took pain pills and fell asleep in the bottom bunk. She was alone when Darcy and Tessa came looking for her. (Emma had a fear of heights, and had taken a sleeping bag to the common room rather than sleep in the top bunk.) Darcy shook Bel awake and told her to get her ass in gear. She was helping them with their prank, like it or not. Rose and Skyler were the targets, because Bel had to extra-double-prove her loyalty now as punishment for being late, by going after her own twin. They yanked Bel out of bed, and—

Heath walked back into the room, carrying a tray. He'd brought some Tylenol, a container of applesauce, a carton of chocolate milk, and a bottle of water. He put the tray on a wheeled table and moved it into place, so she could reach it.

"The nurse said Tylenol is okay, but nothing stronger," Heath said, looking down at her.

Bel took the pills under his watchful eye, ate the applesauce and drank some chocolate milk. The infusion of sugar brought the color back to her cheeks. Or maybe it was Heath's presence that did that. The room was quiet, and so still that she could count the motes of dust hanging in the air. This moment felt beautiful and surreal—just the two of them, alone in the mellow, old room. But the spell was bound to break. This was not a social call.

He went back to his chair.

"Do you know why you're here?" he asked.

"I did something wrong?" Bel asked, pushing the table aside.

"Not exactly. Hold on, I need to ask you something sensitive," Heath said, and got up to close the door.

"You're in the infirmary because you took too many pills last night, Bel," he said, sitting back down and fixing her with a solemn gaze.

"How many did I take?"

"You don't remember?"

"No."

"There were eight in the bottle the doctor gave you. You were supposed to take one every four to six hours, but you took all eight at once, last night."

"No wonder I feel so tired."

His blue-green eyes were full of concern. "I'm worried

about you. You basically overdosed. They had to make you throw up, and administer Narcan."

"Ick."

"Do you remember that?" he asked.

"No."

"Bel, did you take those pills by mistake? I need to know."

"What do you mean, 'by mistake'?"

"I mean, did you take too many on purpose? For whatever reason. You can tell me. I won't judge you. The most important thing is to get you the help you need."

Heath wasn't accusing her of taking the pills recreationally, Bel realized. He thought she'd tried to kill herself. What's more, he seemed to actually care whether she had. Bel had a vague recollection of taking the pills. Darcy had told her to take something, so she wouldn't have to face the crappy thing they were going to make her do, whatever it was. (And what the hell was it? She'd done something bad, she knew. Was she in trouble?) But the reality was, Bel took the pills for a different reason. She wanted to blot out the pain. Not the pain in her knee. The pain in her heart. Was that the same thing as suicide? She hadn't really intended to die. She could tell Heath this. He would understand.

"I didn't exactly try to kill myself. Not straight up like that. I just wanted to—not be here. Not think, not feel, or remember. I wanted the pain to stop."

"That's what I was afraid of," Heath said, and the words sounded like they came from deep in his heart.

She loved talking to him like this, so intimately. It was like some strange fantasy, come to life. Bel felt fragile and shaky enough already, from the aftereffects of all those pain pills. Her longing for him was overwhelming, and she felt herself start to sink into self-pity. Why was her life so dark? Why did her parents have to die? Why did she get sent here, only to fall in love with a man she couldn't have? Boys chased her, and she barely noticed. Heath was the only one she wanted.

"I'm sorry to be so sad," she said, her eyes welling. "I hope you're not disappointed in me."

He flushed. Her tears got to him, she could tell. They had before, too—at the Arts Café, when he took her in his arms. Bel wasn't crying on purpose. She truly felt hollow inside. But the sympathy in his eyes when she cried made her cry harder, in the hope that he'd hold her again.

Heath leaned forward in his chair. "I'm going to tell you something very personal about myself. Nobody at Odell knows this, and it would be bad for me if they found out. You can't tell anyone. Do you promise?"

"I'll never tell. You can trust me to keep a secret, any secret. I promise."

"I tried to kill myself, once. I did it with pills, just like you."

As his words sank in, Bel realized that the two of them were so much alike. Heath was her soul mate, really. She didn't feel like a girl when she was with him. She felt like a woman—his equal. She could ask him anything now, and he would answer honestly.

"Why?"

"There was something I wanted, more than I'd ever wanted anything in my life," Heath said. He met her eyes, speaking steadily and comfortably, as if telling her his darkest secret was the most natural thing in the world. "And just when it was in my grasp, I lost it. The worst part was, it was my own damn fault. I'd done something wrong, you see, and I got caught. Everybody turned on me. I can't say they weren't justified, but it was awful to feel so abandoned. Not just by the people I'd been working with. But my wife, her parents. Everybody blamed me. I couldn't take the humiliation, to be honest. And the loss. See, I have this idea that I'm meant to do important things."

"Oh, you are. You are, I just know it," she said breathlessly.

"So, to fail like that, was extra difficult for me. I decided I'd rather end things. That was a mistake. Fortunately, my wife found me, and called an ambulance."

Heath looked away. He was so close, but she couldn't comfort him the way she wanted to, with her fingertips, her lips against his skin. It was so unfair.

"Thank you for telling me," Bel said, her hands twitching to touch his beautiful face. She'd done that, just yesterday. She could still feel the warmth of his cheek under her fingers.

"I told you that because I want you to know there's hope," he said. "That you're not alone. That things can get better. That one day, you'll be happy again."

"I'm happy now. I'm happy being here with you. I'm happy that you trust me enough to tell me that."

He looked back at her, his eyes lingering on her face as the tears rolled slowly down her cheeks.

"If you're happy, then why are you crying?" he asked.

"Because I love you, and you don't love me back," she whispered.

Heath was out of his chair in an instant, sitting on the edge of her bed.

"I do love you," he said, his voice low and intimate. "I care about you so much, Bel."

"No, but I love you, for real, Heath. Not like a teacher and a student. I want us to be lovers. I know that's wrong to say."

She saw the look of pleasure, of gratification, in his eyes. But he shook his head. "I wish I could let you say it. But already, I think of you too much. You remind me of songs, of poems. 'Her beauty and the moonlight overthrew you.' Your beauty could bring down kings, Bel, but I can't let myself fall. That's why we can never be together," he said.

"Please don't say that."

"It's true. I'm married. I'm your teacher. You're too young. All those reasons."

"Not because you don't want to?"

"I *do* want to, but I have other obligations. Like leading this school. It's something I've been working toward for a long time. Deep down, I'm still the poor kid with my nose pressed up against the glass, dreaming of being on the inside. Maybe if I could run this place, I could finally banish that demon. I know you understand. You understand me so well."

He brushed at her tears with his fingers. His hands were shaking, she noticed—what did that mean? Glancing quickly at the open door, he leaned forward and touched his lips lingeringly to her forehead. Bel couldn't believe this was happening. Was it real, or just a beautiful dream? It was *real*. She could feel his weight on the mattress, his warm breath on her skin. He kissed both her cheeks, then the tip of her nose. Her insides melted. He grazed her lips with just the merest taste of a kiss, before pulling back.

"I shouldn't have done that," he said, moving back to his chair.

"Yes. You should," she said, smiling through her tears.

"You can never tell anyone."

"Of course not. Never. I would never tell about anything we do," she said.

He got up and paced the narrow strip of floor, drawing deep breaths.

"I need some air," he said, pointing to the window. "Do you mind?"

"Go ahead."

Heath cracked the window, and cool air rushed in.

"I have to ask you about a difficult subject," he said. "The slipper attack. Last night. Do you remember?"

Bel turned her face to the pillow. "Sort of. I'm not sure. Was it bad?"

"Yeah, it was pretty bad. Darcy and Tessa stripped Skyler Stone's clothes off and spanked her. You filmed it. Snapchatted it. Your phone has been confiscated. The school will have the phone examined, and if they can prove you shared that video, well, normally—"

"I could get suspended?"

"They're looking to crack down. Suspended. Maybe even expelled."

Bel started to tremble. "I can't," she said. "I don't want to leave you."

"I don't want that to happen to you," he said. She was bereft that he made it sound so impersonal. Like he would only be sad for her if she got kicked out. Not for himself.

"You'd miss me, right?" she asked, the tears starting up again.

"We're not talking like that, okay? But I can protect you. I can help you get out of this, Bel, if you do what I say."

"I'd do anything you say."

"Pay careful attention. We're convening the Disciplinary Committee soon. You'll be called in and asked about the slipper attack. Here's what you say."

Heath proceeded to script her entire statement for her. Bel was to claim she'd mistakenly taken too many pills, and that, as a result, the entire night was a blank. She mustn't say anything against Darcy and Tessa because Heath didn't want her getting blamed for any punishment they received. Her best course was to claim full and complete memory loss, and throw herself on the mercy of the Committee. She might have to agree to counseling, but that was nothing, and not a bad idea anyway, given how depressed she'd been.

"Are we clear?" Heath said.

"Yes. Thank you. I'll say it just like you told me. But, what's going to happen to Darcy and Tessa?" Bel asked.

"Normally, they'd just be suspended, and get a notation on their disciplinary record. But Skyler Stone's parents are threatening to sue the school. Darcy and Tessa may need to be sacrificed. They'll probably be expelled."

"Expelled, my God," Bel said, collapsing back against her pillows.

"What's the problem? They're a terrible influence on you. They attacked your sister, and got you in serious trouble. You ought to hate them."

"I *do* hate them. But they're my only friends."

Heath laughed. "Silly girl, no they're not. You have me."

"I have you?" she asked wistfully.

"Yes, you do. How many times do I have to say it?"

Heath smiled, and laugh lines formed around his beautiful eyes.

"I'm lucky, then," Bel managed. She was mesmerized, and having trouble forming thoughts.

"But you have to help me," he said.

"How? I'll do anything."

He looked sober suddenly. "Just be good, Bel. That's how you can help. So I'll be strong enough to be good, too."

19

Four days after the slipper attack, Bel was called before the Disciplinary Committee to explain herself. As she sat alone in the gloomy anteroom waiting for her interview, she felt almost calm. Heath had been appointed acting dean of students, which meant he would be the person running the disciplinary hearing. He'd pulled her aside after English class yesterday, explained how things would go, and went over one more time exactly what she should say. That's why she didn't feel afraid. This would be like taking a test for which she'd been given the answers in advance.

As she watched, the door to the inner conference room started to open. Bel drew in a long breath, holding on to it like that could help her stay calm. It was daunting to think of sitting in the hot seat, facing a long table of disapproving faculty members, explaining how she'd taken an overdose of pills. *It was an accident,* she was supposed to say, *a mistake. I was . . . tired, in pain, confused. I never meant to take those pills. I can't remember anything that happened afterward. I don't remember the attack, the Snapchat. I don't know who I sent the video to. You can look at my phone. Please look at it—I have nothing to hide. But I can't be much help. It's as if none of this ever happened. I'm terribly ashamed to have been involved with something so sordid. It was a dreadful mistake to take those pills. I'm no longer friends with those girls. My mother died recently. I'll be more careful with prescription drugs in the future. I would like to make amends. I wrote a letter of apology to the victim. Please forgive me. All I want is to move past this and contribute to the Odell community.*

What if they didn't believe her? None of it was actually true, after all. She'd taken the pills accidentally on purpose because she knew something ugly was about to go down. When Darcy and Tessa came for her, Bel was too doped up to resist, but she'd planned it that way. She wanted to make it easier to do what they said. And she did remember. She remembered everything. She'd kept that to herself. Nobody knew, not even Heath. She hadn't been entirely honest with him, but only because she cared so much what he thought of her. That was understandable, right?

Today wasn't about being honest, anyway. The point of her testimony was to make sure she could stay at Odell, so she could be close to Heath. Otherwise, Bel wouldn't have given a shit whether she got expelled or not. She didn't feel guilty or remorseful, either. Darcy and Tessa were the ones who'd planned the attack, and they were the ones who deserved to be punished. It was only fair. Bel had faith. She would follow the course Heath had laid out for her. He'd get her through this. He knew best.

This must be him now, coming to collect her, to squeeze her hand supportively, to whisper that she shouldn't worry as he led her to her chair.

But it was Rose who stepped out of the conference room.

Bel sprang to her feet. This was her first chance to speak to her sister face-to-face since the attack, though not for lack of trying. Rose had been avoiding her. Bel might not feel guilty, but she felt sad. She missed her sister. The worst thing about this stupid prank was that it had come between them.

"Get away from me. The last thing I need now is *you*," Rose said, her voice full of contempt. She tried to push past, but Bel blocked her way.

"Wait," Bel said. "I came to your room three times to explain what happened, and every time Skyler chased me away."

"That's right. I told her to."

"You don't get to just freeze me out. You have to let me explain. I'm your sister."

Rose snorted. "Like that counts for anything with you?"

"It does. It means a lot."

"What about the part where I'm *your* sister? Shouldn't that mean something, too? Like, don't bring your sleazy friends to my room in the middle of the night to physically attack me?"

"Rose, I was drugged out of my mind."

"If you want to fry your brain with that garbage, be my guest. But don't use it to justify what you did to me."

"To *you*? It was Skyler they attacked."

"*They*? Like you weren't even there? Are you really so unable to take responsibility for your actions, or is this some kind of ploy?"

"I'm sorry. I admit, I was there."

"Of course, you were there. I saw you! And for your information, Skyler's not the only one who got hurt, Bel. I had to fight them off, or I would've been next. I have bruises to prove it. And now, instead of studying for finals like I ought to be, I have to spend my time testifying in front of the Disciplinary Committee. You know what that means, right? Everybody thinks I'm a rat. Your precious Darcy even threatened me. She threatened my safety. That's the mess you dragged me into."

"I can explain. I was given pain meds for my knee. I didn't get high on purpose. I took too many, by mistake. Honest, I was like a zombie that night. I had no idea what was happening. Darcy and Tessa showed up to my room, they said go, and I went. It was all them. Swear to God."

Rose hesitated. Bel saw doubt in her sister's eyes, and felt a flicker of hope.

"You know it's true," Bel said, grabbing Rose's hands. "You came by my room before the attack. I know you did because you left me food, and a note. I was out cold, right? Dead to the world? Please, Rose, you have to believe me."

Rose pulled away, sighing wearily. "I *don't* believe

you. That's the problem. You sided with those girls against me before, and then promised things would change. But they didn't. They got worse."

"I hate Darcy as much as you do at this point. I'll testify against her, too. Then we'll be rats together. Would that help? Would that prove my loyalty?"

"If you go in there and actually tell the truth? It would be a start."

Heath cleared his throat. The girls looked over to see him standing near the closed conference-room door. It was unclear how long he'd been there, or how much he'd heard.

"The Committee is waiting for you, Bel."

"One second."

Bel turned back to Rose.

"Go," Rose said.

Then she walked away, a disgusted look in her eye, without wishing Bel luck or even saying good-bye.

Heath and Bel were alone in the anteroom. He walked over and placed his hands on her shoulders, gazing down into her eyes. Heath was the only person who mattered now. If she could just focus on that one fact, everything else would fall into place, and her life would make sense.

"Don't worry about Rose," Heath said. "She'll come around. Just say what I told you to say, and everything will work out fine."

20

Rose woke up at five a.m. on Sunday to catch the bus to Connecticut for Thanksgiving break. It was dark and quiet in the dorm room, and she was jittery. Skyler had left last night to fly to her grandparents' house in Florida, and Rose was afraid to be in the room by herself. With all the fallout from the slipper attack, she'd been sticking close by Skyler, who was the only person at school people hated more than they hated Rose.

The Disciplinary Committee had taken its sweet time about making a decision, but a week earlier, they'd finally announced that Darcy and Tessa were expelled. Turned out, that decision was not popular among the student body. Go figure—just because the Moreland seniors were nasty and vile didn't mean they lacked for admirers. In the days since the decision had been made public, stuffed rats had started appearing in Rose and Skyler's room on the regular, perched in their desk chairs or sitting on their beds. It freaked Rose out that people were sneaking into her room when she wasn't there, and doing something so sinister. (There were no locks on the bedroom doors at Odell because, supposedly, it wasn't the sort of place where you needed a lock—*right*.) In the dining hall, people made squeaking noises when Rose and Skyler walked by. Skyler received an anonymous note that read: *Snitches get stitches*. And in the middle of the night last week, someone yanked their door opened and threw slippers at their heads as they slept. Whoever did it ran away before they could see her face.

Rose and Skyler talked it over and decided not to file a complaint about the harassment. If they complained again, things would only get worse. It was hard to know whether they were in actual, physical danger. Emma Kim had told Rose that Tessa Romano had been spotted on campus, even though she was now forbidden to return. That was just gossip, but it had the ring of truth. Unlike Darcy, who lived in Connecticut (not far from Grandma, actually), Tessa was a local girl. A townie, from a family that owned several restaurants in town. Rose had heard through the grapevine that Tessa would be enrolling in the local high school after Thanksgiving break, which meant she'd be a mere ten-minute drive from the Odell gates. Close enough for a drive-by attack. But there was no actual evidence that Tessa was planning to retaliate. That was speculation, or gossip. And as for the things Rose did have evidence on—the rubber rats, the nasty notes—she didn't know who was behind them.

Rose's hair was still wet, and it was pitch-dark out as she dragged her suitcase from Moreland to the parking lot in front of the library, where several buses sat belching exhaust into the damp, chill air. Odell ran buses to New York, Boston and the closest airports every school holiday. The New York bus stopped in Westport, where Rose would get off. (Spring Hill, Grandma Martha's estate, was a fifteen-minute drive from there.) Presumably Bel would be on the same bus, although Rose was no longer on speaking terms with her twin. No longer? Better to say, yet again, since Bel kept doing things that made it impossible to stay her friend. Standing outside the conference room that day, Bel had led Rose to believe that she would tell the Committee the truth about Darcy and Tessa, and back up Rose and Skyler's claims about the attack. Rose had actually been stupid enough to believe that. But Skyler's father had seen the transcript, in which Bel claimed to be so doped up that she had no memory of the entire night. Bel lied her ass off, basically, because she was a goddamn coward. She left Rose and Skyler twisting in the wind, the lone rats. So much for sisterly loyalty, for being on the same team. It was one betrayal too many. Bel could be bleeding on the ground now, and Rose would walk by without stopping. No, she *would* stop—long enough to look down and laugh. That's how hurt she was, that's how furious. That's how much she hated her sister.

Hate was not too strong a word.

Rose stood on line at the side of the bus, waiting to put her suitcase in the luggage hold. Without warning, somebody bumped her hard from behind. The impact sent her feet skidding out from under her on the slippery sidewalk. If the girl behind her hadn't grabbed her arm, she would have landed flat out on her butt.

"Thank you," Rose said. "Sorry!"

"It wasn't your fault," the girl said. "That was weird, it was like he went out of his way to bump you. What's his problem?"

They stared after the boy who'd bumped Rose, who was now boarding the bus. His Frankenstein-like head looked familiar. *That was Brandon Flynn, Darcy's boyfriend—wasn't it?*

"Are you okay?" the girl asked.

"Oh, yeah, I'm fine," Rose said, nodding, not wanting to cause a fuss. But she knew now that the bump was no accident, and it unnerved her.

Rose climbed the stairs onto the bus. It was a luxury long-distance bus, with a bathroom in the back and plush seats and television screens that showed movies the whole way. Rose had her earbuds, so if nobody talked to her, she would zone out watching movies and try not to mind.

Rose was moving forward, scanning the seats for friendly faces, when she tripped over something in the aisle and went flying. She landed on her hands and knees on the narrow strip of floor, the breath knocked out of her. Her backpack swung around and clonked her on the head. For a split second she was stunned, but then she got to her feet, praying nobody had noticed her flame out like a total klutz. No such luck. Brandon Flynn sat in an aisle seat right next to where she'd fallen, smirking. Zach Cuddy, the cute boy from her bio class, sat across the aisle from Brandon. Rose was mortified because she'd developed a serious crush on Zach. He was tall, dark and handsome, except with glasses, and smart as a whip. Her idea of the perfect man. She talked to him every chance she got, and found herself blushing like an idiot, palms sweaty and heart racing. Perfect Zach had now seen Rose trip like a bumbling idiot while the jerk who tripped her sat there laughing. Zach probably knew *why* that asshole tripped her, too. It was a small school, and gossip traveled like fire in the wind.

"What the fuck was that?" Zach Cuddy demanded.

Rose's heart stopped, but Zach's words weren't intended for her. He was glaring across the aisle at Brandon Flynn.

"Mind your business, Cuddy," Brandon said.

"You tripped her. I saw it."

"I did not."

"So, you're a liar as well as a thug?"

They both jumped to their feet. Brandon was built like a jock, as tall as Zach, but thicker and more muscular. Rose stood in the aisle between them, quaking in her UGGS. She glanced up to the front of the bus, but the driver was outside, handling the students' luggage, and there was no other adult in sight. All around them, kids were getting up, leaning into the aisle, craning their necks to ogle the confrontation.

Emma Kim sat one row behind. She stood up, too.

"He's right, I saw you do it," Emma said. "You tripped her on purpose. That's bullying, Flynn. You want to get expelled, like your skanky girlfriend?"

"Shut up," the senior said. "Enright's a snitch, she deserves what she gets. You want some, too, Emma? Come and get it."

Brandon Flynn had just admitted to tripping Rose intentionally, and called her a snitch in front of the entire bus. There was no way out of this nightmare. As much as Rose might want to deny it, everybody in the school knew she'd told the Disciplinary Committee what Darcy and Tessa did. She might as well stand her ground, and keep her self-respect.

"I'm not afraid of you!" Rose said, right to his ugly face, as loudly as she could. "You want to hurt me? Just try it. You'll wind up expelled, too."

"Attagirl, you tell him what's what," Zach said, and took her arm. "Back off, Flynn. This girl is not afraid of you. Rose, come sit with me, in the back where the company is better."

"I'm coming, too," Emma said, gathering her things. "I refuse to sit near a bully."

"You're gonna regret crossing me, Cuddy. I know where you live," Brandon said.

"He just threatened you," Rose whispered.

"Yeah, he pulls shit like that on the regular. He's like the worst of the jock thugs. I hate his guts," Zach said, guiding Rose toward the back of the bus.

"Should I be worried about him coming after me?"

"Like Emma said, he's a bully. If you stand up to him, hopefully he backs down. And you did stand up to him. I thought you were gonna punch him out."

Zach smiled at her. He had a lovely smile. She was

even more smitten with him now that he'd stood up for her.

"I *wanted* to punch him. I can't believe he called me a snitch in front of everyone," Rose said, her hands still shaking from the encounter.

"Brandon Flynn's a douche, anyway. Nobody gives a shit what he thinks," Zach said.

"He's just mad because Darcy got expelled, and no other girl is stupid enough to date him," Emma said.

As they made their way down the aisle, Rose spotted Bel about halfway down, leaning against the window and pretending to sleep. The sight of her sister made her angry all over again. Bel wore dark sunglasses and had a black pashmina draped over her head like some reclusive movie star hiding from the paparazzi. Her belongings were piled on the seat beside her so nobody could sit there. Who the hell did she think she was, some tragic celebrity? Granted, Bel's best friends had been expelled—her only friends, as far as Rose could tell. But that was her own damn fault for being friends with assholes. Rose's life at Odell had become a living nightmare because of what Bel and those girls did. Meanwhile, Bel got off scot-free. She hadn't been punished at all, and nobody seemed to blame her. It wasn't fair.

They found a row in the back where all four seats were empty. Zach slid into the window seat on the left, and Rose sank down beside him. Emma took the aisle seat on the right, and leaned across to them, smiling.

"Anybody want breakfast? I raided the New last

night," she said, pulling fruit and granola bars from her backpack, and handing Rose an apple.

Emma thought of everything. She was so cool, so self-assured, in her baggy sweater, black leggings and white sneakers with no socks, despite the cold. If only Rose had been assigned to room with her instead of Skyler, none of this would've happened. Nobody would dare pull a prank like that on Emma. She carried herself with too much dignity. People didn't like Skyler, that was the problem, and Skyler's bad karma had rubbed off on Rose. As soon as she thought that, Rose got mad at herself for victim-blaming. The people responsible for this epic disaster were the ones who'd pulled the prank: Darcy, Tessa—and *Bel*.

"So, *I* heard," Emma stage-whispered conspiratorially as the bus pulled out of the driveway and headed to the main road, "that ever since Heath Donovan got appointed acting dean of students, he needs to make a name for himself. So he's taking a really hard line. Skyler's parents weren't satisfied with just expelling Darcy and Tessa. And Bel got away with everything. The Stones want the school to go after the boys who shared the video, too, or they're gonna sue. Donovan's agreed to do it, to prove how tough the school is on hazing."

"That video was a Snapchat. Snapchats disappear after ten seconds. They can't prove who shared it. They can't even prove it was sent. Right?" Zach said, with a sick look on his face.

"Oh, an expert can recover a Snapchat with a special search," Emma said, nodding knowingly. "Besides, they know it was sent. Some boy who got the Snapchat told Skyler about it. He was like, *Hey, bitch, my dorm saw you naked.*"

"What dorm?" Zach asked.

"Huh?"

"Which dorm was the kid from, who said he got the Snapchat?"

"Cushman. Why? That's not yours, is it?"

"No. Not mine. Absolutely not." Zach looked relieved. "Seriously, though, what kind of idiot would tell Skyler he saw her naked?"

"An expelled one, now," Emma said, smiling ruefully and tossing her glossy black hair. Rose couldn't imagine being so cavalier about something so dire, but then again, Emma had nothing to fear. She had no personal involvement in the incident, unlike Rose or—judging by the expression on his face—Zach.

"Expelled? Jesus," Zach said.

"Why are *you* worried?" Emma asked suspiciously. "You didn't view the video, did you?"

"You know, if someone sends you something, and you open it, that's not a crime."

"You viewed it?" Rose asked. "Why would you do that? It's an invasion of privacy. Skyler's more wrecked over that than over the attack."

"I never said I saw it. If I did, I wouldn't confess. I'm not a moron."

"Oh, come on, Cuddy," Emma said. "You saw it. It's obvious. At least tell me if Rose was as epic as they say. I heard she beat the crap out of those seniors."

Emma winked at Rose.

"I stuck up for my roommate, that's all. You would've done the same," Rose said.

"For Bel?" Emma said. "Nope. She's one of the bad guys. I don't even like rooming with her."

Rose was uncomfortable discussing her sister with Emma, so she steered the conversation to their plans for the break. While it was a relief not to be talking about the investigation, she was anxious for more information. Was it really possible the boys who watched the video would get expelled? If that happened, Rose's life at Odell would go from living nightmare to living hell.

21

"Come into the parlor, dear. There's something we need to discuss," Grandma Martha said, poking her head into the hallway as Rose passed by the parlor door.

It was the Monday morning of Thanksgiving week, Rose's second day at Spring Hill. She'd been on her way to the kitchen to scrounge breakfast from the housekeeper. Grandma's estate sat on twenty manicured acres in the Connecticut countryside, and consisted of a charming old clapboard-and-stone manor house, as well as a stable and paddocks, a pool, pool house and tennis court. The house was gracious, spacious and elegant, but sadly it wasn't large enough to sneak down for breakfast without being discovered.

Rose stepped into the parlor, a beautifully proportioned room with tall windows, expertly decorated. It was a cold, gloomy day outside, but a fire crackled cheerfully in the fireplace. Grandma's lawyer, Warren, whom Rose had met on several occasions, sat on the sofa in front of the fire, looking dapper in gray slacks and a navy blazer. Grandma was elegantly turned out as well, in a pretty blue dress and pearls, leaving Rose—still in her pajamas, hair not brushed, with morning breath—at a distinct disadvantage.

Grandma took a seat beside Warren. They both wore disappointed, long-suffering looks, like parents about to deliver a scolding to a misbehaving child. Rose wracked her brain and couldn't think of a single thing she'd done wrong. Her grades were excellent, and she'd never been in trouble. She'd only been the victim of trouble. Bel was the one who needed lecturing, not Rose. Yet, Bel wasn't there.

"You remember Warren Adams, my attorney," Grandma said.

"Of course. Good morning, Mr. Adams. Nice to see you again," Rose said, and shook his hand.

"Likewise, Rose. Please, have a seat," he replied.

Rose sat down in an armchair, folding her hands in her lap and looking at them attentively. Odell had taught her that a simple display of manners would get you far in this life. People might not be good at Odell, but they were polite, and they got away with murder on a lot of fronts because of it. Something to remember, and use to her advantage when possible.

"Your grandmother received some troubling legal news, which she's asked me to advise on," Warren began. "It's about your roommate, Miss Stone."

Terrible thoughts flooded Rose's mind. Skyler had

hung herself, she'd slit her wrists in the bathtub. Or she'd decided to withdraw from Odell and leave Rose as the lone target of retaliation.

"Is Skyler all right?" Rose said.

"As far as I know. That's not the problem. Her parents have filed suit against Odell Academy, and the girls who attacked her," Warren explained.

Rose slumped with relief. "Oh. Thank God, I thought she was hurt. But a lawsuit—I heard they were doing that."

"You knew they were planning to sue?" Warren asked.

"I didn't know for sure. But Skyler said it was a possibility. Her dad's a lawyer, and he's sued people before over stuff. What does this have to do with us?"

With *me*, she meant.

"Quite a bit, unfortunately. Your grandmother is a named defendant."

"Why? You weren't there," Rose said, turning to Grandma, who'd averted her eyes, and was looking out the window as if she'd rather not look at Rose.

"Bel was there," Warren said. "Your grandmother had been named in the lawsuit because she's Bel's legal guardian."

"This was done to all the families," Grandma said, turning to give Rose a hurt look. "Darcy Madden's family is named because of Darcy's conduct. I know the Maddens quite well from the club. They're extremely upset, as you can imagine. Not just because their granddaughter's been expelled and referred to the police—though they're beside themselves about that. But mainly because anybody who's named, well, their assets are at substantial risk. These Stone people are asking for *twenty million dollars*."

That enormous number seemed to float out of Grandma's mouth and hang in the air between them. They sat for a moment, staring at one another in horror, both at a loss for words, as the gold clock ticked on the mantel. Above it hung a portrait of Rose's grandparents with her father, painted when Brooks Enright was no more than ten or eleven. He'd been a handsome boy–square jaw and fair hair, wide forehead. (Rose looked a lot like him, though his features didn't sit quite so well on a girl.) Brooks looked like someone who'd be a reliable friend in your hour of need. If only he were alive to defend Rose now.

"I had no idea," Rose said.

Skyler, that bitch. She could've at least given me a heads-up. Is there nobody I can trust?

"As you can imagine," Warren said, "the lawsuit puts *you* in an extremely awkward position, Rose. Your grandmother is a defendant based on your sister's conduct, and you will surely be called to testify for the other side."

"Well, if they ask me to testify, I'll just say no. I'll refuse," Rose said.

"I'm afraid that won't be possible. Not if they subpoena you, and I expect they will," Warren said.

"Well, then. I'll say it never happened. Or that Darcy and Tessa did it alone, and Bel wasn't there."

Warren and Grandma glanced at one another sadly.

"Let's assume for a moment that what you're suggesting wouldn't amount to perjury, since obviously, perjury is frowned upon," Warren said, raising an eyebrow. "That more favorable version of the facts would unfortunately come too late, since you've already given a statement to the Disciplinary Committee saying exactly the opposite."

"You know about that?" Rose asked.

"It's quoted in the lawsuit. In your statement, you made quite clear that Bel was involved in the attack. Though, frankly, I'm not sure why you thought that was necessary, given that the three attackers wore ski masks, and Bel never spoke."

"You could have said you weren't sure," Grandma said.

The bottom fell out of Rose's stomach. She'd been promised confidentiality if she spoke to the Committee. She never thought anyone in her family would find out about her statement. She certainly never thought that Skyler would put it in a lawsuit for the whole world to see. If she'd known that, she would've kept her mouth shut. But why was this Rose's fault? All she did was tell the truth. Bel was the one who caused the trouble. She ought to get the blame.

"This is not my fault!" Rose blurted. "They told me I had to tell the truth about what happened, or I'd get hit with a code-of-conduct violation. I follow the rules, Grandma. I'm the good sister. You should be mad at Bel, not at me. She went along with those girls voluntarily."

"She says she was drugged."

"She took some pills. Big deal. They stripped Skyler

naked and hit her with a slipper, and Bel was awake enough to film it."

Warren chuckled. Rose and Grandma both gave him shocked looks.

"Come on, you have to admit that's funny," he said. "In my day, people would've been embarrassed to make such a fuss about a silly prank."

"Don't you understand, Bel *Snapchatted* the whole thing," Rose said, horrified.

"What is that? Some Facebook sort of thing?" Grandma asked.

"It's a video-sharing app. They took a video of Skyler, stark naked with her privates showing, and sent it to a bunch of boys. *Bel* did that. Skyler is completely humiliated."

Grandma looked pained. "I agree, that's not nice. But it wasn't Bel's *fault*. She'd taken pain medication for her knee that made her not in her right mind."

"Believe what you want, Grandma. But I was there. Bel was in her right mind enough to break into our room with her trashy friends, take video, and forward it to a bunch of boys. I don't know what else I can say."

"Ugh, it was that awful Darcy," Grandma said. "She's a bad influence."

"That's who Bel hangs out with. I told her not to," Rose said.

"Rose, I hate to say it, but you're starting to sound like a tattle, and it's not attractive," Grandma said. "I don't like Darcy, either, but I don't like hearing you speak against your sister."

So, that's how it's going to be. Just like with Mom, when push comes to shove, Bel is Grandma's favorite. It isn't fair.

"Can we focus on the lawsuit, please?" Warren said. "I don't care what happens to Darcy Madden, but I do care about your grandmother."

And her money, Rose added mentally.

"Your statement corroborates Skyler Stone's account of Bel's involvement," Warren said. "Without it, it would be Skyler's word against Bel's. With it, they have a strong case. There could be an enormous payday for Skyler Stone's family, at your grandmother's expense, because of what you've said. I'm not sure that we can overcome the statement you already gave. But I have an associate looking into ways to strike it from the record. In the meantime, Rose, you're not to speak to anybody about this matter—not the Disciplinary Committee at Odell, not the police—without calling me first. Do you understand?"

"That could get me in trouble at school. Have you read the handbook? It says that refusing to cooperate with a disciplinary investigation is grounds for suspension, or even expulsion."

"That's a risk we'll have to take," Warren said.

"Risk my Odell education?" Rose said, appalled. "I'm not taking that risk."

"Without your grandmother's money, there is no Odell education," Warren said.

"This isn't about money," Grandma said coolly. "It's about family loyalty. Enrights stick together. Bel may have poor taste in friends, but she didn't take sides against this family. *You* did, Rose. I don't like it, not one bit, and it stops now."

Bel *had* taken sides against her family. Bel had taken sides against Rose, and attacked her in the dead of night, but nobody cared. Grandma certainly didn't. All she cared about was money, and her darling, manipulative Bel, who weaseled out of every problem, and never paid the price.

22

Transcript of Witness Interview conducted by Lieutenant Robert Kriscunas, State Police—Major Crime Unit, and Detective Melissa Howard, Odell NH, PD, with Mrs. Sarah Donovan.

Kriscunas: We've heard that the Stone family's lawsuit caused a big breach between the sisters. Do you have any insight into that, Mrs. Donovan?

Donovan: The lawsuit changed a lot of things at Odell. It brought tremendous scrutiny of how the school handled disciplinary matters. Historically, Odell preferred to counsel kids who got into trouble rather than punish them. These are teenagers, right? They're still learning. For a first offense, they might be assigned therapy, or rehab. Or some sort of community service. In extreme cases, kids would get suspended and it would go on their permanent records. After the *slipper incident, though, the school did get tougher. Odell expelled two of the girls involved and actually reported the incident to the police.*

Kriscunas: We're aware of that. What I'm asking you is: Did it lead to hostility between the sisters? Or, more broadly, did you ever witness any open hostility or violence between them? Anything at all?

Donovan: Oh my, no. Nothing like that. You seem to have the wrong impression. Violence among our students is unheard of. I mean, with a few exceptions obviously. The slipper attack, and this awful murder. Other than that, no, there's absolutely nothing. And just let me say that Rose, in particular, was always a quiet, gentle girl.

Kriscunas: Getting back to the slipper attack, I wanted to ask you about the aftermath. Two students got expelled, and from what we've heard, they were extremely angry at the Enright girls over that. Do you think it's possible Darcy Madden or Tessa Romano were involved?

Donovan: Involved in the murder?

Howard: Yes.

Donovan: They were expelled the week before Thanksgiving. As far as I know, they haven't been on campus since.

Howard: Tessa Romano hasn't been on campus since?

Donovan: Tessa does live in town, so I suppose it's possible. It's an enormous campus. She could be here every day, and I wouldn't know. On the other hand, I haven't heard anything to say that she was.

Kriscunas: What about Brandon Flynn, Miss Madden's boyfriend?

Donovan: I don't know much about him, or his involvement.

Kriscunas: Fine, let's get back to what you do know. You were saying that the lawsuit affected your family. In what way?

Donovan: Well, my husband got promoted, for one thing. Heath—my husband—had advocated for a tougher approach to the girls who were involved in that attack, and I guess the school felt that's what was needed. The dean of students was out on sick leave, and ultimately couldn't return to the position. Heath was appointed to the position. At first temporarily, then permanently.

Kriscunas: You say he got the job because he was going to get tough on discipline. But we've heard from another witness that there was disparate treatment of the girls involved in the slipper attack. Bel Enright was not disciplined for what she did, and her conduct was not reported to the police. Can you shed any light on that?

Donovan: From what I understand, the night it happened, Bel Enright was having a bad reaction to some pain medication she'd been given for an athletic injury. The feeling was, she wasn't thinking clearly because of that, and so she was excused.

Kriscunas: That's it? And do you feel that was an adequate response?

Donovan: Uh—I'm not sure what you're getting at.

Kriscunas: We've had a witness suggest that favoritism

was shown to Bel Enright in the disciplinary process, in particular, by your husband. Do you think that's a fair assessment, or not?

[PAUSE]

Kriscunas: Mrs. Donovan, do you need me to repeat the question?

23

"Is everything all right with you and Heath?" Sarah's mother asked in a low tone, eyes shining in anticipation of bad news.

It was five o'clock on Thanksgiving Day, and darkness had fallen outside the windows of Sarah's childhood kitchen. She stood washing the good china in soapy water, as her mother collected dessert forks and teacups, getting ready to serve the pie. The kitchen was warm and cozy, smelling of turkey and cinnamon and wood smoke from the fireplace in the parlor. Sarah could hear the kids in there, shrieking with laughter as they rolled around on the floor with Max, the dog, who'd been thrilled to make the two-hour journey to her parents' house in Massachusetts, where he'd barked at the neighbors' dogs before nabbing a cozy spot by the fire. Normally, Heath would be down on the floor causing an uproar right along with them. But things weren't normal today, and they weren't as idyllic as they seemed. Heath was shut up in the guest room, talking on his phone. He'd been in there for nearly an hour. And her mother's inquiry wasn't concerned or sympathetic. She just loved to dig in the knife.

"Things are fine, Mom. He's busy with work," Sarah said, in a clipped tone designed to get her mother to back off.

"On Thanksgiving Day? You'd think he was a lawyer or an investment banker instead of a schoolteacher," her mother remarked dryly.

"I'll get him," Sarah said with a sigh, drying her hands on a dish towel. "But I won't have you disparaging him. If you do that, we're going to leave."

"You're overreacting. I just wondered what was taking so long, that's all."

Yeah, sure. Nothing rallied Sarah to Heath's side like her mother's disapproval. For one terrible moment five years ago, when she found out that Heath had lied to her about the problems with his book, Sarah thought about leaving him. She stayed because she loved him, but also because she *really* hated the thought of listening to her mother say *I told you so* for the rest of her life. Her parents never believed Heath was worthy of marrying into their exalted family. They were awful snobs—so awful that Sarah hated to think they could ever be right.

Lately, though, Heath's behavior was starting to worry her again. He was upstairs on crisis-management phone calls over the Stone family's lawsuit against the school. The crazy thing was, the Stones were only suing the school because of Heath. They were livid over the naked video, and the fact that Bel Enright had barely been punished for it. But that leniency was Heath's doing. The Disciplinary Committee let Bel off with counseling because Heath convinced them she was too drugged to think straight on the night of the attack. That wasn't necessarily a lie, but it wasn't an excuse, either. Judging from what Rose said about her sister, Bel was in league with the Moreland bad girls of her own free will. She'd probably taken the pills on purpose, too. Sarah would have told Heath that, if he would have listened. Instead, he shut her out of the process, and she only learned of the Committee's vote after it already happened. Heath apologized for not keeping her in the loop. The slipper attack had turned the school upside down, he said, and he'd needed to move fast to restore order. But the apology felt insincere. Heath had made up his mind to treat Bel leniently, and he didn't want Sarah interfering. That's why he didn't consult her.

So, why the special treatment for Bel Enright? It could be sympathy. Bel was an orphan, new to the school, an outsider, and Heath had been an outsider at Odell himself, back in the day. It could be that Bel took the pain meds because of an injury suffered on Heath's watch, and he was worried about blowback. But no matter the reason, Sarah didn't like it. She didn't like feeling that he was keeping things from her. It reminded her too much of old times. *Bad* times.

Sarah went upstairs to get Heath off the phone, pausing on the carpeted landing outside the guest room. The door was firmly shut, but she could hear his voice coming from inside. Something in the way he was speaking made her pause. She held her breath and stepped closer, listening with her ear to the door.

"Don't worry. It'll be different when you come back," Heath was saying.

There was something strangely intimate in his tone. Was that the headmaster on the phone?

"Because. With Darcy and Tessa gone, you can start fresh. You'll have me to guide you."

There was a pause, and then Heath laughed. He laughed often, but this particular laugh was one she hadn't heard from him in years—flirty, sexy, confidential. Like he was talking to a woman. A lover.

"Not that way, silly girl. You promised."

Silly girl. Girl.

Heath wasn't talking to Simon Barlow. Sarah turned the knob and flung open the door. Heath sat on the edge of the bed, a goofy smile on his face. He looked up, and for a split second, his eyes were like a startled animal, caught. Then his face changed, and he assumed an expression so bland and normal and innocent that Sarah thought she must be imagining things.

"I should be going," he said into the phone, holding up a finger toward Sarah. "Thanks for taking the time to give me your feedback. Appreciate it. Yep, talk Monday. Thanks, Simon."

Sarah's hands felt cold, and her mouth was dry. She stood there, paralyzed, waiting for some terrible truth to crash into her. But Heath just stood up, and thrust the phone into his pocket, smiling at Sarah so artlessly that she could almost believe she hadn't heard what she'd heard. *Silly girl*. And yet, if she'd heard right, her marriage—her whole life—was in trouble. She didn't want to believe her own ears.

"Dessert ready, babe? Sorry I've been holed up in here," he said.

"Who was that on the phone?" Sarah asked. It took effort to get the words out.

"Simon. We're talking about putting out a press release on Monday, announcing a new anti-bullying initiative. What do you think? Is that a good idea, or does it look defensive?"

Silly girl. The words had been perfectly audible. That wasn't Simon Barlow on the phone, which meant he'd just lied to her. If what she'd overheard had an innocent explanation, why would he lie about it?

"I don't believe you," she said.

"Really? I thought it was a pretty good idea. Decent, anyway."

Heath sounded jokily hurt, like this was just some work thing. Sarah searched his eyes, looking for the truth. Heath could be very convincing when he wanted to be. He'd lied to her before about a matter of great importance, and she'd believed him with all her heart. This time, she didn't. But was that wisdom, born of experience? Or paranoia?

"Sarah?" her mother called from downstairs. "Dessert is on the table. Please come down and collect your children."

Heath raised an eyebrow and smiled conspiratorially. "Your mother may be hard to stomach, but at least the pie will be good. Let's go," he said, calling on their old solidarity.

Sarah gave a sick smile in return. If she'd heard what she thought she'd heard, Heath was involved with another woman—no, not a woman, a *girl*. Bel Enright—it had to be. And yet, that wasn't possible. There had to be some other explanation because the Heath she knew wouldn't do that.

They went downstairs for dessert. Sarah couldn't eat any pie, but nobody noticed.

For the rest of the holiday weekend, Sarah went through the motions, playacting the happy wife, mother, daughter. She made pancakes for breakfast, and let Harper help, using the same colored mixing bowls Sarah had loved as a girl. Everybody went for a horse-and-buggy ride at the local orchard. They bundled under blankets and had hot chocolate and cider donuts afterward for treats. Sarah and her parents sat around reading the newspaper, while Heath went for a run, and the kids played on the floor nearby.

Soon it was time to pack up the car and say their good-byes. On the surface, everything looked serene and happy, but inside, Sarah was in tatters. If Heath was having an affair, her marriage and her family were a charade. And if it was with a young girl, a student— well, that was unthinkable. Not just unthinkable, *illegal*. She wanted to disbelieve her own ears because to do otherwise, she would have to accept that Heath could stoop that low. And she didn't accept that. True, he'd lied before, but in an instance of poor judgment by someone with an inordinate need to prove himself.

He'd always been faithful. And he'd never shown signs of being a creep or a pedophile. Maybe she'd heard the words right, but they meant something else, something other than an affair. She had to find out.

Heath kept his phone close by him all weekend. Was that normal? She couldn't remember. She'd never paid attention to that before, since she'd never had cause to distrust her husband. Well, occasionally she questioned his judgment, but she'd never felt the need to snoop on him, until now.

The only time Heath left his phone unattended was when they stopped for gas on the way back to Odell. It was late, and the temperature had plummeted. He opened the car door, letting in a blast of cold air, tinged with the sharp smell of gasoline. Sarah watched him through the window as he pumped the gas, stamping his feet against the night air, his breath coming out in clouds. The kids were asleep in their car seats. Max was asleep in his kennel in the far back. Heath paid for the gas with a credit card, then walked off toward the mini-mart. Was he going to buy a coffee? Use the restroom? How much time did she have to search his phone? She couldn't afford to hesitate. As soon as the glass door swung shut behind him, she grabbed the phone off the console, and typed in his passcode—their Odell graduation year.

It didn't work. She stared at it. Tried again, and again. It warned her that it might shut down if she kept entering the wrong passcode.

He'd changed his passcode. Heath had had that same passcode as long as she could remember, and now, suddenly, he'd changed it? Did that mean her worst fears were true? She saw him heading back, carrying a coffee and a bag of chips, and dropped the phone back onto the console like it was fire.

"Want some, babe?" he asked, holding the bag out to her, as he slid into the driver's seat.

"No, thanks."

They drove off into the cold night just as it began to snow. Sarah stared out the window, sneaking glances at Heath when he wasn't looking. His face in the light from oncoming cars was more familiar to her than her own. She'd always been in awe of its physical perfection, while taking pride in seeing the vulnerability underneath. Nobody else saw that. Other people thought Heath was a rising star, charming, a natural leader. Only Sarah knew the needy guy beneath the perfect exterior, who was plagued with self-doubt. She'd thought so, anyway. Heath had slept beside her every night for more than a decade. Was it possible she didn't know him as well as she thought?

24

As the bus rolled back onto campus Sunday evening, Rose looked out and saw rows of television vans parked just outside the school gates. Odell Security cars were lined up facing them, blocking the entrance to campus, like a standoff. The security cars pulled aside to let the bus pass, then moved back into position. Before Skyler's lawsuit, nobody outside the school knew about the slipper attack. Then Skyler's lawyers held a press conference to announce they were suing the most famous boarding school in the country. The tale of rich girls gone wild was now a tabloid and Internet sensation, to the point that the school had to hire extra security to keep the press from storming the campus.

Rose had sat with Emma Kim on the bus, and now she stuck close by her as they walked back to Moreland Hall through the lightly falling snow. The memory of Brandon Flynn tripping her as she walked down the aisle was still fresh in Rose's mind. But things were different since news of the lawsuit hit, and it turned out she needn't have worried. Kids shot her curious looks, but they kept their distance all right—to the point that nobody would speak to her.

"What am I, radioactive?" Rose asked Emma, after a group of sophomore girls they knew said a perfunctory hello and scurried past.

"People think you're part of the lawsuit, so they don't want to associate with you," Emma said.

They were pulling their suitcases down the icy, brick path toward the Quad. The sky was a vivid violet-blue, the lightly falling snow visible in the glow from the lanterns along the path. The beauty of the scene made Rose's eyes sting. Her love for Odell burned all the brighter now that the school community seemed to have closed ranks against her.

"Why would I be part of the lawsuit, when it's *my* grandmother being sued?" Rose lamented.

"Your grandma's getting sued because of what Bel did, which came to light because you and Skyler complained. You're seen as aligned with Skyler. Not by *me*. I totally get why you talked. It's a code-of-conduct violation not to be truthful with the Disciplinary Committee, and you have to look out for yourself first. But other kids aren't as understanding as I am."

"I had nothing to do with her stupid lawsuit. I'm sorry I ever backed up her story. Everyone blames me, even my own grandmother. She says I'm taking sides against the family."

"Gosh, that's awful. And now the threats, too."

"Threats? You mean, kids calling me a rat?"

"No, I'm talking about what Darcy posted on Facebook. What an ass."

"Darcy posted something about me?" Rose asked, a shiver going through her. This was getting worse and worse.

"You didn't see it?"

"I'm not Facebook friends with her."

"Let's check in, then I'll show you."

They'd reached Moreland. They reported to the common room to sign the check-in sheet, then trudged up the stairs with their suitcases. At the second-floor landing, where they normally parted ways, Emma stopped, and took out her phone.

"Hold on, I have to find Darcy's post," she said, scrolling. "Hmm, that's weird."

"What?"

"It was there this morning. She must've deleted it."

"Deleted *what*? Emma, tell me what she said."

"It wasn't words. It was a picture. She took your head shots from the student directory—yours and Skyler's—and photoshopped them onto a picture of dead bodies, like from a war or something."

Rose grabbed the banister. "Oh, my God. That's a threat on my life. I can't breathe."

"Don't be so dramatic," Emma said. "You're panicking for no reason. Darcy's in Connecticut. Expelled students aren't allowed on campus. She can't hurt you."

"Who would stop her from coming here and trying?"

"Did you see all those security cars at the gate?"

"They won't do anything!"

Emma grabbed her by the shoulders. "Rose, chill. You're getting hysterical. People will see you act this way and think you're guilty."

"'Guilty'? Of what?"

Just then, a junior named Becca, who lived down the hall from Rose, burst through the swinging door onto the landing. Rose and Emma stepped apart.

"Oh, hey, guys," Becca said, looking at them curiously as she headed down the stairs.

"Hey," Emma said.

"See?" Emma said to Rose, once Becca was out of earshot. "Now she's going to tell people you're acting sketchy."

"I'm not acting sketchy. I'm an innocent bystander, whose life just got threatened. I need to report it."

"Why report the post? Darcy already took it down. She's a bitch, but if you complain about a deleted post, you look like the crazy one. Don't make things worse than they already are. You need to behave like everything is normal. Ignore the assholes, keep your head down, do your schoolwork and this will blow over. I promise. Now, go unpack, and let's meet up in the common room later. I bet there'll be cookies. Are you with me?"

"All right."

"Good. Remember, the best revenge is straight A's and a cute outfit."

Emma gave Rose a quick half-hug and headed up to the third floor. Rose stood looking after her, feeling shaky and slightly ill. But then she heard girls coming up the stairs behind her, and hurried to her room.

Emma was right. She shouldn't be seen acting scared. If nothing else, she had her pride.

Inside, the room was dark, and Rose's heart sank. Skyler was supposed to be back from Florida by now. Her flight must've been delayed. Drat, Rose really didn't want to be alone. In the dim glow from the window, the sense that something was different filtered into Rose's consciousness. She reached out and flicked the light switch on, and it hit her like a punch in the stomach. Half of the room was bare. Skyler's bed was stripped. Her bulletin board and posters were gone. Her desktop and dresser top were swept clean. Rose ran to Skyler's wardrobe and flung the door open. Skyler's clothes were gone. This wasn't light packing for vacation. *Skyler* was gone. She'd taken all her things and left the school, without saying good-bye.

25

On Monday, Rose went down the food line in the New, heaping her plate high. Maybe a double portion of mac and cheese and a big piece of chocolate cake would quell the nervous flutter in her stomach. News of Skyler withdrawing from Odell Academy had been circulating since last night. Kids were looking at Rose funny today, keeping their distance, like she had a contagious disease. She lingered after French class to wait for Emma because she dreaded walking to lunch alone. But Emma blew her off with the excuse of violin practice. In the middle of the day? Come on. Emma obviously didn't want to be seen with Rose, at the moment when Rose most needed a friend. Rose was actually afraid to be alone, that's how much she worried that Darcy Madden would show up and make good on her threat.

"Enright? Have you become undead, or are you just ignoring me?" said a voice from behind her.

Rose turned to see Zach Cuddy in all his glory—bright blue eyes behind nerdy glasses, lanky frame, oddly formal manner. Normally, Zach speaking to her would give her a rush, but today she was so distracted by her problems that Zach barely registered.

"I just said your name, like, three times," he said.

"Oh, sorry. I didn't hear you."

They reached the end of the food line, and stepped over to beverages. Rose filled her glass with chocolate milk from the dispenser. Zach got an ice water. He had a salad and some lentil soup, which made her ashamed of the enormous pile of carbs on her plate.

"Are you sitting with anyone?" Zach asked.

"You mean, for lunch?"

"What else would I mean?"

She'd been wanting to have lunch with Zach Cuddy, like, forever. Yet, she found it odd that he would suddenly be interested in having lunch with her on the very day that other kids decided to treat her like a pariah.

"Are you asking to sit with me? I usually sit at the Moreland sophomore table," Rose said. "But—"

But, I might not be welcome there today, she thought, *and, I've been dreaming of sitting with you my entire Odell career, so yeah.*

"If you don't want to sit there, I'll sit with you somewhere else," Rose said.

"I need to talk to you about something in particular," Zach said.

"About bio?"

"No. It's rather sensitive, actually, so we can't discuss it here. How about if we eat separately, then meet outside, in say, fifteen minutes? We'll find somewhere to talk privately."

That didn't sound like a lunch date. It sounded ominous. On the bus, going home for Thanksgiving break, Zach stood up for her against Brandon Flynn, at some cost to himself. Brandon had actually threatened Zach as a result. But it also seemed likely that Zach had shared the Snapchat of the slipper attack. Was he now in trouble over that? Did he blame Rose? Did he think she was a rat? Maybe she shouldn't go somewhere alone with him. On the other hand, she'd had a crush on him since September, and here he was asking to spend time together, privately. If she said no, she'd always wonder.

"All right," Rose said.

They nodded, and went their separate ways to eat. Fifteen minutes later, still with no idea why Zach had sought her out, she met him on the plaza in front of the dining hall. They walked to Benchley Hall, because Zach had a key to the lit mag office on the top floor.

The old building was largely deserted at lunch hour. As they climbed the stairs, Rose was perspiring. She both liked Zach *and* felt anxious to be alone with him in a deserted building. The office was at the back of the fourth floor. It felt attic-like, high up, with grimy dormered windows that looked across to the library. A light snow had started to fall in the minutes since they'd come inside. Zach closed the heavy wooden door behind them. He moved a pile of papers off the sofa to make space for her to sit down, then perched on the nearby desk, facing her. She looked up into his eyes.

He really was handsome.

"This is about your sister," Zach said.

Rose's hopes, which had been tearing along at a frantic pace, crashed. Why did everything have to be about Bel?

"I wish you told me that before," she said, getting to her feet. "I wouldn't've come."

"Please, sit down. Let me just explain my predicament, okay? I'm throwing myself on your mercy here."

"All right." She sat.

"To begin at the beginning, Bel and I hooked up back in September, and we used to Snapchat. She'd send me pics. Nothing too porny, just fish lips and bra shots, you know?"

"*Ugh,*" Rose said.

"You didn't know?" Zach asked.

"Whatever. It's just gross."

"Well, to be honest, I'm exaggerating. Slightly. She sent me one Snapchat, once. But the point is, Bel was in my phone, and there was a history of her Snapchatting me. So, on the night of the slipper attack, when a Snapchat came in from Bel, I recognized it and opened it, expecting to find a picture of her, like the fool I am. Instead, I saw Skyler getting spanked. Bel's message said to forward it, so I forwarded it to some other guys. Stupid, I know. I let myself get used, in this twisted game she was playing. And now I'm in deep shit."

"You're in trouble for the Snapchat."

"Yes. A lot of trouble. The Disciplinary Committee is meeting about it right before Christmas break, which means I could get a very unpleasant Christmas gift.

You have no idea what it would do to my family for me to get expelled from Odell. I'm not a fifth-generation rich kid like you. My dad owns an auto-repair shop. My family sacrificed so much to send me here. They'd be crushed. Not to mention that I'm a total misfit at home. Odell is the only place I fit. I just *can't* get expelled."

Zach's speech made Rose like him more. She wished her life at Odell could be normal for once. That there was no slipper attack, no threat of retaliation against her for ratting, that Zach Cuddy liked her, instead of Bel. Was that so much to ask? Rose's problems were really Bel's fault, when you thought about it. Her life would be much better if Bel just wasn't around.

"Just so you know, I'm no fifth-generation rich kid, either," Rose said. "I'm a poor relation, here on my grandmother's charity. And now Grandma's furious with me over Skyler's lawsuit, which, when you think about it, is Bel's fault. So, I hate Bel, too."

"Good. We can agree that Bel is responsible for our problems—*both* of our problems. Now, have you ever wondered why Bel got off with just counseling, yet Darcy and Tessa got expelled?"

"They decided it that way because Bel was high on pain meds during the attack."

"I heard that, too. But does it make any sense? Since when does abusing drugs before you haze someone get you a more lenient sentence?"

"What's your point, Zach?"

"The point is, *Donovan* is protecting her. I know that

for a fact because one of the student reps on the Disciplinary Committee is a friend. He knows I'm in jeopardy, so he's keeping me apprised."

"What do you mean, he's protecting her?" Rose asked.

"From what my friend says, Donovan spoon-fed a bullshit drug-reaction story to the Committee. He manipulated the outcome to favor Bel. Now, why would he do that? There has to be a reason. Something's going on there, don't you think? Some special relationship?"

Rose remembered the moment when she confronted her sister outside the disciplinary hearing, and then Donovan came out to get Bel. Had there been a flash of something between them then? She'd been hearing the gossip for weeks now, about Bel and Mr. Donovan making eyes at each other in English class. Back when she was trying to be friends with her sister, she'd made a conscious decision not to ask her about that. It was too over-the-top, too embarrassing. And besides, Rose hadn't really believed it.

"You must be basing that on the gossip about them staring at each other in class," Rose said. "I heard that, too. But even if it's true, it hardly means they're having an affair. I don't believe that."

"Why not? *I* do."

"Zach, I basically hate my sister's guts right now. You could probably convince me she'd do something as depraved as sleep with a teacher. But *he* wouldn't do it. He has too much to lose. Mrs. Donovan is my advisor. I go to their apartment for tea. I've seen them together. I've seen him with his kids. He's a family man."

"You don't understand men, then. Plenty of loving husbands have a sidepiece. And your sister is very pretty."

"This conversation is starting to creep me out," Rose said. She was about to get up again, but Zach waved her down.

"I have proof," he said.

"What proof?"

"I saw him kiss her. When she was in the infirmary, the day after the slipper attack."

Rose's jaw dropped. "Kiss her, like, how?"

"He sat on her bed. It was a romantic kiss."

"You were in the room?"

"No. I was—outside."

"Were you spying?"

Zach blushed. "I wanted to visit Bel, but they said no visitors. So, I went around the back. I was going to knock on the window and say hi. Instead, I saw that."

"You saw Mr. Donovan kiss Bel, in a romantic way?"

"Yes."

"Wait a minute, I'm not buying this. Why would you even visit her?"

"What do you mean?"

"You say Bel sent you that Snapchat the night before. You already knew she did something that could get you into trouble. So why visit her?"

He blushed deeper. "I guess, well, honestly—I don't know. I'm a sap?"

"This sounds fishy. And I *still* don't get what it has to do with me."

"Rose, whatever's going on between Bel and Donovan is happening inside Moreland Hall, at night."

"Wow, you've really thought about this."

"Yes, and you should, too. It's not good for her. You could find out what's really going on."

"You want me to spy on my sister."

"I'm asking you to help me figure out what the truth is. If Donovan's sleeping with a student, a vulnerable young girl, he should be made to stop, don't you agree? And if I had real evidence, like a picture or something, I could—" He stopped.

"You could what?"

"I could get Donovan to back off me."

"To back off *you*?"

"Yes. Otherwise, he's going to expel me."

"You want me to spy on my sister, get a photo of her having—ugh, *sex*—with a teacher. And not just any teacher. The dean of students, the head of my dorm. Then you want me to give you the photo, so you can blackmail him into not punishing you for sharing a nude video of my roommate, that made her leave school."

"When you put it that way, it sounds bad, but—"

"Yeah, no. I'm leaving."

Rose stood up.

"I'm a nice person, really," Zach said, walking backward in front of her as Rose headed for the door. "I hope you'll think about it. We could talk more. Get to know each other. I'd like for us to be friends. Rose, please? We have a lot in common. I could message, or FaceTime you. We could grab coffee."

She laughed bleakly as she stepped around him into the hallway. The boy she'd been crushing on all year finally wants to call her, and it's about *this*? What the hell, maybe she should let him. Her life was out of control already. She might as well get something out of it.

"Go ahead," Rose said. "It's a free country."

26

December

It was only because Bel received a card in the mail from Grandma with a check for a hundred dollars inside that she remembered it was her birthday. She was turning sweet sixteen. But she didn't feel much like celebrating, and even if she had, there was nobody to celebrate with.

It was the middle of finals week, cold and snowy out, and people were busy. They bustled by without saying hello. After Darcy left school, the seniors had let Bel know she wasn't welcome at their table in the dining hall. When that first happened, she kicked around the New in search of another home, randomly sitting with kids from her classes or from cross-country. Everybody seemed to look askance at her, and who could blame them, given her sketchy reputation. Finally, Bel gave up, and passed her mealtimes alone in the Quiet Nook, an alcove in the Commons where you could go to read or study while you ate. It was a gloomy spot

where geeks and psychos lurked, but nobody bothered her there. Bel ate her birthday dinner in the Quiet
Nook, with her geometry textbook open in front of her
for company, silent and alone.

When she'd finished and was walking through the
New to take her tray to the conveyor belt, Bel spied
Rose at one of the sophomore tables, sitting between
Emma Kim and Zach Cuddy. Since when were Rose
and Zach friends? There was a cupcake in front of
Rose with a lit candle stuck in it. Bel watched her sister blow out the candle, smiling as Emma clapped and
Zach rubbed her back. An electric-green bolt of jealousy shot through her. By rights, they ought to be Bel's
friends, not Rose's. Yet, she had to admit, it was her
own fault they weren't. She'd squandered them. She'd
made big mistakes, and her life at Odell was off the
rails. But since she couldn't see a way to salvage it,
why not double down?

Bel hadn't seen Heath alone since he'd visited her
in the infirmary on that dreamlike afternoon, nearly a
month ago now. She'd given up cross-country because
of her knee injury, which meant giving up her solo runs
with him. And since becoming dean of students, Heath
had been too busy to find time for an advisor meeting.
They'd exchanged cell numbers, and Heath had called
her, unexpectedly, over Thanksgiving break. That had
been wonderful, until he started talking funny, and she
realized he'd been caught in the act. He hung up abruptly,
and when she got back from break, he told her they
needed to stay away from each other because people

were starting to talk. She tried to be understanding, but it was hard. When she called him now, his phone went straight to voicemail. If she asked to meet with him alone, he made an excuse to avoid her. She thought nonstop about the time he kissed her, to the point that the memory had become faded from overuse. It was her birthday and the only thing she wanted was for Heath to kiss her again. To make that happen, she'd have to take matters into her own hands.

Bel knew where he usually sat to eat dinner—in the area they called the faculty corner, with his family. She scraped her plate, and dumped it on the conveyor belt. Then she fluffed her hair, squared her shoulders and marched over there to find him.

She put her hand on his shoulder, and he turned. From the corner of her eye, she caught the shocked look on his wife's face. But Bel was entitled; this was her advisor, and she needed advice.

"Mr. Donovan?"

"Bel. Hello. What can I do for you?" he asked, alarm in his eyes.

"I have an important question about the final paper. Can I talk to you for a minute?"

"Certainly."

"Alone?"

"Oh. All right. Excuse me, I'll be right back," he said to the table, which was full of faculty and their children.

He followed her toward the vestibule where the coat-racks were. Heads turned as they walked through the dining hall together. Bel knew they were the subject of gossip. She liked that; Heath probably didn't. Too bad, he shouldn't have encouraged her, then.

They stopped between the coatracks. Hidden from view by puffer jackets and parkas, she turned to him.

"What is it? Is everything all right?" he asked, frowning.

"Today's my birthday."

"Happy birthday. You really can't come up to me like that. It'll make people wonder."

"I wanted to see you. You never take my calls."

"Bel," he said, shaking his head.

"When can I see you?" she pleaded.

A kid getting his jacket looked at them with frank curiosity.

"I can't do this here," he said.

"Then tell me when and where to meet you, and I'll go away now."

"Tonight. Meet me in the laundry room in the basement of Moreland. Two a.m. That's late enough that the dorm will be asleep."

She nodded, and he turned and walked away.

Bel found her coat amidst the others on the rack. She shrugged it on and stepped out into the frosty night air, feeling like she was floating. *Two a.m. Two a.m. I'm meeting Heath at two a.m.*

A strange feeling made her turn and look back over her shoulder at the dining hall. Through the plate-glass window, she saw Zach Cuddy standing in the vestibule where she and Heath had stood a moment before. He was staring after her, and a chill ran down the back of her neck. But she was being silly. With the glare of bright light on the inside of the window, Zach probably couldn't even see her. He was staring at his own reflection, that was all. Bel put Zach out of her mind, and headed to the library, where she would do her best to concentrate on studying for finals, not because she cared about her grades, but because she needed to pass the slow, endless hours until her meeting with Heath.

Bel slipped silently out of her room just before two, making sure not to wake Emma. Outside the windows on the landings, snow fell steadily. Inside, all was quiet, except for the creaks and sighs of the old building. She used the flashlight on her phone to find her way down the stairs to the Moreland basement. The laundry room was creepy—pitch-dark and smelling of mold and dust—and her flashlight threw crazy shadows up on the walls. Bel had never been down here before, since Grandma paid for a laundry service. She sent her clothes out each week and got them back, pressed, folded and dry-cleaned, hanging on racks in the common room along with those of the other rich girls. Thankfully. Given the creepy state of the laundry room, she would hate spending time down here just to get laundry done. But a secret tryst was another matter. For that, this place was perfect.

She heard Heath's footsteps before she saw him. He walked into the laundry room and flipped on the light. He was wearing faded jeans, and a gray T-shirt that clung to his shoulders and chest. His hair was mussed, like he'd just come from his bed—which, presumably, he had. She'd never seen him dressed so casually, and he looked gorgeous.

"You're standing here in the dark?" he said.

"I thought that's what I'm supposed to do. Aren't we having a secret rendezvous?"

"Is that what this is?" he said, walking up to her.

She was trying to sound jokey, but he seemed almost angry. Her heart started pounding so hard that the front of her camisole twitched.

"I was hoping," she said. "It is my birthday."

"How old are you?" he asked.

"Sixteen."

"Well. That *is* the age of consent in this state," he said.

"Are you all right? You seem—"

"What?"

"Mad at me."

"Do you know what you're doing to me? Ever since I got caught talking to you on the phone, I've been afraid of what might happen. I tried to put you out of my mind. I can't. Then you come up to me in the dining hall tonight, so brazen. God, that was crazy, Bel. You can't do that."

He took her by the waist and pushed her backward till she banged up against a counter that was used for folding clothes. He grabbed her and lifted her up onto it.

"What are you doing?" she said, her voice shaking.

"You asked to be alone with me. Isn't this what you want? It's what I want."

He put his hands in her hair and yanked her head back, and started kissing her neck roughly, until she moaned. It hurt, but it also felt good. Just like that afternoon in the infirmary, she was in a dream state. This couldn't be happening. She didn't know what she'd expected, but not that he'd actually have sex with her. How could he? He was her teacher. But when he pressed against her, he was hard.

"If you want me to stop, tell me now," he said.

His voice was harsh, like it belonged to a different person. She *did* want him to stop, or at least slow down. But if she said that, he might leave, and she didn't want that, either. Before she could decide what to say, his hands were on her breasts. He kneaded them roughly through her Henley, as his mouth closed on hers, and his tongue pushed in. She couldn't speak, couldn't breathe. His hands moved to her hips now, and he tugged her leggings down, her panties coming along with them. She'd hooked up with boys before—on the beach back home, with Zach in the woods after that dance. But hooking up in Bel's parlance just meant making out, or heavy petting. Bel was still a virgin, and this didn't feel right. But it was happening. She heard rather than saw him unzip his jeans. There was a snapping sound as he pulled on a condom—he'd *planned* for this. Before she could protest, he grabbed her bare legs and pulled her toward him, then plunged inside her. She cried out, and he slapped a hand over her mouth. A movement in her peripheral vision caught her attention. She turned to look, and could've sworn she saw somebody duck out of the room. Heath hadn't noticed. His eyes were closed, and he had a look of rapture on his face as he moved against her. Then he groaned, and it was over.

"You okay?" he whispered, standing up straight.

She nodded, but there were tears in her eyes. He stepped back and looked at her appraisingly.

"Was that your first time?" he asked.

You'd think he would've asked her that before. She nodded again. He turned away and rearranged his clothing.

"I'm sorry if I was rough," he said, turning back to her. "You're so beautiful, I got carried away. Next time will be better. I'll take you somewhere that we can be alone, properly. Where we can talk. Somewhere with a bed. I'll show you things, make sure it's good for you, too, okay? C'mere."

He took her in his arms and kissed her softly, first on the forehead, and then the lips.

"I'm crazy about you," he said.

She sighed and leaned against him as he stroked her hair. Bel realized that this was really what she'd wanted. To be held and caressed and kissed by him. To be petted and cared for, and *seen*. She'd wanted that, not the roughness, not the sex, not this man she didn't know, so different from the one she'd been fantasizing about.

"Now, go back to your room," he said. "And don't tell anybody."

He left. Bel stayed in the laundry room alone for a while—how long, she couldn't've said. Maybe five minutes, maybe ten. She was trying to wrap her head around what had just happened, and how she would go on from there. Finally, she dragged herself back up to the third floor, where she went into the bathroom, took a long, hot shower and cried. Maybe none of that actually happened, she thought to herself. But the ache in her body told her it was real.

27

Sarah was happy at the moment the girl walked up to Heath in the dining hall. She would remember that later.

The Donovan family was having dinner in the faculty corner with the Mendezes—Eduardo, who taught social studies, his wife, Mercedes, who worked in admissions, and their four-year-old son, Diego, who went to the on-campus day care with Harper and Scottie. The Mendezes were fun, young, witty, stylish. Having dinner with them was one of the best things about moving on campus. The faculty corner looked out through big windows over the lawn behind the New. Outside, the snow was falling, and it got them talking of sledding and skiing. Harper and Diego were making a snowman from mashed potatoes, with peas for the buttons and eyes. The grown-ups were having a good laugh over the time Heath tried to teach Eduardo (who hailed from Miami) to ski. Then Sarah turned around, and Bel

Enright was standing there with her hand on Heath's shoulder, looking into his eyes, asking to talk to him alone. The way he looked back at her—Sarah's heart stopped. The whole world stopped. She watched them walk from the dining hall together, saw heads turn to follow them. Caught the alarmed glance that Eduardo and Mercedes exchanged.

Was something really going on, then? Did everyone in the school know about it but her? She couldn't really claim not to know, not after overhearing that phone call Thanksgiving weekend. When she asked who was on the phone, Heath lied to her. If that wasn't a sign, what was?

But. He'd been so devoted since then that she had put it out of her mind. He'd been loving toward Sarah. Adorable with the kids—getting their breakfast every morning, pulling them to day care on the sled, with the dog cavorting along behind. He made a fire in the fireplace every night after the kids went to bed, and they'd sit and watch it crackle while they graded papers, or ordered Christmas presents online. Their life together felt real, normal, good. Now, this. She didn't want to believe it. She didn't *have* to believe it. A student seeks you out at dinner to ask a simple question. That could happen. It didn't need to mean anything drastic. And the phone call over Thanksgiving—it was probably nothing. She could have misheard. At most, maybe there was a silly little flirtation. Nothing that needed to shake her world.

"Diego's tired," Eduardo said to Mercedes, although there was no evidence of this in the boy's behavior. "We should go."

The Mendezes got up and collected their trays.

Mercedes stopped at Sarah's chair and gave her a concerned look. "If you need anything, you know you can call me, right?"

"Oh, sure. Likewise! You can always call me, too," Sarah said, with forced heartiness. Mercedes nodded, puzzlement in her eyes, and turned away.

Sarah hated to be pitied, especially over something that wasn't proven. It might not actually be true. Her life might not be over; her marriage might not be a charade. Sarah instinctively felt the need to defend Heath to their friends. Innocent until proven guilty. Besides, if there was truly something wrong, somebody would have said something by now. Right? But Sarah was quiet and introverted, raised in a proper Yankee household. She didn't discuss private matters with anyone, so nobody felt comfortable approaching her. Heath was the only person she really talked to. If she couldn't trust *him*, then she was alone.

Heath came back, carrying a plate of brownies for the kids. Normally, Sarah would protest that it was too late in the day for sugar. But she was too numb with panic to care about the routine. Heath passed out the brownies and sat down. As he joked around with the kids, his manner was off, his voice full of false cheer. They were alone at the table. Sarah glanced around, pitching her voice low so nobody would overhear.

"What was that about?" she asked.

"What was what?"

"Bel Enright. Why couldn't she just talk to you here?"

"Oh. She's freaking out about her term paper," he

said casually, taking a bite of a brownie. "You know how it is—finals week. She asked for an extension till after break."

His voice sounded natural, but he wouldn't meet her eyes.

"Did you give it to her?" Sarah asked.

"Huh?"

"The extension. Did you give her the extension?"

"Oh. No. Then I'd have to do it for everyone, right?"

She had the definite feeling that he was lying. But there was nothing more she could do or say to be sure, at least not here and now in the dining hall. The kids finished their brownies, and they went home.

At seven-thirty, the doorbell rang. It was Rose Enright, showing up for an extra-help session that Sarah had completely forgotten about. Heath volunteered to give the kids their bath so Sarah could tutor Rose in the kitchen.

"Sorry, I don't have tea or cookies," Sarah said to Rose, as they sat down at the kitchen table. "I have to confess, I forgot about our appointment."

"That's okay," Rose said, though Sarah could tell she was disappointed. "I know how busy you are. Thanks for meeting with me."

"The good news is, judging by your problem sets, you're in terrific shape for the final," Sarah said.

"I hope so. I don't always feel that way."

Rose opened her textbook. Sarah could hear the water running and the kids giggling in the hall bathroom.

Heath said something to them that elicited a squeal, but his voice was muffled, and Sarah couldn't make out the words. It tore at her heart to listen to him, in there with the kids, like everything was normal.

Rose asked a question about square roots of negative numbers, but Sarah had a hard time focusing, and gave the wrong answer, which fortunately, Rose caught.

"You seem distracted," Rose said. "How are you? Is everything okay?"

Dear, sweet Rose, worrying about Sarah, when it ought to be the other way around. She couldn't let her personal problems get in the way of doing her duty toward this girl.

"No, how are *you*?" Sarah said. "I'm sorry I haven't checked in on you recently. Things have been crazy since the slipper thing, but that's no excuse. I apologize. This must've been harder on you than anyone—witnessing the attack, losing your roommate."

"Yeah, it has been rough. Not just the attack. The lawsuit, too. My grandmother's getting sued because of what Bel did, and she's mad at me for telling on Bel to the Disciplinary Committee."

"I don't get it. Bel's actions caused the problem. Once she did what she did, you had no choice but to tell the truth about it. Or else, *you* could get expelled."

"Yeah, tell that to my grandma."

"Do you want me to? I could talk to her, and explain what the handbook says."

"Honestly, it wouldn't accomplish anything. Grandma's on Bel's side. I'm used to it. My mom really favored Bel. She makes herself seem helpless, then they help her. Like with the slipper thing. Grandma believes Bel had a bad reaction to the pain medication, so nothing is Bel's fault."

"Do you believe that, Rose?"

"Not really. Do *you*?"

"I wasn't there. But you've always said Bel has poor judgment. It's possible she went along willingly, and the drugs were an excuse, after the fact."

"That's what I think. So, why did the Committee go easy on her? She's my sister, I know I'm supposed to take her side. But Bel does what Bel wants, and she gets away with it. No matter who gets hurt."

Rose gave Sarah a searching look when she said that. Did she know something about Heath and Bel, about their relationship? The subtext was there in the air between them, but it would be an enormous risk to bring it into the open. Sarah couldn't ask a student about a possible affair between her husband and another student without violating all sorts of boundaries. Yet, if her worst fears were true, Heath was committing a much greater abuse than Sarah would be simply by asking Rose a difficult question.

"Is Bel doing anything else that might . . . cause hurt?" Sarah asked. "To herself, to someone else? Is someone hurting *her*?"

Rose looked down at her hands and blushed.

"You can tell me," Sarah said. "No matter what it is. I'll figure out what to do."

There was a long pause. The water had stopped running in the hall bath, and the kitchen was dead quiet as Rose visibly struggled with what to say. If Heath was listening, he would be able to hear their conversation. Just then, Harper came running into the kitchen, stark naked, dripping wet, followed by Max, barking like crazy. Heath was a step behind, carrying Scottie wrapped up in a towel.

"Get back here, you little demon," Heath said, chasing Harper around the table as she squealed with laughter.

Taking in the family scene, Rose got to her feet abruptly, a pained look on her face.

"I should go," she said. "I came at a bad time."

"No, stay, it's fine," Sarah said.

"Really, I should go study. Thanks for the help, Mrs. Donovan," Rose said, and ran out the door.

Sarah awoke in darkness, sensing she was alone. She rolled over, and patted the empty space on Heath's side of the bed. The red numbers on the clock read two-thirty. *Do you know where your husband is tonight?*

She stuck her feet in her slippers and tiptoed into the hallway, worried about waking the dog, who'd bark and wake the kids. But Max was already up. He loped toward her, nails clicking on the hardwood floors, and thrust his wet nose into her hand.

"Hi, buddy. Where's Daddy?" she whispered, petting him.

There were no lights on anywhere in the apartment. She checked the bathroom and the kitchen anyway, praying Heath was here somewhere, sitting in the dark. But he wasn't. She went to the front hall and flipped on the light. His parka was hanging on the hook near the front door, and his Sorels were in the shoe tray. Wherever he'd gone, he hadn't left the dorm, not in this weather, with no coat and no boots. He was still in the building. Heath—the love of her life, the father of her children—roaming around a girls' dormitory in the middle of the night. Why would he do that?

"Lie down," she said to Max, pointing at the dog bed next to the shoe tray.

The dog obeyed, whimpering as he turned around and settled in. Sarah felt the same way.

She turned off the light and went to sit on the edge of her bed. Should she go looking for him? That would require leaving the kids alone, but presumably only for ten or fifteen minutes, until she found Heath. But found him where? Doing what? The thing she feared—ugh, did she want to know the truth? Years ago, when Heath could have had any girl, he chose Sarah. She'd always felt loved by him. She'd never known him to pursue another woman. Woman? *Girl*. But how could that be? He just wouldn't do that, and if he would, then nothing was how it appeared. She couldn't imagine her life if Heath was involved with Bel Enright. The world would make no sense.

Maybe she was wrong. Maybe he heard a noise, and went to check on it.

She heard his key in the lock, dove under the covers and pretended to be asleep. He went into the bathroom first. She heard the water running. A few minutes later, he came to bed. He smelled of soap. She had to ask where he'd been. This wasn't just any night. It was the night Bel Enright had come up to Heath to ask to speak to him alone. It was the night that everyone in the dining hall turned to watch them walk out together, as if there was already suspicion surrounding those two. If Sarah didn't ask, this would eat at her.

She rolled over and looked at him, but it was too dark to see his face well. Otherwise, she might have been able to look in his eyes and know.

"Hey," she said, in a false-hoarse voice, to make it sound as if she'd just woken up. "Where were you?"

"Just now? In the bathroom," he said.

That was true, and yet it wasn't. The cleverness of the answer worried her.

"No, before. I woke up, and you were gone. You weren't in the apartment."

He paused. She could almost hear him thinking, there in the dark.

"I heard a noise, and went to check it out," he said. "But it was nothing. Go to sleep, hon."

Heath rolled over. Within minutes, his breathing became even, and he was deep in sleep. But Sarah lay awake for a long time, knowing she was being lied to, wondering what she could possibly do about it. She hated herself for feeling paralyzed. But she was starting to hate Heath—and Bel, too—more, for making her feel like that.

28

After their strange conversation in the lit mag office, Zach Cuddy didn't simply message Rose. He started to hang out with her, regularly. This thrilled Rose to no end, since she'd been crushing on Zach all year. He'd wait for her after bio class, and walk with her wherever she was going. They'd study together in the library, or grab coffee at the Arts Café. He even held doors open for her when they walked. People began to assume they were dating. Rose wished that were true. Zach was one of the top students in their grade, good-looking and charming. The girls in Moreland were obsessed with guys on the football and hockey teams, but Rose thought those boys were Neanderthals. Give her a man like Zach Cuddy—refined and gentlemanly, and not too macho to scribble lines of poetry or draw cartoons in the margins of his notebook.

Zach's attentions had the added benefit of improving Rose's social standing. Before Zach, she felt like an outcast because of the blowback from the slipper attack. But when she started hanging out with a cute guy, all of a sudden, girls who'd been cool toward her warmed up noticeably. Having a boyfriend was a status thing, apparently. Of course, Zach wasn't her boyfriend. He only wanted to be friends. But she didn't tell people that.

On the Monday night of finals week, Rose and Emma were in the Moreland common room studying French, when Rose's phone buzzed with a text.

"It's Zach," she said. "He wants me to meet him in the library. I should probably go. The bio exam is before the French exam, so it takes priority."

Emma raised an eyebrow. "I think what you mean is, Zach Cuddy takes priority over boring old me."

Rose laughed.

"Word to the wise. Be careful," Emma said.

"We're not doing *that*, not yet."

"I didn't mean sex. I meant, you know, watch out."

"Watch out for what?"

"Well . . . Doesn't it seem . . . *odd* . . . how Zach is so into you, all of a sudden?"

It took a second for Emma's meaning to sink in.

"You don't think he actually likes me, do you?" Rose said with an accusing tone.

"I didn't say that. But Zach can be a smooth operator, more than you'd expect. Don't forget, he hooked up with your sister."

"What's that supposed to mean? Like, I'm sloppy seconds or something. Or, no, wait a minute. You think he's still into her. That he's using me to get to her."

"I don't know that for sure. I *do* know he followed Bel around obsessively after they hooked up in September. And he may still be following her."

"You're wrong. That was nothing, and it's over."

"You sound mad, Rose."

"I *am* mad. I thought friends were supposed to support each other. Way to build me up, Emma."

"I'm only trying to protect you. I apologize if I offended you. That was not my intention."

Rose slammed her French book closed. "I'm going to the library."

"Suit yourself. I need to work on my English paper anyway."

Rose walked to the library through steadily falling snow. The path was deserted, but she was relieved to be alone, or at least to be away from Emma. What a killjoy. Emma was just jealous that Rose had a guy interested in her, so she wanted to undermine their relationship. Well, it wouldn't work. Rose caught fat flakes on her mitten and lifted them to her tongue, trying to banish the bad feelings. But the snow tasted of cold, bitter air, and the campus felt desolate, with the wind sweeping across the plaza, and the lights of the library disappearing in the white gusts.

Zach was waiting for her near the periodicals. She saw him through the window as she hurried up the stairs. He smiled when he saw her coming, and held up a key.

"I nabbed us one of the private study rooms," he said.

Rose had heard of kids hooking up in those rooms, though you had to be brazen, since the doors had big glass windows. What the hell, Rose could be brazen. She was tired of being the good girl, the quiet one, the one people felt sorry for. How dare Emma imply that Zach would never be interested in her for herself. Zach hadn't even mentioned Bel since their meeting in the lit mag office, which was weeks ago now.

The study room was a windowless cubicle on the third floor, with a Formica table, a lamp and two swivel chairs. Zach opened the door and held it for her. It felt like a date. She wished she'd worn something cuter than leggings and a sweatshirt. She draped her wet parka over the back of her chair. They spread out their textbooks and lab notes on the table, and sat down side by side.

"Listen, before we get started, I have to ask you something," Zach said.

She leaned toward him. His eyes were very blue behind his glasses. "What is it?"

"You're not gonna believe this. Tonight, at dinner, I overheard Bel and Donovan arrange an assignation."

This *was* about Bel! He'd brought her here to talk about her twin after all. Her cheeks burned. She wanted to slap him.

"Don't talk to me about her. I don't give a shit what Bel does," Rose said.

It was true. Her wounded pride overwhelmed any concern for her twin.

"How can you say that? She's your sister."

"Zach, enough. We do bio, or I'm leaving."

"No, wait a minute. You need to hear this. Tonight, at

dinner, I saw them walk out of the dining hall together. It was so blatant that I followed them. They were near the coatracks, arranging to meet in the Moreland laundry room at two o'clock in the morning. I mean, two a.m. in the basement—that's for sex, obviously. This is the guy who's sitting in judgment on the rest of us? Who might kick me out? He's exploiting her. He ought to be in jail."

Hold up. Maybe this wasn't about Bel after all. Maybe it was about Zach's own disciplinary issues.

"Why are you telling me this, Zach?" Rose asked. "Is this about Bel? Or about your Snapchat problem?"

He gave her a measuring look.

"It's about my case, definitely. If I can prove that something's going on between those two, I'll have leverage over Donovan, who runs the Disciplinary Committee. That's why I need a picture."

"A picture? You mean, a photo?"

"Yes, I said that before. A picture of the two of them—doing whatever. I know it's a lot to ask."

"You're talking about blackmailing a teacher. I can't get mixed up in that."

"You wouldn't be involved in the blackmail part. I'm really just asking you to go down to the basement and check on your sister. I'd do it myself, but I'd have to leave my dorm after curfew, sneak across campus, and break into a girls' dorm. I'd end up expelled, which is what I'm trying to avoid."

"I won't do it."

"Why not? If somebody sees you, you say you

couldn't sleep and you decided to do laundry. You can't get in trouble for that. You're allowed to walk around your own dorm."

"Why is this worth the risk for me?"

"Do you want me to get expelled?"

"Of course not. Do *you* want *me* to get expelled?"

"It's not gonna happen because I would never tell that you took the picture. But if saving my ass isn't enough motivation for you, think about your sister. If Bel is really having an affair with a married teacher, don't you want to know, so you can help her? I get that you two are on the outs. But, come on."

Rose sighed. She was sick and tired of Bel making her life complicated. Yet, he was right. Bel was still her sister, and her only real family.

"If Bel's meeting Donovan in the laundry room at two o'clock in the morning, yeah, I'd be concerned. But I don't believe that's true. You must've misheard."

"It is true, and I didn't mishear. Could you just go check?"

"Look, I'll think about it, but no promises. Don't bring it up again, or it's a definite no. Can we study, please?"

They studied for an hour, then Rose had to head back to Moreland for an appointment with Mrs. Donovan, the timing of which couldn't have been worse. Why hadn't she made up some excuse to cancel? Rose rang the doorbell of the Moreland faculty apartment, and listened as cheerful sounds of the dog and the kids floated out to her. How was she going to look Mrs. Donovan in the eye after what Zach told her? Or make small talk with *Mr.* Donovan? But it was too late to run. The door swung open, and Mrs. Donovan welcomed her into their happy domestic scene. The lights on the Christmas tree twinkled. The kids ran around naked, about to get their baths, their toys scattered everywhere. This was Rose's dream of what a family should be, and now it seemed like it might be a sham.

At the kitchen table, Rose could tell that Mrs. Donovan was upset about something. When the conversation turned to the slipper attack, and then to Bel, it became apparent what. Mrs. Donovan basically came out and asked Rose what was going on between Bel and her husband. Okay, her words were guarded, but that was clearly what she meant. Rose wanted to say what she knew. And she might have, if Mr. Donovan hadn't come into the kitchen right then. It was so upsetting to see him at that moment that Rose had to make an excuse to leave. That *creep.*

Rose's disgust decided something for her. She would go down to the basement tonight to see if Zach was right. Her sister's well-being was at stake, as well as the happiness of her favorite teacher. She wouldn't take a picture, or help Zach in his blackmail scheme. The point was to do the right thing. If Mr. Donovan was preying on her sister, and hurting his wonderful wife—who was like a second mom to Rose—then she'd find a way to make him stop.

At one forty-five that night, the alarm on Rose's phone went off. She got out of bed, pulled a hoodie over her nightgown, pulled on her UGGs and tiptoed down the stairs to the Moreland laundry room. Rose had been down in the basement several times, but never at night, and it was scarier than she'd imagined. Shadows leaped at her. Strange noises made her jump. She nearly lost her nerve, but decided instead to put in the bare minimum amount of time so she could honestly tell Zach she'd tried. She'd stay till 2:05, and when they didn't show, she'd run back upstairs to the comfort of her bed.

On the off chance that someone actually showed up, Rose needed a hiding place. There was a closet in the corner of the laundry room, used to store baskets, detergent and such. She slipped inside it, leaving the door ajar so she could see what happened without being seen, setting her phone to silent so she wouldn't make noise inadvertently. A large pipe inside the closet gave off the sound of rushing water, which made her nervous. Rose flicked her phone light on to examine the pipe, and could've sworn she saw something scurry in the sudden burst of light. *Eek.* The pipe wasn't leaking, but it was dusty and covered with cobwebs. She moved to get away from it, and felt something brush up against the back of her neck. *Cobwebs, spiders.* Rose yelped, then heard a noise, and held her breath.

Someone was coming. She heard footsteps, and saw a flashlight beam sweep across the floor. She was in a freaking closet, and someone was out there with a flashlight. Heart skittering, Rose peeked out the crack in the door. It was her sister. Okay, Bel was actually here, in this basement, at two a.m. Zach might really be right. Then Mr. Donovan walked in, and Rose saw the awful truth.

He switched on the light, and walked up to Bel. Rose couldn't make out their words over the sound of rushing water from the pipe. As she watched, that man put his hands on her sister, lifted her onto the counter and started ripping off her clothes. And Bel *let* him. Bel was too young. Donovan was too old. He was her teacher, and he was *married*—to the nicest person Rose had ever met. Carefully, she opened the closet door and stepped out, thinking she really ought to do something to stop this travesty. But the second she left her hiding place, she lost her nerve, and shrank back against the wall. What could she do, after all? Yell, scream, attack them? She didn't want to watch this. She needed time to think. She had to get out of here.

Heart pounding, she tiptoed toward the stairs. Bel and Donovan were too wrapped up in each other to notice her. At the last minute, Rose turned and snapped a picture with her phone. For a terrified instant, she worried that the flash would go off, but thank God it didn't. She had no idea why she took the picture, since she couldn't imagine showing it to anyone, ever. Zach had somehow planted the idea in her mind. Then she hurried out, and ran up to her room, where she barely slept for the rest of the night.

29

Transcript of Witness Interview (continued) conducted by Lieutenant Robert Kriscunas, State Police—Major Crime Unit, and Detective Melissa Howard, Odell NH, PD, with Miss Emma Kim.

Kriscunas: Miss Kim, we've heard from another witness that the sisters may have had a conflict over a boy. A Zach Cuddy. Can you shed any light on that?

Kim: Over Cuddy? Who told you that?

Kriscunas: I'm afraid we can't reveal our sources.

Kim: Was it Skyler Stone? I know you talked to her because she posted about the interview on Facebook.

Kriscunas: Did she? We request witnesses not to talk about what's said in here. I hope you won't.

Kim: I won't, but Skyler did. She's not super trustworthy. I'd take anything she says with a grain of salt. Skyler left school at Thanksgiving break. She has no clue what happened here after that because nobody ever spoke to her again.

Kriscunas: Are you saying that there was no conflict over Mr. Cuddy? You never heard that both sisters liked him, but he preferred Bel, and that caused problems?

Kim: I mean—yes, that's true. Look, this interview is very uncomfortable for me. I don't like to rat on my friends.

Kriscunas: We understand it may be uncomfortable to give information that may implicate friends or classmates. But this a very serious situation. A young girl is dead.

Kim: I know. I want to help. But—

Kriscunas: Just tell us the facts, that's all we ask. It's up to us to see where that information leads.

Kim: Okay. Yes, Zach and Rose were pretty friendly. After Thanksgiving, they started hanging out a lot, working on some sort of project together, I think. I won't lie. Rose was super into him. She had a crush that wouldn't quit. Zach wasn't that into her. To be honest, he was obsessed with Bel. Everybody knew it. And sure, you should follow up on that. It was borderline creepy.

Kriscunas: Mr. Cuddy's obsession with Bel was creepy.

Kim: Yes.

Kriscunas: Would you say he stalked her?

Kim: At times. But Zach's not the only—it's not the only—he's really not—

[PAUSE]

Kriscunas: What is it? Is there something else you want to tell us?

Kim: I don't feel comfortable. This is, like, big.

Kriscunas: If you're concerned about repeating gossip, again, let me assure you that we would never act on any information without corroborating it first.

Kim: It's not that. Some topics are just very sensitive.

Kriscunas: That sounds like something we need to hear. This conversation is confidential, if that's your concern.

Kim: You promise, nobody will know this came from me?

Kriscunas: Absolutely not. Scout's honor.

Kim: Okay, there's a rumor. Well, more than a rumor. I know there's something to it, because Rose and Bel had a big fight one night in front of me, and it wasn't over Zach.

Kriscunas: Over another boy?

Kim: Not a boy. It was over Mr. Donovan.

Kriscunas: Mr. Donovan? The headmaster?

Kim: Yes.

Kriscunas: Why would they fight over Mr. Donovan?

Kim: Ugh, I'm sorry. I'm uncomfortable talking about this. I need to call my mom, and get some advice. Can I have a break?

Kriscunas: Certainly. Take the time you need. We'll wait.

[TAPE STOPPED]

30

January

The sadness of her first Christmas without her mother weighed Bel down. At Spring Hill over break, the lawsuit hung in the air, and Grandma seemed to want to be rid of her. Whenever they crossed paths in the big house, she'd shoo Bel outside to go skating or snowshoeing. But Bel hated the cold. She holed up in her overheated room, headachy and lethargic, watching old *Seinfeld* episodes on her laptop and reading a musty copy of *Tess of the d'Urbervilles* that she'd found on a shelf in the parlor. Grandma didn't believe in making a fuss, so there were few signs of the season to lighten the mood. Each twin received a gift of a hundred dollars, deposited directly to her bank account. Grandma told them not to bother getting her anything, since she was fond of her own taste, and didn't want them wasting their spending money on something she would never wear. She hadn't put up a Christmas tree since Grandpa John died years ago, and didn't plan to start now. A red runner on the dining-room table and a ham for dinner on Christmas Eve, courtesy of the prepared-foods counter at the grocery store, were the sole concessions to the holiday.

Bel heard from Heath only once over break. He sent a text on Christmas morning that read, "I think of you." Nothing more. It was a reference to the Shakespeare sonnet he'd read aloud in class, the one she loved so much, where the man twined flowers in his lover's hair: "I think of you as the day wanes, and as the sun sinks deep into the ocean, and as the stars turn round above." Heath knew she loved that poem, and he knew he could use it to get to her. As much as Bel wanted to hate him, his text made her heart race every time she looked at it. He'd taken advantage of her innocence. She was just a girl. She was afraid of what might happen next with him. But Heath *saw* her. He was the only person in her life who did. Bel knew she ought to stay away from him, but she also knew she couldn't.

She had just zipped her suitcase, and set her alarm to wake up for the bus the next morning, when Rose knocked on the door unexpectedly. The twins' rooms at Spring Hill were situated side by side at the end of a long hallway, and shared a bathroom, yet Bel had managed to spend the ten days of break living next door to her sister without speaking to her, except at the dinner table, where they made the bare minimum small talk for Grandma's sake. The distance between them wasn't Bel's choice. Rose was still angry over that slipper nonsense, and shut down every attempt. Which was sad, because Bel was in over her head with Heath and knew it. She would have welcomed her sister's advice.

"Hey, come on in," she said.

Was it possible that Rose was ready to make up? Bel thought it was rich that Rose had stayed mad so long, since she had things to atone for, too. Like, ratting out your own sister to the Disciplinary Committee. But Rose had taken so much grief for that from other people that Bel was more than ready to forgive.

Rose sat down in the overstuffed chair beside Bel's bed, like she planned to stay awhile. The room was impeccably decorated in the style of thirty years before. Matching chintz drapes and bedspread and gilded moldings. Cushions everywhere with fringe on them. Precious pictures of dogs and horses in gold frames. The room was claustrophobic in the best of times. Given the tension between them, it felt all the more so.

"What's up?" Bel said, feeling nervous and antsy. She wanted to make up with Rose, but she didn't want to have to go through some big emotional conversation to do it.

"I'm here to give you a heads-up," Rose said.

"Okay. About what?"

"I know you messed around with Mr. Donovan before the break. I'm telling you not do it again, or else I'll have to take action."

The room felt hot all of a sudden, and Bel couldn't breathe. She'd had this fantasy that she could confide in Rose, and get support or advice. But she should have known her own sister better than that. Rose's specialty was judgment and condescension. And apparently also threats. *Yeah, what the hell are you gonna do about it?* Bel was tempted to say. But it would be a mistake to acknowledge that Rose was right about Bel and Heath. Bel had to deny it. Lie. Then Rose would fold her bluff and go away.

"That's just gossip. If you believe it, you're stupider than you look," Bel said as calmly as she could manage.

"Bel. I *know.* All right? I know it's true. I saw you. All break, I've been trying to figure out how to raise it with you."

"You saw me what?"

"I saw the two of you together."

"He's my teacher, my coach, my advisor. We're friends. We spend time together, and there's nothing wrong with that."

"Don't lie to me. I'm trying to help, despite everything you did to me."

"What did *I* do to you? You're the one who ratted."

"Ugh, you and your delinquent friends just about ruined my life with that insane attack. Darcy threatened my life on Facebook, and you expect me to feel guilty for telling?"

"I said I was sorry. And if it makes you feel better, they threatened me, too. Tessa was on campus right before break, lurking around outside Moreland, and she told me to watch my back."

"Tessa was on campus? How?"

"She lives right in town. She probably walked."

"Why would she threaten *you*?"

"They think I cut a deal to rat them out, and that's why I got off easy. I didn't. I told them I didn't."

"God, Bel, you're an idiot. First those lowlifes. And now Donovan. Could you be any more screwed up?"

"Why do you have to be so fucking condescending? If you would act normal, I might tell you stuff."

"I'm starting to think there's no hope for you. Donovan's taking advantage of you, and you let him."

"That's just gossip. Next, you're gonna tell me where there's smoke, there's fire."

"Enough with the bullshit. I *know*, okay? I saw you doing it in the laundry room. The man has a family. If you don't stop, I'll tell Grandma."

Bel flashed on that night in the laundry room, seeing a movement out of the corner of her eye. Wait a minute. Was that a person? Was it Rose? Was she there that night? If it was true—Jesus, Heath would freak the hell out. He'd said a million times, nobody could ever know about this. It couldn't be true. Bel felt the crushing weight of panic in her chest.

"You better not tell. Grandma hates you already because you're such a tattle. She'll kick you out this time."

Rose's face went red. Bel had hit a nerve.

"You think you're so smart," Rose said, near tears. "I can prove it. I have pictures."

"Pictures of what?"

But Rose wouldn't answer.

"Pictures of *what*, I said?" Bel demanded.

"Oh, now you're worried. Tough shit, I'm not telling," Rose taunted.

Nobody could push her buttons like Rose. Bel moved toward her twin with fists clenched.

"Stay away from me!"

Rose jumped up and ran for the door. She was faster than she looked, and made it to her room before Bel could take out her frustrations. As the door slammed and the bolt shot home, Bel raised her fist to pound on the door, but stopped short. Grandma's bedroom was directly below them. If Grandma heard a ruckus and came upstairs to investigate, Rose would spill about Bel and Heath. She might even show Grandma this supposed picture. *If* it existed. (It couldn't exist, please don't let it exist, Rose was making that up.) And then what? Would Grandma tell the school? Would Heath get in trouble? Would he blame her if he did?

God, she could kill her sister.

31

Rose put her head down and huddled into the hood of her parka as she left Moreland for the library. It was a bitter evening, raw and wet, and Bel's terrible secret was weighing on her. She was completely stuck as to what to do, and yet, she couldn't ask for advice. Who could she talk to? What would that conversation even sound like? *Hey, Emma, my sister's sleeping with a teacher. I have a picture of them on my phone. It's blurry but it's also pretty graphic, and I don't know what to do with it. How do you handle situations like that?*

Nope.

She could try to talk to Bel again. But they hadn't spoken since their fight at Spring Hill, and even when they did talk, Bel never listened. She could show the photo to Mrs. Donovan, but Rose loved her teacher too much to bring her the news that would ruin her life. That left the obvious move—confront Donovan with the photo, and tell him to quit it or else she'd go public. But Rose was too much of a coward to face down a teacher, especially one creepy enough to have sex with her sister, in the Moreland laundry room, no less. If Donovan could sink that low, God only knew what else he was capable of.

Rose wished she could be more like Zach Cuddy. Zach was the person who'd told her to take the photo in the first place. He would have no hesitation to blackmail Donovan with it. But Zach didn't know the sex picture existed. Rose had never told him about it. She'd never even told him about seeing Bel and Donovan together that night.

It had been a relief to come back from break and see that Zach was still at Odell. Rose had refused to help him with his blackmail plan, but apparently he'd found some other way to avoid getting expelled. All the boys who'd shared the Snapchat had gotten off with no punishment. Nobody knew for sure how they'd done it. A rumor was going around that Brandon Flynn's dad had paid for a computer expert to wipe their phones, though it seemed unlikely that Brandon Flynn would help out Zach. Zach and Brandon had been at odds ever since their confrontation on the bus at Thanksgiving break, when Brandon attacked Rose, and Zach defended her. Anyway, if Zach was brazen and sneaky enough to evade punishment, then he might just be the ally Rose needed. He'd have the guts to confront Donovan, and he'd probably be willing to do it, if only to show off for Bel. But that was the problem. If Zach still had a thing for her sister, Rose didn't want to encourage it. On the other hand, who else could help her with this bizarre predicament? She couldn't keep the secret much longer. It was so upsetting and distracting that she could barely study. And midterms were only three weeks away.

She stopped under the light of a lamppost, whipped out her phone and texted Zach to meet her in the library. "I have something to show you," she said. There, that would get his attention. Rose started walking again, but she was immediately plagued with doubts about showing him the photo. Zach wasn't someone she could control. He wouldn't necessarily handle this the way she wanted him to. He'd have an agenda of his own. *Ugh*. She didn't know what to do. She probably shouldn't show it to him. But she'd already texted. He'd been ignoring her lately; maybe he wouldn't show up. And if he did show, she could claim she only wanted to compare bio notes.

It started raining harder. Rose turned off the main path to take a shortcut that ran between Anson Hall and the woods. She usually avoided the shortcut at night because it was dark and the woods were scary. But the narrow passageway was bordered by tall pines whose boughs formed a sort of tunnel, sheltering the path from the rain. Head down, hood up, lost in her thoughts, Rose didn't hear them approaching until two large figures stepped up on either side of her.

"See, Tessa, I told you there were rats in these woods," Brandon Flynn said, taking Rose by one arm.

Rose gasped. Brandon was burly and well over six feet tall. His grip was powerful enough to hurt. Rose tried to pull her arm away, but he wouldn't let her.

"Big, ugly rats, too," Tessa said, taking Rose's other arm.

"Let go! What do you think you're doing?" Rose struggled to break free, her voice shrill with fear.

"Don't bother fighting, you're not going anywhere till we say so," Tessa said, tightening her grip.

"Let go, let go," Brandon mocked, in a high-pitched tone.

He had a prominent forehead that gave him an ape-like appearance. Rose had been afraid of Brandon ever since he bumped her and tripped her on the bus. And Tessa was an athlete, tall and strong, and mean-looking, her red hair bedraggled in the rain, her mouth a sour line. Between the two of them, they could hurt Rose if they wanted to, and she wouldn't be able to stop them. *Shit.*

"What do you want?" Rose said.

"I *want* my life back," Tessa said. "Darcy and I are expelled. The police are investigating us. No college will look at us now. I'm working in my uncle's dry-cleaning shop, and it's your fault, rat."

Now, that just pissed Rose off. She'd done the right thing by telling. Tessa had made her own bed. She ought to take some responsibility.

"You did this to yourself, Tessa. But if you need to blame someone, you should blame Darcy. She got you into this mess. I bet she's crying her eyes out on a beach somewhere with an umbrella drink in her hand. She sure as hell isn't working at a dry-cleaner's."

"Shut up about Darcy. Don't you talk about her," Brandon said.

But Rose could see from Tessa's expression that she'd hit pay dirt. Darcy and Tessa might have gotten the same punishment, but it had hurt Tessa a lot more.

"I bet Darcy doesn't even return your phone calls," Rose said.

"Shut *up*." Brandon twisted her arm, making Rose cry out in pain.

"Brandon, stop it," Tessa said, dropping Rose's arm. "Let's ask the question and be done with it. I don't need more trouble. Enright, tell us what we want to know, and we'll leave you alone."

Brandon let go of Rose's arm. She stood between the two of them, shaking with cold and fear, as her breath went up in clouds. If there was a way to escape this situation without getting hurt, she would certainly prefer that.

"Fine. What's the question? I'll tell you, if I know," she said.

"We want to know why *we* got kicked out, and Bel didn't," Tessa said.

"'We'?"

"Me and Darcy."

"Uh, because you planned the attack?"

"Don't get cute, or you'll be sorry," Brandon said.

"I'm not being cute. I'm saying, maybe because Bel was a follower," Rose said.

"Not any more than I was," Tessa said, her words coming out in an agitated rush. "Darcy planned everything. Bel and I both took orders. So why did I get expelled, and Bel get off scot-free. *Why?* I don't buy that bullshit story about pain pills. Normally, if you're high when you break a rule, the Committee just whacks you harder."

"I don't know the answer to that," Rose said. "But if you're implying I lied to help my sister, I didn't. I told the truth about what Bel did, like I did about everything else."

"I'm not saying you lied. I heard Bel slept with Donovan to get out from under the charge. Is it true? I *need* to know. And I need proof. We could use that to get our case reopened," Tessa said.

Rose had the proof on her phone, but she wasn't about to tell these two. Darcy and Tessa launching an appeal, getting reinstated and coming back to campus, was Rose's worst nightmare. The thought made her so furious—at *Bel*, for getting her into this mess—that she didn't have to dig deep to come up with a convincing response.

"You're confusing me with someone who gives a shit about my sister," Rose said.

The venom in her voice was real. Bel just kept screwing up Rose's life. When would it end?

"Is that a yes or a no?" Tessa asked.

"I don't have a clue what Bel did to get off easy, and I don't care. Because of her, I lost my roommate, everybody thinks I'm a rat, my grandmother is pissed at me.

That's Bel's fault, I agree, not just yours and Darcy's. I know you got punished, and Bel got *counseling*. She gets away with shit. She always has. In case it's not obvious, I hate my sister, and I don't speak to her. Bottom line, I don't know if she slept with Donovan. But if you want to tell everyone that, you won't hear a complaint from me."

Somebody was coming up the path behind them. Rose did a double take in the dimness of the trees.

"Well, hello," Zach said, coming up to them. "Not who I'd expect to run into on a rainy night. Especially you, Tessa. I thought you were banned from campus."

"Mind your own business, Cuddy. Odell doesn't tell me what to do anymore."

"Maybe not, but they could charge you with trespassing. Though, criminal charges—no big deal, right? And you, Flynn—"

"Bite me. You wanna fight?"

"If that's the only language you understand."

"You talk like a total twat."

"And you talk like someone who was bashed on the skull with a lead pipe and failed to seek medical attention."

Brandon raised his fists. He was thick as a gorilla, with a wide neck and meaty fists. Zach was no match for him. Rose held her breath, waiting for Brandon to lay Zach out, flat on the path. But in the blink of an eye, Zach whipped a pocketknife from his jacket and held it up, the blade glittering dangerously. Everybody gasped.

"Are you fucking crazy?" Brandon said.

"You started this. I'll finish it if I have to."

"Zach, please, you'll make it worse," Rose said.

Tessa poked Brandon. "Let's go. Enright doesn't know shit, and this is getting ugly. C'mon, it's cold out here."

Brandon backed off grudgingly. "You got off easy this time, both of you," he said. "Better watch your backs. And, Rose, tell your slutty sister that, too. We know she's hiding something, and we're coming for her."

Rose trembled with shock as she watched them walk away. Zach put his arm around her protectively. His presence helped her catch her breath.

"Are you all right?" he asked.

"Shaken up. Thank God you came along. But really, a *knife*?"

"It's just a Swiss Army knife."

"Isn't that a disciplinary violation?"

"Technically, but I need it for self-defense. That thug Brandon's been bothering me."

"Is it because you stuck up for me on the bus? I'm sorry."

"It's complicated. There was stuff that went on you don't know about, with Snapchatting the slipper attack. Flynn was in deep."

"Is it true he paid to have everyone's phone wiped?"

"Rose, the less you know the better. Anyway, I don't want to talk about it."

"Okay, but I'm scared, Zach. They were following me. They waited till they could get me alone. I want to report them. Will you back me up?"

"Bad idea. Brandon's pissed enough already, over Darcy. Imagine how he'd act if we went after him directly. Come on, let's get out of the cold. We can go the library. I want to see this mysterious thing that you mentioned in your text. I'm dying of curiosity."

32

Sarah sat at a long conference table surrounded by members of the board of trustees and the senior administration of the school. Everybody listened attentively to Heath as he gave a PowerPoint presentation about his brainchild, Odell's new anti-bullying policy. Sarah was there in her capacity as head of Moreland Hall, since Moreland had experienced a serious bullying incident. But she was also Heath's wife. So, when her phone buzzed in her pocket, she studiously ignored it. It wouldn't do to check her phone while Heath was in the middle of the most important presentation of his career.

A minute later, it buzzed again. There was a terrible flu bug going around the kids' day care, and she had visions of Scottie and Harper crying out for Mommy as they burned with fever. She eased the phone from her pocket and glanced at it surreptitiously under the table. The alert was for an e-mail, from a sender called

Anonymouse@yahoo.com. *Anonymouse?* Like, *anonymous*, but a mouse? The subject line read only, "Important Message." Must be junk. She shoved the phone back in her pocket.

Heath took questions about his plan, and answered every one of them brilliantly. When his talk was done, everyone applauded enthusiastically, then they adjourned for a ten-minute coffee break. Sarah went up to the front of the room, wanting to congratulate her husband, but she couldn't get close. Heath was surrounded by trustees. They fawned over him to the point that Simon Barlow, the headmaster, looked pink with jealousy under his mane of white hair. Simon had been headmaster for twenty-five years, and people were saying he was stale in the job. Now he had a rival on his tail.

"Masterful pivot," the chairman of the board was saying. "No question, this is going to help us settle the lawsuit."

"I'd like to put you in touch with the school's lawyers," another trustee said. "They could really benefit from hearing your ideas."

"And the marketing firm, too," the chairman said. "I'd like to have Heath repeat his presentation."

Sarah backed away. It was clear she wouldn't get a word in. And this was somewhat hard to watch. As happy as she was for Heath's success, she worried it would go to his head.

Sarah went back to her seat and opened the e-mail she'd gotten a few minutes before. She read it, blinked, and read it twice more. The lights in the room seemed to dim as she stared at the screen.

"Your husband is cheating on you," it read. "He's screwing a student. Everybody knows but you."

Everybody knows but you. Sarah glanced up, afraid that people were watching her. But nobody had noticed her private drama. Was it true, did they know? How could they? Would the trustees be patting Heath on the back like this, if they thought he was *screwing a student*? No, that made no sense. They couldn't know. Nobody knew. Then why did she feel like everybody in the room could read her mind, could see this e-mail?

Maybe because the e-mail hadn't come out of the blue.

Sarah had been fretting about Heath and Bel Enright since overhearing that phone call on Thanksgiving Day. She remembered Bel coming up to him in the dining hall, and the heads swiveling as the two of them walked out together. *He's screwing a student. Everybody knows but you.* Everybody in the dining hall that night had seemed to know—what? *Something.* That same night Heath snuck out of the apartment and didn't return until 2:30 in the morning. But he'd explained where he was. He heard a noise. Plausible, right? She'd been struggling ever since over whether to believe him.

Did this e-mail settle the question once and for all? But how could it? It was anonymous. It could be a prank. People were malicious. They enjoyed inflicting pain. Anonymouse could be a student of hers, upset with the grade she'd given, who'd overheard gossip and decided to use it against her. Or a student of Heath's, who wanted his attention, and got mad when he didn't deliver it. Anonymouse could even be Bel Enright herself. Who was to say? Kids did stupid shit all the time. Maybe this was a lie.

The problem was, she believed it. There were too many signs, and she'd been ignoring them for too long. She looked at her husband now, surrounded by admirers, and felt like she couldn't breathe. A strange weakness swept through her, and she had to hold on to the edge of the table to steady herself. This was real. He was cheating. With a student. Right?

But if he was, and everyone knew, why the hell didn't they say something, or do something? How could the administration of a school suffering its worst-ever scandal ignore evidence that the dean of students was sexually involved with a student? How could her friends and colleagues know that her husband was cheating on her, and not say a word? A conspiracy of silence that big seemed impossible—or at least, implausible. Sarah sat there panicky, shaky, her palms sweaty, not knowing what to do next. How could she go on with her life, not knowing for sure whether the e-mail was true? She had to do something.

She would write back, ask for details, truth-test the sender to see if he, or she, had any real information. She prayed that this would turn out to be a hoax. After all, if this was real, why would Anonymouse withhold the name of the student? Why not come out and say it was Bel Enright? Maybe Anonymouse wanted to play games. Drag it out, toy with her. Maybe Anonymouse was out to get her—or Heath. He was clearly on the rise in the administration. Just look at how they fawned on him. A man with his ambition was bound to attract enemies. There were plenty of reasons to doubt the veracity of this e-mail.

The headmaster went up to the podium and tapped the mic. The meeting was about to resume. Sarah was seated at the far end of the table, closest to the door. If she was looking for a chance to escape, for a moment when they were all distracted, this was it. Quietly, she pushed her chair back, crossed the few steps to the door, turned the knob carefully, shut the door behind her as softly as she could manage, her phone gripped tightly in her hand.

Out in the hallway, she took a deep breath, feeling like she'd escaped from prison. The women's bathroom was in the basement, three flights below, and she started down the staircase, holding tight to the banister because she was light-headed and dizzy. The stairs were steep and ancient, made of marble, worn into grooves by generations of Odell students. Sarah had been among those students once. The younger Sarah—innocent, hopeful. She'd walked these stairs when her romance with Heath was new, imagining the perfect life she'd have with him. That didn't feel like so long ago, but obviously, it was.

The women's room was low-ceilinged, dank and empty. Sarah shut herself in a stall and stared at her phone. She would write back, ask questions. There was barely any reception down here. She opened the e-mail, and clicked Reply. The icon started spinning, struggling to load. Eventually it allowed her to type, "Who are you?" Anonymouse was waiting and wrote right back, but again, there was a frustrating delay before the response loaded, during which Sarah saw that there was a reply in her in-box, but couldn't read it.

"A fly on the wall," Anonymouse had written.

"If you don't have the guts to tell me who you are, why should I believe you?" Sarah wrote.

Again, delay. Then the reply appeared in her in-box. "I'm telling the truth. You know I am. He's weak, surrounded by pretty girls. What did you expect?"

Sarah felt sick reading that reply, but it also made her angry. "Tell me who the student is or get lost," she wrote, and hit Send.

She waited as the icon turned. Nothing.

Her phone rang in her hand, the buzzing so startling that she nearly dropped it. How the hell did Anonymouse get her number? Was Anonymouse someone she knew? But then she had the presence of mind to look at the number, and saw that it was the day care.

"Hel-lo?" Sarah said, her voice shaking.

"Sarah?" a voice squawked.

"Yes?"

"It's Allison from day care—"

Her cell cut out. *The children.* Sarah tried dialing back, but she didn't have enough reception. She ran out of the bathroom, up the stairs and out the door of Founders' Hall.

"Allison? It's Sarah. I lost you," she said, when the call finally connected.

"Oh, Sarah, thank goodness."

"What is it? The flu?"

"I'm afraid so. Harper threw up after lunch. We took her temperature. It's a hundred and two, and she broke out in a rash. We need you to come get her right away."

"Of course. The poor thing! I'll be there in ten minutes. I'll take Scottie, too. He's probably next," Sarah said.

"Thank you. They'll be ready when you get here."

Only after she hung up did Sarah feel the cold. A light snow was falling, and the ground was slick. She'd left her coat and handbag in the conference room. Ugh, she couldn't face going back in there to get them. She hugged herself for warmth and struck out toward the other side of campus, where the day care was located. She'd collect her children and take them home to tend to them. Heath could get her things.

Heath.

Sarah couldn't afford to think about Anonymouse now. Those e-mails would have to wait. She was a mother first, and her babies were sick. She was a teacher, and she couldn't leave her students hanging. She needed to cancel her afternoon classes. The phone was still in Sarah's hand. She opened her e-mail to notify her students, and saw that Anonymouse's reply had finally loaded.

"It's Bel Enright. No way I'm covering for that bitch. You don't believe me? I have proof. Take a look."

With shaking hands, Sarah clicked on the attachment.

33

Transcript of Witness Interview conducted by Lieutenant Robert Kriscunas, State Police—Major Crime Unit, and Detective Melissa Howard, Odell NH, PD, with Mr. Zachary Cuddy.

Kriscunas: What happened to your hand, Zach? That looks serious.

Cuddy: Oh, no, it's just a—uh—squash injury.

Kriscunas: Is it a cut, or—

Cuddy: It's nothing. Look, I really don't have anything useful to tell you, so if you don't mind, I need to get to my next class.

Kriscunas: Zach, I understand that you have some hesitancy about speaking with us. I just want you to know, I did get permission from your parents. Your father faxed me a signed permission form. Would you like to see it?

Cuddy: Yes, I would.

[PAUSE]

Kriscunas: Okay?

Cuddy: I see that's my father's signature. He's not very sophisticated about these things. Just because he signed, doesn't mean I have to talk.

Kriscunas: That's correct. You don't have to speak with us, but let me tell you what I told him, and maybe it'll put your mind at ease. We're just trying to get some background information about the relationship between Rose and Bel Enright, and we understand there might've been tension between them over a romantic relationship with you. We were hoping you could shed light on that.

Cuddy: Yeah, see, that's the thing. You've got the wrong guy, sir. I really have nothing to add.

Kriscunas: Are you saying you're not the Zachary who was romantically involved with one sister, while the other one was pursuing you?

Cuddy: That's right.

Kriscunas: Was it some other Zachary?

Cuddy: I have no idea. All I can tell you is, I wasn't romantically involved, as you put it, with either of the Enright girls. You have bad information. Whoever told you to talk to me was lying, or mistaken. And I'm late for class, so if you'll excuse me.

[SOUND OF CHAIR SCRAPING]

Howard: Hold on, Mr. Cuddy. You're not being straight with us.

Cuddy: I resent that.

Howard: Well, that's the impression you're giving. Sit down for a minute. Tell us about your relationship

with the sisters. Help us square it with what other wit-
nesses have said, or else it looks like you're hiding
something.

Kriscunas: *Detective Howard is right, Zach. We've*
talked to a number of people at this point. We have
a picture of your relationship with the Enright twins
that's more than what you're describing. When wit-
nesses aren't fully honest, we have to ask ourselves why.

Cuddy: *Maybe I was minimizing, but when you say*
romantically involved, that's a crock. Rose was in my
bio class. We were friendly, that's all. I wouldn't even
say we were close friends. Bel and I had a brief—call
it a hookup—months ago. One time, after a dance,
and I've had nothing to do with her since. Okay? I'm
serious, you're wasting your time with me. Looking in
the wrong place.

Kriscunas: *Where should we be looking instead?*
You tell us.

Cuddy: *For starters, Darcy Madden, Tessa Romano,*
Brandon Flynn. Those three have been threatening the
Enright girls for months, and they have a history of
actual physical attacks.

Kriscunas: *Darcy and Tessa we know. Who's this—*
Braden, you said?

Cuddy: Brandon. *Brandon Flynn. Darcy's boyfriend.*
A rich kid, but a real thug. He wrestles and plays rugby.
Enormous guy, maybe six-two, two-fifty. He was livid
when Darcy got expelled.

Kriscunas: *He blamed Rose Enright for it?*

Cuddy: *Yes, because Rose testified before the Disci-*
plinary Committee. But they were mad at Bel, too. All

three of those delinquents hated Bel because she got off with no punishment. They thought she cut a deal behind their backs.

Kriscunas: You think they were capable of violence?

Cuddy: Not just capable. They've been violent all along. Look what Darcy and Tessa did to Skyler Stone. It was practically a rape. And Brandon physically attacked Rose on a bus a few months back. I saw it. He pushed her, he tripped her. There were tons of witnesses.

Kriscunas: When was this?

Cuddy: On the Odell bus to Connecticut and New York for Thanksgiving break.

Kriscunas: You say there were other witnesses?

Cuddy: Dozens.

Kriscunas: Names?

Cuddy: Emma Kim was there, and saw everything. The thing is, this incident on the bus wasn't the only time they attacked Rose. About a month ago, I took a shortcut to the library, and came across Brandon and Tessa Romano confronting Rose on the path. They had her cornered. Nobody was around. If I hadn't come along, they were going to hurt her, it seemed obvious.

Kriscunas: We need the details on that incident. Exactly when and where it occurred, what you observed.

Cuddy: Sure.

Howard: Wait a minute. Tessa is banned from campus, as I understand.

Cuddy: You think she listens? She comes here whenever she feels like it. These three have no shame, no limits. Leave me alone. Go talk to them.

34

Max started barking in the front hall, and Sarah heard Heath's key in the door. It was evening, and the kids had just gone down. For the past three nights, Sarah had slept on an air mattress on the floor of their room, nursing them through an awful virus. She sat on the edge of Harper's bed, and reached out to put her hand on the little girl's forehead. The air in the room felt close and oppressive, and carried the faint tang of vomit. But Harper's temperature was back to normal, and Scottie's would be soon, too. Sarah hated it when her kids were sick. And yet, it had been a relief to sink into motherhood, to hide from her husband and the breakdown of her marriage. The moment was coming when she'd have to face the truth, and she dreaded it. What she feared most was her own weakness. Sarah had to keep reminding herself about that photograph, or she would love her husband again the second she saw him, like she always did.

Heath's shadow fell across the floor. She looked up to see him standing in the doorway.

"How are they doing?" he asked.

"*Shh.*"

"Oh, sorry, babe," he whispered. "Come to the kitchen when you're done. I have great news."

She knew she shouldn't listen to his good news. She shouldn't listen to a word he said until she confronted him, and got an answer to the enormous question hanging over their heads. There was still room for doubt. The image was blurry. It was impossible to tell where the photo was taken, or who the girl was. It might be Bel, it might not. But Sarah believed that the man in the photo was Heath. She knew his body too well not to recognize it in a photograph, no matter how dark or blurry. When you lived with someone for more than a decade, you just knew. And pictures didn't lie.

But force of habit brought her to her feet, to follow her husband down the hall and hear his good news, like any normal day. In the kitchen, Heath stood at the counter, his back to her. He turned around, and she saw a bottle of champagne in his hands.

"What's going on?" she asked.

"We're celebrating."

"Heath, the kids have been throwing up for three days. I'm hardly in the mood to celebrate."

"Poor sweetheart. I wish you'd let me help more."

He had offered to help. But she chased him away. She couldn't bear to watch him with their children, when he was probably having an affair with a girl who was little more than a child herself. *Probably.* In her heart, Sarah hoped desperately for some other explanation. But she didn't expect one.

"I know you're tired, but please toast with me," he said with a smile, and popped the cork.

He arced the perfect spray of champagne into two glasses and handed one to Sarah, smooth as always. Heath was an expert at romance, quick with an endearment, always ready with the perfect quote. He knew when to put on romantic music, or to bring her flowers for no reason. He'd won her heart that way so many times. But this problem was too big to be solved with a bottle of champagne and a winning smile.

"What are we toasting?" she asked.

The temptation to pretend things were normal was almost irresistible. If only she could delete the photo and forget she'd ever received it. But she wouldn't be able to live with herself. She couldn't stand here, gazing into her husband's beautiful eyes, not knowing the truth.

"Skyler Stone's parents settled the lawsuit," he said. "Odell will pay a modest sum to the charity of Skyler's choice, *and* institute my proposed anti-bullying curriculum. My project is what broke the deadlock."

"We're toasting to you, then. To Heath Donovan, savior of Odell Academy," Sarah said, a harsh edge in her voice.

Heath looked at her with concern. "Are you okay?"

"I'm tired. I told you."

"Drink up," he said. "A little bubbly'll lift your spirits."

He clinked his glass against hers, flashing a movie-star grin. Sarah sat down numbly in a chair, and downed the champagne in three long sips. She put the glass down and looked searchingly at him. She was going to ask him about the picture. She really was. She was working up to it.

"The school got off easy," Heath said. "The Stones were never able to prove that the Snapchat was shared. I think those sneaky kids wiped their phones. Without that, the case is just a couple of girls hitting another girl with a slipper. Hardly worth a big payout."

"The trustees must be happy," Sarah said.

He poured more champagne into her glass.

"Thrilled. They've asked me to head up a new anti-bullying task force. Sarah, this is an enormous opportunity for me. They've asked me to expand my role significantly, and take the lead in helping the school change its image. I have a plan to parlay our anti-bullying stance into favorable press. By the time I'm done, Odell will be the poster child for kindness and enlightenment. But that's not all. Wait till you hear this."

He paused for a second, expecting her to squeal with excitement, and beg him to tell. It scared her how much she wanted to.

"Simon is retiring, effective at the end of the school year," he announced triumphantly.

Simon Barlow had been the headmaster of Odell even before Heath and Sarah were students there. He was a former Oxford don, with a charming British accent and wise, sad eyes, who wrote famous books of essays on poetry and the arts. He gave witty speeches, and hosted sophisticated dinner parties for donors, along with his husband, Michael Lazarus, who was head of the theatre department. It was true that Simon was not known as a crack administrator. When things got messy or difficult at Odell, he tended to duck and delegate. But he gave Odell its intellectual panache. Sarah couldn't imagine the school without him. It would be a loss.

"Why? He's not sixty-five for another two years."

"It's part of the deal," Heath explained. "Skyler's parents blame Simon for allowing a climate to develop where the attack could happen. His retirement was floated by the board as a concession, and they jumped at it."

How convenient for Heath if Simon took the fall for this. Sarah wondered whose idea it had been, really. She'd always viewed her husband as an open book. He was outgoing, warm, emotional—too emotional, sometimes. She assumed she knew what he was thinking, where he went, what he did. After seeing that photo, she was no longer sure. If Heath could lie to her about his fidelity, his very love for her and their children, then he could lie about anything. He was certainly capable of scheming to take over the school, while pretending it was the trustees' idea.

"Why only Simon?" she asked. "We were running the dorm, after all."

"What are you talking about?"

"We were the ones in charge of Moreland Hall when the slipper attack happened. Shouldn't we offer to re-sign, too?"

"Simon's not *resigning*. That would be too big an admission of fault. The trustees would never go for it. He's retiring to pursue other interests."

"But I'm saying, why let him take the fall alone?" Sarah insisted.

She didn't have the guts to confront the real problem, so instead, she nagged at him about this. If she were braver, she would ask about the photo.

"Moreland was a problem for years," Heath said, "and Simon let it fester. He's the wrong man to set a moral example, don't you see? We're the ones who turned the tide, you and me, our wholesome all-American family. Nobody blames us, and if you want proof of that, here's the *real* headline, Sarah. I'm in the running to become the new headmaster."

The thought of Heath as headmaster was starting to seem wrong, dangerous even. "You? Headmaster?"

His face changed instantly, his eyes darkening and his chin jutting out. "How can you say that? I'd be great at it. You know I would."

"Your skill set is not the problem."

"You're going to support me in this, right? It's within reach, I can feel it, and I want it so much. You know I'm not happy teaching."

"Heath, you can't be headmaster. Not now, anyway. There's a problem," Sarah said flatly.

Once the words were out, she knew that she had to press on. She had to find out the truth about his relationship with Bel. A man conducting a sexual relationship with a student must not under any circumstances become headmaster of this school. Sarah had an obligation to protect the students, even at the expense of her own husband's career.

If the photo was real.

"You think I'm too young, too inexperienced? But they want a fresh face. Someone with vision and vigor. A wholesome family. The chairman compared me to John Kennedy."

"That has nothing to do with it. I need to ask you something. Wait here."

Sarah hurried to the kids' bedroom and grabbed her phone from the dresser. She pulled up the photo of Heath and the girl (woman?), naked and locked in an embrace, then ran back to the kitchen, and held it up in front of his face.

"What's this?" she demanded.

She watched his eyes focus on the screen. She saw the emotions flit across his face: recognition, fear, then pure panic. But then he stepped back and became guarded.

"I have no idea," he said. "It's impossible to see. Are you suggesting this has something to do with me?"

"That's *you* in the picture. You and . . . *someone else*, having sex."

"Are you crazy? That's not me. Where did you get this?"

"It was sent to me anonymously. Along with an e-mail that said you're sleeping with a student. Bel Enright, to be specific."

"So that's supposed to be a picture of me and Bel Enright having sex?"

"Yes."

He huffed in disbelief. "Bullshit. Let me see that again," he said, and reached for the phone.

She held it behind her back, half expecting him to take it from her by force. But he didn't. Instead, he sat down heavily in a kitchen chair, looking up at her imploringly.

"Sarah, how can you think that I would ever cheat on you? We've been together since we were kids. There's only you. There's never been anyone else. We have two beautiful children together. Does that mean nothing to you?"

Of course, it did. It meant everything. Their love, their life, their family. They'd both wanted children, badly. And it hadn't been easy. Harper had had terrible colic and didn't sleep through the night until she was two. Scottie was a preemie and had developmental delays. But instead of driving them apart, their babies had brought them together. He was such a devoted father. She never would have believed that Heath could betray her—until they moved into Moreland this past September. Before then, everything had been good between them. All she wanted was for it to be good again.

"The idea that you would buy into some anonymous e-mail," he said, shaking his head, his aqua eyes sparkling with unshed tears, "some phony photo—after everything we've meant to each other—I don't know what to say. I'm devastated."

He looked so forlorn that Sarah began to question her own eyes. God, how she wanted to believe him, to believe that he would never look at another woman. That he would never touch a girl whose care was entrusted to him. She stared at the photo again for several seconds. The image was muddy, grainy, underexposed. The girl's face was not visible; neither was Heath's. Maybe he was telling the truth. But—the broad expanse of his back, the curve of his buttocks, the curl of his hair against his neck. She knew them.

"I think it's you. Look," she said in despair, handing him the phone.

If Heath would just say out loud that it was him in the picture, then she would know what to do. If not, then, she was utterly confused. She couldn't take drastic measures that might hurt him, or his reputation, or even destroy his career, or harm their marriage, unless she was sure.

Heath rotated the phone to make the image larger. He expanded and contracted various parts of the frame with the pinch of his fingers, frowning in concentration.

"Look at the guy's ear. That's not my ear at all," he said, finally, showing her the screen, which had been manipulated to display an image of an ear, massively enlarged.

She glanced from the screen to Heath's ear. It was impossible to tell. Sarah worried that he might be manipulating *her*, and yet, he seemed so genuinely hurt that she was tempted to believe him. In times of trouble, we fall back on old habits, and Sarah had been in the habit of trusting Heath for her entire adult life. She started to believe him again, and to doubt her own eyes. Your eyes could deceive you, right?

"I want to believe you," she said finally. "But I just don't know."

"It wasn't me, I swear it. Somebody is trying to undermine my candidacy. They photoshopped this to discredit me."

"Who would do such a thing?"

"Somebody who views me as a threat, obviously. There are plenty of those. I'm in the running to become headmaster. Some people want that job for themselves. Others don't want me to get it because they're worried I'll clean house. And they're right. There's a lot of dead wood around Odell, a lot of policies that need changing. People are afraid of me coming in and shaking things up."

The panic in his eyes seemed genuine. It was true that he had enemies. Was she really going to ruin his career, destroy their marriage, risk his very life (given how he reacted to failure), over an anonymous e-mail and a blurry photo? What if that *wasn't* him?

"I want to believe you. But I don't understand why, if someone wanted to discredit you, they would send this to me, instead of going public?"

"Because they know the picture's fake, and that it won't stand up to scrutiny. If they go public, they'll be exposed. This way, they send it to you, betting that you'll confront me, and that I'll take myself out of the running to be headmaster in order to avoid embarrassment. You're playing right into their hands."

"I see that. But—"

"How can you do this to us, Sarah?" he said. "Don't you love me? Don't you trust me? I can't go on if you don't, baby. If you abandon me—Well, I don't know what I would do."

Heath tossed the phone on the table. He walked over to the cabinet, took out the barely touched bottle of Scotch they'd gotten for Christmas two years ago, and filled his champagne glass to the brim. As she watched him down the Scotch in one long gulp, Sarah flashed back to the worst moment of her life. It was in their New York apartment, shortly after Heath's dishonesty had been exposed. She'd forced him to admit the truth to her, and they had a terrible fight. He started drinking heavily—something he never did—just like now. She went out for a walk to clear her head. When she came back, it was dark in the apartment, and the bedroom door was ajar. She called his name; no answer. She walked into the bedroom, and saw him facedown on the bed, his arm hanging limply off the edge. She flipped on the light. There was an empty bottle of pills on the floor. She ran to him. He was pale white, cold, and lifeless. She dialed nine-one-one. They told her if she'd found him five minutes later, he wouldn't've made it.

She'd begged him to get help. Get therapy, a diagnosis. Medication could help. But he never would. He said he'd watched his mother be slowly sucked dry by charlatans, who'd ruined her mind and her health. Action was Heath's cure. They found a new life at Odell. He nurtured other dreams. Now they had two children together, and he was scaling new heights. Sarah had no choice but to support him. She couldn't ever, ever go through that horror again.

Sarah walked over to her husband, took the glass from his hand and threw her arms around him.

"Maybe I'm wrong," she whispered. "I've been

exhausted. I'm not thinking straight. Heath, if you promise me it wasn't you, I'll believe you."

"I promise, it's not me. I'm devastated that you would ever think that. But at least you told me. Now we have a chance to fight back."

He pushed her away, then took her phone from the table, and started typing. She heard a *swoosh*.

"What did you just do?"

"I e-mailed the photo to myself," he said. "I know a computer forensics expert, from my work on the Disciplinary Committee. I'm going to show it to him, to see if I can figure out where it came from, and how it was faked. I need to know what I'm up against. And that way, just in case they do go public, we can be ready with a defense."

Heath would never give the photo to an expert unless he knew it was a fake. That gave her some confidence that he was telling the truth. But he was still fiddling with her phone. She leaned over to see what he was doing, just in time to watch the photo disappear from her screen.

"Did you—did you just delete that?"

"I have a copy now. There's no need for you to worry about this, Sarah. I have everything under control."

From the bedroom came the sound of Scottie wailing. Her baby needed her. She'd found the strength to confront Heath, and he had given her a reasonable explanation. If she had any remaining doubts, she wouldn't indulge them any further—not now, not without more credible evidence. Heath was right: People were out to get him, so why turn her life upside down over something that was probably a hoax to begin with? Her children were sick, and her husband was more mentally fragile than she'd realized. She had to be strong for them.

"I should go to Scottie," she said. She started to get up, but Heath stopped her with a touch.

"Thank you for trusting me, sweetheart. You won't regret it. All I ask is, if you start having doubts again, you come to me, so we can talk it out. Okay?"

"Yes. I promise."

Heath leaned in and kissed her lingeringly on the lips. With a relieved sigh, she kissed him back. It felt like coming home after a long and difficult journey. She went to take care of her son with a quiet heart.

35

From: HD1234@yahoo.com

To: Anonymouse@yahoo.com

January 14 at 9:15 p.m.

All right, who the fuck is this and what do you want? Leave my wife alone. You deal with me from now on. Do you have some kind of demand?

From: Anonymouse@yahoo.com

To: HD1234@yahoo.com

January 14 at 9:19 p.m.

Hi Heath. Yeah I know it's you even if you're not using Odell e-mail. You think that's gonna keep you safe, keep your name out of this? Not a chance. And yeah, that's you in the pic, but I guess you know that already. What a bad boy you are. 😏 As for who I am, think of me as a little mouse, or a fly on the wall. I see things, I know things. And what I wonder is, why you'd risk it all over that stupid slut Bel. She's nothing special, not even that pretty. Your poor wife—how very sad! You ask what I want. I'll think about that. In the meantime, I love watching you sweat this. You'll be hearing from me.

Xox,

Anonymouse

36

All through January, Bel led a double life. On the surface, she appeared to be a normal Odell student. She went to classes—including Mr. Donovan's English class. She studied for tests, wrote essays, handed in problem sets, got tutored. She played volleyball with a knee brace on, and did physical therapy twice a week. She went to meals, and sat with the motley crew of misfits that ate in the Quiet Nook, who'd gelled into something like a clique. Her surface life was tolerable, but it wasn't one she'd chosen for herself. Her dreams were consumed by the secret life she led with Heath.

That life required subterfuge. Nobody could ever know about them, he told her, and he seemed extra wired about that lately—maybe because he was in the running to become headmaster. Even the slightest whiff of scandal would torpedo his chances. He'd devised a private signal to set up their meetings. That way they didn't have to text or try to steal a moment to speak privately. A conversation could be overheard. A text left a record; he'd learned about that from the Skyler Stone lawsuit, when he consulted with a computer forensics expert. Records could be destroyed if you knew what you were doing, and Heath now knew what he was doing. He made her give him her phone, and he wiped it of any trace of him going back to when they first started communicating privately, around Thanksgiving.

Twice a week, on the days she did physical therapy, Bel was finished early, and could sneak away. If Heath could get free to see her on those days, he'd wear a red tie to class. Red—the color of roses, of hearts, of love. That was her signal to pay attention and wait for a coded message. He would make a list on the whiteboard of literary devices, or future assignments, or things that kids said in class—anything, really—and label the items on the list 1, 2, 3, 4 and A, B, C, D. Then he'd underline a letter and a number—as if just to emphasize a point as he spoke—to tell her when and where to meet him. The number he underlined told her what time he could meet her, and the letter told her where. "A" meant the parking lot behind the Alumni Gym—easy to get to, but exposed, and therefore risky. "D" meant the parking lot on Danbury Road. Heath liked that one better because there was little chance of being observed. But getting to it required Bel to walk out the back door of Founders' Hall, slip into the woods, and hike to the Danbury trailhead on the other side of the nature preserve. It could be difficult in the snow, especially with her knee. But she'd do it anyway, and she'd wait in the cold until he showed, as long as it took—a half hour, even an hour once. She didn't mind.

It was nearly February, which would normally be dead winter, but there had been an unseasonable thaw. The paths were slick and wet. The snow had melted all over campus, exposing bare brown lawns in need of tending. Heath signaled Bel to meet him at four o'clock at the Danbury Road lot. A chill rain fell as she left Founders' Hall through the seldom-used back exit, and hurried the fifty feet to the woods. As she slipped between the trees, darkness swallowed her. The afternoon was gray and blustery. Fortunately, the snow that had covered the ground since December was gone, except for patches here and there under the trees that never saw the sun. Icy trickles of rain dripped from the trees onto her hair, and she pulled the hood of her puffer jacket up. She'd gotten used to the woods when she ran cross-country, but then the other girls had always been within earshot, so she'd never felt alone. Now, hearing the drip of rain and the moan of the wind in the trees, Bel's heart raced, and she quickened her pace. She got to the crossroads, where the trail split, and paused to look at the wooden sign. The path to the left continued through the woods to the meadows and Lost Lake. That was one-third of a mile. The one to the right was a quarter mile, and went out to the trailhead on Danbury Road, which had a little parking lot. Heath would be waiting for her there.

As Bel read the sign, she heard a rustle behind her, and a strange prickle ran down the back of her neck.

But when she looked over her shoulder, nobody was there. She was being paranoid.

Bel set off toward the trailhead. A hundred feet down the path, she heard the rustle again. This time she was certain. She stopped abruptly, turning around slowly, a full 360 degrees, and scanning the woods. There was nothing. Nobody. But then the sound came again, from off to the side, and her eyes flew to it. She could've sworn she saw . . . *something*. What? A shape, a shadow. It was probably an animal, but it was enough to spook her. Feeling foolish, Bel turned toward the trailhead and took off at a slow jog, cursing herself for not wearing her knee brace. Without it, she didn't dare break into a sprint. The path was flat and clear, and she made it to the trailhead in a matter of minutes. She was pretty sure she'd left whatever-that-was behind, and breathed a sigh of relief. She should try to feel happy. The silver glint of Heath's Subaru was visible through the trees. He was there, waiting, and they would go to the motel. It would happen again. She slowed to a walk, catching her breath, wanting to remember this moment, right before they'd be together.

Then, behind her, she heard a ruckus in the woods, and stopped dead. That was no squirrel. Her skin crawled, and she took off in a burst of speed that sent pain shooting through her knee and down her leg. Right before she left the woods, she looked back over her shoulder and saw a figure slipping between the trees. She was certain now. It was a person, a human. Not an animal. Somebody had followed her. She emerged from the trees into the trailhead parking lot, and made a beeline for Heath's car, jumping in and slamming the door hard.

"What happened? You look like you saw a ghost," he said.

It wouldn't do to tell him she might've been followed. He wouldn't like that.

"I heard a noise," she said. "An animal."

He laughed, then stopped abruptly, glancing in the rearview mirror. "A car's coming. Get down."

She ducked into the passenger-side footwell, and rode down there the whole way to the motel.

Afterward, at the motel, Bel had a moment of melancholy, wondering why she was doing this. The sex was always rougher than she expected, and less fun. Yet she went through with it every time. There had been three times since that first time in the laundry room. When they did it, she would feel far away, like she didn't know him, didn't know herself. But afterward they would lie in bed and talk, and that was the good part, the part she waited for. The thing she lived for, really. Heath Donovan, the most beautiful man she'd ever seen, the teacher that every girl in school was mad for, would stroke her hair, kiss her eyelids, tell her things he told nobody else. She would listen to that voice, gaze into those eyes, and feel seen and listened to by him. That part was worth any sacrifice.

Heath was explaining to her something about the board of trustees. He was plotting to become the next headmaster.

"I don't understand," she said. "If you become headmaster, what happens to Dr. Barlow?"

"He gets put out to pasture."

"But he's been here, like, forever."

"That's just the point. Don't you see, Odell can't recover from the slipper mess with Barlow at the helm. He's tainted goods. The bad stuff all happened on his watch."

"That's true. You'd be way better. Everybody's in love with you. Dr. Barlow's old and kind of ugly," she said.

He smiled and kissed her ear. "My little love. You *would* think that, but the trustees have other considerations in mind when they make their selection. One of them is that the candidate have a sterling reputation. In other words, there can't be the faintest whiff of scandal about me. Do you hear what I'm saying?"

"Yes, you've told me that a million times, nobody can know about us. It's why you never text me anymore. It's why I never text you, either, or come up to you in the dining hall, like I did that time. I hate it, but I understand."

His face darkened, and he looked away. "About that night, there's something I have to ask you. Something serious."

Bel held her breath. Whenever he talked like this, she became terrified that he would end their affair, and she couldn't bear the thought of life here without him.

"Ask me anything," she said.

"The first night that you and I were together, down in the laundry room, was anybody else there?"

"Anybody else in the laundry room? That's ridiculous," Bel said, and laughed harshly.

He turned and looked at her sharply. Had the laugh been too much? Did she oversell it? Bel gazed back at him innocently, her mind replaying that moment when she saw a movement from the corner of her eye. And the time Rose taunted her that she had proof of her illicit relationship with Heath.

"You're sure?" he said, searching her face.

"I would have noticed. But why are you asking?"

"No reason."

He twined his fingers in her hair, leaned in close and started kissing her neck. Under the blanket, his hands traveled over her body. She went warm and liquid at his touch.

"You're a delight, an obsession, an addiction. But one that has to stay secret. If you ever have any reason to think somebody knows about us, you must tell me right away. You understand?"

He grabbed her hips under the covers and pulled her tight against him, his fingers digging into her flesh.

"Heath, you're hurting me," she said. But she wanted him, she did.

"Say yes."

"Yes."

"We've got half an hour before we need to go back," he said, his breath warm against her ear. "Let's not waste it. I'll go slow this time, I promise."

Late that night, Bel sat at her desk, finishing a problem set that was due in a matter of hours. Emma had gone to sleep long ago, and the room was dark, except for the glow from Bel's laptop. A soft tone sounded, and a message box popped up on the screen, informing her that she had an e-mail. From someone called *Anonymouse*.

Stupid name.

Bel assumed it was a prank from one of the geeks in the Quiet Nook. They were the types to think goofy stuff like that was funny. She was on their group chats now, and got looped in when they sent around group texts or e-mails. It was usually Harry Potter–themed, or *Game of Thrones*. She'd thought about asking to be left off because, really, they were such geeks. But they were the only friends she had left at this stupid school.

She ignored the e-mail, since she ought to get this problem set finished and grab a few hours' sleep. But then it occurred to her: What if it wasn't the Quiet Nook geeks? *Anonymouse*. The name, silly as it was, gave her a queasy feeling. She remembered Heath's nervousness this afternoon about the possibility of a third person in the laundry room. What had him so worried all of a sudden? He never explained. The connection, vague as it was, bothered her enough to distract her from the problem set.

She clicked on the e-mail.

"Lookee, somebody followed you, LOL," the subject line read, and she got a chill.

The noise in the woods had been real. She'd tried to put it out of her mind. But she'd been right to be afraid. She'd been followed. There was an attachment in the e-mail. Terrified, she held her breath, and opened it.

It was a photo, of Bel getting into Heath's car. The

shot was wide-angle and well-framed. You could see Bel's face clearly. She looked frightened, upset even. She remembered vividly how she'd felt in that moment—how she'd gotten spooked and ran, how her knee hurt and her breath came in gasps as she barreled toward Heath's car. Someone had been behind her in the woods. It wasn't her imagination, and it wasn't a coincidence. Somebody followed her, stalked her and photographed her.

But Bel wasn't the only subject of the picture. The license plate on Heath's car was plainly visible. You could see the back of his dark head in the driver's seat. You could just make out the blurry writing on the sign for the Danbury trailhead. You could see the muddy gravel of the parking lot, and the trees. A young female student, getting into a teacher's car in a deserted, off-campus parking lot. It was irrefutable evidence that they were meeting, in secret, in a way they shouldn't.

Rose. It had to be Rose who followed her. Over Christmas break, Rose had made that threat. She was going to expose them; she had proof. She never came out and said that her proof was a picture of them together, but wasn't it obvious? She'd photographed them once before, and now she was doing it again. Bel had been foolish not to take Rose seriously as a threat. Rose was a twisted person who'd always been bitterly jealous of Bel—of her closeness to their mother, her looks, her clothes, the fact that Grandma liked Bel better. You name it. It was crazy when you thought about it. What was there to be jealous of, after all? Bel wasn't happy (except maybe in those stolen moments with Heath, but not even then). Yet it seemed to be true. Rose was out to ruin everything that Bel cared about. Rose wanted her kicked out of Odell; that's why she'd snitched about the slipper thing. Instead of facing facts, Bel was weak enough to miss her sister, and think about making up with her. She'd been naïve, and let the situation fester. Now Rose had more evidence. She had to do something about it before Rose actually followed through and went public.

That would destroy Heath's career. And if that happened, she'd kill her.

37

With Skyler gone, Rose had a room to herself, but living alone was bleak and depressing. Rose couldn't get comfortable at school after all that had happened. Granted, the large-scale bullying had ended. Nobody threw toy rats into her room anymore, or made squeaking sounds when she walked by, or sent messages that snitches got stitches. But since the night that Brandon Flynn and Tessa Romano snuck up on her on a deserted path, she didn't sleep well, and constantly looked over her shoulder. She buried her unease by keeping busy. She studied hard, did lots of extracurriculars, got excellent grades and socialized frenetically at meals in the New, as if to convince herself that she had real friends.

That night, she'd been up late, studying for a French test. When the clock hit one, following a rule she'd made for herself to always get six hours' sleep before a test, she turned out the lights and got in bed. But she took her laptop with her, and reviewed flash cards on-line until her eyelids got heavy, and closed.

She was in the middle of a bad dream, being chased down a long hallway, when she felt a presence in the room and opened her eyes. Groggy with fatigue and stress, not sure if she was awake or in a lucid dream, she called out for Skyler, forgetting that Skyler was gone. There was no answer.

Rose turned toward the wall, and slept again. A minute passed or five or ten—she couldn't've said. She became aware that someone was standing over her bed, and rolled over to see a looming shape in the dark. This was real. She felt a hand beneath her blanket, sat up and screamed.

"Shut up!" the intruder said.

It was Bel. She'd grabbed something from on top of the blanket. Rose's laptop! Rose reached out to snatch it back. In the dark, she missed, and Bel ran out the door, taking it with her.

"What the *hell!*" Rose said.

What did Bel think she was doing? Stumbling out of bed, Rose got tangled in her blankets and stumbled, landing on her hands and knees with a *thud*. Why would Bel take her laptop? Did she just hate Rose so much that she wanted to sabotage her? All her work was on there. The French flash cards she'd made, the social studies essay that she'd spent all of yesterday afternoon working on. It was due third period; she had to get it back. Barefoot, Rose ran after her sister. In the hall, she saw the door to the landing swinging shut. Bel was heading for her own room on the third floor.

Rose sprinted up the stairs after her, blood pounding in her ears, full of rage. She ran down the hall, and heard the door to Bel's room slam. It must be three a.m. She'd wake up all of Moreland. Rose got to the door of Bel and Emma's room, panting. Rose shoved the door open. Bel stood at her desk with Rose's laptop open in front of her, paging through e-mails. She looked up at Rose. In the glow from the laptop, Rose saw sheer hatred on her sister's face.

"Where is it?" Bel said.

"Where's what?"

"You know. You fucking know."

"I don't know what you're talking about," Rose said, though in that instant she realized she did. The picture of Bel and Donovan in the laundry room—that's what Bel wanted. But why was she coming for it now, when Rose had told her about it more than a month ago? Okay, maybe not *told* her, but heavily implied.

"Yes, you do so. You know exactly what I'm talking about," Bel said.

"That's my laptop. I want it back. Give it to me."

"Come and get it," Bel said, stiffening like she was preparing for battle.

Emma sat up and rubbed her eyes. "What's going on?"

"Ask *her*," Rose said, advancing on her sister. "She stole my laptop. Give it back, Bel!"

"You followed me, you *bitch*. Where is that picture? You delete it right now or I swear, I'll kill you."

"Jesus, calm down both of you, before someone hears. Do you want to get in trouble?" Emma said.

Rose reached for the laptop just as Bel snatched it

off the desk. Rose grabbed the edge of the laptop, and for a moment they both held on to it, wrestling back and forth. Emma jumped out of bed, her mouth falling open in shock.

"Stop it. What is wrong with you?" Emma said.

Rose managed to wrest the laptop from Bel's grip, and bent over it, hugging it to her chest. Bel lashed out with her fist just as Emma stepped in between them, catching Emma on the side of the face.

"Ugh, you hit me. Are you crazy?" Emma said, her hand flying to her eye.

"Get out of the way," Bel said. "Give me that!"

Bel grabbed Rose by the hair. Rose yelped and lashed out blindly with one hand, gripping the laptop tightly with the other. Without warning, Bel kneed her in the stomach, and Rose doubled over in pain, retching. She let go of the laptop, and it fell to the floor with a clatter. Bel snatched at it, and Rose fell on top of her to stop her from running away with it. Bel grunted and writhed, trying to throw her off.

"Give it back or I'll kill you!" Rose said, tears welling in her eyes as she struggled to contain her sister.

"This is fucking crazy. I'm going to get Donovan," Emma said, her hand still over her eye.

"No!" Bel said. "Wait. I'll stop. I'm stopping."

Bel went limp beneath Rose. Rose didn't trust Bel, and stayed put.

"Get off me, you cow. I can't breathe," Bel said.

"Give me my laptop, and I'll get off you," Rose demanded.

"If you want the laptop, give me the picture."

"What is she talking about?" Emma said.

"I don't know. I don't care. I hope she dies down there."

"Come on, Rose. Get off me, *please*," Bel pleaded.

"Here, give *me* the laptop," Emma said, holding out her hand. "I'm a neutral party."

"Emma's not neutral," Bel said.

"Do you want me to let you go, or not?" Rose said. "Give it to Emma."

Slowly, Bel pushed the computer out from under her stomach. Emma leaned down and snatched it up, retreating a few feet, so she stood next to the door.

"Now, you both behave, or I'm going to get Donovan," Emma said, one hand on the doorknob.

"I don't care if you do," Rose said. "She's the one who's freaked out about that." But she rolled off her sister and sat up. She was exhausted, and tired of this folly.

They both got to their feet, breathing heavily, each watching the other warily.

"What is this picture that Bel wants so badly?" Emma asked Rose.

"A picture of her and Donovan. It proves they're having an affair."

"Oh my God. For real? I thought that was just malicious gossip," Emma said.

"It is gossip. It's a lie!" Bel said.

"If it's a lie, then why do you care so much about the picture?" Rose demanded.

"It's just a picture of me getting into his car, but you're going to twist it, and make it into something shameful. People are stupid enough to believe you."

"What? It is not a picture of you getting into his car," Rose said.

"You were getting into Donovan's car?" Emma asked, looking shocked.

"Yes, it is. You followed me," Bel said.

"I admit I followed you. But the picture's of the two of you in the laundry room, before Christmas break," Rose said.

Bel went pale. "Shit. You really have that? I didn't believe you," she said.

"I told you. But it's not on my laptop. It never was."

"Where is it? You have to delete it," Bel said. Her eyes looked wild, and her fists were clenched.

"I refuse to. That picture is my leverage to get you to stop the horrible thing you're doing," Rose said.

"Why do you give a shit what *I* do, Rose?"

"I don't. But I care if you ruin Mrs. Donovan's life. She's a wonderful person, who's been kind to me, and I won't let you hurt her. If you don't break things off with him, I'm going public with that picture."

"No. I don't believe you. If you were going to do that, you would've done it by now," Bel said, a desperate look in her eyes. "Right?"

"Maybe. But I'm not the only one who has that picture."

"Somebody else has it? Who? Is it *you*?"

Bel turned on Emma, who raised her free hand to proclaim innocence. "First I'm hearing of any of this."

"Then who? Please tell me. I'm begging you. Rose, you can't go public. It would be a huge mistake. It'll ruin everything."

"God, this is just like the slipper thing," Rose said. "You do something completely evil, then cry bloody murder that I told, like the whole problem was my fault."

"Who else has the picture? Did they follow me in the woods today? Tell me, you have to tell me," Bel said, distraught.

"Now you want me to tell, after months of calling me a tattle? No way," Rose declared triumphantly. "You're screwed, Bel. The whole world is going to know about you and Heath Donovan, and there's nothing you can do to stop it."

38

Transcript of Witness Interview conducted by Lieutenant Robert Kriscunas, State Police—Major Crime Unit, and Detective Melissa Howard, Odell NH, PD, with Miss Emma Kim (continued).

[INTERVIEW RESUMES]

Kriscunas: Are you ready to proceed, Miss Kim?

Kim: Yes. I called my mom to ask for advice. And I'm sorry, but she told me I need to be careful here. Not to get mixed up in things that are over my head.

Kriscunas: What does that mean? You don't want to talk to us anymore?

Kim: I can tell you the basics of what happened in this fight, but I'm not going to get into what it was about.

Kriscunas: I'm afraid I don't understand.

Kim: They were fighting over something that—that's just very sensitive, and my mom told me to mind my own business about it, okay? She says she doesn't want me gossiping about people in authority, that I could get in trouble. The whole school knows about this, anyway. An entire institution is keeping this secret. Why should it be up to me to tell?

Kriscunas: Tell us what? It's hard for me to evaluate your position, if I don't know what ballpark we're playing in.

Howard: Look, Bob, we know what this is about.

Kriscunas: We do?

Howard: Yes. Based on what Miss Kim said earlier, right before she went to call her mom, this fight between Bel and Rose was over Heath Donovan. The headmaster. Am I right?

Kim: I want to take that back. I just don't want to go there. Go ask someone else. Ask a faculty member. Ask Mrs. Donovan. I'm telling you, everybody knows about this, including her. But here's what I am willing to tell you about the fight. It was around three o'clock in the morning. I had a French test at eight o'clock, and I got woken up by the Enright twins—in my room—shouting and having an actual, violent physical altercation. They were struggling over a laptop. Apparently, Bel snuck into Rose's room while she was sleeping to steal it. Rose woke up and chased her back to our room, where they fought over it.

Howard: Why would Bel take Rose's laptop? Didn't she have her own?

Kim: She did, but there was something on Rose's laptop that Bel wanted.

Howard: What was it?

Kim: A photo.

Howard: A photo, having to do with Heath Donovan?

Kim: I can't talk about that.

Kriscunas: Were they fighting with words, or are we talking about actual violence?

Kim: Violence, yes. When I tried to intercede, Bel punched me right in the face. You see this? A black eye. It's faded now, but it was pretty bad. I've never been hit before in my life. Can you believe that, here at Odell? What a nutjob.

Howard: Bel was the aggressor in this fight?

Kim: Bel started it, by stealing Rose's laptop. When Rose tried to get it back—which frankly was justified, I mean, her schoolwork was on there—Bel got violent. She tried to punch Rose, and ended up hitting me in the face. Then she—I don't remember exactly, but I think she punched Rose in the stomach. Then the two of them were down on the floor rolling around, wrestling over it. Rose ended up on top. She was sitting on Bel. Rose is—I won't say she's heavy, but she's a solid girl. Bel kept saying she was choking, she couldn't breathe, and Rose said, "I hope she dies down there." It was insane. I got them to stop, but it wasn't easy. I mean, these girls were threatening to kill each other, and to me, it sounded like they meant it.

39

From: Anonymouse@yahoo.com
To: HD1234@yahoo.com
January 31 at 11:46 p.m.
A fun pic for you!
Hi Heathie. It's your little mouse friend again. Told you I
have eyes and ears everywhere. Some of them happen to
be kickass photographers. I hope you enjoy this great pic of
Bel Enright getting into your car. Personally I love the fram-
ing of this bc you can see Bel's face and your license plate
at the same time. Naughty naughty. More to come.
Love,
Anonymouse

From: HD1234@yahoo.com
To: Anonymouse@yahoo.com
February 1 at 12:11 a.m.
A fun pic for you!

I'll ask you again. What do you want? If you want to make a deal, tell me. Better yet, come out and meet me right now. If not, I'll come looking for you, and that won't be a happy ending.

From: Anonymouse@yahoo.com
To: HD1234@yahoo.com
February 1 at 12:14 a.m.
A fun pic for you!
Yeah, nice try. Meet you, alone, at night—I'm not stupid. You'll be hearing from someone soon with my demands. They won't say it's the mouse, but you're a smart boy, you'll figure it out.

40

February

Bel was crossing the Quad, heading to her fifth-period class in Founders' Hall, when a text from Heath lit up her phone. It was a raw afternoon, blustery, with temperatures in the thirties and ice-blue skies. She stopped in the middle of the path to read the text, as students streamed by her on all sides.

"I need to see you. As soon as you can get away, now if possible," the text read.

It was exactly the sort of message Bel dreamed of getting from Heath, full of desire and urgency, all the more precious since he'd gotten paranoid about texting her recently. It made her heart skip a beat and her breath come faster. She was surprised that he'd violated his own rule, but she was too thrilled to question it. She immediately wrote back.

Just say when ♥♥♥ B

ASAP at the trailhead parking lot, came the reply, within seconds.

That would mean cutting fifth period, which would earn her an attendance demerit. Bel didn't really care about that. But meeting at the parking lot was a bad idea. Rose knew that was their spot. She'd followed them there before, and had e-mailed her a picture to prove it. Not that Bel planned to tell Heath about that. It would upset him too much.

Why pkg lot—r we driving? she asked.

No—need to see you ASAP, office too risky, he replied.

There were other places they could see each other that would work just as well, and involve less risk of being seen. They could meet at Lost Lake, at the beautiful hikers' shelter that faced the water. It was built of bleached cedar, and smelled of pine. Bel loved that place, and often daydreamed of spending time alone with Heath there.

Pkg lot 2 visible. How abt Lost Lake shelter? 15 mins, she texted.

He said yes, and her heart leapt. Bel shoved her phone in her jacket pocket and continued toward Founders'. Once everybody else was in class, she'd slip out the back door and into the woods. She slowed her pace, pretending to stare at her phone, letting the other kids pass her by.

"Bel! *Mia bella,*" a voice called from behind her.

She turned. Zachary Cuddy, just what she needed.

"Hey, Zach," she said, her lack of enthusiasm apparent in her voice.

"Where're you headed?" he asked, smiling ingratiatingly.

"History class. You?"

"English. I have Renfrew. She's a bore," he said.

"I know. You told me that before."

"Did I? Hey, we should hang out. Are you busy after class?"

"Since when do you want to hang out with me? I though you hated me because of the Snapchat. Remember?"

"I didn't get in trouble, neither did you. It's water under the bridge. And there's something urgent I need to discuss with you."

"It's not a good time."

He looked positively stricken, way more than was justified by her refusal. She was tired of being hounded by Zach, but he never seemed to get the message. They'd reached the grand limestone steps that led up to Founders' Hall. Bel mounted them alongside Zach, pretending for his benefit that she was going to class. They joined the crowd flooding through the enormous double doors. At this rate, she would be late to meet Heath.

"Gotta go, Zach," Bel said as they entered the echoing marble foyer.

She waved dismissively, marching toward the back of the building. But he was right beside her.

"Wait a minute, where are you going?" Zach said. "You're in Watson's history class, right? That's on the third floor."

"How do you even know that?"

"You must've told me at some point."

"No, I didn't. Back off."

"I'm just curious as to why you're heading in the wrong direction."

"I'm going to the bathroom, okay? Satisfied? You're creeping me out."

"Sorry."

The fifth-period bell rang.

"Did you hear that? You'd better get to class," Bel insisted.

"You should, too. You'll be late," Zach said.

"Jesus. Get lost! Do I have to scream in order to get rid of you?"

"Fine," he muttered, finally turning around and leaving her alone.

Bel lurked near the girls' bathroom, waiting until the halls emptied and fell silent. Then she ducked out the back door and ran to the woods. The trees closed around her, and she breathed easier. It was dark in there, and peaceful, smelling of rain and decaying leaves, and she was going to see the one person in the world who cared about her. Bel had a secret fantasy about running away with Heath. If she told him about it, he'd just get solemn and condescending, and explain how it could never be. So she kept it to herself. In her fantasy, they were outlaws. They stole an old camper, and drove on back roads all the way to California. She showed him the places she had loved as a child—the beach, the mountains—and they slept under the stars, and cooked over campfires. But her dream would never come true. It was too perfect.

At the sign at the crossroads, she went left. The path

was narrow and uneven, and her knee ached. But soon she emerged into the wide meadow surrounding Lost Lake. The path cut through a flat, open area of sodden grass, running down to the water's edge, where it continued around the lake's perimeter. The shelter where she would meet Heath was visible now in the distance, surrounded by a beautiful stand of white birch trees. She hadn't been there in a while. Last time, the lake was frozen solid, but with this weird thaw they were having, it had started to melt. Ice bobbed and floated in thick snow-covered chunks.

As Bel approached the shelter, Heath stepped out and scanned the horizon. He beckoned her, then stepped back into the shadow. She ran the last twenty feet, ready to throw herself into his arms, but his expression when she got there put her off.

"What's the matter?" she said.

"Did anybody see you?"

"No. I was careful."

"Good. Have a seat. There's something we need to discuss," he said.

This was not the welcome she'd been dreaming of.

The shelter was a rough wooden structure with a roof and three sides. The front of it was open to the air, and provided a lovely view of the lake. A built-in bench ran along the back wall. Bel sat down on it, and Heath sat beside her. He took her hands, but not in a romantic way, more like he was preventing her from running away.

"I've tried to deal with this without bringing it up to you, because I didn't want to alarm you. But something's happened, and we need to talk."

"What is it?" she asked.

"A while ago, somebody sent my wife a picture of us having sex in the laundry room. Was that you? Did you do that?"

He spoke matter-of-factly. But there was a coldness to his tone that chilled her. She wondered what he would do if the answer was yes. Fortunately, she wouldn't find out.

"Me? N-no. Of course not. Why would I?" she said.

"Some misguided idea of breaking up my marriage. Having me to yourself."

"God. No. That's crazy. Heath, I would never do that."

He stared her in the face stonily. Then he breathed out. "I believe you."

"Well, yeah. You should. But—what happened? What did your wife say?"

"The image quality was poor. I was able to convince her that it wasn't me in the picture. That might not be true the next time."

"The *next* time?"

"That's right. There's a second picture, of you getting into my car. It hasn't been sent to Sarah yet, or I would know. But somebody followed us, and photographed us, and is trying to hurt us by exposing our relationship. Just because they haven't succeeded yet, doesn't mean they'll stop trying. Who is it?"

Of course Bel knew who was doing this. It had to be Rose. She'd admitted following them in the laundry room. She'd obviously followed Bel into the woods, too, and snapped the picture of her getting into Heath's car. But Bel couldn't tell Heath that. Not with the way he was behaving. He'd explode.

"Who did it, Bel?"

"I don't know," she said, but her voice was shaky, and she could see he didn't believe her.

"I think you do know. It must be a student. Somebody close to you, or someone who has a grudge against you." He tightened his grip on her hands. "This isn't a game. We have a problem, and we have to take care of it. Who sent the picture, Bel?"

"It—it might've been Rose who took it."

"Might have been? Or it was?"

"She said she had a picture like that. I didn't believe her."

"Which picture?"

"I don't know, it's confusing. I think both."

"When did she tell you this?"

"Last night."

"That night in the laundry room was nearly two months ago. If Rose took that picture, why would she only tell you now? Are you lying to me?"

"No, I swear."

"You were lying a minute ago when you said you didn't know who sent the picture."

"Stop. You're hurting my wrists. You're scaring me."

Heath let go of her hands. "I'm sorry. This subject is very upsetting."

Bel had tears in her eyes. She'd never seen him like this. He was terrifying this way.

"We were having a fight," Bel said. "That's why Rose brought up the picture. She hadn't done anything with it in all that time. She was just using it to threaten me."

"Threaten you how?"

"I don't know. Show it to someone, maybe."

"Jesus Christ," he said, dropping his head into his hands.

"No, it's okay. We made up. Rose and I are friends again. She didn't do anything yet, and she won't now, I'm sure."

Better to lie to him than have him this upset. He looked up, but his eyes were still troubled.

"I can't rely on that, Bel. The board of trustees meets in a week to vote on the new headmaster. I can't have any problems, don't you see?"

"Yes. Of course."

"No, I don't think you do. I need that picture. I want it deleted. Where is it? Is it on her phone?"

"I don't know. I never saw it."

"You have to get it."

"I mean, all right. I can try."

"Not *try*. You *have* to get it. Do you understand the magnitude of this problem?" He glared at her like there was something wrong with her. "No, you know what, Bel? Forget it. I would be foolish to trust you to handle this situation. Have Rose come out here. I'll talk to her myself."

"Come here? Now?"

"Not now. Tonight."

"Won't that be—awkward?"

He laughed bitterly. "*Awkward*? For Chrissakes, this is what I get for sleeping with a dumb kid. Your sister is going to blackmail me with this photograph, and you're worried it'll be awkward?"

"I really don't think she would blackmail you, Heath."

"You just told me she threatened to do exactly that to you."

"No, not exactly. I mean, sort of. But—"

"I don't have time for this nonsense, Bel. I'm going to tell you what to do, and you're going to do it. Do you hear me?"

Her hands were shaking. "All right."

"Here's the deal. You make up a story that will convince Rose to meet you here tonight, at this shelter. I don't care what you say. Just make it convincing, and whatever you do, don't mention the photos. And don't mention my name. Got it?"

"Okay. What time should I tell her?"

"After check-in, once it's dark. I'll send you a text with the time." He paused. "That reminds me. Give me your phone."

She handed him her phone, and told him her passcode. He deleted their texts from earlier.

"Do you happen to know your sister's passcode?" he asked, casually.

"Why do you need that?"

"Just in case she refuses to delete the photo. I might have to do it for her."

"Do it for her? How? What do you mean?"

"I mean, I might have to take her phone and delete the photo."

"You won't—" She began, but she was afraid to ask the terrible question that had formed in her mind.

"Won't what?" he said, standing up next to her.

"You wouldn't . . . *hurt* Rose, would you?"

"Of course not, baby. I just want to have an honest,

reasonable conversation with her, in the hope I can convince her to delete the photo. That would be in everybody's best interests, don't you agree?"

She breathed out in relief, realizing only then that she'd been holding her breath. "Yes. You're right. Thank you," Bel said.

"What is Rose's passcode?"

"I know what it used to be, like, a long time ago. When we were close. We don't talk much lately."

"What was it before?"

"When we were younger, her lucky number was seven. It was four sevens. I don't know if she changed it."

"Let's hope she didn't. Thank you, little love, thank you for trusting me," he said.

Heath put a finger under her chin and tilted her face toward his.

"I'm sorry if I was short with you. I've been under a lot of stress. Forgive me?" he said.

He leaned in and kissed her tenderly. At the touch of his lips, her fears melted like ice on the lake. Heath cared about her, and so long as Bel did as he said, everything would be all right.

41

Because of her awful fight with Bel, Rose's friends were treating her with a noticeable reserve, almost as if they were afraid of her. Emma had obviously told everyone that the fight got violent, as if that was Rose's fault at all, in the slightest. Bel was the one who'd snuck into Rose's room in the dead of night, stole her computer with all her important work on it, then punched and pummeled Rose when she (quite understandably) tried to retrieve her property. Bel was the dangerous, unstable sister. Rose was the studious, quiet one, the good citizen, the reliable friend. But nobody seemed to see that. Kids kept their distance now. Not just now. *Again*. Just when Rose had gotten past the trouble over the slipper incident. Bel had started that one, too, yet Rose wound up taking the blame. That happened every single time, throughout her entire life. It was so unfair.

At dinner on Tuesday night, Rose once again sat at the Moreland table, only to find her so-called friends politely ignoring her. She blinked back tears, not wanting anyone to see how hurt she was. But she wouldn't sit here and suck it up for longer than absolutely necessary. She'd go to the library, and study by herself until check-in. She gulped down her meat loaf and green beans, then rose and said a terse good-bye.

Rose bused her tray and went to find her coat. Zach Cuddy stood near the coatracks, like he was waiting, or watching for something. He'd been avoiding her, too, though for a reason that had nothing to do with her fight with Bel. He caught sight of her now, and turned away.

"I see you over there, Zach," Rose called. "Don't try to sneak away."

"I'm not sneaking."

"Yes, you are," she said, coming up to him. "You've been avoiding me."

"That's nuts, Enright. I deny that completely."

But he *had* been avoiding her, and she knew why. He owed her an explanation, and he obviously had nothing to report.

The night that Zach stopped Brandon Flynn and Tessa Romano from threatening Rose on the path, she was feeling shaky and vulnerable. He took her to the library, and bought her a cup of hot chocolate from the vending machine. They found some cozy chairs in a quiet corner, and he sat with her as she calmed down. He was so attentive, so protective, that her qualms about confiding in him evaporated. That was before her big fight with Bel, when Rose's main thought was to get Donovan to leave her poor sister alone. She made the mistake of showing Zach the photo of Bel and Donovan having sex in the laundry room. He stared at it with such rage that he almost scared her. His voice as he promised to take care of Donovan left Rose no doubt that he'd do something about it. If anything, she feared he'd do something stupid. But instead, it appeared he had done nothing. It had been more than a week since she gave him the photo. As of last night, when they had their huge fight, Bel was still involved with Donovan. So, what gives?

"Zach, I've messaged you at least four times to tell me what's going on about that photo. You ignore me."

Rose had done more than just message Zach repeatedly. She'd lurked near classrooms where she knew he'd be, gone to meals at times he liked to go, looking to bump into him. But he'd developed a sixth sense for when she was nearby. He always managed to leave her staring at his back as he beat a hasty retreat. Not this time.

Zach looked about jerkily. "Jesus, shut up. Somebody might hear."

"Nobody's listening. And if they are, I don't care. I trusted you, and you did nothing. Except stalk my sister."

"You're mental."

"She told me about the second photo. Of her getting into Donovan's car. Tell me that wasn't you. What game are you playing, Zach?"

He grabbed her arm and pulled her behind the coats. There was an odd look in his eyes.

"The second photo? How did Bel know about that?"

"I have no idea. I assumed you told her."

"Where is she now?" he asked. "She hasn't come to dinner yet."

"Is that why you're skulking there? Waiting for Bel?"

"I'm not *skulking*," he said indignantly. "I just need to know where she is. I have to ask her something."

"What about confronting Donovan with the sex picture? When are you going to do that?" Rose demanded.

"Will you keep your voice down?" he said, in an angry whisper. "That picture from the laundry room sucks, Rose. You can't even see their faces."

"That's why you haven't done anything?"

"We need better evidence if we want to move against Donovan. And that's not the only problem. Something's weird with my phone. I think maybe it's bugged. I think Donovan's on to me."

"You're wigging out, Zach. No, wait. You're using this, as an excuse to follow Bel around. If I gave a shit about her, I might worry about her having a crazy stalker. But I'm done with her, and I'm done with you," Rose said, grabbing her parka from the rack. She shrugged into it, and headed for the door. "See ya," she said.

Outside, the weather had changed yet again. This climate made her head spin. The day had dawned chilly, blustery and clear. In the late afternoon, the sky clouded over, and began to snow, in wet, heavy flakes that quickly coated the trees and the lawns. A half hour ago, when she'd entered the dining hall, Odell had looked like a winter wonderland. But while she'd been inside, a warm front had moved in. The air was balmy now, and the snow was melting fast, giving off a strange, wispy mist. Rivulets of water dripped from the eaves of buildings, and the fog was thickening. It was almost eerie. Rose decided to skip the library. She went straight back to Moreland, where she studied in her room until eight, then went down to the common room for check-in. She was on her way back upstairs, when her phone buzzed. She saw with surprise that she had a Facebook message from Bel.

"I need to talk to you," was all it said.

Rose went back to her room, and sat at her desk, staring at the message, thinking about what to say. She'd just about decided not to reply when the phone buzzed again, with a single-word message this time.

"Please," Bel had written.

"Why should I?" Rose wrote back.

"We're sisters. I'm sad at how things are."

Rose had been sad about that for a while now, wishing things could change. But after that fight last night, she was so angry that she didn't know if she could get past it. Something felt different, like maybe she'd given up on Bel for real this time.

"Used to be sad, now just pissed," she wrote. "People blame me bc of u, they think I'm crazy bc of our fight."

"Rose, please. I'm desperate. Can you come to the shelter at Lost Lake now please pretty please," Bel wrote.

"Are you crazy? It's dark, and I don't go out of bounds," she wrote, using Odell slang for leaving your dorm after check-in. "If ur there now, ur out of bounds too so u better come back or I'm telling."

"I can't come back."

That gave Rose pause. "Why not?" she wrote.

"BC of him," Bel replied.

"Who him? Donovan?" Rose asked.

"Yes. I need ur help."

She paused. Was it possible that Bel was truly in trouble? That she was involved in something with Mr. Donovan that somehow put her in danger? Or was this just some scam, a way to seek revenge by getting Rose to leave the dorm, and get in trouble.

"Things are so bad, just come, I need u," Bel wrote.

Rose didn't reply. Yes, there was something seductive about being asked for help. But she didn't trust Bel. How could she, when they'd come to physical blows? She still ached from where her sister punched her in the stomach. Rose waited, trying to decide what to do. Her phone lit up again.

"Pls—I'm scared," Bel had written.

The message gave Rose a chill. She was about to message back, when the green light next to Bel's name blinked off. *Active 1m ago*, Facebook said.

"Bel????" Rose wrote.

She waited, her heart pounding. There was no answer.

Rose always followed the rules. She would normally never consider leaving the dorm after check-in without a pass from a teacher. Sneaking out was a disciplinary offense, and she planned to graduate from this school without a single black mark on her record. Plus, she didn't like the woods around Odell. They were thick and dark and spooky, even in the light of day. The thought of walking into them at night, in the cold and fog, was horrible to her. And yet . . . as the minutes ticked away, as Rose messaged Bel several times more and received no reply, as she dialed Bel's phone and got only voicemail, she began to think she had no choice. Bel was the only family she had left in the world—other than Grandma, who didn't think much of Rose, and would think even less if she failed to help her sister. She had to find Bel.

Rose put her coat on. Then she had second thoughts, and took it off again. Bel couldn't be trusted. This was a scam. Bel was trying to get Rose in trouble, or get her alone, in order to steal Rose's phone, and get that photo. Rose shouldn't fall for it. She should look out for herself, and stop worrying about Bel. Everything that happened to Bel was her own fault anyway.

But what if Bel was in real trouble?

Rose could go, but go *prepared*. She would proceed carefully. Check things out each step of the way, before proceeding further. Be on alert, in case this actually was some kind of setup. She entered the number for Odell Security into her phone so it was ready to dial at a moment's notice. Her phone already had a flashlight, but she also downloaded a compass, and a map of the Odell grounds and the adjacent nature preserve. Then she put on her coat.

She was almost ready. Just one more thing. She needed a weapon. Something sharp, to defend herself with if things went bad.

42

Rose crept down the stairs and paused on the first-floor landing. It was milk-and-cookies night, and cheerful voices emanated from the common room. The smell of Mrs. Donovan's chocolate-chip cookies wafted into the hall, and Rose felt a pang of longing. She wished she could go to Mrs. Donovan now, eat a cookie, share her troubles. Right, and say what? *Your husband is a monster. He has my sister under his sway. I think she's trying to lure me into the woods. I want to blackmail them, but I'm too much of a wimp.* Things were so far beyond that. All Rose could do was sigh as she tiptoed down the hall and out the front door of Moreland.

On the Quad, the fog had grown even thicker, eerily backlit by the full moon. She hoped it would give her cover for sneaking out, and make it less likely she'd get caught. In the event that she did, she had a story ready. She was on her way to do layout for the lit mag. Rose's reputation as dependable and levelheaded would give her some leeway. It was unlikely any teacher would demand that she produce a pass.

Avoiding the path down the center of the Quad, Rose clung to the sides of the buildings as she made her way toward Founders' Hall. The perimeter of the Quad was dotted with gracious iron lampposts. They gave a yellow light that looked viscous against the fog. The dorms lining both sides of the Quad were fuzzier than usual, as the glow from their windows dissipated in the mist. When Rose passed Founders', and reached the open field behind it, the lights disappeared completely, and the night closed in. She reached the place where the path passed into a dense wall of trees, and lost her nerve. The fog was collected in patches on the ground, and hung in the air. Now that her eyes had adjusted, she could see— somewhat—by the light of the moon. But the natural sounds of the night were strangely distorted. The dripping of water, the rustling of branches came at her from all sides. Rose thought she heard the crunch of footsteps behind her and whirled, her heart racing, to find nobody there.

She was imagining things.

She took out her phone and turned on the flashlight. Fog caught in its beam, swirling like smoke. But the cheery shine gave her some comfort. She took a deep breath, squared her shoulders, and entered the woods.

Mist from the hollows under the trees engulfed her clinging to her eyelashes, dampening her hair. A strange smell—cold and metallic—filled her senses. There was a chill in here that went beyond temperature. It floated in the air, penetrating her clothes, getting into her bones. She forced herself to put one foot in front of the other, using her phone to get her bearings, navigating in the direction of the crossroads. She couldn't afford to miss the turn. The trees were tall as buildings and met overhead, blocking the moonlight that had guided her out on the field. She kept the flashlight beam trained down at the ground in order to avoid tripping on the thick roots and sharp rocks that jutted underfoot. But that meant she couldn't see beyond its beam. If she somehow missed the sign for the turnoff, she'd wander deep into the woods, and be lost, as the night closed in, as temperatures plunged. She might die of exposure, or be attacked by a wild animal.

She could still find her way out if she turned back now.

Then just ahead, she saw the sign, and walked up to it, shining the flashlight directly on it. The sign lit up, and leached light from the path around her, making everything else seem black in comparison. LOST LAKE, 1/3 MI, the sign read. The very name seemed ominous.

Rose couldn't do it. She simply couldn't. She turned around, and took a step back toward campus, toward Founders' Hall and the lights of the Quad. Then she saw it. The figure of a person, on the path in the distance, standing between her and the exit from the woods. Saw *him*—from the height, it was a him. He moved toward her, and she heard the sound of feet crunching on icy ground. A man was following her. Her skin crawled.

"Who—who's there?" she said.

The figure froze in place, and said nothing. Then the clouds shifted, and she could no longer see the figure

amidst the trees. *Was* it a person, or were her eyes playing tricks? But no—she'd heard the crunch of footsteps. That, she could not have been imagining.

"Is anybody there?" she said, but her voice, shaking
with fear, was barely audible.

Terrified to get any closer to the shape, Rose stood
rooted to the path. Then suddenly, she heard a scream
from behind her. A long, thin shriek that rang out and
hung in the fog-thick air, making all the fine hairs on
her body stand on end. The scream was definitely human, not an animal. And it sounded like her sister.

Rose grabbed the weapon from her pocket, whirled
and bolted toward Lost Lake. She forced herself not to
look over her shoulder for the figure in the woods. But
she didn't need to. The crashing sound behind her told
her he was real, and he was following her. Ahead in the
distance she saw a spectral glow. The opening to the
meadow wasn't far. She had to make it to the meadow
before he caught her. She had to get to Bel.

Rose ran flat out, her flashlight beam bouncing wildly
off the trees. Within seconds, she'd stumbled on a root,
and went down hard on her hands and knees. She got to
her feet, stunned and in pain, but she was too late. He
was already on her. He grabbed her from behind. He
was wiry and strong. She screamed, but he clapped his
hand over her mouth. She jerked sideways, got her arm
free, and lashed out with her blade, making contact. He
cried out in pain and let her go. She saw his outline in
the moonlight.

"You fucking bitch," he said, an edge of hysteria in
his voice.

"*Zach*? Are you crazy? What the hell are you doing?" Rose said. She was breathing hard, her heart thundering.

"You cut me. I'm bleeding. I could cut you, too," he said, clutching his hand.

"We have to find Bel. Did you hear that scream?" she said, struggling to catch her breath.

"Screw her. She deserves what she gets. I'm sick of you both."

His tone terrified her. Rose backed away, and then turned toward the opening to the meadow, expecting that he would try to stop her. But he didn't. Instead he turned, as if to leave. Rose walked a few steps, putting distance between them. Twenty feet ahead, she stumbled out into the open, onto ground squishy from the melting snow.

The moon was bright, but this close to the water, the fog was thicker. Her flashlight reflected back at her, like she was swimming in clouds. Her breath, harsh in her throat, made it hard to hear. She knew from having been here before that the lake was straight ahead, but she couldn't see it. She thought the scream had come from that direction, but there had been no sound since then—at least, not that she'd been able to hear over her struggle with Zach. Was it Bel who'd screamed? Was she still out here? Or—God forbid, had something happened to her?

Then Rose saw a light up ahead, bouncing in the fog. It was a flashlight beam. Somebody was up there. For a split second, the beam picked out a stand of white birch trees, and the side of the wooden shelter, and Rose knew where she was. Bel had originally asked to meet at that shelter. Maybe she was still there. Rose walked forward. The bouncing flashlight had disappeared in the mist, but her own flashlight bounced along in front of her.

"Bel?" she called. "Bel?"

The lake was at her feet, to the left. She saw the water, black and oily as it caught a glint of moonlight, and heard it lapping at the shore. The fog was so thick here that it seeped into her lungs, making her sputter and cough. Suddenly, she was face-to-face with the wooden shelter. She had almost walked into it. She went inside. There was nobody there. She shone her light all around. A dark spatter marred the back wall. She walked over to it and examined it under the light. Then she took off her glove and touched it. Her finger came away wet, and crimson. She started to shake with terror.

"Bel?" she said, but it came out a whisper.

Rose's entire body shook with panic. She stepped out of the shelter, onto the path. Then she saw it. The *thing*, at the edge of the lake. A lump, a mound, something unnatural pushing down the grass. She took a step closer. The moon escaped from behind a cloud, and she saw clearly now. She saw her sister's face, white and still, the long hair fanned out, the many rents in her jacket where the knife had gone in, the darkness of blood in the snow all around her. Rose saw a glint of silver in the snow, reflecting the moon. Instinctively, she reached for it, then stared down in numb horror at a large knife, covered in blood. She held it in her hand, not wanting to understand what it meant. Rose dropped to her knees beside Bel's inert body, a strange keening sound coming from her own throat. She knelt over her sister, gathered her close, whispered.

"Please, Bel, please, wake up. Bel, please, please, wake up."

She waited. But Bel didn't move. She put her cheek to her sister's nose and mouth. Nothing. Not a whisper of breath escaped. Had this evil knife taken her sister's life? But a knife didn't act on its own. There was someone standing behind her. He'd been there for a minute or two, but she hadn't allowed herself to know that. The hair on the back of her neck stood up. She was paralyzed with fear, like in a nightmare, and couldn't turn to look. He took a step back, and she heard the sound of a solid object whizzing through the air, coming at her. As if it was happening to someone else, Rose thought that this was the man who'd murdered her sister, and now he was coming for her. Pain exploded in her head, at the same moment that her heart exploded, because she knew now, she knew for certain.

Bel is dead, she's dead, she's dead!

part
two

. . . .

43

She'd picked up a second job working as a dispatcher for the Odell Security Department three nights a week, on the four-to-midnight shift. She liked it because it was quiet, and she could sit down the whole time. Her job as a cashier at the Food Giant had her on her feet all day. She answered the phones, took down information, and relayed it over the radio to the security cruiser on duty. The calls were always routine—lost valuables, a car speeding on Campus Drive, that sort of thing. Staying awake was the biggest challenge.

The security office was off on its own, across the enormous parking lot from the Alumni Gym, in a one-room brick building that backed onto the woods. It was an open plan inside, with desks for the chief and the two officers. She sat at the reception desk, right when you walked in. On her shift, there was only her and the one security officer who worked the late shift. He was a retired cop from Massachusetts, nice enough guy for a big-city type. He came in twice a night for breaks, and they would chat. The rest of the time she was alone. The building was old, and it creaked something awful on windy nights. Crazy thing, the door didn't lock. A lot of buildings on the Odell campus were like that—no locks—because it was so safe here. Supposedly. The fact was, it made her nervous, being there alone at night.

About ten o'clock, the wind kicked up. It came through the old windows in places, making an eerie, whining sound. She turned up the space heater to fight off the draft, and draped her coat over her knees. She'd forgotten her book at home, and her phone was out of juice so she couldn't check Facebook. With nothing to do, and the heat turned up, she found herself nodding off.

Wouldn't do to have the officer come in and find her sleeping. She got up from her chair at the reception desk, and went to the kitchenette at the back of the office. The kitchenette was really a just a counter with a microwave, a coffeepot, and a mini-fridge. The officer would be coming in in the next hour, so she made a fresh pot. She was just stirring some creamer into her cup when she heard a noise behind her.

"You're back early—" she said, turning as she spoke.

She froze. A girl stood there, covered in blood. It was on her face, in her hair, on her coat, on her pants, like something out of a Stephen King novel. Slowly, the girl raised her hands. In one of them, she held a large kitchen knife, slick and red with blood. The dispatcher opened her mouth to scream. Her throat worked, but no sound came out. She thought she might wet her pants. The girl took a step toward her.

"Put the knife down! Get back!" the dispatcher said, finding her voice.

She held her cup of coffee in front of her, the hot liquid her only weapon. The girl swayed on her feet, her eyes oddly fixed and dilated.

"So much blood," the girl said, and collapsed in a heap on the floor.

44

It was eleven-thirty when Heath got home. Sarah had left the bedroom door ajar, so she would hear him come in. She was in bed, pretending to sleep. But she'd been lying in the dark for more than an hour, and hadn't closed her eyes.

Sarah hadn't gone to dinner tonight because the kids were still recuperating from that awful flu. She'd subsisted on grilled cheese and canned soup and milky tea for the past four days, as she cared for them. She texted Heath around dinnertime to ask him to bring her some dinner from the dining hall. That was at least five hours ago. He never replied.

There was a milk-and-cookies social in the common room tonight. Sarah had baked for it when the kids went down for their naps in the afternoon. She'd been planning to host, and hadn't arranged for any other faculty member to cover for her. Heath knew that. He was supposed to come home to watch the kids. When she still hadn't heard from him by quarter-to-seven, she dialed his cell. It went to voicemail.

"Uh, hey, it's me. I have to go to milk and cookies. Where are you? Call me."

Ten minutes later, she still hadn't heard from him. She dialed his office phone. No answer. She put on a clean shirt, and some lipstick. It was past the kids' bedtime. She'd been planning for Heath to put them down. She couldn't leave them, not even to go down the hall. She tried getting them into the stroller in their pajamas. Scottie whined and fussed. Harper fought her, bouncing up and down, and kicking. Sarah was breathless and exhausted by the time she got them strapped in. She put the trays of cookies in the bin under the stroller, and rolled down the hall to the common room. She'd have to ask Rose Enright to take the kids right back to the apartment before they melted down completely.

There were about twenty girls in the common room tonight. But Rose was not among them.

Neither was Bel.

Sarah stood there looking around the room like a fool, wondering where Bel Enright was, and if she was with her husband. She'd been lying to herself about the photo. That was Heath; she knew his body too well to keep denying it. If the girl in the picture was Bel, that meant Heath was involved with a minor. That wasn't just an affair, or Sarah's personal tragedy. It was a crime. But she had no evidence. You couldn't see the girl's face, or any more of her body than one leg, wrapped around him. And besides, Sarah didn't even have the photo anymore, since Heath deleted it.

What was her fear based on, other than paranoia and gossip run amok in the hothouse environment of this crazy school?

The head of the math department, Pat Banks, had been threatening for some time to come to the Moreland social to sample Sarah's famous chocolate-chip cookies. Of course, she had to pick tonight to show up, when Sarah could hardly think straight and found it impossible to make simple small talk. Pat, with her brittle manner and thin, ascetic face, was not the motherly type, but she watched Sarah with worried eyes, and eventually found a moment to draw her aside.

"What's wrong?" Pat said. "If you're feeling ill, I can take over."

"No, no, I'm fine."

"Sarah, you don't look well. I know you've been nursing those kids for days. Where's your husband? Why isn't he here to help?"

"I'm not sure. Maybe he had a meeting and forgot to tell me," Sarah said, and her eyes filled with tears.

"Come outside," Pat said.

They stepped into the hall.

"What's wrong? This is more than fatigue. You're not happy about Heath being in contention for headmaster, are you? I know it's a sacrifice."

Sarah took a deep breath. She could continue floundering in the dark, or she could aggressively seek information. If Heath was really having an affair with a student, if the whole campus knew about it, but wasn't willing to tell her, maybe she should do the obvious thing, and ask.

"It's not that," Sarah said. "Pat, this is going to sound crazy. I know it comes out of the blue. But I'm worried about something. I've been trying to ignore it, but it's weighing on my mind."

"Go on."

"Have you heard any gossip lately? Gossip, about Heath in particular?"

"I *might* know what you're talking about," Pat said, raising an eyebrow.

"About Heath, and a student? You've heard it, haven't you?"

"Well, sure. But so what? It's nonsense."

"It isn't true?" Sarah said with relief.

"My dear, how would I know whether it's true or not? What I mean is, I don't pay attention to gossip. If I did, I'd constantly be questioning my colleagues. Every good-looking teacher gets gossiped about. It's a professional hazard. Until a student files a complaint, or a credible witness makes an accusation, my advice is: Ignore it. Or it'll drive you crazy."

"You think so?"

"Absolutely." Pat looked at her sharply. "*Unless*, you know something I don't."

Sarah hesitated. She could tell Pat about the photograph, but that would trigger a major investigation. Even if the investigation ended up clearing Heath, and finding him completely innocent, it would take him out of the running to be headmaster. Losing his dream would destroy their marriage. It would destroy *him*. No. She couldn't take such a drastic step—not unless she was sure that the girl in the picture was Bel. And she wasn't sure.

"No, I don't know anything. I was just—wondering."

"You're a levelheaded girl, Sarah. You know your own husband. If you trust Heath, that's good enough for me. And, by the way, if he gets this job, there'll be a lot more scrutiny. You need to stay strong, and take care of yourself. I can tell you're exhausted. Go home. Put those kiddies to bed, and then get some rest. I'll stay and clean up."

"Pat—"

"I insist."

"All right. Thank you."

Sarah hugged her boss awkwardly. Then she took the kids home, put them to bed. And waited for Heath.

Her eyes were wide-open now in the darkness of their bedroom. There had been more commotion than usual when Heath entered the apartment. Max started barking like crazy. When he wouldn't quiet down, she heard the front door open, close and open again. Heath must've let Max out onto the Quad. They did that sometimes, though only during the day when they could keep an eye on him from the window. Never at night. Sarah thought about getting up and saying something, but she couldn't bear speaking to Heath right now—not until she decided how to handle things. Instead, she lay there and listened to him move around the apartment. She heard him in the kitchen, opening cabinets one after the other. What was he looking for? Then she heard him in the bathroom, turning on the shower. After a few minutes, the shower went off, the bathroom door opened, and he went back to the kitchen. What was next—the refrigerator? But no. To her surprise, she heard a scraping sound that she immediately identified as the louvered door to the closet that held the washer and dryer.

What the hell?

Heath was good about taking care of the kids, making breakfast, loading and unloading the dishwasher. But he wasn't big on doing laundry. That was Sarah's job. Was he really going to wash his clothes, at this hour? Apparently, yes. She heard the screech as he turned the washer knob, the rushing sound as the machine filled with water. Then she heard him in the living room. She couldn't really tell what he was doing. But several minutes later, a whiff of wood smoke reached her nose, and she thought maybe he'd built a fire in the fireplace. They sat in front of the fire most nights, but tonight she wouldn't join him, not with the doubts she was having.

A half hour passed before Heath came to bed. In the interim, he went back to the bathroom, and then to the front hall. She heard him leave the apartment and return with Max, who was whimpering. When Heath finally came into the bedroom, Sarah was lying with her back to the door and her eyes firmly shut, fighting the urge to ask what was up with the dog. The bed dipped as he

got into it. The covers pulled taut. He didn't say a word.
An acrid smell tickled her nose, and she suppressed a
sneeze. It took a moment to realize what that scent was.
Bleach?

Sarah was in the process of gathering her courage
to ask why the hell he was doing laundry at midnight,
when she realized the bed was shaking.

Heath sobbed quietly. She could tell he was trying
not to wake her, and she lay there, frightened, listening. Was he falling apart again? Like his mother had
before him, like he had himself, the last time his career went south? Sarah flashed on the silent apartment,
on Heath's arm, hanging off the bed. She couldn't go
through that again, ever. This time, she would know
the signs. She would ask him to get help. She would say
something—now.

"Heath?" she said. "Are you all right?"

He turned toward her and buried his head against her
shoulder. She held him as he cried.

"I'm so sorry, baby," he said through his tears.

"Sorry for what?" she asked, her voice cold. Was he
about to admit to cheating?

"For not being there," he said. "I love you so much,
Sarah. You and the kids, you're all that matters. I promise, I'll never let you down again."

This wasn't just about missing the milk-and-cookies
social. No, this was Heath's confession. He wasn't just
telling her he'd cheated, though. With the way he cried,
like his heart was breaking, he was saying that he'd
ended it, and he was truly sorry. After all they'd been
through together—the long years, the troubles, the

children—if Heath came back to her now, broken, remorseful, wiser, could she forgive him?

Yes. She could. She would.

She drew him closer, and kissed his hair.

"It's all right," she said. "Everything will be all right."

45

Rose awoke in a dingy room with a searing pain in her head. The bright light that filtered through the gaps in the blinds hurt her eyes. It must be the middle of the day. But which day? She wasn't sure where she was or how long she'd been here. After a moment, her vision cleared. She saw that she was lying in a hospital bed in the Odell Infirmary. But she couldn't remember how she got there. Vague images filled her mind. She was on a stretcher. They put a needle in her arm, and a cold feeling spread out from her vein. In its wake, she was hollow inside, and couldn't think or feel or remember. When was that? Yesterday? Last night?

Last night. She sat up abruptly. A sharp pain radiated behind her eyes, and the room swam. She sank down against the pillow, overcome by a wave of nausea. Her mind was hazy, but she remembered Bel—her white, still face. The blood everywhere. Blood on her own hands. The horror rose up inside her, and she started to scream. A woman ran into the room, then a man. They held her down. She fought and flailed.

"Bel!" she screamed. "Bel!"

They plunged another needle into her arm. She felt tired and numb and like she was separated from the world by a gauzy veil. Whatever happened felt long ago and far away. She remembered fog, and the wetness of blood. She remembered holding a knife, saw it glitter in the moonlight. Then she slept.

Rose opened her eyes. The room was dimly lit by the bulb of a single bedside lamp. The gaps in the blinds showed black. It was night. The last thing she remembered was holding a knife. Thinking hurt her head. Everything hurt her head. Her mouth was dry, and she was hungry. The room smelled of antiseptic. Gingerly, Rose shifted in the bed.

"You're awake," a voice said.

She turned her head, and then closed her eyes momentarily to fight the nausea. When she opened them again, she saw her grandmother, sitting in a chair, her phone lighting her in a circle of darkness. Somebody stood behind her.

A phone, a light, the path through the woods. A man behind me.

The man. She wanted to scream. She had screamed then. There was a man here now.

"I'm going to turn on the overhead light, so we can see each other," he said. His voice was familiar.

"Please, no," Rose said.

Her own voice sounded funny to her ears—thin and reedy and weak. Carefully, she touched the spot on the back of her head where the pain lived. A knob the size and shape of an egg protruded from under her hair, which was dry and crusty. *Blood?* Putting pressure on the tender spot made Rose feel sick.

The man flipped on the overhead light anyway. The glare seared Rose's eyes, and she cried out. He switched off the light and opened the door to the hall. A bright yellow bar fell across the foot of the bed, but it didn't reach Rose's eyes.

"Is that better?" he asked.

It was Warren Adams, Grandma's lawyer/boyfriend. His presence didn't reassure her. Bel had always said he wanted them out of Grandma's life, so he could have her to himself.

Bel!

"Yes."

"I'm glad to see you so alert, Rose," Warren said, going back to stand beside her grandmother's chair, putting a hand possessively on her shoulder.

Grandma wouldn't meet Rose's eyes.

"We need to have a serious conversation, Rose," Warren said. "The sooner the better. If you're able, I propose we do that now."

"I'm—not feeling very well."

Rose looked down and saw that she wore a hospital gown. What happened to her clothes? She remembered blood, so much blood. Had that been real, or a terrible dream? She pulled the blanket back.

"Why am I here? What happened?" Rose said, a bubble of hysteria rising in her throat.

Her grandmother made a small, frightened noise. It was Warren who answered.

"You don't remember?"

"Were *you* there?"

"Was I where?"

"I remember being outside, at night, and it was foggy. A man was there. Was it you?"

"Me? No, of course not."

"I saw Bel. She looked—hurt. Someone was behind me. I don't remember anything after that. Or really, even, much before that." Rose paused, a terrible thought forming in her mind. "Is Bel all right?"

"You don't remember what happened?"

"No."

"Your sister is dead. She was murdered last night," Warren said.

As she struggled to process his words, life with Bel passed before her eyes. *My sister, my twin, no no no.* Lying in bed with Bel, comforting each other, after Dad died and they moved west. Playing in the courtyard of the apartment building in the shade of the palm trees. Riding the bus together to a new school. They grew apart, but then came back together when their mother got sick. Rose remembered the night their mother told them. She remembered holding on to Bel as they cried. For all their differences, they had turned to each other. They had come east—to live with Grandma, to go to Odell—together. Bel was her only family. The only person who truly knew her. But then Bel took sides against her, and they fought, terribly, over—what? Such a waste. She loved her sister, more than she loved anybody in this world. And now Bel was—*dead?*

"Dead? How?" Rose asked.

"I'd like to ask *you* that," Warren said. "But I won't. You're in serious legal trouble, and the less you say, the better. Even to us."

"Legal trouble— *Why?*" Rose asked, gulping for air. She found it hard to breathe all of a sudden.

"I would think that's obvious, given what happened last night."

"I said, I don't remember what happened. Didn't you *hear* me?"

Rose hated this man. His coldness, his condescension. Why wouldn't her grandmother speak, or look at her?

"Grandma," Rose said.

Warren touched Grandma's shoulder again. It was a hushing sort of touch that said not to worry her pretty head because he had everything under control.

"Rose, you walked into the Odell security office last night, covered in your sister's blood, holding a large kitchen knife," Warren said. "You proceeded to tell the dispatcher where to find Bel's body. The police went there, and they found her. Stabbed. Seventeen times."

Rose closed her eyes and moaned. In the blackness of her mind, she saw the knife, felt the stickiness of blood. It couldn't be true. She wouldn't do that. She loved her sister. There was somebody behind her. But she couldn't remember who.

"I didn't do it," she whispered.

"The evidence suggests otherwise. They're awaiting test results on the murder weapon, and they expect to find your fingerprints. The police also took your clothes to the lab to be tested, so they can prove it's Bel's blood on them. They're beginning to interview your classmates, to gather evidence about motive. From what I know of your relationship with your sister, they'll find plenty. The bottom line, Rose, is that the police will be able to prove you killed Bel."

"But I didn't. I would never hurt Bel. I love—*loved* her. Grandma? You believe me, right?"

Rose looked at her grandmother, who turned her head to the side and began to cry silently. Warren handed her a handkerchief.

"Your grandmother is a generous woman," Warren said. "She won't abandon you, even with this horrible thing you've done."

"But I didn't do it!"

"You may think you didn't. Your mind is disturbed. The approach we're going to take is that you need psychiatric help."

"You want to say I'm crazy?"

"That makes it sound very stigmatizing. Our doctor will place your actions in the context of the trauma of losing your mother. The damage it caused to your mind. Nobody is blaming you. We're trying to spare you, and more importantly, your grandmother, the pain of an arrest, incarceration, trial, and so forth. This is the best way. The only way."

"I didn't do it. You're trying to make people think I did. You just want me out of the picture."

"Rose, I'm trying to keep you out of *jail*. You're sixteen years old. For a crime as serious as murder, they'll prosecute you as an adult. You could end up with life in prison if we don't handle this properly. Finding a specialist who'll say that your actions arose from severe mental disturbance brought on by your mother's death is your only chance. Do you understand?"

Rose looked past Warren, trying to make eye contact with her grandmother, who still refused to look at her.

"Grandma, I swear. I didn't hurt Bel. I'm begging you. You have to believe me."

"Rose," Warren Adams said, "you were holding the knife. It was covered in her blood. You told the police where her body was. And you say you're not guilty? Do you see how crazy that sounds?"

"I can't explain right now. I'm having trouble remembering. My head hurts. My brain is messed up. But I know in my heart, I didn't hurt her. I want to talk to the police. I can make them understand."

"Absolutely not, that would be a terrible mistake," Warren said. "We keep you *away* from the police. They let you stay in the infirmary because I convinced them you're injured and incoherent. The second you start talking, they'll see that's not true and lock you up. Do you understand?"

"But I'm *not* crazy."

Grandma turned and finally met Rose's eyes. Her face was sunken and wet with tears, and she looked much older than the last time Rose had seen her.

"Rose, your mind is disturbed," Grandma said. "I

blame myself for not realizing. If only I'd seen it, I could have gotten you the help you needed, and your poor, sweet sister would still be alive. I won't abandon you, Rose. But we both need to follow Warren's advice. He knows what's best."

"Grandma, I'm innocent!"

Grandma made a strangled sound and buried her head in her hands. Then she got up and left the room—without a hug, without trying to comfort Rose, without even saying good-bye.

"Rose, your grandmother is very upset. They woke her with the news in the middle of the night, then we drove up here from Connecticut to identify Bel's body. Now, we have to make funeral arrangements. She's exhausted, she's in shock. She needs rest. We have to go. I'll be back tomorrow, with the psychiatrist. Don't talk to *anybody* without consulting me. You understand? Not the police, not anybody."

"No. Please, Mr. Adams. Wait."

Warren ignored her and walked out, pulling the door closed behind him. Rose heard a brief staccato of voices from the hall. Then the lock turned.

They'd locked her in.

Hysteria built inside her, until she thought she might scream. But screaming would only bring the nurse, and the needle. Her sister was dead. They thought she was the killer. Her own grandmother believed she'd murdered her twin. If everyone believed it, could it be true? She needed to think clearly. Rose remembered holding the knife, seeing its deadly glimmer in the moonlight.

She remembered being angry, to the point of hating Bel, and picking up a sharp object—an X-Acto knife—and putting it in her pocket. She went to the lake with a knife in her pocket. Not the same knife that she remembered holding later. Where did that one come from? Had she killed her own sister? Was it possible? She lifted the covers again and held up her hands before her eyes. She remembered seeing her hands last night, covered in blood, and started to shake.

And she remembered something else. The man standing behind her. The memory felt so real that it sent a convulsion of fear through her body. He'd been holding something. Something hard—a stick, a baseball bat? She remembered the sound as it cruised through the air, the crack as it connected with her skull, the explosion of pain and darkness. She touched the raw, crusty spot on the back of her head. The bump was real. *He* was real.

Her sister's killer was still out there.

46

The jangle of Heath's phone woke Sarah at five o'clock the next morning. He grabbed it so fast that she realized he must've been awake already. It was cold in the apartment, and he wore only boxers. But he got out of the warm bed and took the phone into the living room, so he wouldn't disturb her. Sarah reached a hand out and caressed the empty spot he left behind. Something had shifted between them last night. She felt it as he shook in her arms, his tears wet against her neck. He was sorry for what he'd done. He loved her, and the kids, more than ever. She wanted to forgive, and as she held him last night, she thought she could. But the more awake she got, the less certain she became. Was she forgiving an affair with a grown woman, or a relationship with a teenager? Those were two very different things. And how could she be comfortable that whatever it was, was over, when he wouldn't talk about it?

Heath tiptoed back into the bedroom, and dressed in

the dim light that filtered from the hall. Watching the curve of his back, the breadth of his shoulders, Sarah remembered that photograph, and her mind went to a dark place. Maybe it *wasn't* over. Why had he taken the phone into the other room? Was there something he didn't want her to overhear? The possibilities weighed on her mind.

Heath sat on the bed and put on his shoes. He was leaving. At five a.m.

"Where are you going?" she asked, the panic rising in her voice. "Who was that on the phone?"

Her throat was raw and dry. She noticed for the first time that her eyes burned, and her head hurt. Was she getting the virus, on top of everything?

"It was Simon. There's some sort of emergency," he said.

"What emergency?"

"I don't know. He didn't give details. Get some sleep."

He kissed her on the forehead. She watched him go with a hollow feeling inside her.

Sarah pushed the stroller across campus toward the day care. It was the kids' first time back since getting sick, and they were out of sorts. It had turned bitterly cold again. Sarah pulled the plastic weather cover forward to protect them from the wind, which made Harper whine that she couldn't see, and Scottie try to kick it off.

"Leave it be," she said, more sharply than she'd intended.

Sarah hadn't taught in nearly a week, hadn't checked in with the substitute to find out what material had been covered, and hadn't reviewed her lesson plans. Heath had been gone for three hours, and he didn't answer when she texted him to ask about the emergency. Her eyes stung from the cold, her head pounded, her throat hurt.

She had half a mind to turn around and go back to bed.

The flashing lights didn't register until she practically stumbled over a police car. Four cruisers were pulled up at odd angles near the entrance to the old carriage road that ran through the nature preserve. Sarah had never seen that many cop cars on campus in all her years at Odell. Two officers stood together, leaning on the front of a cruiser, consulting a map. Sarah pushed the stroller right up to them.

"Excuse me. I teach at the school. What happened?"

"We can't comment, ma'am. Move along now."

Could this be related to Heath's emergency phone call? If the emergency was real—if he'd been telling the truth—that would give her some comfort. Maybe she'd let her imagination get the better of her, like Pat Banks had said last night. Don't listen to gossip, she said. Wait for someone to file a complaint, or produce real evidence, before jumping to conclusions. Sarah ought to take a page from Pat's book. Be rational. Skeptical. Life would make more sense then, or at least, be easier to bear.

At day care, Harper ran right in, but Scottie kicked and hit Sarah as he resisted getting out of the stroller.

Allison, the director, had to come outside and help her wrestle him through the door, then out of his snow-suit, as he screamed the entire time. Sarah felt like the world's worst mother for leaving him.

Allison was down-to-earth, with frizzy hair, a big bosom, clogs. Normally Sarah could count on her to be sunny on the face of chaos. Not today.

"Are you sure he's ready to come back?" Allison asked sharply, after Scottie's small, pummeling fist caught her on the side of the head.

"It's been five days. He's been fever-free for twenty-four hours," Sarah said, but she was having her doubts.

"We're short two teachers because of the virus. We don't have a lot of bandwidth to deal with meltdowns."

"I think he'll be fine once he settles in. But if not, call me and I'll come get him."

Sarah trudged across campus toward her office. The paths were empty. The bitter wind that swept the plaza in front of Digby Hall nearly knocked her down. Sarah was glad at least that she didn't teach until second pe-riod, and would have time to catch her breath.

Inside the airy lobby, groups of kids had gathered in clusters in the seating area. It took a moment to grok that they shouldn't be there. It was the middle of first period: Why were they out of class? They looked stricken. Some cried, some hugged each other, some gesticulated wildly. Sarah approached the nearest group with a growing feeling of foreboding, remem-bering the police cruisers out on the road.

"What's going on?' she asked.

Maisie Chan, a Moreland freshman with glasses and spiky hair, stepped forward eagerly.

"You don't know? I assumed it would be all over campus by now," the girl said.

"What would?"

"Classes are canceled. The police are on campus, and they're bringing in grief counselors."

"Did someone die?"

"Rose is locked in the infirmary. They say she killed her sister."

"Rose *Enright*?"

"Yes. Stabbed her with a knife in the woods last night is what we heard."

Sarah's heart stopped beating for a split second. "I-I can't believe that."

"I know, right? She seems so nice."

It was surreal. From what Sarah knew of Rose Enright, this was completely impossible. There had to be some other explanation.

"Why do they think *Rose* did it?" Sarah asked.

"I have no clue. Nobody knows anything. We're all in shock."

It made no sense. This was *Rose Enright* they were talking about—quiet Rose, the A-student, whom Sarah trusted so much that she'd asked her to babysit her children. It had to be a mistake.

But, wait a minute. Rose killed—*Bel*? Bel Enright was dead?

"Rose killed her sister, you said?" Sarah said, shaking her head in disbelief.

"Yes. Somebody heard that from a teacher, so we think it's true. We've been talking, and nobody's seen Bel or Rose since last night. Emma Kim told a kid in my Mandarin class that Bel never came to bed," Maisie said.

Bel Enright, dead. If Bel was dead, and if Heath had been involved with her, that meant it was over. *What the hell, Sarah?* It was wrong to think that way. Despicable. A young girl had died. Just because Sarah had gotten herself all worked up last night, when Heath didn't come home and Bel wasn't at the social, didn't mean—

Last night.

Last night, Bel was missing. So was Heath. He didn't answer her calls. He came home late, put the dog out, took a shower, did *laundry*. And sobbed in Sarah's arms. This morning, he got a phone call, and seemed almost to be expecting it. And now she learned that Bel was dead. Not just dead. Stabbed. *Murdered.*

Sarah let the meaning of those things sink in.

No.

She started to shake all over. Her vision blurred and the room tilted as Sarah collapsed.

47

Sarah came to. She was sitting in a chair. Students crowded around her, looking worried.

"She's waking up. Somebody get her a glass of water."

"Why did she faint?"

"The Enright twins were in her dorm. Rose was her advisee."

"*Is* her advisee. Rose didn't die."

"Yeah, but she's a murderer. You get expelled for that, right?"

Somebody thrust a paper cup into Sarah's hand. "Mrs. Donovan? Can you hear me? Drink this."

Sarah took small sips of water. Her vision slowly cleared. Then it came back to her about Heath and Bel both going missing last night, and her head started to swim all over again. That couldn't mean— Could it?

"Put your head between your knees and take deep breaths," Maisie Chan said.

Sarah bent over, breathing in and out and trying to

get a grip on herself. She was panicking, and for no good reason. The only thing she had evidence for was that her husband had cheated. And even that was open to question. Heath claimed that photo was doctored by his enemies to stop him from becoming headmaster. Maybe that was true. But whether it was true or not, the girl in the picture was completely invisible, hidden by the man's body (admittedly, a body that looked just like Heath's, but still). Sarah had no evidence that the girl was Bel—other than gossip, and Pat Banks had told her not to listen to gossip. To conclude that her own husband murdered a young girl based on—what? The fact that he came home late on the night of the murder, and did laundry? That was insane. She needed to calm down and find out what had really happened last night.

She needed to talk to Rose Enright.

Still shaking, Sarah struggled to sit up, then tried to get out of the chair. "I have to go talk to Rose."

"Are you sure? She's, like, a crazed killer," Maisie said.

"It can't be Rose. That's impossible. Rose was always the good sister. She was the quiet one, the one who studied and made perfect grades. I'm sure there must be some mistake."

Sarah reached out her hands, and a couple of boys pulled her to her feet. They steadied her as she got her balance.

"Mrs. Donovan, you don't look well," Maisie said.

"I have to see Rose. She's all alone. I need to go to her. Thank you all," Sarah said, and stumbled toward the door.

The five-minute walk to the infirmary through the

bitter cold left Sarah weak and trembling. The intake station was deserted. She pushed the buzzer, and Kim Kowalski, the head nurse, came bustling out to greet her. Kim, with her round, cheerful face and thick thatch of gray hair, had been a nurse at Odell for so long that she'd treated Sarah in her student days. She now doled out ear drops and lollipops to Sarah's children when they were sick.

A big grin lit up Kim's face when she saw who it was.

"Sarah, I'm thrilled to hear the news," Kim said, coming out from behind the window and giving Sarah a bosomy hug. "I always knew Heath would do great things. Cream rises to the top."

"What are you talking about?"

"Well, I'm talking about your hubby. The new headmaster of Odell Academy."

"What? Who told you that?"

"Was it supposed to be confidential? But the announcement e-mail went out not five minutes ago. I was just in the back, reading it, and doing a happy dance. You must be so proud. *Mrs.* Headmaster—guess that makes you First Lady."

Heath, headmaster? It was too much to absorb, especially when she suspected him of cheating, possibly with a student. And of— No, not *murder.* She didn't actually think that, and she'd come here to rule it out entirely. But still, until this was resolved in her own mind, the idea of Heath as headmaster seemed plain wrong. And how was it even possible?

"I don't understand," Sarah said. "Simon's not retiring till the end of the school year."

"Simon resigned, not a minute too soon, you ask me. This murder is a huge black mark for the school, and Simon's poor leadership is directly responsible. He let bad behavior fester for too long. We need new leadership around here. Fresh blood, *young* blood. I can't imagine anyone better than your husband. Youngest headmaster in more than a hundred years, the e-mail said. And the best-looking, too," Kim said, with a wink.

"My God," Sarah whispered.

Bel Enright was dead, and Heath's dreams were coming true. Was that a coincidence? She had to steady herself against the wall, so she didn't fall over in a faint again.

"Honey, you don't look so good. Here I am, gabbing away and not realizing you got the bug. That's why you're here, right?"

"Oh, no. I came to see Rose Enright."

"Why would you want to see her?" Kim said, her face clouding over. "I have a note in the file—no visitors except family."

"I'm not a visitor. I'm her faculty advisor, here on official business. Somebody needs to check on her. I imagine she's terribly upset."

"Yeah, I'd be upset, too, if I just killed my own sister and was about to go to jail."

"Oh, Kim. Rose could be innocent. We don't know what happened out there."

"*I* do. The security guy who brought her in is my next-door neighbor, and he gave me the inside scoop. Rose Enright stabbed her sister to death out near Lost Lake, then showed up at the security office with the bloody knife in her hand, and gave them directions to the body."

Sarah stared at Kim, speechless, unable to comprehend what she'd just heard. It was impossible to reconcile that bloody image with the loving, responsible girl she knew. Sarah and Rose chatted every week—about classes, grades, school activities. Rose babysat for Harper and Scottie regularly. She sat in Sarah's kitchen, drank tea and gabbed like an old chum. Sarah knew everything about Rose's personal life—or thought she did, anyway. She knew there was tension between her and her sister, but never in a million years did she imagine it would boil over into violence. Rose was one of the most considerate, intelligent, caring girls in the school—simply incapable of hurting another person.

"That can't be true. I know this girl very well. There must be another explanation," Sarah said.

"It *is* hard to believe. But my friend assured me, it's murder, plain and simple. Let me say it again. Rose had a bloody knife in her hand, and led 'em right to her sister's body. I'm sorry if this upsets you on your big day. But sometimes we don't know people as well as we think we do."

Bel was dead, and Rose was the killer. Was it possible? Maybe it was. *Please, God, let it be true,* Sarah thought fiercely, then immediately felt ashamed of her selfishness. It would be a tragedy if Rose Enright had murdered her sister. It would be a nightmare for poor Rose, and the worst thing that had ever happened at Odell Academy. It was wrong of Sarah to see any silver lining at all. But it went to show how terrified she was, how uncertain of her own husband she was, that she felt a big surge of relief.

Rose's guilt meant Heath's innocence.

"Now that you know she did it, you still want to talk to her?" Kim asked.

"I'm her advisor, so yes, I think I should."

"Okay, but I have to warn you. She could be suicidal, or dangerous. We're on strict orders to keep the door locked and sharp objects out of her room. I was told they'll move her out today or tomorrow, and I can't wait. I'm short-staffed from the virus, I got twelve kids admitted with it, and I'm supposed to be checking Rose Enright every thirty minutes, for the suicide watch."

"Suicide watch, ugh. Awful."

Sarah knew too well what that was like. If Rose was suicidal, it would be wrong to turn away and leave her to her own devices. Sarah had gone there for selfish reasons, looking for information to exonerate Heath. Now that she had it, she couldn't just walk away, basking in her relief. She ought to stay, to help a poor, disturbed girl who was in bad trouble.

"It is awful, and I don't have the manpower to monitor her properly," Kim said. "I told them that. I'll take you to see her, but I want to take your temperature first. I've been dealing with this virus all week, and I know the signs. I'm almost certain you got it. Wait here."

Kim went away, and came back wheeling a machine. She stuck a plastic probe under Sarah's tongue. After a moment, the machine beeped.

"Uh-huh, just like I thought. A hundred point nine. Home to bed, miss, and that's an order."

"After I talk to Rose."

"Sarah, you're not listening. This one's as bad as flu gets. High fever, dizziness, nausea, lethargy, brain fog. You won't be able to stand up, let alone think straight."

"All the more reason to visit now, while I'm still on my feet."

"All right, but make it quick, and here, use some Purell first. Follow me. We put her all by herself at the end of the hall."

48

Rose awoke from a nightmare, with tears in her eyes and a scream ringing in her ears. It wasn't her own scream. It was Bel's. The sound felt horribly real, because it *was* real. She remembered now—hearing that shriek of terror in the woods, last night when Bel was murdered. No wonder Rose was crying: She'd been reliving her sister's death. They blamed her for it. But Rose didn't murder the one person left on the planet whom she'd really, truly loved. She could never do that. Whoever did was out there right now, walking free.

The blinds were drawn, and the line of light around the edge of the window told her it was daytime. Her grandmother and the lawyer hadn't come back, which was just as well. The lawyer wanted her gone, and Grandma went along with anything he said. Nobody would help her. If Rose wanted to get out of here, if she wanted justice for her sister, she'd have to help herself. The only way to do that was to *remember*.

The sound of the scream was so clear that it carried other memories within it. Rose remembered running through the dark and the fog, as a crunching sound followed behind her. The sound of footsteps on icy ground. Someone was chasing her. She remembered the feel of frozen ground under her knees, and relived the bolt of fear she felt as someone stood behind her. She'd been kneeling on the ground, when she heard the whir of a hard object, traveling through the air. Then, boom. Darkness.

Why was she kneeling on the ground? Who hit her? *Think.*

Rose remembered leaning over Bel's motionless body, holding her, begging her to wake up. She recalled picking up an object and staring in horror as it glinted in the moonlight. *A knife.* The murder weapon, the deadly blade used to stab her sister. The killer had chased her through the woods. She'd stumbled upon Bel's body, and the bloody knife. The killer smashed her in the head to stop her from telling. To silence her. He wanted her *quiet.* He succeeded. Rose lost consciousness. Later, in shock, covered in her sister's blood, she went for help, the bloody knife still in her hand. And now they thought she'd done it, when it was him.

Him. She thought it was a man. Why did she think that?

She had to tell the police.

Rose threw off the scratchy hospital blanket and swung her legs over the side of the bed. A wave of nausea hit, and she had to sit very still until it passed. Slowly, she got to her feet, walked to the door and tried to open it. It wouldn't budge. She put her ear to the door, expecting to hear the bustle of the infirmary, but it was surprisingly quiet.

She knocked. Then pounded. "Hello? Hello? Can anybody hear me? Let me out, please let me out!"

Nobody came. Trapped, Rose paced the narrow room until her legs grew weak and shaky. Then she fell back into bed, and turned her face to the wall.

Rose had been languishing for what felt like hours when she heard a key turn in the lock.

"I need to check her before you come in," the nurse said to someone behind her, stepping into the room.

As the nurse took her vitals, Rose vowed not to tell Grandma and her lawyer what she'd remembered. They'd only accuse her of lying, or worse. No. She needed to find a way to get out of here, and talk to the police on her own, without them knowing.

"You can come in now," the nurse said. "I'm going to lock the door while I get her a breakfast tray. I'll be back in ten minutes to let you out, okay?"

Rose looked up to see Mrs. Donovan standing on the threshold.

"Is it okay if I come in?" Mrs. Donovan said with a concerned look on her kind face. "I just wanted to check on you, but if you're not up for a visit, I'll come back some other time."

Is it okay? Are you kidding me?

Mrs. Donovan was the one person in the entire world Rose trusted to help her. She wanted to turn back time, to go back to her afternoons in Mrs. Donovan's kitchen. If only she could taste the chocolate-chip cookies again, hold that adorable baby in her lap, hear the thump of the dog's tail. If she could stay forever in that moment, if none of this had happened, if she could live a normal girl's life. Then things would be all right. Instead, Bel was dead, and they thought Rose had murdered her own sister. The weight of it hit her at the sight of her teacher's face, and all the tears she'd been holding back came flooding out.

Mrs. Donovan rolled the small visitor's chair closer to the bed and sat down. She leaned forward, gathered Rose into her arms, and held her till the storm passed.

"It's okay," she whispered. "Let it out."

Eventually, Rose stopped crying, and realized that Mrs. Donovan was speaking to her softly.

"Oh, Rose, I'm so sorry," she said, in a quiet voice. "I know you loved her. I know it was complicated. Sometimes, we do things we can't explain. You need a friend. I'm here to listen, not to judge."

Rose looked up in shock. "You believe them. You believe that I murdered Bel. What did they tell you?"

"We don't need to talk about that now. You're upset."

"I *am* upset because I didn't kill my sister. Somebody else killed her, and he's still out there."

"But—that's—not possible," Mrs. Donovan said, in an oddly strangled voice, her eyes wide with fear. "They say you were covered in blood. That you had a knife in your hand."

"That part is true. I was in the woods, searching for Bel. But when I found her, she was already dead."

Rose told her story in a fierce rush. The footsteps behind her as she heard Bel screaming. Running through the fog. Finding the body, kneeling over her dead sister, holding her, begging her not to die. But she was gone. Seeing the knife, staring at it in horror as she felt the presence of the killer behind her. Then the whizzing sound as he struck her in the head.

"Everything went black," Rose said. "When he hit me in the head, I lost my memory. That entire night vanished like it never happened. But then I woke up this morning, and I remembered. I'm remembering even more, talking to you now. He grabbed me, just when Bel screamed. I lashed out and cut him, and he let me go."

"You *cut* him? With the knife?"

Rose stopped short. She had a vivid memory of picking up the knife from the ground as she knelt beside her sister. But that was later. So how was it possible?

"No, I found the knife later," she said. "Let me think."

She stared at the wall, willing her mind back into the fog and the fear. And suddenly she knew.

"I had an X-Acto knife. I took it from my room because I was afraid to go into the woods alone at night."

"If you were afraid, why did you go?"

"Because Bel texted me and begged for help."

"Help with what?"

"I can't remember. Oh God, where's my phone?"

Rose looked around frantically. She sat up on the edge of the bed and fumbled in the drawer of the bedside table. It was empty. Gingerly, she walked over and threw open the door of the small wardrobe, which was empty, too. She looked down at herself and realized she was wearing a hospital gown. Where had her clothes gone? They'd taken them, when she was unconscious.

"I can't find my phone. And where are my clothes?" Rose asked.

"I don't know. Maybe the police took them. They might want to—"

"Test for blood?" Rose said, her stomach lurching.

The wheels of justice were spinning. Time was running out to prove her innocence, and to find the real killer. Soon it would be too late.

"I need that phone," Rose said. "It's incredibly important. I could show you Bel's texts, and prove what happened. But I remember a lot more now. I cut him with an X-Acto knife. I cut *Zach*."

"Zach?"

"Yes. *Zach Cuddy*. He followed me into the woods. He grabbed me, right when Bel screamed, and I cut him, to make him let me go. I told him we had to help her, and you know what he said? He said Bel 'deserves what she gets.' He also said he could cut me, if he wanted. He carries a Swiss Army knife. Mrs. Donovan, I think Zach Cuddy murdered my sister. I have to tell the police."

49

Transcript of Witness Interview conducted by Lieutenant Robert Kriscunas, State Police—Major Crime Unit, with Mr. Brandon Flynn, represented by Lisa Walters, Esq. Ms. Walters also present.

Kriscunas: Lisa, so we meet again. Seems the two of us are involved in every major murder case in this state.

Walters: Bob, good to see you. I know you're not one for pleasantries, so let me cut to the chase. Your colleague, Detective Howard, informed me that Brandon is a person of interest in the Bel Enright murder. I'm here to tell you he had absolutely nothing to do with it. You've got the wrong guy.

Kriscunas: Person of interest, huh?

Walters: That's what she told me over the phone. Is that wrong?

Kriscunas: With all due respect to Melissa, this is her first homicide. It's not the term I'd choose. What

I can tell you is: Your client held a grudge against the Enright sisters because his girlfriend was expelled over the slipper attack. We just wanted to ask him, in a friendly way, where he was on the night of the murder. That's all.

Walters: Okay. Look, we don't admit he had a grudge, as you call it. But for the sake of argument, say that he did. If he did, it was against Rose Enright, not Bel. Rose was the one who snitched. It was her testimony to the Disciplinary Committee that got Darcy Madden expelled. My client had no beef with the dead sister whatsoever, and nothing to do with killing her.

Kriscunas: Witnesses say he had a grudge against both sisters. Hear me out. We know that your client twice physically confronted Rose Enright. The first time occurred on a school bus at Thanksgiving break. We have at least five witnesses to that incident, and what they describe amounts to a chargeable physical assault.

Walters: Okay, okay, this is the first I'm hearing of this. But even if that's so, you say it pertains to Rose, correct? Rose? Not Bel.

Kriscunas: Yes, but we're talking physical assault here. He punched and tripped her within the sight of witnesses. Then he followed her a second time, along with Miss Romano. They cornered her on a deserted path at night. I don't know how familiar you are with the Odell campus, Lisa. But it's huge, and empty at night. Nobody's gonna hear you scream. Your client was prevented from doing harm by a bystander who fortunately came along and interrupted the confrontation—

Flynn: Cuddy.

Walters: Brandon, keep your mouth shut.

Kriscunas: That bystander heard Mr. Flynn make a specific threat to Bel Enright. Apparently, Mr. Flynn was incensed that Bel was not punished as severely as his girlfriend. So, there is a beef there, plus evidence of prior willingness to use violence. I ask you again, where was Mr. Flynn on the night of the murder?

Walters: I request a recess to consult with my client.

Kriscunas: Sure. Take your time.

[PAUSE]

Kriscunas: You've had time to consult?

Walters: Yes.

Kriscunas: What would you like to tell me?

Walters: My client would like to know if this information comes from Zachary Cuddy. Because Mr. Cuddy is not a reliable witness, and bears a grudge against my client.

Kriscunas: I don't reveal the names of witnesses. You know that, Lisa.

Flynn: It is Cuddy. I can tell by the look on your face. Dude's a frigging liar. You should ask him where he was that night.

Kriscunas: Mr. Flynn, I can assure you that all leads will be followed in this investigation. If there's evidence you can offer against Zachary Cuddy, I'd be happy to listen. But this interview is really about you and your conduct. This is your chance to exonerate yourself by providing an alibi. You can choose to do that, or not. If you don't, we will view you as a person of interest, in which case we'd consider seeking other charges against you—charges we might not pursue otherwise—in order to hold you while we continue our investigation.

Flynn: What's he saying?

Walters: He's saying he can charge you with assault for tripping Rose Enright on the bus.

Flynn: Fuck, man, that's harsh.

Kriscunas: It's reality, Brandon.

Flynn: No reason to screw me, man. I didn't kill her. That night, I was in my room, by myself. You can check the dorm log.

Kriscunas: We did that already. The log shows you checked in at eight-thirty. We believe the murder occurred somewhat later than that. You could've snuck out without being seen. Was anybody else with you that night, say between nine and eleven p.m.? Someone, anyone, who can corroborate your alibi?

Flynn: Nah, man. I don't have a roommate. I was in my room by myself, chilling. Watched some YouTube, did a little homework, ate some Cheetos. Nobody saw me.

Kriscunas: So, nobody can verify that?

Flynn: Nope. Now what? You lock me up? 'Cause that's bullshit. Whatever Cuddy told you was to cover his own ass. He was obsessed with Bel. He used to follow her around. He took pictures of her. Ask anyone.

Kriscunas: Pictures? What kind of pictures?

Flynn: Yeah, you know, that gets sensitive. I need to ask my lawyer something.

Walters: Request a recess.

[PAUSE]

Walters: My client has nothing to say about any photographs.

Kriscunas: These photographs exist, but he won't talk about them? Or they don't exist?

Walters: Next topic, Bob. Or we walk.

Kriscunas: Do you have any specific evidence connecting Zachary Cuddy to the murder of Isabel Enright?

Flynn: Any actual, like, evidence? I wish I did, but no. He's a slimy little twit, and he deserves to go down. I think he probably offed her. Unless it was Donovan.

Kriscunas: Donovan?

Flynn: Yeah. Heath Donovan.

Kriscunas: The headmaster? Why would he murder a student?

Flynn: To keep her quiet. Why do you think Bel got off so easy in the slipper attack?

Kriscunas: You tell me, Brandon.

Flynn: Because Donovan was doing her. That's not gossip, it's a known fact. You're wasting your time with me. Go ask Heath Donovan where he was that night.

50

Sarah stepped into the hallway, closed the door to Rose's room and leaned against it, weak with relief. Rose knew who killed Bel, *and it wasn't Heath*. It was Zach Cuddy. Bel had gotten mixed up with a boy her own age, and when she rejected him, he lured her to the woods and stabbed her to death. It was the oldest story in the book, and made Sarah's suspicion of Heath seem laughable. Sarah had listened to gossip, and had let her imagination run away with her. She'd believed a hoax photo sent to her by someone calling himself *Anonymouse*. Interpreted an innocent conversation in the dining hall as an affair with an underage girl; turned a load of laundry into murder. To doubt her own husband over such nonsense, the father of her children, the man who'd been by her side since they were teenagers—what was *wrong* with her? She ought to be ashamed.

She would make it up to Heath, and be the best wife

he could imagine. But first, Rose Enright needed her help. Holding Rose as she sobbed, Sarah viscerally felt the girl's innocence. Rose's grandmother had let some lawyer convince her that an insanity plea was the only hope to avoid jail. They wouldn't listen to a word Rose said, and refused to let her talk to the police. Sarah had to do something. She'd talk to Mrs. Enright first, but if that didn't work, she'd go to the police, whether the family wanted that or not. Rose's freedom was at stake, and that wasn't even the worst problem. Rose claimed another Odell student had murdered her sister. Zachary Cuddy was somewhere on campus, potentially a danger to other students.

"You, there." A white-haired man in an expensive suit strode down the hall, looking so angry that Sarah started with alarm. "Were you in Miss Enright's room? I *said*, no visitors."

This had to be the man who was trying to railroad poor Rose into taking the fall for her sister's murder. He had a sneering, aristocratic look about him, and she hated him on sight.

"Let me guess. You're Mrs. Enright's lawyer," Sarah said.

"Yes, Warren Adams," he said, surprised. "And you are?"

"Sarah Donovan. Rose's faculty advisor and the head of her dorm. Rose doesn't want to see you, and she doesn't want you speaking for her. I need to ask you to leave."

"I'll do no such thing," he said, and tried to go around her.

Heart racing, Sarah stood her ground. She was afraid he'd push her, but he backed off a step, and glowered instead.

"Get out of my way."

"I can't do that. I have an obligation to my student, and if you can't respect her request, I'll call security."

"How dare you? Martha Enright is my client. She hired me to represent her granddaughter on a very serious matter. This girl is accused of murdering her own sister."

"But she didn't do it. She's innocent."

"That's ridiculous. Rose walked into the security office covered in blood, carrying a knife, babbling like a lunatic. She told them her sister was dead in the woods, and that was the last coherent thing she said."

"I just spent half an hour with Rose. She's perfectly coherent, and she can explain everything that happened that night. She needs people who believe her and support her. I don't know what game you're playing, Mr. Adams, but you're not acting in Rose's best interests. She wants to talk to the police, but she says you won't let her."

"That's right. And if you knew the first damn thing about defending someone from a murder charge, you wouldn't, either. This is none of your business, so butt out."

While they were arguing, a young woman had appeared. She approached them, holding up a badge.

"Don't mean to interrupt, but I just heard someone say that Rose Enright wants to talk to the police. That would be me. Detective Melissa Howard with the town police department."

The detective was in her twenties, with a pleasant face, an athletic build and short, blond hair. Sarah had seen her standing by the police cruisers earlier, at the entrance to the woods. She wore a boxy, black pantsuit perfect for concealing a holster under her arm.

Adams made a harrumphing sound, and handed the detective a business card.

"Rose won't talk to you," he said. "I'm her lawyer, Warren Adams, and I'm invoking the right to remain silent on her behalf."

"Don't listen to him, Detective," Sarah said. "Rose is desperate to talk to you, and he won't let her. She says she didn't kill her sister, but she knows who did, and he's keeping it from you."

The detective's eyes went wide in bemusement. "Uh, sorry. You are?"

"Sarah Donovan, Rose's academic advisor. I just spent the last half hour with her. She can explain everything that happened the night of the murder."

"Donovan, I know that name." The detective took out a notebook and flipped through the pages. "Okay, you're the cohead of Moreland Hall, right? Married to Heath Donovan, formerly the dean of students, now the headmaster?"

"Yes."

"You're on my list of witnesses to interview. I wanted to speak with Rose first, but unfortunately Mr. Adams here just mucked up my plan by invoking Miranda."

"But Rose *wants* to talk to you," Sarah said.

"Rose is a minor. We don't interrogate minors without

the consent of the parents, so I have to check with who-ever's the legal guardian. Which I assume is not him."

"No. It's Martha Enright, Rose's grandmother. She backs me, a hundred percent," Adams said.

"Fine, then. Give me her number, and I'll confirm it."

Adams wrote down a phone number and handed it to the detective.

"Until I talk to the grandmother, I don't want you speaking to Rose, either," the detective said.

"You can't keep me from my client."

"Actually, I can. Rose is confined here in lieu of being sent to state prison. She's technically in police custody. I'll clear this up quickly, but until further notice, nobody but Odell Infirmary medical personnel are allowed in Rose's room."

"*Unacceptable,*" Adams said. "I have a psychiatrist coming up from New York this afternoon to evaluate her."

"Do you have a court order for that?"

"No, but—"

"Then get one. Or else you can wait until I figure out who represents Rose. Now, I have to ask you to leave."

To make her point, Detective Howard stepped in front of Rose's door, squared her shoulders and rested her hands on her hips. She was tall and strong-looking enough that she might've played basketball in college. The glint of a gun peeking out from her jacket added to the impression. Judging by his shocked expression, Adams wasn't used to being told no, especially not by a woman packing heat. He backed away huffily.

"Fine, but you'll be hearing from me," he said, with an injured air, and walked off.

"Don't let the door hit you on the way out," Detective Howard said, under her breath, her eyes twinkling, as they watched him leave.

"Don't you hate guys like that?" Sarah said. "It was great to see you put him in his place."

"Oh, he'll be back. That one's not done making trouble. If you're free to talk, Sarah, I'd appreciate that interview now. My colleague and I are set up in a conference room on the other side of campus. I won't try to question Rose. But I'd very much like to hear what she told you about her sister's murder, the sooner the better."

51

Word of Heath's appointment had spread. As Sarah crossed campus with Melissa Howard, people stopped her with hugs and handshakes and offers of congratulation. Colleagues on the faculty, secretaries and administrators, buildings and grounds guys, kitchen workers, students—they all had the same message. It was an awful time for the school. But now they had hope. Simon Barlow was tired and burned-out, and didn't have the vision to get them through the terrible crisis of a student being murdered. Heath would save them. Sarah must be so proud. Please let him know, everyone was behind him, everyone was pulling for him, everyone believed in him. Heath Donovan was the man to lead Odell out of the wilderness.

"You're married to a rock star," Melissa said.

"It's crazy. I'm not used to it," Sarah said.

It was only just starting to sink in that Heath would be running the school now. It was a meteoric rise. But he'd also be incredibly busy, and under tremendous scrutiny. So would Sarah, for that matter. They would be expected to entertain. To move into the headmaster's house—a grand and gloomy old monstrosity that she didn't even like visiting. How on earth would she live in that mausoleum with small children? Sarah had been so preoccupied with Rose's problems that she'd forgotten her own. But now, with her fever spiking, too, life felt overwhelming. All she wanted was to go home to bed.

But first, she had to give this interview, to help Rose. The school's security office had been commandeered by crime scene investigators, so Detective Howard was using a conference room in Founders' Hall, the main administration building, to interview witnesses. Leaving the brightness of the Quad for the dim, dusty vestibule of Founders', the detective explained that Sarah would be interviewed not only by her, but also her partner, a lieutenant from the state police.

"Odell PD is small and, I'll be honest, this is my first homicide. We called in the staties for assistance. Lieutenant Kriscunas is an old-timer, knows the ropes. He can be a little brusque, maybe. Don't take it personally."

"Got it."

Since classes had been canceled, the building, which normally would've been bustling with students, was quiet and echoing. Sarah followed the detective past the first floor, where classrooms were located, to the second. When they got to the landing, Detective Howard turned toward the headmaster's office.

"Where exactly are we going?" Sarah asked, a nervous note creeping into her voice.

"Your husband hooked us up with the conference room next door to his office."

"*His* office," she repeated.

Sarah hadn't seen Heath since the early hours of the morning, when he'd rushed off in response to that emergency phone call—which, Sarah now realized, must have been about Bel's murder. In the meantime, Heath had suddenly been elevated to the position of headmaster of Odell, and was apparently already moving into the headmaster's office. It was enough to make anybody's head spin, so if the thought of seeing him for the first time since all that happened made her uncomfortable, that should only be expected. Her suspicions had turned out to be fantasies. She could trust him. Not only that, she owed it to him to congratulate him with a sincere heart, and to stand ready to help him, however he needed. It was the least she could do, after she'd failed him by convicting him of murder in her own mind.

In the walnut-paneled anteroom, Betsy Pirello, Simon Barlow's secretary, was taping shut a cardboard box. When Sarah walked in, Betsy dropped was she was doing and ran over, smiling broadly.

"Sarah, I'm so delighted you stopped by. Heath's on the phone, but I'd be glad to buzz him, or send in a note if you prefer."

Betsy, a trim, pretty woman in her thirties with unnaturally bright blond hair, had always seemed to look down on Sarah, but now she sounded strangely eager to please. Of course—Betsy was *Heath*'s secretary now. Sarah was Heath's wife, and therefore a personage to be reckoned with. And yet, she now had to go through a gatekeeper to speak to her own husband. It was a brave new world.

"I'd love to say hi to him. But I'm here to get interviewed by the police, so it needs to be quick."

"I'll buzz him right away."

Just as Betsy picked up her phone, Heath stepped out of Simon's office—which was now his.

"Hey, I thought I heard your voice," he said to Sarah. "Want a quick tour of the new digs? Or are you here for something else?" he asked, looking back and forth between Sarah and Detective Howard, his expression growing wary.

"Yes, the police want to interview me."

Heath gave the detective an ingratiating smile. "Is that really necessary, Officer? Our kids have been under the weather, and my wife is exhausted. Anything you need to know about Moreland Hall, I'd be happy to tell you myself."

"I'll try to make it quick, but we do need to cover the bases. Protocol and such."

"All right. Can you give me a minute with my wife, and then I'll send her into the conference room."

The detective nodded. Sarah followed Heath into his new office. She stopped short, gasping, as she took in the tall casement windows with the grand drapes and sweeping view of the Quad, the imposing mahogany desk, the portraits of former headmasters on the wall. It was all so splendid and regal.

Heath watched her face, brimming with pride. "Amazing, huh?"

"Gorgeous. I've been here before for meetings. But to think, it's all yours now."

"It's all *ours*, sweetheart. C'mere."

He held out his arms, and she stepped into them. He held her for a moment, kissed the top of her head, then stepped back and looked down at her with an oddly guarded expression.

"What does this detective want with you?" he asked.

"To talk about Rose, I think."

"Why ask *you*, though?"

"I'm her advisor. Plus, I spoke with Rose earlier today, and the detective knows that."

"You spoke to her? You mean, on the phone?"

"No, I visited."

"You went to *see* Rose Enright? I thought she was locked in. Why didn't you tell me?"

She looked at him, confused. "I just told you now."

"You should have consulted me first."

"Why would I do that? Rose is my advisee. She's all alone, in a terrible situation. It was my responsibility to visit. You would never tell me not to. Would you?"

"Yes, I would. You're the headmaster's wife now. This girl is accused of murder. You can't go anywhere near her. Think about how it looks."

Sarah was shocked that Heath would try to keep her from seeing her advisee. It was because of his new position, obviously. Anything that reflected poorly on the school was bound to upset him. But this didn't bode well for how he would handle the pressure.

"I understand why you're worried, honey, but Rose needs my help. She's innocent."

"That's crazy, Sarah. That's just wrong. They found her with the knife in her hand."

"She can explain that. And, there was somebody else in the woods when Bel was murdered."

Heath went deathly pale. "That's impossible. Who told you that?"

"Rose told me herself."

"She's making it up," he said, beginning to pace the floor frantically. "She's lying. She had no memory of the murder whatsoever. I was told that, quite clearly, by the doctor."

"Only because she had a concussion. Her memory is back now. Heath, what's the matter? You look like death all of a sudden. Is it the flu?"

He took a deep breath, wringing his hands together, struggling visibly to control his emotions. God, she wished it was the flu, but no, it was Heath's instability, rearing its ugly head. *Be careful what you wish for, because you might just get it.* Heath had wanted this job so bad. If any position was prestigious enough to make up for the collapse of his writing career, headmaster of Odell was it. Unless the pressure destroyed him first.

"What exactly did Rose tell you?" he asked.

Sarah needed to be careful what she said about Zach Cuddy. If Heath heard that a *different* Odell student was involved in the murder, that could send him into a tailspin.

"Rose saw somebody in the woods, but she's sketch

on the details. She asked for my help in going to the police because her grandmother won't let her."

"She wants you to help her disobey her grandmother?"

"You make that sound so bad. Rose just wants to tell the truth."

"Sarah, listen to me. Your meddling in this investigation is dangerous for the school. The evidence proves Rose guilty. Her family has a plan for dealing with the police in what is a very tricky situation. It's not up to you to subvert that. If you interfere, Odell could be looking at another lawsuit."

"A lawsuit. Really?"

"Yes. Families sue at the drop of a hat these days. Don't you see why I'm worried? I have to lead defensively if I want to succeed in this job. I need you to tell that detective you've reconsidered, that it's not your place to come between Rose and her family. Can you do that for me? Can you do it for *Odell*?"

"Heath, she's my advisee. I promised to help her."

"You're a dedicated teacher, so naturally, you want to help. But we have to put the school first now. I'm headmaster. You're my wife. It's our job to protect Odell as an institution. Will you support me in this? Please, darling?"

He made it sound like a reasonable request. "I guess so. All right," she said.

"Thank you," he said, and kissed her forehead tenderly.

But as Sarah crossed the anteroom to the conference

room where the investigators waited, she was ridden with guilt. Keeping her promise to Heath meant breaking her promise to Rose. The worst part was, she was acting out of selfishness. Not to protect the school, but to protect her husband's fragile mental health and emotional stability. Mere hours into the new job, and the signs were already there. Heath was falling apart.

52

Sarah hadn't been in the headmaster's conference room since that awful day when Heath had given his presentation, and she had checked her phone to find Anonymouse's prank e-mail. The dark paneling and dusty smell, the wind rattling the old windows, flashed her back to that terrible moment, and made her feel more nervous than she already did about this interview. She was about to face a difficult moral choice, in a room that was bad luck for her. The combination made her feel ill, though that could also be the virus coming on.

A thin, balding man with glasses sat at the head of the table, jotting notes. Detective Howard introduced them. Lieutenant Kriscunas placed a tape recorder in front of Sarah and inserted a tape.

"So, Detective Howard tells me you have a message for us from Rose Enright," Kriscunas said.

Sarah flushed, her stomach knotting more intensely.

Was she really going to abandon Rose, for the sake of protecting Heath's job? She didn't know if she could, or how she would live with herself if she did.

"But I have to ask you not to relay that just yet. I'm waiting for a legal opinion from the county attorney's office on whether it's okay for us to take Rose's statement from a third party, given that her lawyer said she's exercising her right to silence."

"Wait. Did I hear you correctly? You don't want me to tell you what Rose said, about being innocent? About who really killed her sister?"

"Ma'am, I feel terrible about that. It goes against my every instinct as an investigator not to pursue relevant information. But I've also learned if you take shortcuts with a defendant's rights, you wind up blowing the case on a technicality. So, bottom line, we'll hold off on that for now."

A defendant's rights. He called Rose a defendant. Did that mean he already believed she was guilty? Looking on the bright side, though, if they wouldn't let her relay what Rose said, at least it wouldn't be by her own choice. She wouldn't be withholding information to help Heath's career. Sarah felt a bit better at the thought, although the room was hot and cold at the same time, and her vision had funny black dots in it.

Kriscunas began with routine questions. How many girls lived in Moreland Hall? What were Sarah's duties as dorm cohead? She found herself weighing her answers, checking her words before she spoke, asking whether what she said might put the school in a bad light, or upset Heath. At least she didn't need to worry that her answers would hurt Rose. But when Kriscunas turned to the topic of Rose and Bel's relationship, Sarah started to get upset. Everything he asked seemed to assume Rose's guilt. Did the lawsuit cause a breach between the twins? Did Sarah observe hostility between them? She wanted desperately to stick up for Rose, but he didn't give her the chance. She was almost about to stop the interview, when he suddenly turned to asking about the girls who did the slipper attack. Had Sarah seen Tessa Romano around campus since she was expelled? Was it possible that Tessa or Darcy or even Darcy's boyfriend, Brandon Flynn, might have wanted to kill Bel? Wow, they were way off base if they thought Tessa Romano killed Bel. But Sarah couldn't steer them in the right direction without revealing that Zach Cuddy was in the woods that night. And she couldn't tell them that without repeating what Rose said.

She was stuck watching the police go off on a tangent. It was excruciating, but then it got worse.

Kriscunas wanted details on the disciplinary process surrounding the slipper attack. He started asking about why Bel Enright got off easy, and Sarah started to sweat. She glanced around the conference room, her eyes landing on the seat she'd occupied when her phone buzzed in her pocket so fatefully during that meeting. She remembered opening the attachment to Anonymouse's e-mail, seeing the photo of Heath or, if he was to be believed, not-Heath. She never quite believed him over the evidence of her own eyes, and yet she let him convince her that the photo was a fake. She let herself accept an obvious excuse, a fabrication. Why? Because otherwise her life would change, forever, and she couldn't accept that.

"We've had a witness suggest that favoritism was shown to Bel Enright in the disciplinary process, in particular, by your husband. Do you think that's a fair assessment, or not?" the lieutenant asked.

Perspiration trickled down her back. In the chill of the room, her clothes were clammy against her skin. Her vision blurred, and the lieutenant's voice echoed weirdly. Sarah was back at her parents' house, over Thanksgiving weekend, just after the Disciplinary Committee had met. Eavesdropping on Heath through the door, his voice as he spoke to the girl so tenderly it was almost a caress. *With Darcy and Tessa gone, you can start fresh. You'll have me to guide you . . . silly girl.* He had been talking to Bel. Who else could it possibly be? There was something off in the exchange—something *wrong*. She'd known it then; she knew it now. Other people knew it, too. In the dining hall, they turned and stared. Yet everybody kept the secret. Sarah kept it, too, and now the girl was dead. She should tell them. She should tell them about Heath and Bel, about Anonymouse's photo.

But no, then they'd think he was a murderer, when he wasn't. Heath didn't kill Bel Enright. Zach Cuddy was in the woods that night. Rose said so. Sarah clung to that fact like a life raft, as the room spun around her.

"Mrs. Donovan, do you need me to repeat the question?"

"I-I don't feel well," she said, and bolted for the door.

53

Sarah was on her knees, heaving in a bathroom stall, when she heard the door to the ladies' room open. Her body shook with fever, and tears leaked from her eyes. She threw up again, and flushed the toilet, then stopped to listen. Somebody was standing outside the stall door.

"Hello?" she said.

"Mrs. Donovan? It's me, Melissa Howard. Are you all right in there?"

"No, I'm—not well."

"Would you like me to take you to a doctor?"

Sarah wiped her eyes and mouth with a piece of toilet paper. "It's the flu. My kids had it. It just has to run its course."

"I can take you home. My car is parked near the gym."

Home, and bed, sounded very good right now. Sarah struggled to her feet and staggered out of the stall. The detective reached out a hand to steady her.

"Whoa there."

"I'm okay. Just—I need some water."

Sarah rinsed her mouth and splashed her cheeks. The cold shock against her skin helped a little. As she dried her face with a paper towel, she looked in the mirror and saw Melissa Howard watching with a shrewd, steady gaze.

"You seemed really upset, up there. When the lieutenant asked about your husband."

The intelligence in the detective's eyes was disconcerting. If Sarah lied, this woman would probably know it. But she wasn't lying. She just wasn't telling every fact she knew. Not yet. Not until the mental fog of the fever went away, and she could decide more carefully what to say, and what not to say.

"I'm actually really sick. There's an awful virus going around this school. I'm not making that up."

"I believe you. The nurse told me about it."

"My apartment is closer than the parking lot. So, if you'll excuse me, I'm going to walk. I'm going home, to bed."

"Let me escort you. You're so unsteady that you might not make it on your own."

Sarah took one lurching step, and nearly toppled over, proving the detective right. She nodded.

With the detective supporting her firmly under one arm, they made it up the stairs and out onto the Quad. They walked along the columned portico, hugging the buildings to keep out of the wind. The headmaster's office was on the top floor of Founders' with a commanding view down the length of the Quad. If Heath happened to glance out his window right now, the portico would block his line of sight, and he wouldn't be able to see Sarah with the detective. He'd been so worried about her speaking to the police because he wanted to protect the school. That made her uncomfortable, but at the same time, she was glad he wouldn't see her. Why upset him, when she wasn't going to say anything, anyway. The police wouldn't listen to anything about Zach Cuddy being in the woods that night until they got their legal clearance. That made it impossible to tell them about the anonymous photo, or anything else that might implicate Heath in a relationship with Bel Enright. She would be painting a false picture. A worse picture than the actual, horrible truth. The police would suspect her husband of murder, when really all he had done was—what?

If Sarah was honest with herself, she didn't know what Heath had done.

At the outer door to Moreland, Sarah leaned against the wall and fumbled in her bag for her card key, as the detective looked on.

"That was a big help, but I'm fine from here," Sarah said.

"Sarah— May I call you Sarah?"

"Sure."

"You know, about these card keys."

"What about them?"

"There are virtually no surveillance cameras on Odell grounds. Did you know that?"

"I didn't. It doesn't surprise me, though. There's no crime here—uh, until recently."

"Very few cameras, but all the dorms use these card keys. Each use creates an electronic record. If we want to figure out who was where, and when, these little buggers can give us a pretty good picture."

"Why are you telling me this?"

"Can I come in? Just five minutes. There are a few things I think you should know."

That sounded bad. Sarah didn't think she could handle the truth right now, in her muddled state.

"I need to get to bed."

"Five minutes of your time."

"No. Really—"

"Look, Sarah, you're worried about Rose Enright getting jammed up for a murder she didn't commit, right? So am I, but the lieutenant, not so much. He's an old-timer, and experienced cops love those obvious explanations. Can't say I blame 'em. Nine times out of ten, they're the right ones. If the victim's been stabbed, then the girl with the bloody knife in her hand is the killer, right? Makes sense. Well, the lieutenant is working backward from that assumption. If Rose did it, then any evidence that doesn't fit needs to be explained away."

"But Rose didn't do it. It sounds like you know that. Why don't you tell him?"

"Because I *don't* know that. What I do know is: There are problems with the evidence against Rose. But just because I can poke holes in it, doesn't mean I have evidence against somebody else. And until I do, I can't say for sure that Rose is innocent. If you and me join forces, pool our knowledge, maybe we could get somewhere."

"Okay, come in. But I'm warning you, five minutes is the most I've got in me."

"Understood."

Sarah led the detective into the apartment. She sat down hard on the sofa and put a hand to her forehead. Her skin was burning.

"I'll try to make this quick," the detective said.

"The best thing is if I just tell you what Rose said this morning. I know you're not supposed to ask about it. But it's the only thing I know. I have no other information."

Melissa jiggled her knee anxiously, which shook the couch, and made Sarah dizzy.

"Are you nervous?" she asked, and the leg stopped jiggling.

"This is a tough one, Sarah. See, I think you might know more than you *think* you know."

"Huh? Sorry, but I'm too exhausted to understand that."

"Maybe if I tell you what *I* know, it might shake something loose."

"Okay."

Melissa searched Sarah's face, seemingly trying to decide whether to trust her. Her short hair and lack of makeup made her look girlish, like a friend Sarah might have had in high school. But she wasn't a friend. Sarah worried that she'd let her guard down too far by allowing the detective in the apartment, by trusting her more than she should. Especially when she was in such a weakened state.

"This could get me in trouble. You can't tell anyone. Do you promise?" Melissa said.

"Sure."

"All right. Down at Lost Lake where we recovered Bel Enright's body, we found three sets of footprints."

Sarah breathed raggedly, her heart fluttering with fever—or was it fear. *Three sets.*

"Whose footprints?" she asked.

"To determine that, we need shoes to compare them to, right? So, one set was Bel's. One was Rose's. But there was a set of male footprints that we can't identify. There was also male DNA, recovered from Bel's body by our forensics team. Not just from outside her clothing, but from—well, *inside.* You get the picture?"

The detective was telling her that Bel Enright had sex before she died. Why on earth would she tell *Sarah* such a thing?

Anonymouse's photo flashed before Sarah's eyes.

She'd been lying to herself. That was Heath's body in the photo. She knew it as well as she knew her own. As to who the girl was, she had no way of knowing. And yet—

A wave of nausea overpowered her. Sarah stood up, stumbled to the bathroom and vomited copiously. She lay on the floor afterward, weak and shivering. The detective knocked on the door.

"Are you okay?"

"Yes. Just a minute."

Sarah used the side of the tub to haul herself to

her feet. She washed out her mouth with Listerine and reached for the doorknob. She had to protect her husband. Not because he was guilty, but because she couldn't risk being the one to implicate him. Not now, not when her brain was so foggy with fever that she couldn't think straight, or know what various facts and pieces of evidence might add up to. She could tell Melissa what Rose said about Zach Cuddy. That, she knew was important. And she also knew it was true; or at least, that Rose claimed it was true. Let the police work on that lead, for now. Then, once Sarah's mind cleared, she would comb through what she knew about Heath, and decide whether there was anything that needed telling.

Melissa wasn't in the living room. Sarah followed the sounds to the kitchen. She found the detective bent over, looking in the dishwasher.

"Uh, can I help you?" Sarah asked, alarmed.

Melissa jumped up. "Oh, uh, I was thinking of getting a new dishwasher. Do you like this model?"

Even in her fevered state, Sarah recognized that as a lie. What the hell was Melissa Howard doing? Looking for evidence of some kind? In the dishwasher? It made no sense. But nothing made sense to Sarah's flu-addled brain.

"Look, I'm not feeling so great. You should go," Sarah said.

"You're right. One last thing, though. About those card keys—"

"What about them?"

"They show us when Bel and Rose left Moreland last

night. And Bel left more than an hour before Rose did. That's what I wanted to ask you. Where was Bel? Who was she with? Is it possible that Bel went to the lake first, and then somehow told Rose where to find her?"

"Well, I would say how should I know. But I do know. That's what happened. Bel went to the lake first," Sarah said.

She was feeling dizzy again and had to sit down.

Melissa's eyes widened. "You *do* know. I thought so."

"Yes. Rose told me. She said that Bel texted her."

"Oh," Melissa said, seeming disappointed. "Rose told you."

"She says, find her phone. It'll prove what happened."

"We have Rose's phone. Bel's too. The texts show Rose texting *Bel* to meet her at the lake. But based on evidence from the card keys, the texts were sent nearly two hours after Bel left Moreland, and an hour after Rose did. It makes no sense. And there are weird time gaps in the texts on both phones, like stuff was erased. I sent the phones to the lab, to see if they were tampered with. Kriscunas thinks I'm crazy, but I think, whoever killed Bel rigged the phones to frame Rose for the murder."

There was a layer of gauze between Sarah and the world that the detective's voice couldn't penetrate. There was something important she was supposed to convey. Right—about Zach Cuddy. Sarah had better tell the detective that, right now. She couldn't hold out against this fever much longer.

"Zach Cuddy," Sarah blurted.

"Cuddy? What about him?"

"Rose told me that—I think she said, he was in the woods that night. He chased her, and—and she cut him. Yes, definitely, now I remember. Zach was in the woods. Rose cut Zach with an X-Acto knife."

Melissa stared at her. "Well, that explains something. We did find an X-Acto knife with traces of blood, not far from the scene. The blood wasn't Bel's though, and the X-Acto knife wasn't the murder weapon. Thank you for clearing that up."

"You see what it means, right? Rose is innocent. Zach's the killer."

But Sarah was too muddled to explain why it meant that. And the detective looked unconvinced.

"The murder weapon was a kitchen knife, with a ten-inch blade," Melissa said. "Henckels, to be exact. I checked with the kitchen supply store in town. They don't carry that brand. Hard to see how Rose gets her hands on it, living in the dorm. Zach either."

Through her feverish haze, Sarah sensed that Melissa was making an important point about the knife. It meant something, but she had no idea what.

"You said Rose babysits for you, Sarah?"

"What?"

As she watched, the detective grew smaller and farther away.

"I have to lie down."

Sarah staggered down the hall and collapsed onto the bed. Eventually, she heard Melissa Howard moving around in the front hall, then the sound of the door closing. The detective had left without asking a single question about Heath. That was good, right? If they suspected him, they would ask her about him. Heath was innocent. He had to be. It was Zach Cuddy in the woods that night.

With the room spinning, Sarah couldn't focus. The murder investigation was complicated. So many facts, floating in her addled mind. She closed her eyes, and let the fever sweep her away.

54

Rose opened her eyes. It was dark in the room, except for a small sliver of light filtering under the door to the hallway. The light wasn't enough for her to see in the room, and she didn't hear anything. And yet she lay there, certain that she wasn't alone.

"Is—is somebody there?" she called in a shaky voice, reaching out her hand.

She sat up. A dark shadow fell across the sliver of light, and Rose watched it move. It was a man. He was coming toward her. She screamed at the top of her lungs, and the next second he was on her, pushing her down, pressing something soft—a pillow?—over her face. She fought as hard as she could. Lashing out, hitting at him, kicking, screaming. The lamp toppled over with a loud crash. But the more she struggled, the harder he pushed down, till she felt the fight going out of her.

The world was hot and airless. She kicked one last

time, and connected. He stepped sideways, and his hand was right next to her face. She bit down, tasting blood. He gasped, and let up for a split second. She tried to break free. Then he punched her, hard in the head, and she went down.

"Stop it," he said, and she knew who he was.

The pillow was on her face again. This time, he wouldn't let go. Red dots danced before her eyes. She blacked out.

55

There were two *men in the woods.*

Sarah woke from a fevered sleep, knowing that fact with terrible certainty. How did she know? Simple math. One plus one equals two. Numbers. Time. The problem existed on an axis. She could graph it, if only she had paper and pencil.

She staggered out of bed, heading toward the kitchen. A long time later, she arrived there, having forgotten why she came. She went to the sink and filled a glass with water, taking tiny sips. Keep hydrated. That was important with this flu. She remembered that from when the babies were sick.

The children. They were at day care. But no, they couldn't be. It was dark beyond the kitchen window, and the Quad was as empty as midnight. Sarah needed to call Heath, to tell him to pick the children up. But where was her phone?

Her eye fell on the knife block, beside the sink. Something was off about it. It registered just enough to seem significant, but she couldn't make sense of why. She remembered the detective, here in the kitchen, looking inside the dishwasher. It was a puzzle.

Oh, right—paper and pencil. Pencil and paper. She rummaged in a drawer, found the pad she used to write the occasional grocery list. Groceries. When had she last eaten? Not for a long time, but the thought of food made her want to—

She was in the bathroom, on her knees in front of the toilet.

"Mommy?" Harper said from the doorway.

The kids were home. Where was Heath?

"Go back to bed, sweetheart. Mommy's sick."

"I take care of you now," Harper said, coming to stroke Sarah's hair.

"Stop it. You'll catch my germs. Is Daddy home?"

"No. But Max is."

"Max is a dog. He can't help me. Close the door and go back to bed, Harps. Do it for Mommy. *Please*. Mommy needs to throw up now."

"Yuck," Harper said, and left.

Sarah threw up for what seemed like a very long time, her body wracked and heaving, then crumpled sideways to the floor. Her eyes were wide-open, staring, unfocused; her breathing was shallow. Her clothes smelled, and her mouth tasted sour, but the tile of the floor felt clean and cool against her cheek.

She would rest there for a bit, before making the herculean effort to get back to her bed.

Sarah closed her eyes for a minute. When she opened them again, she was staring right at the smudges.

On the bottom of the bathtub, just above the point where it met the floor, far enough back to be hidden from view by the toilet, there were three large smudges of what looked like blood. The only way you would see them was by getting down and putting your face in exactly this spot. Her head was hot and her eyes were burning, but she didn't think she was hallucinating. She crawled closer, her limbs aching with fever, and stared at them. The smudges were an inch or two long, and feathery, as if blood-soaked fabric had brushed up against the smooth porcelain of the tub. She put a fingertip to one. It was crusty, just like you'd expect from dried blood.

Those smudges are real.

This was not a dream, and it wasn't her imagination. As far away as Sarah's mind had traveled in the grip of her fever, it came rushing back, clear as day and full of terror. She'd seen the pieces of this puzzle, and allowed herself to dismiss them. Heath came home late on the night of Bel Enright's murder. The dog went crazy, and Heath put him out. Heath did laundry, which he never did, and came to bed smelling of bleach. There had even been the smell of fire. She should check the fireplace for signs that he'd burned his clothes.

What else did Sarah know? She wanted paper. Why? Because she knew about the sounds, in the woods. Rose had told her about them in great detail. She needed to graph the sounds. But where was the paper? She'd forgotten it, in the kitchen.

Sarah grabbed the side of the tub and pulled herself to sitting. That minimal effort drained her, and she had to stop and rest her face against the cool porcelain. When she'd caught her breath, she levered herself to standing. Her legs were like rubber, and the room swayed, but she managed not to topple over. In the hallway, she steadied herself against the wall to keep her balance, and stumbled to the kitchen, where she grabbed some paper and a pencil and sat down at the table. Strange lights danced before her eyes.

Sarah drew horizontal and vertical axes, then sat and stared at her handiwork. In her befuddled state, it took several minutes to realize that what she wanted was not so much a graph, as a timeline. Her fevered epiphany was all about timing: the timing of the sounds that Rose heard in the woods, when Bel was murdered.

What did Rose say? She heard footsteps behind her, crunching on snow, as she walked toward the lake. Somebody was following Rose through the woods. Sarah made a mark on the X-axis, close in to the Y-axis, and labeled it "Footsteps Behind Rose."

Next, Rose heard a scream that she recognized as Bel's. It came from the direction of Lost Lake. Sarah made a second mark, farther out along the X-axis, and labeled it "Scream from Bel—at Lost Lake."

Then what? Right after the scream, Zach Cuddy grabbed Rose from behind, and Rose cut him with the X-Acto knife to get away. Sarah made a third mark, and labeled it "Zach Grabs Rose/Gets Cut."

Well, there it was, in black and white. Zach was *behind* Rose at the moment Bel screamed. Sarah went back to the mark labeled "Footsteps Behind Rose." and added "Zach." Zach had been behind Rose the whole time. Zach was *still* behind Rose, on the path in the woods, when Bel screamed. But Bel was already down at the lake. And she screamed at just that moment—presumably in terror, or in pain.

What next? Rose ran toward Bel's scream. But Zach didn't follow or Rose would have mentioned hearing his footsteps behind her, which she didn't. Wherever Zach went next, it wasn't to the lake. Rose got there in a mere minute or two, and saw a bouncing light, which then disappeared. *Someone else*—not Zach—had been down at the lake at the moment Bel screamed. Someone who was alive, moving, using a flashlight, at the moment Rose arrived. But it couldn't've been Bel because the next moment, Rose found her sister—*already dead*. Sarah made another mark and wrote, "Rose Finds Bel Dead at Lake (Zach Not Present)." Then she went back to the mark for Bel's scream, added, "Second Man at Lake?" and underscored it three times.

Bel died at Lost Lake, while Rose and Zach were still in the woods. Rose found the body. She found the murder weapon, picked it up, held it in her hand. And then somebody hit her in the head.

Zach was gone at that point.

There was a second man.

Heath.

Sarah wrote her husband's name. Then she crawled back to bed and sank down into fevered dreams, filled with blood.

56

Sarah tossed in a haze of delirium. The kids were here somewhere; she heard their piping voices, and was glad they were far away from her, healthy and safe.

It was bright in the room. Daytime. At some point, her vision cleared, and Heath stood over her, holding a piece of paper. He was asking her something she didn't understand, lips moving, face screwed up in a fury she'd rarely seen from him. Was this real? Sarah cried, and begged him not to talk so loud, because her head was about to explode.

She woke up sometime later. There were strange men in the room, carrying a stretcher.

"We're moving you to the hospital, babe. I'm worried about you," Heath said, in such a loving tone that she knew she'd imagined those awful things before.

"What? No. I'm fine."

"Sarah, you need an IV. You're terribly dehydrated."

They told her to cross her arms across her chest, but

her body wouldn't listen to her mind. They took her under the arms and thighs and lifted her. She floated in midair, then she was on the stretcher with Heath looking down at her.

"We're moving to the headmaster's house," he said. "I'll see you there."

Sarah didn't even try to understand. She just gave in to darkness.

57

Transcript of Witness Interview conducted by Detective Melissa Howard, Odell NH, PD, with Mr. Zachary Cuddy. [NOTE: Interview conducted at Odell Infirmary; DNA sample taken and transmitted to lab per chain-of-custody form.]

Howard: FYI, I'm recording this on my phone. Thanks for meeting with me, Zach.

Cuddy: You didn't give me much choice. The subpoena said show up and give a DNA sample, or be held in contempt. I'm requesting a lawyer, Detective.

Howard: Yeah, sorry, kiddo, you're not entitled to a lawyer for this part. It's not an interrogation, just a simple cheek swab. Noninvasive. Your dad gave his permission in writing.

Cuddy: I told you before, my father is not sophisticated enough to look out for my interests in this situation. He's kneejerk pro–law enforcement. The cops are always right in his book. If you want my DNA, he assumes I did something that I ought to be punished for. Do you understand? He's not about to help me.

Howard: Do I hear you saying that you didn't do anything terrible?

Cuddy: I didn't kill Bel Enright, that's for sure.

Howard: But you were in the woods that night.

Cuddy: Don't you have to tell me I have the right to remain silent before you ask me something like that?

Howard: You're not in custody, Zach, so—no. But if it makes you feel better, I'll read you your rights.

Cuddy: No, thanks.

Howard: I'll be up front with you. I have information that you sustained a cut to your hand in the woods the night of Bel's murder, and I'm investigating that to prove your whereabouts at the time of Bel's death.

Cuddy: Rose Enright tell you that?

Howard: You know I can't confirm or deny witness identity.

Cuddy: God, what a bitch. I covered for her, too.

Howard: Covered how?

Cuddy: I could've said she was there. But I didn't. I told you about that thug Brandon Flynn instead. He is a thug. Did you interview him, like I said?

Howard: You just admitted to obstruction of justice, Zach, you realize that?

Cuddy: Lucky for me, you never read me my rights.

Howard: You're a little too smart for your own good. Ready to confess?

Cuddy: Confess to what? I didn't do anything. I'm innocent. I actually had feelings for Bel. I would never hurt her.

Howard. All right, then. If you're innocent, this swab will exonerate you.

Cuddy: Oh, really? How is it going to do that?

Howard: By not matching the samples. The person who murdered Bel left forensic material in and on her body.

[PAUSE]

Howard: Are you okay?

Cuddy: Forensic material. What kind of material? Was it—semen?

Howard: Is there something you need to tell me, Zach?

58

*R*ose!

Sarah startled awake in a hospital bed with an IV in her arm, and Rose Enright's name on her lips.

But why? There was something she was supposed to do. What was it? She'd already spoken to the detective. She had relayed the message. Zach Cuddy was in the woods that night. She'd fulfilled her promise to Rose.

No. It was something else.

She looked around and realized she was not in the Odell Infirmary. A buzzer hung from a cord at the head of her bed. She pressed it repeatedly until a nurse came, but it was a male nurse, with a mustache, wearing scrubs and Crocs. Nobody she recognized.

"Is Kim here?" she asked.

"I don't know any Kim, ma'am. Is there something you need?"

"Where am I?"

"County Hospital, receiving intravenous fluids. That

virus going around the school is so bad, the infirmary is full, so they brought you here."

She remembered two men, a stretcher. And Heath.

Heath.

She'd told Heath that Rose had regained her memory. She'd made a graph of the sounds from the woods, and Heath had found it. He'd asked her about it, yelled at her, in a rage. Heath knew what Rose had seen, what she'd heard.

"Where is my husband?"

"Sorry, I really don't know. I only came on duty fifteen minutes ago."

"I need to get out."

"Do you need the bathroom?"

"No. I need to leave here, right away. There's something important I have to do."

"You're not leaving till the doctor clears you. Dehydration is no joke. If you don't follow instructions, you'll relapse. So, please, calm down, and rest."

He left.

Sarah took in her surroundings. She was alone in this room, wearing a hospital gown. She didn't see a clock, didn't have her phone, and there was no landline visible in the room. Based on the weak light filtering through the window blinds, it might be early morning or late afternoon. She had no idea what day it was, and she was worried for Rose's safety. Why? There was a nagging twinge in the back of her mind, a memory that she needed to bring forward. It had to do with the apartment in Moreland, and the detective.

The detective, looking in the dishwasher.

The murder weapon was a kitchen knife, with a ten-inch blade, Henckels, to be exact, she'd said. Sarah owned a set of Henckels knives, received years ago as a wedding gift. They lived on the counter beside the sink. Melissa Howard had been looking right at them when she made that comment. Later, Sarah had stood in that same spot by the sink, at the height of her fever, staring at the knife block, feeling like something was wrong—off, missing. She closed her eyes and visualized.

Sarah gasped. The slot farthest to the left had been empty.

She hadn't been able to process it then, to realize the significance of what was right before her eyes. Normally, that slot held a ten-inch chef's knife. *It was gone.* That's why the detective had looked in the dishwasher. When she saw that the slot was empty, she went looking for the knife. But she wouldn't've found it. The Donovans owned few precious things; the ones they did own were tenderly cared for. Heath, even more than Sarah, would never in a million years put the good knives in the dishwasher. If that knife was gone from its slot, then it wasn't in the apartment.

Had their wedding gift been used to end Bel Enright's life? The idea was awful in itself. Even if a complete stranger had stolen that knife and used it to murder a young girl, that would be devastating. It took her fogged mind a moment to take the next terrible step. If the knife was used to kill Bel, then she had to grapple with who had used it.

Two people had access to Sarah's kitchen, other than herself. Rose. And Heath.

Rose had unfettered access to that knife only when she babysat for the children, which she hadn't done for probably two weeks, prior to Bel's death. Rose would have had to plan far in advance to steal the knife, and count on Sarah not figuring out that it was missing. The fact was, it hadn't been missing—not for long anyway, or Sarah would have noticed.

That left Heath. Her husband. The man she'd loved since they were practically children, as young as Rose and Bel were now.

As young as Bel *had been*.

Could the man that Sarah loved, the man she'd stood by through highs and lows, the man who slept beside her every night, who adored their children and quoted poetry and made a fuss over her birthday, could that man be capable of such evil? Did Heath take a wedding gift from their kitchen, the kitchen where they ate breakfast with their children every morning, and smuggle it out to the woods, intending to commit murder? To kill a student, a young girl in his charge, to keep her quiet about their sexual affair? And having intended such a thing, did he carry it out? Did he have it in him to plunge a knife into that girl's body until her blood ran out into the snow? Until the life left her, and she was dead?

Sarah thought about the plain facts. The evidence seen with her own eyes, heard with her own ears. The intimate phone call at Thanksgiving. The photograph of Heath making love to a young woman. His mysterious absences at critical times. The dog going crazy the night Bel was murdered. The late-night laundry. The smell of bleach. And now, the missing knife, and the smudges of blood on the bathtub. She thought about the lies she'd told herself so she could continue believing in her husband. In his fidelity, his basic goodness. But that was ridiculously simplistic. No person was all good or all bad. Heath least of all. He was capable of deceit, as Sarah well knew. He'd deceived her before, about a matter of great importance. And as loving as he could be, as adoring a husband and father, he could never see past himself, or get out of his own way. He was profoundly selfish.

Selfish enough to murder his young lover, in order to silence her, to further his own ambition?

If the answer to that was yes, then Sarah was complicit in Bel's murder. She didn't know how to live with that, but it would be true. She could have outed Heath, revealed his affair, destroyed his career, and prevented him from being in a position to do harm. Instead, she had worked diligently to explain away every damning fact. Her need to believe in him had taken priority over protecting a young woman's life.

Could that happen again? If Heath murdered Bel, it wasn't much of a leap to thinking he might seek to silence Rose in the same way. That would also be Sarah's fault, even more directly. Sarah had told Heath about Rose regaining her memory. She'd drawn a timeline, written Heath's name on it, shown him exactly how Rose could implicate him. If Rose was in danger now, it was Sarah's absolute duty to protect her, to warn her.

Sarah lay there and stared at the IV in her arm. The intravenous fluids were holding off the worst symptoms of the virus, but she felt ragged and exposed, like her nerves were on the outside of her body. She couldn't imagine standing up, let alone getting to the infirmary to warn Rose. But Rose's life could be at stake. She had to take action.

That nurse would never let Sarah leave here without a fight. She'd have to sneak out.

With her fingernails, Sarah carefully pried the adhesive tape from around the catheter at the crook of her elbow. A light bruise surrounded the site where the needle penetrated her skin. Just looking at it made her dizzy and nauseous, but waiting wouldn't make this any easier. She grabbed a Kleenex from the box on the bedside stand, and gently tugged on the catheter. It didn't budge, so she pulled harder, crying out in pain as she yanked it from her arm. She clamped down with the Kleenex, which swiftly turned red. She lay back on the bed to collect herself and wait for the bleeding to stop.

She found her clothes and shoes in a plastic bag that hung from the foot of her bed, and dressed as quickly as her clumsy, unresponsive fingers and limbs would allow. She searched the room, but her coat, wallet and phone were nowhere to be found. It was snowing outside the window, and she was fifteen minutes by car from Odell. But taxis idled in the turnaround area. There wasn't a moment to waste. If the nurse caught her, he'd stop her from leaving, and she would lose her chance to warn Rose. She cracked the door, peeked into the hall. It was empty, and she headed for the stairs.

59

Transcript of Witness Interview conducted by Detective Melissa Howard, Odell NH, PD, with Ms. Kimberly Kowalski, head nurse, Odell Academy Infirmary.

Howard: Okay, I got the recorder going now. This is Detective Melissa Howard. I was here on another matter, when I was approached by Nurse Kowalski, who asked to file a report about a disturbance in Rose Enright's room last night. Ma'am, can you repeat what you just told me?

Kowalski: Okay, this was maybe ten, ten-thirty last night, and the girl wrecked her room. I'm reporting this because I would appreciate her being removed from this facility ASAP.

Howard: From the beginning, please. Just the facts. What you heard, what you saw.

Kowalski: Okay. I was the only person on duty. I worked a double shift yesterday because we've got four *nurses out with the flu. I'd been on since eight a.m., on my feet the whole time. So, I took a little lie-down in the only empty room in the house, which happens to be at the far end of the hall next to Rose Enright's room. We purposely have her isolated down there, under lock and key, given the, uh, situation and all. You know, I keep asking when she will be removed from my facility because I'm not equipped to handle this. She's medically cleared to go at this point. For the life of me, I don't understand why she's still here.*

Howard: Why is she still here?

Kowalski: You tell me. We're waiting for charges to be filed.

Howard: Look, ma'am, no warrant has been filed. We can't make you keep her here if that's not medically necessary. You can discharge her whenever you like. Just give us a heads-up, so we can keep track of where she goes in case we do decide to arrest her.

Kowalski: Where does she go? Back to the dorm? I mean, this girl's a murderer.

Howard: Maybe, maybe not. Just so you know, we have not made a determination yet as to who committed this murder. So, when it comes time to release Rose, I assume you'll call her family.

Kowalski: I doubt they want her. The grandma was in here yesterday, upset out of her mind. The one granddaughter, stabbing the other. Terrible thing.

Howard: Right. So. Back to the details. Ten, ten-thirty last night. You're sleeping. What happened?

Kowalski: Not sleeping. Maybe I dozed off for a minute.

Howard: Okay, dozing. Then what?

Kowalski: I heard a commotion.

Howard: Can you be more specific?

Kowalski: A crashing sound. Like, someone was tearing up the place. I got up out of bed to investigate. Maybe it took me a minute or so before I found my shoes and my glasses. Then I went out to the hall, and I saw the door to Rose's room was open.

Howard: Open all the way, or—?

Kowalski: No, like, a few inches. But that door's kept locked, so it scared me to see that. Rose scares me. I didn't know what I would find when I went in there.

Howard: Did you call Odell Security?

Kowalski: No, I didn't. I was in too much of a hurry. See, if that girl did something—suicide, violence, whatever—because I made a mistake and left her door unlocked, that comes back on me. I didn't have time to wait for security to show up. I just went charging in there.

Howard: You're saying, you left the door unlocked.

Kowalski: No. I'm saying I'm very careful, and I remember locking it.

Howard: How did the door wind up open then?

Kowalski: Rose found a way to open it herself. Has to be.

Howard: Okay. What happened when you went in there?

Kowalski: I found the room a disaster, and Rose fast asleep in her bed.

Howard: Disaster, you say. Can you be more specific?

Kowalski: The IV pole tipped over. The water jug

and cup on the floor with water everywhere. The covers kicked off. Pillow over her face—

Howard: Pillow over her face? You didn't mention that before.

Kowalski: I was just getting to it—

Howard: Was she all right?

Kowalski: Yes, she's fine. I woke her up to make sure. And honestly, to ask her what the hell she thought she was doing, wrecking the place. She claimed a man broke in and tried to kill her.

Howard: What? Why didn't you tell me that immediately?

Kowalski: Because it's not true. It's impossible. Maybe it's possible I left Rose's door unlocked, through an oversight. Very remote possibility. But there is no way some outsider got in there.

Howard: Outsider? Why not someone from Odell? Surely people have keys.

Kowalski: The doctors and nurses do. You're not gonna convince me that one of them attacked Rose Enright.

Howard: I'm not saying that. What about Odell faculty? Any of them have master keys?

Kowalski: I have no idea. Security could probably help you out with that.

Howard: I'm not supposed to interview Rose, so I have to rely on you. Tell me exactly what she said. There was a man in her room? How did he get in? Could she describe him? What did he do? Did he say anything?

Kowalski: I didn't ask her a lot of questions because I didn't believe what she was telling me. Long story

*short, she wakes up, there's a guy in her room, and he
tries to smother her. She fights him off, which is what
caused the ruckus, and he splits before she can get a
look at him.*

Howard: He tried to smother her?

*Kowalski: Yep, and then he punched her. She claims.
Which, I will admit, she does have a mark on her face.
But she could've done that to herself. You're looking
at me funny. I'm telling you, there's no way for anybody to get in. The infirmary has two entrances. The
back entrance is always locked. The front entrance is
locked after five p.m., and it was locked last night. I
was the only person on duty after four p.m. Anybody
who got in, I had to buzz them in. We had two students
admitted, and a few more kids in and out for meds.
But everybody who wasn't admitted was gone by eight
o'clock. Nope. Didn't happen.*

Howard: Unless they did so without your knowing.

*Kowalski: Whatever. I said what I think. Anyways,
Detective?*

Howard: Yes?

*Kowalski: This girl is a problem. I want her out of
here. You're telling me I don't have to keep her, I'm
calling her grandmother to have her discharged. Wait,
where are you going?*

*Howard: I need to talk with my partner. Something's
going on here that we need to get a handle on. Don't
release Rose without telling me first.*

60

The door to Rose's room was ajar. That nurse had left it unlocked. Rose could hear them just outside in the hallway, talking about her, playing with her fate like she was a toy. Her grandmother, the lawyer and the nurse, who made no secret of disliking Rose, hating her even, because she believed Rose had murdered her own sister. The nurse could've stopped the real killer, when he came to Rose's room last night, if she'd had an open mind, and paid attention. But she was lazy as well as blind. People saw what they wanted to. The nurse accused Rose of punching her own face, wrecking her own room. She wouldn't believe in Heath Donovan's guilt even if she'd personally witnessed him standing over Rose's bed, smothering her with that pillow.

"I want her out by the end of today," the nurse was saying. "There is no medical reason for us to keep her, and I'm full to bursting with flu patients. I need that bed."

"The police will have something to say about that. They don't want her out on the street," Warren Adams said.

"This isn't a jail, Mr. Adams. If the police want to arrest her, they can be my guest. But if she's medically cleared to go, she's not staying here. I'm discharging her."

"We're not set up to care for her properly," Grandma said, in a tremulous voice. "We need to make arrangements. Talk to a psychiatrist, find her a bed in a facility. That could take weeks."

"Ma'am, where this girl goes next is not my problem. Four p.m., she's gone, and that's all I have to say."

Four o'clock wasn't soon enough. Rose couldn't even wait that long to get out of this place. She wasn't safe here. He'd come to her room last night, done his best to silence her, and presumably thought he'd succeeded. But he'd been careless. At the first signs of the nurse coming, he'd run off without finishing the job. The second he found out that Rose was still alive, he'd be back. She had to be gone before then.

Grandma and Mr. Adams were alone in the hallway now, discussing what to do about Rose's impending release.

"You can't just take her home. She's dangerous," Warren Adams said.

"We don't know that for sure. We haven't gotten an opinion from a psychiatrist yet. Maybe it would be all right."

"You don't need a psychiatrist to tell you that a girl who stabbed her sister seventeen times is a danger. It's common sense, Martha. We can't let them release her. I say we go talk to Heath Donovan. He was just named headmaster. New headmasters need to prove themselves as fund-raisers. Dangle a big enough cash contribution in front of him, and he'll keep Rose locked up here forever."

He'll keep Rose locked up here forever. She panicked, her heart racing. Heath Donovan was now headmaster, and they were going to *tell* him that Rose was still alive, about to be released, out of his control. He'd murder her before she could put her shoes on. Rose needed to get out of here, fast. But she needed help. She had no money and no clothing other than a hospital gown. Outside her window it was nearly dark, and the sky was spitting a frigid-looking rain. She was in the middle of the vast Odell campus, which Donovan now ruled. If she tried to run, her fellow students would turn her in in a heartbeat, either because they were nasty backstabbers or blind rule-followers. Most of them were.

Maybe not everyone.

The nurse, eager to be rid of Rose, had gotten careless. She left the door unlocked, and Rose strolled out of her room, easy as pie. There were kids sleeping on stretchers in the hallway, with no adults in sight. She stopped to pilfer a pair of rain boots and a parka from the coatroom near the front door. Nobody saw her. Her bare shins protruded from her hospital gown as she exited into a gust of bitter wind. Stinging sleet blew into her eyes and scored her skin. She shivered with cold as she hurried on stiff legs, unused to walking after a couple of days in bed, forced to take the much longer back route to avoid being seen.

Once upon a time, Rose had lived for Zach Cuddy, and in those innocent days, she'd made it her business to know everything about him, including which dorm was his, and which window. He lived on the second floor of Ashcroft Hall, in a room accessible from the ramshackle fire escape that snaked up the back side of the building. By the time Rose reached Ashcroft, she was soaking wet and blue-tinged. She stood and stared at that fire escape. During her ill-fated crush on Zach, she'd imagined climbing it, though never in a million years would she have done it for real. (Sneaking into a boys' dorm outside of official visitation hours was a major disciplinary offense.) She'd been a good girl then, but now she had bigger worries than getting suspended.

The fire escape was steep and narrow with rusty metal steps. She climbed quickly, the wet hospital gown flapping around her bare legs and the too-big boots slipping. When she reached the landing, she looked in the window and saw that Zach's room was empty. Her spirits plummeted. When she'd decided to ask Zach for help, she'd assumed she would miraculously find him in his room. But there were a dozen other places on campus he might be, including the library, the gym, a snack bar, a friend's room. If Rose went looking— recognizable as she was, dressed like a hobo, spattered with mud—there was a likelihood approaching a certainty that she'd be caught. And sent to *Donovan* for discipline.

The wind gusted and lashed cold rain into her face. Rose huddled into the lee of the building, shivering. She couldn't stay here, but she had nowhere else to go. With the next gust of wind, the ancient part of her brain told her to seek shelter, so she threw up the window sash and climbed through into Zach's room.

The room was warm and messy, and smelled like dirty laundry. In the midst of the horror show that her life had become, she recalled, as if from long ago, what it felt like to be smitten with Zach. She immediately knew which side of the room was his. It was piled with books and papers, the walls hung with posters for indie bands and an Ansel Adams photograph of snow-covered mountains. The other side, covered with sports memorabilia, clearly belonged to Zach's roommate, a hockey player Rose considered beneath him. She walked around for a moment, mesmerized, running a finger over Zach's bed with its navy-striped comforter, imagining how she might have sat on this bed during visitation hours had things gone differently between them.

A noise in the hallway reminded her that she could be caught. Heart racing, she dove into the closet on Zach's side of the room, squeezing in amongst shoes, sports equipment and dry-cleaning bags. Her movements stirred up dust, and she sneezed, stifling the sound with her hands, terrified that someone might hear. But nobody came to investigate, and she settled in, making a nest for herself on the floor. In a laundry bag stuffed in the corner, she discovered a pair of sweatpants and an Odell sweatshirt, slightly tangy with sweat but warm and dry. Maneuvering carefully so as not to make noise, she got out of her wet things, and dressed herself in Zach Cuddy's clothes.

It was warm and stuffy in the closet. Rose tucked the laundry bag behind her head, leaned back and closed her eyes. Just for a minute.

Sometime later, voices woke her. Zach and his roommate were in the room, talking about whether to go over to the dining hall or order a pizza. Zach's voice was right outside the closet door now. If he opened it and discovered her, with his roommate watching, she was done. But he moved away. He was sitting at his desk now, from the sound of it. He told his roommate to go on to dinner without him, that he'd be along shortly.

Rose waited until the roommate was gone, then eased the door open. Zach sat with his head on the desk, cradled in his arms, like he was upset. Rose stepped out.

"Zach," she said.

He jumped out of his chair and backed away. "Jesus Christ, what the hell are you doing here?" he said, shutting the door to the hallway. "Did they let you out?"

"No, I escaped."

He looked at her, horror-struck. "You're wearing my clothes. You're scaring me, Enright. People say you're a fucking loon, and I defend you, but now I have to wonder. Maybe you did kill your sister."

Rose raised her hands placatingly. "No, I swear to God, I didn't kill her. Zach, you know that. It was Donovan. It has to be. Last night, he tried to kill *me*."

"What the hell are you talking about?"

"He came into my room in the infirmary while I was sleeping, and tried to suffocate me with a pillow."

"Did you call the police?"

"No. There's no phone in my room, and I was locked in. I told the nurse. And guess what, she accused me of trashing my own room, punching myself in the face and making up a story to cover my ass. That nurse hates me. But now that Donovan's headmaster, *nobody's* gonna believe me. That's why I came here, because I knew *you* would. I need your help, Zach. My phone is missing, but you have those pictures, right? We have to give them to the police right away. We have to get Donovan arrested, before he comes after me again. Or after you."

"Hate to burst your bubble. But I gave the cops the pictures. Nothing happened."

"When?"

"This morning."

"How do you know they didn't arrest him?"

"I saw him on the Quad half an hour ago. It was like seeing the devil walking the earth. I actually got a chill."

"When you gave the police the pictures, did they say anything about what they planned to do?"

"No. She said thank you, but it didn't mean shit. She thinks I did it, given that I got hauled in to give a DNA swab, all because of *you*. What's up with that, Enright? I thought we were friends, and you claim *I* killed Bel. Why did you lie?"

"It wasn't a lie, it was a *mistake*. I saw you in the woods, right before I found her. When somebody came from behind and hit me in the head, naturally, I thought it was you."

"Why would you think that? You know how I felt about her."

"You always denied it. Besides, I actually thought you were stalking her, so that sort of made it more likely you were guilty. But now that I remember what happened, I know the truth, and I'll tell them. I'll clear your name, I promise."

"A day late and a dollar short. I saw you in the woods, too, you know. You actually *cut* me, but I didn't tell on you. I told the cops to go after Flynn instead."

"Why would you do that, if you thought *I* killed Bel?"

"I never believed you would hurt her. In my heart, I knew it was Donovan, that fucking creep. He killed her to shut her up."

"Then why not tell the police it was him? Why implicate Brandon Flynn?"

"Flynn," Zach said with a bitter laugh. "That asshole torments me. I'm pretty sure he tapped my phone somehow, when I gave it to him to be wiped. But that's another story. Honestly, I wanted to make trouble for him. Plus, I didn't think they would believe me about Donovan. Donovan walks on water, as far as the rest of the world is concerned. What do we have to put up against his angelic reputation? Pretty much nothing. The photo from the laundry room is so blurry that it sucks as evidence. And the picture of Bel getting into his car doesn't prove anything. I could have great photos, and I bet you nobody would buy it. Donovan's like Teflon. Nothing sticks to him. He charms everyone. Just look where we are now. Bel is dead, and Donovan is on top of the world. He *won.*"

"Don't say that. You can't give up. We owe it to Bel to stop him."

"What do you suggest we do? I gave the pictures to the police this morning. I think we would have heard if they arrested him. Instead, the scuttlebutt is, he's moving into the headmaster's house as we speak."

"I could tell the police he tried to kill me last night."

"Be my guest. I'll give you the detective's phone number, even dial the phone. But the nurse didn't believe you, so why would the police?"

"You know who would believe me? Mrs. Donovan. She trusts me. She knows I didn't kill Bel. That I wouldn't make this up. We should go talk to her."

"We can't. Mrs. Donovan has dropped from sight. Nobody knows where she is."

"That's not possible. I just saw her— Wait, what day was that?"

"I wouldn't know. Kids in the dining hall were speculating that she's out with the flu. But Emma says she's not in Moreland, and the Donovan kids got sent to their grandparents' house. Their stuff is getting moved to the headmaster's residence, but the secretary is handling the move. Mrs. D isn't in the infirmary. I heard that from a guy in my dorm who just got discharged this morning. It's bizarre, like she vanished."

"What are you suggesting?"

"I might be willing to give your idea a try, Enright. But in order to do that, we have to find her. I'm thinking maybe Donovan doesn't want to risk that happening."

Rose stared at him, as the fear spread like cold liquid through her body. "Like, he *did* something to her?"

"The guy is a psychopath. I wouldn't put anything past him. If Mrs. Donovan knew something, yeah, he could go after her. For the same reason he killed Bel."

"What's that?"

"Like I said. To keep her quiet."

61

Sarah asked the taxi driver to take her directly to the infirmary, and to wait for her while she checked inside. But when she got there, Rose had already left. Kim Kowalski claimed that Mrs. Enright took Rose without asking or signing discharge papers. Nobody saw her leave. Sarah found this troubling, but her mind was cloudy from the virus, which came on with terrible ferocity, it seemed, each night when the sun went down.

Kim took one look at Sarah, and told her to go home to bed. Sarah promised to do so, and borrowed money to pay for the cab. She needed to go home anyway, to find her phone, and call Rose to make sure she was all right.

At the turnaround area behind Moreland Hall, a large moving van blocked the road. As Sarah got out of the cab, the door to Moreland's rear entrance flew open, and a mover came out, carrying the oval mirror from Sarah's bedroom, wrapped in Bubble Wrap, and the bunny lamp from the kids' room.

"Wait a minute, those are my things," she said. "Where are you taking them?"

He was a young guy, beefy, with tattoos, and a harried look. "Headmaster's house, ma'am."

"Who gave you permission to do that?"

"Betsy, the headmaster's secretary. We were told to move the stuff from this apartment over to the headmaster's house."

"But that move isn't happening yet," she said.

"Yeah, it is. I'm doing it right now."

Was this for real? It felt like a bad dream. Like Sarah had returned home after a long absence, to find strangers living in her house.

"But those are my things," she repeated, on the verge of tears. "Put them back. I don't want them moved."

"I'm doing my job here, lady. You got a problem, take it up with Betsy," the mover said, turning to go.

"*Wait.* Where are my kids?"

"I don't know your kids from Adam."

"Are they inside?"

"Nobody's in there. They already moved," he said, looking at her like she was crazy.

Her fever spiking, Sarah forgot about Rose, and thought of nothing but the fact that her children were missing. *Find the children. Find the children.* She ran down the path and out onto Founders' Road, toward the headmaster's house. It was a ten-minute walk under the best of circumstances, but now it felt endless.

Like Sisyphus with the boulder, the more she walked, the farther behind she fell. A mix of sleet and freezing rain made the road slick. The old loafers she'd worn in the hospital seemed to have glass soles. She took baby steps on shaky legs to avoid slipping and falling, and got colder with every step. She couldn't stop to rest. She had to get there, to find her babies. What came after that, she didn't know. If what she suspected was true, they couldn't stay with Heath.

The headmaster's house was a brick-and-limestone folly, extravagantly ornamented with turrets and gargoyles. It sat on a slight bluff at the head of Founders' Road, at an inconvenient distance from the main Quad, with a wide front lawn that sloped down to the street, and dark woods in the back. People said it was the crown jewel of Odell architecture. But Sarah saw it in the distance and shivered. With its windows lit from within and glowing a turgid yellow, it looked evil. Like a haunted house. Or the house of a killer.

She was panting and soaking wet by the time she got to the front door. When it swung open as she reached for the bell, she might have been living a nightmare.

Heath stepped back and pulled Sarah into the double-height entry foyer. It was massive, with a chandelier and sweeping staircase, but Sarah wasn't impressed. She'd grown up in a fancy house, and knew the coldness of such places. Her main memories of her childhood home were of being scolded for tracking mud on the expensive carpet or leaving fingermarks on the walls. But Heath would love it here, she suspected. It would feed his delusions of grandeur.

"Where have you been?' he said. "I've been worried sick. You pulled out your own IV and walked out of the hospital? Are you crazy? I had to leave my meeting to go driving around, looking for you."

Through the fever-haze, she noted that he had not called the police. Odd behavior from a man truly worried for his wife's safety.

She heard the dog barking. The sound came from far away.

"Is Max in the basement?" she asked.

"Let's get you to bed."

"Heath, why is the dog in the basement?"

"He's been misbehaving."

"Since Bel died, right? Why did you do laundry that night? And what happened to the knife from our kitchen?" Sarah asked.

His face contorted. Or maybe that was a trick of her eyes. The checkerboard marble floor came up to meet her.

Sarah woke up alone, in a strange bed, in a strange room. It was dark outside, and quiet, but the bedside lamp cast an orange circle that lit the room sufficiently to see. From the height of the ceilings, and the fussiness of the décor, she knew—she remembered—that this was the headmaster's house. But where was Heath? Where were the children?

Sarah dragged herself from bed and staggered across the Persian carpet to the door. The knob wouldn't turn. Was she that weak? She tried again. It wouldn't budge.

Had Heath locked her in here? She put her forehead against the door, and tears flooded her eyes. The man she'd loved for her entire adult life was keeping her prisoner? She couldn't let him do this to her. Sarah lifted her fist and pounded.

He came in an instant. She heard the key turn, and fear clutched at her throat. Fear, of her own husband. Heath entered the room and took her by the shoulders, steering her firmly back to bed.

"Babe, you shouldn't be up," he said, pushing her down, and not gently.

Her legs collapsed under her, and she fell back onto the bed. Heath loomed over her. He was larger than her in every way—taller, broader, stronger. Before, always, she'd found that comforting. Even in their lowest moments, she'd felt physically protected by him. But now she saw that he could use that strength against her. He could turn on a dime, with no warning. All men could. That comfort, that trust, would then turn to terror in her heart. Presumably that was what happened to Bel Enright, the night she died.

Sarah shook so hard that her teeth chattered. She pulled the blanket over her, and pulled it up to her chin. But it did nothing to make her warmer, or less afraid. She was also angry. She'd given him the benefit of the doubt for so long. What kind of fool was she to give him a pass like that, when the signs were so clear? And he'd taken advantage.

"You locked me in here," Sarah said.

"Yeah, because I'm not about to risk you trying to get up, and falling down that staircase."

"Why not? Then I'd be dead, like Bel. Isn't that what you want?"

"Sarah, you're delirious."

"What have you done with the children?"

"Your mother picked them up. She wasn't happy about it, but when I told her I got named headmaster, and I was busy meeting the trustees, she came around."

"You killed that girl, Heath."

He sat down on the edge of the bed. He could reach down and strangle her easily, if he chose to. But Heath wasn't angry. He seemed merely hurt.

"Sarah, you need to stop saying these things. Nobody can overhear right now, but if they did—"

"So what? It's the truth."

"That's the flu talking. It's making you say crazy things," he said.

She wasn't surprised he would lie. He'd lied the last time she'd confronted him about something enormous. She'd had proof then, too. And still, he denied it. He denied until denial became impossible, at which point, he went for the coward's escape. And failed. This man, whom the world viewed as a great success, was actually a failure at everything he did. Sarah kept trying to fix him. It hadn't worked, and it was time to stop.

"Heath," she said, in a weak voice, struggling to get the words out. "*Please*, if you have any respect for me, any self-respect, stop lying. I know what you did. I won't close my eyes any longer. I only want to understand, and make it right."

He looked away. When he wouldn't meet her eyes, she knew, a hundred percent. Her last shred of denial went up in smoke, and she shook with rage, and grief for what they could have had, but lost.

"You were always stronger than me," he said, and hung his head. "That's why I love you so much."

"*Why*? Why did you do it?"

His eyes shimmered with tears, and his shoulders started to heave. This was the real Heath, the Heath she always saw at the darkest moments, weak and vulnerable and filled with self-pity.

"I did it for *you*," he said, sniveling.

"*No*," she said, and her voice, in her sickness and her shock, came out in a hoarse croak.

"I did! For you, for us, our kids, our life together. I made a terrible mistake. Okay, that part, I take responsibility for. I slipped up with that girl. Bel came into my life at a moment when I just really needed—I don't know—confidence, affirmation? You didn't believe in me, Sarah. You looked at me with doubt in your eyes."

"Don't you *dare* make this about me."

"The way Bel adored me—it was like a drug."

"I have to throw up," Sarah said.

The bathroom was en suite, or she wouldn't have made it in time. She slammed the door, and heaved. There was nothing in her stomach anyway. Time passed. She lay against the bathtub and thought of all the ways he'd failed her and their children and himself. She wished him gone. She even wished him dead. But from the floor, as she pushed the door open much later, she saw him standing just outside.

"Go away," she said.

"Here, let me help you back to bed."

She didn't have the strength to resist.

He sat down beside her again, and started to talk in a low, comforting voice, like one would use with an invalid, or a child.

"I never intended to hurt Bel," he said. "I was trying to fix the problem I created. I know what I did was wrong, but that came out of the fact that I always did right. I'm not a player. I'd never cheated before. I was foolish enough to think I could keep the affair a secret, that nobody would find out. But then Rose threatened to expose it. She'd been sending me anonymous messages, too. She had that photo, the one you showed me, and another one, of Bel getting into my car. At least, I thought she did, though I only found the one on her phone. I couldn't let her expose me. It would have been unfair to *you*, Sarah. I asked Bel to get Rose out to the woods, so I could talk some sense into her. Convince her to delete the photos. That's all I ever intended. But Bel got there first, and she was so—uncooperative. She said she was afraid of me, that she'd decided what we were doing was wrong, and she was going to file a complaint with Simon. I panicked. I just lost it. I couldn't let her do that to us. And before I even knew what was happening, Bel was—she was—well, there was blood, everywhere."

Sarah listened in horror to his litany of excuses. Heath blamed everyone but himself. Sarah was responsible because she failed to worship him sufficiently, and drove him into the arms of a young girl. Rose was responsible because she threatened to expose him. Bel was responsible—for *her own death*—because she wouldn't keep quiet. And on and on, his eyes lit up with self-pity. The only person *not* responsible was Heath. Every time, he let himself off the hook. Every time, he lied, like he always had. And she let him, and forgave him. Sarah couldn't bear it any longer—not just Heath's lies, but her own complicity.

"There was blood because you stabbed that girl to death. Heath, you *planned* it. Why else bring the knife?"

He looked momentarily startled, then his face settled into an adolescent pout, like he was the true victim here, if only Sarah were understanding enough to see it.

"Well, I needed it to scare Rose," he said, like it should be obvious. "I had no intention of *using* it. I feel worse about this than you do, Sarah. I feel terrible."

"So terrible that you showered, and did laundry, and wiped down the bathroom with bleach?"

"And burned what I couldn't clean. Yes. I had to do that, or it would pull us all down. I couldn't hurt you like that."

Thankfully, she was lucid enough to stop herself from confronting him about the hidden bloodstains in the bathroom. He'd run right over there and get rid of them. It was obvious he felt no remorse. Not a shred.

He took her hand, gazing into her eyes, pleading. Her heart felt that old tug toward him, the desire to try to fix him with her love. But it was too late.

"Nobody suspects me," he said. "It's a miracle that Rose showed up when she did, and picked up the knife. Her fingerprints are all over it. She even has motive. Everybody knew those girls were at each other's throats. The cops believe Rose did it. All we have to do is keep our mouths shut, and things will go back to normal. We forget this ever happened, never mention it again, and we can finally have the life we want. The life we deserve. We can be happy, Sarah."

He expected her to go on as if nothing had changed. To *stay* with him. The thought made her skin crawl.

"Rose knows you did it," Sarah said.

"If she tries to talk, nobody will believe her. Under that sort of pressure, who knows. A young girl might snap. She might even kill herself."

His words sent a chill through her, worse than the shivers of fever. Downstairs, the doorbell rang. The sonorous boom of it echoed up the staircase, and brought a frown to Heath's face. He was not expecting company, apparently. He opened the drawer of the bedside table, pulled out a small silver handgun, and tucked it in the waistband of his pants. Where the hell did that come from? They didn't own a gun. Sarah had never wanted one in the house, and neither had Heath, or so he claimed. He'd obviously had a change of heart. She could ask where he got it and when and why. But the answers wouldn't matter, and besides, she already knew them. Guns were easy to come by. And Heath was a violent man.

"What are you doing?" she asked, her heart pounding with fear.

"Stay here."

He ran out of the room, locking the door behind him so she had no choice but to obey his command.

62

Zach suggested performing what he called a welfare check, to find out if Mrs. Donovan was all right. Given everything that had happened, Rose had no intention of returning to Moreland. But Zach needed to be back in his dorm for check-in, which was in a little more than an hour. She climbed out the window and down the fire escape. He met her below. They hurried through the rain to the headmaster's house, where Rose crouched behind a bush and Zach rang the doorbell. As far as Donovan knew, Zach had nothing to do with any of this. He ought to be able to walk up to the front door and ask about Mrs. Donovan without arousing suspicion. His behavior might seem weird, but it wouldn't put him in danger, the way it would if Rose paid a call. They had come up with a plausible story to explain his visit—or so they hoped.

When nobody answered the door after a few minutes, Zach rang the bell again. Rose heard it echo in the massive house. Still, no answer. What was taking so long? Her legs started to cramp up from the squatting and the cold. She shifted position, jostling the bush and sending a shower of frigid raindrops onto her hair. An icy trickle ran down inside her jacket.

Finally, the door opened. A bar of yellow light fell across the dark lawn. She couldn't see from her hiding place who had answered. If it was Mrs. Donovan, Rose would come out and speak to her. But if it was *him*—well, they'd have to see. Rose's heart was beating hard.

"Good evening, Mr. Donovan, or I guess I should call you 'Headmaster' now, right?"

It was him. The words carried past Rose and dissipated into the air. She strained to hear better.

"Zach, right? What can I do for you?" Donovan said.

"Sorry to bother you, sir. I'm actually looking for Mrs. Donovan. I was told she's no longer on duty in Moreland Hall, so I thought I would check here."

"It's a little late, isn't it? If you're in her math class, e-mail and make an appointment. She doesn't meet with students at this hour."

Zach was not in Mrs. Donovan's math class. They'd banked on her husband not knowing that, which, luckily, it seemed he didn't. But now Zach would have to float the more elaborate story, which had to do with an upcoming test, and a tutor coming down with the flu.

"Yeah, sorry, but this is fairly urgent."

"Classes are canceled for the rest of the week. What's so urgent?"

The wind gusted, carrying off Zach's reply. A squall was rolling in. Bitter rain mixed with sleet lashed

Rose in the face. She pulled her hood tight, and huddled against the bush. They were still talking, but she couldn't hear a word. She stood up and stretched her legs. A minute later, the door slammed. The angry sound of it gave Rose an awful jolt. She prayed the wind had taken it. If not, a slammed door could mean that Donovan had found them out.

He must have, because Zach didn't wait for her. He bolted down the front path like he'd been shot from a cannon, without so much as a glance over his shoulder to see if Rose was following. She panted with fear and retreated into the bush, wedging herself between the scratchy branches and the cold brick of the house. To follow Zach to the road, she'd have to walk down the middle of the front lawn, which was completely open to view to anybody inside the house. To *him*, and he'd already tried to kill her once. Twice, actually, if you counted the blow to the head, in the woods, the night Bel died.

Rose needed to wait long enough that he would lose interest and stop watching. Five minutes passed. The rain came down harder. The wind shifted, and she thought she heard someone calling her name. Rose poked her head out and scanned the lawn. Beyond the perimeter of light cast by the house, it was too dark to see anything. There were only tall trees, swaying in the wind, outlined against the stormy sky.

"Rose. *Enright*, over here."

The sound had come from the edge of the woods. Rose turned, and saw a figure move. It was Zach, beckoning to her. She tucked her conspicuous blond hai more securely into her hood, and ran for the trees. Zach grabbed her the second she reached him, pulling her into the underbrush where they wouldn't be seen. From his expression in the moonlight, and his taut grip on her arm, she felt his fear.

"What happened?" she asked, keeping her voice low. "I couldn't hear anything after he told you to e-mail her. Then he slammed the door."

"I tried to talk my way in, but that tutoring story didn't hold water. He knew I was up to something, and he started to ask questions. Then I heard this pounding coming from upstairs. Like someone was banging on a door, begging to be let out. I think I even heard a scream, but it was windy. Once that happened, he told me to get lost, and he shut the door in my face. Rose, she's up there. It had to be her, and I think he's got her locked in. Plus, you're not gonna believe this."

"What?"

"He has a gun."

"How do you know?"

"I saw it. When the pounding started, he turned to look, and the gun was stuck in the back of his pants. That's when he slammed the door. He must know I saw it."

"We should call the police."

"Ugh, I tried, but my phone's dead. We have to find Detective Howard. She seems reasonable, and I think she would want to help. She's working out of the Odell Security Office."

"We can't go there. Odell Security reports to Donovan now."

"Well, we can't stay here. You heard what I said. He has a gun."

"You go, then. I don't want to leave Mrs. Donovan alone with him. I'm afraid he'll hurt her."

"What can you do? If you go in there, he'll kill you."

"I'm not planning to storm the house. I'll stay right here, and keep an eye out."

"But you can't even see anything from here."

"Then I'll go around the back, and look in the windows. Maybe I can get her attention."

"*No.* That's crazy. If you want to stay, you've got to keep out of sight. I'll get the detective, as fast as I can. If something happens, if you see him coming, *run.* Get to the road, flag down a car. But only if there's an emergency—otherwise, stay in the woods, where he can't see you. Promise?"

"Yes. I understand. Thank you, Zach."

"Be safe, Enright."

Zach tapped her apprehensively on the arm, and turned to go.

63

Heath was at the front door for what felt like a very long time. This was a drafty house. Sarah knew that the door was open, and that Heath was still standing there, presumably talking to whoever rang the bell, because the wind gusted in and rattled the walls. As she lay in the bed in the throes of fever, shivering with each fresh blast, the image of Heath tucking the small silver handgun into his waistband played on repeat in her mind.

It meant something. Something specially for her.

Heath had asked Sarah to forgive and forget. To pretend he never had an affair with a vulnerable young girl. Never stabbed that girl to death and left her to bleed out in the woods. Never allowed her poor sister—Sarah's dear Rose—to take the blame for his crime. Sarah should behave as if nothing happened, stand by Heath's side, cover up his lies. That's what he wanted from her. What he expected of her.

But what if she didn't?

That's what the gun was for.

Why else would he have it? Who else was left for him to threaten, to kill? Maybe Rose, but Rose was beyond his reach now, safe with her grandmother—thank God. Sarah was the prisoner here. The children were gone. The dog was locked in the basement. There would be no witnesses. And as far as the world at large knew, Sarah had run away from the hospital and had not been seen since. With her illness, with the weather as dire as it was, it was possible that she'd meet an untimely end, and that her body would never be found. He wouldn't want another body to explain. He was smart enough to realize that.

But, come on, that was the fever talking. Heath was her husband. They had two children together. If he begged her to forgive and forget, it was because he still loved her, and wanted to save their marriage. He would never hurt her.

Bel Enright thought the same thing. And Heath stabbed her seventeen times and left her lying in a pool of her own blood.

The fact was, Sarah didn't know what Heath was capable of, or what he intended. She never would have imagined that he could kill someone, yet he had. He admitted to it, freely, making Sarah's willful denial seem ludicrous and pathetic. What a fool she'd been, to believe him for so long. Heath had a gun. Why have it, if he didn't plan to use it on her when she refused his demands? Not only was he armed, but Sarah was weak as a kitten. If he decided to hurt her, she wouldn't be able to protect herself. She needed help. There was a person at the door now, and they wouldn't be there for much longer. If she hoped to attract attention, this was her chance.

Sarah pulled the bedspread back, and the effort of doing so left her faint. She gathered her strength, then placed her feet squarely on the floor and used the bedside table to lever herself up to standing. The room swam, and her eyes teared up. How could she manage this? She hung her head in despair. If she died here, by her husband's hand, her children would never know. They'd grow up without her, fed a false story of her death. Heath would remarry, of course; he didn't like to be alone. He was the sort of man who needed a wife. Someone like Sarah, wholesome and solid, dazzled by his brilliance, buying his lies, raising his children. They were so little that they'd forget her entirely, and call the new woman Mommy.

She made it to the locked door and pounded with every ounce of strength she had left. She screamed her throat raw. And nothing happened.

64

After a while, a shadow fell across the slit of light under the door, and Heath came in. She'd gotten back in bed, and lay there with her eyes closed and her heart pounding, pretending to sleep. He saw through that one easily enough, or else he just didn't care. He crossed quickly to the bed, grabbed her arm and shook her viciously.

"What the hell was that?"

She cried out in shock and opened her eyes. Heath gripped her arm so hard that his fingers dug into her flesh.

"Please, let go," she said, in a shaking voice.

But he grabbed her by both arms and yanked her to sitting. She nearly passed out.

"Sarah, I tried to make peace with you. I begged forgiveness. I humbled myself. What did I get in return? Betrayal. You scream like a banshee, you bang on the door, like you're trying to attract the cops? How can I trust you after a stunt like that? Where's the good faith? Where's the love?"

His tone was so wounded, so disappointed, that it terrified her. He thought he was right. He thought Sarah was the one in the wrong. She wanted to tell him how insane that was, but she didn't have the strength.

"Please, leave me alone," she whispered.

"I can't do that. You're trying to ruin me, and I have no idea why. All I ever did was love you, and try to protect you. Everything could've been fine, but no, you had to go and destroy my trust in you. Now I see that the first chance you get, you'll go to the cops. I thought we were teammates. I thought we would tough this out together. But you're not on my side, and that makes you my enemy. I never thought it would come to this, but I have no choice. I'm actually really sad, for myself and the kids, that you're making me do this."

Tears glittered in his eyes as he raised the gun. Sarah said a silent prayer and waited to die.

Outside, Max started barking like mad.

"What the hell."

Heath lowered the gun and walked to the window.

"The dog got out," he said. "Somebody's in the woods. If it's that kid, swear to God, I'll kill him."

Heath ran from the room. This time, he forgot to lock the door. With tremendous effort, Sarah got out of bed and walked to the window to see who was out there. If she knocked on the window, would they hear?

At that moment, floodlights came on, lighting the perimeter. Heath must have turned them on. Sarah squinted, but saw only trees. The window faced the backyard, and the woods beyond, which extended as far as the eye could see. The light stopped at the edge of the woods, making the woods appear especially dark and ominous, which felt appropriate. Those trees hid a multitude of horrors. Lost Lake was out there, less than a mile as the crow flies, where Heath had stabbed Bel Enright, and left her bleeding in the snow.

Max stood at attention at the edge of the woods and barked incessantly. Maybe a person was in there, or maybe it was an animal, but there was definitely something. Heath emerged from the house. Sarah gripped the sill as she watched him cross the lawn, heading for the spot where the dog stood. The rain had turned to snow. The lawn was white with it. He slipped a couple of times as he made his way, and had to right himself, but he was there in a minute.

A thought penetrated her fever fog. Why the hell was she just standing here? She should take advantage of his distraction, and run for the road. But her body was slow to obey her thoughts, and in that moment of hesitation, Heath reached Max, and started yelling. A person emerged from the woods, a girl, with her hands up. It was Rose. He had the gun pointed at her.

Sarah made it down the stairs, and stopped short in the entry hall, unsure of where to go. Her legs were like water. She didn't have an ounce of energy to spare. This house was enormous, and she didn't know her way around. *Think.* Heath had exited directly from the house to the backyard. There must be a rear exit.

A stiff wind blew through, coming from the back of the house. She followed it, creeping down a long hallway past darkened rooms, her hand on the wall to keep from falling over. She couldn't think about her illness now. She wouldn't give into it. She had to think of Rose, who'd come here to help her and gotten caught.

Sarah made her way to the kitchen. It was vast, industrial, and dark, but she couldn't turn on the light, for fear of attracting Heath's attention. Near the sink, beside a window, something glittered. Knives, hanging from a magnetic strip. She grabbed a big one, and the heft of it in her hand was terrible. She pushed the thought away, not wanting to know what it felt like when he stabbed that poor girl to death.

Outside, Rose screamed, and Sarah rushed to the back door. It stood ajar, leading from the hall behind the kitchen onto the snow-covered terrace, and lawn beyond. Heath faced the woods, his back to Sarah, his gun still trained on Rose. As she walked out the door, a powerful gust of wind nearly pushed her back inside. The snow was falling harder now. Neither Heath nor Rose had noticed her. She picked her way across the lawn in sodden loafers, one step at a time, praying that she could sneak up on him from behind. She might have succeeded. But Max woofed at her, and Heath turned. She crossed the last few steps, staring at the barrel of his gun.

"Run," she said to Rose, raising her knife as if she'd attack him. But he had a gun, and she could barely hold the knife up.

Heath stared at her in surprise. "What are you doing? Don't be foolish. Give me that thing," he said.

When Sarah didn't budge, he put the gun to Rose's head. "Sarah, don't make me do things I don't need to do. Drop that on the ground right now," he said.

And she did.

"Inside," he said, waving the gun toward the house.

When Rose cowered, and dug her feet in, Heath sighed.

"Look, this gun thing, it's just to make you listen. It's freezing out here. Let's go inside, and try to work this out."

Sarah looked at Rose for the first time. The girl was shaking and crying. She'd just spent five minutes out here alone, with Heath. Maybe he planned to kill them, no matter what, and Rose knew that. Maybe he'd already told her.

"I want to know what you're going to do," Sarah said.

Heath turned to her. She looked at his familiar, much-loved face, and didn't see her husband there. She knew the answer. He was going to kill them inside. The certainty of that stopped her breath.

"Just go," he said.

When Sarah didn't move, Heath reached out and grabbed her by the arm. Sarah went limp and fell to the ground, forcing him to bend down to try to drag her up. Rose saw that he was distracted, and bolted toward the house, screaming and shrieking. As Heath took aim, a powerful blast of wind hit him hard, and he staggered backward. A shot rang out. Wood chips flew. He'd fired at Rose, and hit a tree. Rose's cries spread out on the wind, echoing in all directions. Heath pointed the gun straight down at Sarah. His face was wet. She thought he might be crying.

"I didn't want it to be like this," he said.

"Police! Drop it!"

Detective Melissa Howard stood ten feet from them, pointing her own gun at Heath's head. He didn't move.

"Drop it or I'll shoot," she said.

Sarah stared up at her husband. She pulled herself up on an elbow, finding his eyes.

"Do what she says. I'll help you. I'll stand by you. I promise."

"I'm sorry. I can't face it," he whispered.

Heath pressed the gun to his own chin and pulled the trigger.

65

One Year Later

At a bend in the road, just before the gates of Odell Academy came into sight, Grandma looked at Rose and saw tears on her face. She pulled over in the driveway and took Rose's hand.

"You're sure about this, dear?" she asked, her soft voice barely audible over the blast of the heater, and the swish of the windshield wipers against the glass.

"The memorial was my idea, Grandma."

"I know. And it's a beautiful one. But the dedication ceremony is simply a formality. You don't have to go. I can call, and say our flight was canceled. Or I can drop you back at the hotel, and go by myself. I don't mind. This place holds no memories for me, the way it does for you. Maybe it's better if you never see it again. What do you think?"

"I'm not sure. I wanted to come. To be here for Bel. But now, thinking about seeing the place, the people . . . it just seems hard."

Rose stared out the window. Grandma handed her a Kleenex, and she wiped her eyes. Just the sight of snowflakes, melting on the windshield, reminded her of things. Where they lived now, there was no snow, just as there hadn't been any in California, when she and Bel were growing up together. The only cold place in her life was this one.

When Grandma had realized the truth, she asked Rose how to make amends for not believing her. *Take me far away from here*, Rose said. They lived in Florida now, just the two of them, together. Grandma dumped that lawyer once she saw how he tried to come between her and her granddaughter. She showed him the door, and seemed relieved to do it. Rose and Grandma were close now. They traveled together on school breaks. They had designed Bel's memorial together. They helped each other through their grief, sometimes just by cooking a new recipe, taking a walk on the beach or just watching a funny show on TV. They lived in a modern house, stark white, with minimalist furniture, no mementos, and no photographs, except for a single photo of Bel in a silver frame with a black ribbon across it, that Grandma kept on her bedside table. Rose went in and looked at it sometimes, when she needed to.

Things were getting better, slowly. The quiet of her new life helped. She had a bedroom with a view of the ocean, a good therapist, and a new school, completely different from Odell. Very small. She'd made some new friends. The kids there were artsy and bohemian. They reminded her a little bit of her sister.

"What does Judith say?" Grandma asked, after a while.

Judith was Rose's therapist. She was old and wise, with bright blue eyes surrounded by wrinkles. Rose had had qualms about Judith at first, because of her age, which she knew was unfair, but still. She'd imagined someone young and hip, like a friend to talk to. But Judith came highly recommended, so they tried her out. And it turned out she knew a lot of things, and was exactly the right therapist for Rose.

"Judith says it's up to me. That it might be traumatizing. But it might be healing. Only I can decide."

"You decide then, Rose. Take your time. They can wait."

Grandma sat quietly with her hands folded in her lap, while Rose thought. She thought about the card that came in the mail, a few months back. Rose wasn't the only one whose instinct for self-preservation counseled her to flee. The card was from Mrs. Donovan, postmarked from the town in Oregon where she now lived with her children. She didn't say much about herself, or what she was doing. She only apologized, profusely, for not preventing Bel's death. She held on to so much guilt that Rose felt sick at heart for her, and wrote back immediately, a letter full of forgiveness and sympathy. Rose told Mrs. Donovan about the memorial, though she stopped short of inviting her former teacher to the ceremony. That would be impossibly painful. What Sarah Donovan went through was worse than what Rose went through herself. The only person who'd suffered more than Sarah at the hands of Heath Donovan was Bel.

Bel. Rose thought about her beautiful, sad, maddening twin. She'd been working hard to banish her own guilt, yet the negative feedback loop was powerful enough to suck her in, even sitting here in this car. Her thoughts got away from her so easily, still. If only she'd been there for Bel when it mattered. If only she'd done more. If only she hadn't taken every little slight from Bel so personally. If only she hadn't gotten offended, and pushed Bel away, so that she ended up dying alone, without support, because of Rose's selfishness.

It would be all too easy to go down that road again. But Rose was learning how to stop. She reminded herself of the things Judith said, to help her through this. Rose had heeded Bel's cry for help that awful night. She'd ventured into the dark woods, despite a real fear for her own safety. She had found her sister, and confronted the killer. Rose still had nightmares about that night at the headmaster's house. But she did all those things because she loved her sister, and had wanted to do her best for her. What more could one sister ask of another? If Bel were alive, she'd tell Rose that.

Rose thought of Bel every day. This memorial was her tangible tribute. She had to be strong, and see it through.

Rose turned to Grandma.

"I want to be there for her. I have you with me. We can handle this. We should go."

Grandma nodded, and pulled back onto the road. As

they approached the Odell gates, she took Rose's hand. There were tears in Grandma's eyes. Not tears of sadness, so much as tears of pride.

"You're very brave, dear. This isn't easy. But it's right. We'll remember her, together."

Epilogue

There are things I wish I could tell Bel. For instance, I never wanted her to die. I never expected that. I always liked her. Naturally, I did—she was my little minion. She did my bidding. It reflected well on me. Until she started disobeying. Until she started trying to take *him* away from me. He was mine by right. Everybody in Moreland knew it. Bel knew it, too.

Not just by right. Heath Donovan *was* mine. I won the contest. Nobody knew it because he told me not to tell, like I'm sure he told her. Only, I listened. I know how to keep my mouth shut. You'd think he would have valued that quality in a girl. But after the slipper prank, Heath turned on me. He took *her* side. He wanted her, more than he wanted me, I guess. It made no sense. I'm better in bed. Bel was a little priss, way too uptight. And like Anonymouse said in those e-mails, Bel wasn't that special. She wasn't that pretty. I'm way prettier. Seriously, people always say to me: Darcy, you're the most beautiful girl I've ever seen. That happens, like, all the time. It's a mystery why Heath sided with her, but I couldn't let it slide. Nobody who knows me could possibly think I would.

I'm Anonymouse, if you haven't guessed by now. Like, anonymous, except a mouse? Cute, right? Okay, maybe a little dorky, but I liked it.

I lucked out, getting my hands on those pictures of Heath with Bel. It was all because Brandon had a beef going with that sneaky twit Zach Cuddy. When Zach gave Brandon his phone to be wiped after the slipper attack, Brandon decided to keep an eye on Zach, and had his computer guy clone the phone. We could see everything Cuddy did. He was right in the thick of it with those Enright girls. How he got that sex pic, I have no idea, but it was the bomb. It freaked Heath the hell out—which, I have to admit, I enjoyed. The car photo was good, too. I didn't even need Brandon to physically follow Bel to get the goods on her. Cuddy did all the work for me, without even knowing.

Once I got those pics, Heath Blue-Eyes Donovan was wrapped around my little finger again. I was just about to make my demands—exoneration, reinstatement, graduation—when he killed her. And then himself.

I didn't ask for any of that. I would much rather have had my demands met. I would much rather have blackmailed him into submission, returned to Odell in triumph and graduated. And, oh, yeah, I would rather have Heath Donovan in my bed again than have him dead. He was worth it, even if he hurt my feelings. And I wouldn't have killed Bel, either. I might've punished her somehow. Exactly how, I'm not sure. But not with *death*. That's just so extreme, so over the top. And they say *I'm* a drama queen.

But, you know, plans go wrong sometimes. My little blackmail scheme set Heath off. I never took him for crazy, just reckless. Turns out, I was mistaken. Don't expect me to cry over it. Bel was a big girl, she knew what she was getting into with him. As for Heath, he got what he deserved in the end. He paid the price.

I guess we all did.

Though, I can't say I suffered too badly. I'm heading off to college soon. And by college, I do mean a party school, in a sunny climate, working on my tan.

Read on for an excerpt from

A STRANGER ON THE BEACH

the new novel by Michele Campbell,
now available in trade paperback
from St. Martin's Griffin!

1

There was a stranger on the beach. He was standing in front of my house, staring at it like he was casing it to rob.

Sometimes fate sneaks up on you. But Aidan Callahan didn't sneak up on me. He was brazen. He stood there in the middle of the sand, staring up at my brand-spanking-new beachfront house, looking like he was up to no good. I saw him clearly as I looked through the wall of windows, over the infinity-edge pool, to the ocean beyond. Yes, he was gorgeous. But I was a married woman of twenty years' standing who loved her husband, and I barely noticed that. What I noticed was that this guy looked strong. Dangerously so. And he dressed like a townie. Baggy athletic shorts, tank top, the glint of a gold chain at his neck. People like him resented people like me, and sometimes, they robbed them. There had been a string of robberies recently, of some of the big houses. The summer people thought the local cops were dragging their feet about solving them, maybe because the culprits were local boys. When I saw Aidan standing there, those robberies were the first thing that leapt to mind, and a chill went down my spine.

I'll tell you everything that happened, starting from the beginning. My first impression of Aidan was that he was a potential thief. If only I'd listened to my instincts, I would've turned and run in the opposite direction. But that's not what I did. I walked toward him. And I will always blame myself for what came after.

2

It was a hot, sultry day, two weeks past Labor Day, and the bluff had cleared out. The summer people were all back in the city, leaving only me, and my next-door neighbor, old Mrs. Eberhardt. She lives in a salt-box shack on a wide lot that's coveted by every real estate developer in the East End. I live in the type of place that people build after they tear down houses like hers. She has a yappy little dog that wakes me up at five thirty every morning. As you can imagine, we didn't have much to say to one another, so basically, I was at the beach alone.

I'd been waiting around all day for the technician from the burglar alarm company to show up for the installation. The house had that fresh-paint smell. Details were still being attended to, and the alarm was one of the last items on the punch list. The company gave me a window from ten to two for installation, which I said was fine, because I had work to do preparing for the huge housewarming party I would be throwing in a matter of days. Finalizing guest lists, working out catering menus, scheduling the delivery of the tent, negotiating with the valet parking company, angling to get a photographer from *Avenue* magazine to show up and take pictures for the society column. On and on. Hours passed, and the alarm guy still hadn't showed. At four, I called to complain, and they told me the technician was overbooked, and they'd have to reschedule for next week. *Typical.* I thought about reaching for the bottle of gin in the cabinet and mixing myself a nice strong cocktail to ease my frustration. But it was hours till sunset, and I decided to be good. I'd go for a run on the beach instead.

As I laced up my sneakers, I got the urge to text my daughter. Hannah had just left for college, and I was having trouble letting go. I gave the hair elastic on my wrist a good snap to feel the clarifying sting. My sister had taught me that trick. Aversion therapy. She'd used it to quit smoking, and now I was using it so I wouldn't be a helicopter mom. It worked. The urge passed. I walked through the French doors onto the terrace and took a deep breath of the salty air. The ocean was visible beyond the bluff, the crash of the waves audible from here. The surf was rough today, yet it never failed to calm me.

And I needed calming. Hannah's departure had set me adrift, leaving me all too conscious of how alone I felt in my life. My husband, Jason, traveled constantly for business. He'd never actually spent a single night at the beach house, despite the fact that we were pouring all our money into it. The house was a big source of stress between us. It was my dream, not his. We'd stretched to buy the land, which was postage-stamp-sized but in a primo location. We'd stretched even more to build the perfect house on it. Things weren't right between me and Jason, but in all honesty, I didn't fully know that yet. It was just a nagging feeling lurking in my heart, making me antsy and discontented. But I fought it. I told myself, *He works a lot. He's a good provider. A good father. And hey, somebody's got to pay for the house, right? I shouldn't complain.*

I picked up the pace, fighting the pull of the sugary sand against the bottom of my sneakers, legs working, oxygen pumping through my veins. A shaft of light broke through the clouds, illuminating the water to a sparkling green. I lived on the part of the bluff closer in to the main road, where land was "affordable" at a million-plus an acre. (I won't say how much beyond a million.) The route I liked to run took me down the beach away from the road, toward the point, where the true mansions were. There was a house out there that last traded at forty million. You couldn't see it, though, because of the tall, perfectly groomed hedge that its famous owners installed for privacy. I'd never met those people, and I guessed I never would. Jason and I didn't rate. He was an investment banker, but not one of the famous ones who hung out with celebrities and owned a fleet of jets. I was an interior designer, but not the type with a million Instagram followers and houses featured in *Architectural Digest*. I'd stopped working when Hannah was born and had only recently gone back, trying to get my business off the ground, but facing headwinds. Jason and I moved in well-to-do circles, but we weren't at the top of the heap. The thing about being rich is, there's always someone richer.

I ran a mile-plus down the beach, not letting myself stop till I was out at the point. Then I doubled over, panting and holding my sides, till I caught my breath. I'd be forty-three in November, and I liked to think I still looked good. But lately there were hints of middle age coming on. Fine lines in the mirror that I covered with makeup, gray hairs peeking through that I masked with highlights. But you can't fake exercise. I needed to get back to Pilates class, or hire a trainer. Getting the house finished had taken too much time and energy. With Hannah gone, I should focus on *myself.*

The clouds were rolling in over the water, turning the sky black. I could smell the rain coming. I hadn't checked the forecast before I left, but generally they were saying to expect a stormy fall and a bad hurricane season. My superstitious mother had left me with a fear of electrical storms, to the point that I wouldn't turn on a faucet if it was lightning out. So, when the first peal of thunder sounded, I turned around and headed back.

Ten minutes later, I was back on my stretch of the bluff, with a clear line of sight to my house. A huge thunderclap sounded, and a vivid bolt of lightning split the sky. And there he was again, like some demon who'd materialized from thin air. The stranger I'd seen an hour earlier from my kitchen window. Staring again. The sight of him stopped me short. I could tell he was a townie, that he didn't belong in my neighborhood.

Maybe that sounds snobbish. But I don't come from money, and I didn't mean it that way. As a matter of fact, Aidan that day reminded me of my own people. My brothers and their friends, playing street hockey back in the day on hot afternoons in front of our house. I loved those guys, but they were no angels. I know what I'm talking about. I know casing when I see it, and when I saw Aidan, I knew exactly what he was doing.

I'm not a shrinking violet, and I can take care of myself. I walked toward him, determined to say something.

"Hey! Hey, can I help you?" I yelled.

The wind took my words away. But somehow he heard, and turned and smiled at me. The smile, I definitely noticed. It was like the sun breaking through the clouds, and all my suspicions melted away. He fooled me. Anybody can get fooled.

"That's your house?"

He spoke as if he already knew the answer. I should have noticed that, and realized it was odd. But I didn't see it. I only saw him.

"Yes," I said.

"She's a beauty."

"Thank you."

"I'm Aidan," he said, and held out his hand. I took it.

"Caroline."

"Caroline. Pretty name."

"Thank you."

His hand was warm. His eyes were very blue. He looked at me searchingly. I felt tongue-tied. He had to be ten or fifteen years younger than me. He seemed like he was about to say something more. But then the skies opened, and it started pouring.

"You should get inside before you get soaked," he said.

"Yes."

That was it, our whole conversation. He gave me a little wave and turned and hurried off. He was so casual about it, so nonchalant, that I forgot all about the idea that he might be a burglar. The beach where he'd been standing was public. He had a right to be there, and I figured he was just a guy who stopped to look at a beautiful house. Twice. Okay. But that's not a crime. I went inside and tried to put him out of my mind, but I didn't entirely succeed. My interest had been piqued. My guard had been lowered. My life was not in order. The combination of those things would prove to be my downfall.